The

DYSASTERS

ALSO BY P. C. CAST
AND KRISTIN CAST

The Dysasters

HOUSE OF NIGHT

Marked

Betrayed

Chosen

Untamed

Hunted

Tempted

Burned

Awakened

Destined

Hidden

Revealed

Redeemed

The Fledgling Handbook 101

Dragon's Oath

Lenobia's Vow

Neferet's Curse

Kalona's Fall

The DYSASTERS

[THE GRAPHIC NOVEL]

P. C. CAST
and
KRISTIN CAST

Art by

ANTONIO BIFULCO

**WEDNESDAY
BOOKS**
NEW YORK

To SA

You've reawakened my creativity
and love for writing.

I am forever grateful for what you've
taught me and continue to teach me.

We are the ultimate team.

Watch out, world!

First published in the United States by Wednesday Books, an imprint of St. Martin's Publishing Group

THE DYSASTERS: THE GRAPHIC NOVEL. Copyright © 2020 by P. C. Cast and Kristin Cast. Art copyright © 2020 Antonio Bifulco. All rights reserved. Printed in the United States of America. For information, address St. Martin's Publishing Group, 120 Broadway, New York, NY 10271.

www.wednesdaybooks.com

The Library of Congress Cataloging-in-Publication Data is available upon request.

ISBN 978-1-250-26877-8 (trade paperback)
ISBN 978-1-250-19758-0 (ebook)

Our books may be purchased in bulk for promotional, educational, or business use. Please contact your local bookseller or the Macmillan Corporate and Premium Sales Department at 1-800-221-7945, extension 5442, or by email at MacmillanSpecialMarkets@macmillan.com.

First Edition: February 2020

10 9 8 7 6 5 4 3 2 1

[ACKNOWLEDGMENTS]

This graphic novel wouldn't be what it is without our amazing team at Wednesday Books. Monique Patterson, Anne Marie Tallberg, Jennifer Enderlin, Mara Delgado-Sanchez, Michelle Cashman, Paul Hochman, Jessica Preeg, and the rest of Team Cast are some of the hardest-working humans in publishing. I appreciate you each so much!

My fabulous Curtis Brown family has a special place in my heart. Ginger Clark, Jonathan Lyons, Sarah Perillo, Holly Frederick, and Maddie Tavis all *kill it* on a daily basis. I am so grateful to have this powerhouse team in my corner.

Humongous, squishy hugs to Theo Downes-Le Guin and GC, for not only being generous and fantastic humans, but also for making my partnership with Steven Salpeter a real-life thing.

Steven, I adore you! I'm trying to think of something profound and moving to write here, but I keep coming back to Dr. Evil's "you complete me" scene. I feel like that's too much, but not really. So, you complete me (professionally speaking)! You're a superb agent and I cannot wait to see what the future holds for us.

As always, I send so much love to my dearest Auntie M.

To our readers: Remember, you are *powerful!* Your choices *matter.* Thank you for choosing Team Cast.

The
DYSASTERS

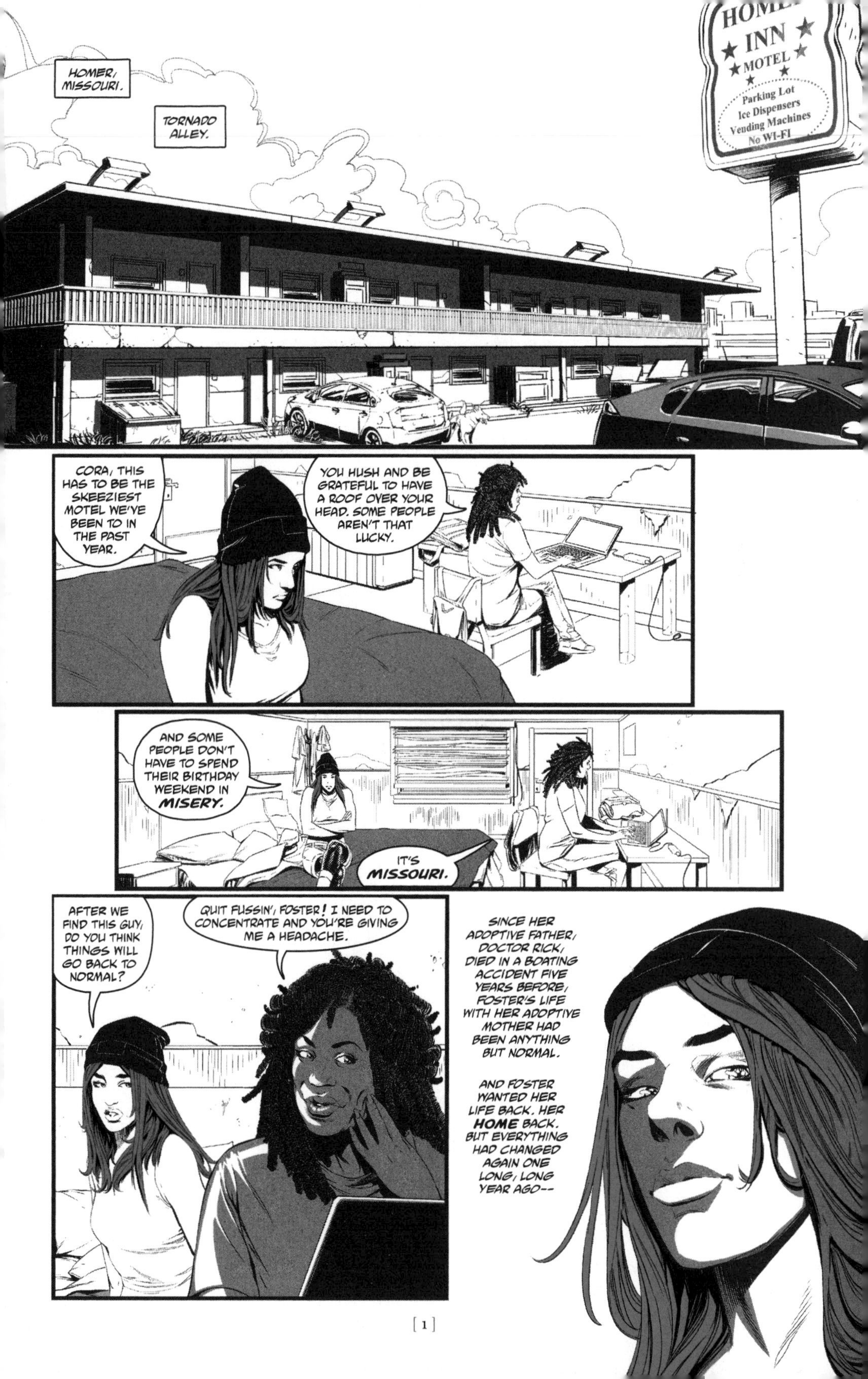

HOMER, MISSOURI.
TORNADO ALLEY.
HOME INN MOTEL
Parking Lot
Ice Dispensers
Vending Machines
No WI-FI
CORA, THIS HAS TO BE THE SKEEZIEST MOTEL WE'VE BEEN TO IN THE PAST YEAR.
YOU HUSH AND BE GRATEFUL TO HAVE A ROOF OVER YOUR HEAD. SOME PEOPLE AREN'T THAT LUCKY.
AND SOME PEOPLE DON'T HAVE TO SPEND THEIR BIRTHDAY WEEKEND IN MISERY.
IT'S MISSOURI.
AFTER WE FIND THIS GUY, DO YOU THINK THINGS WILL GO BACK TO NORMAL?
QUIT FUSSIN', FOSTER! I NEED TO CONCENTRATE AND YOU'RE GIVING ME A HEADACHE.
SINCE HER ADOPTIVE FATHER, DOCTOR RICK, DIED IN A BOATING ACCIDENT FIVE YEARS BEFORE, FOSTER'S LIFE WITH HER ADOPTIVE MOTHER HAD BEEN ANYTHING BUT NORMAL.
AND FOSTER WANTED HER LIFE BACK. HER HOME BACK. BUT EVERYTHING HAD CHANGED AGAIN ONE LONG, LONG YEAR AGO--

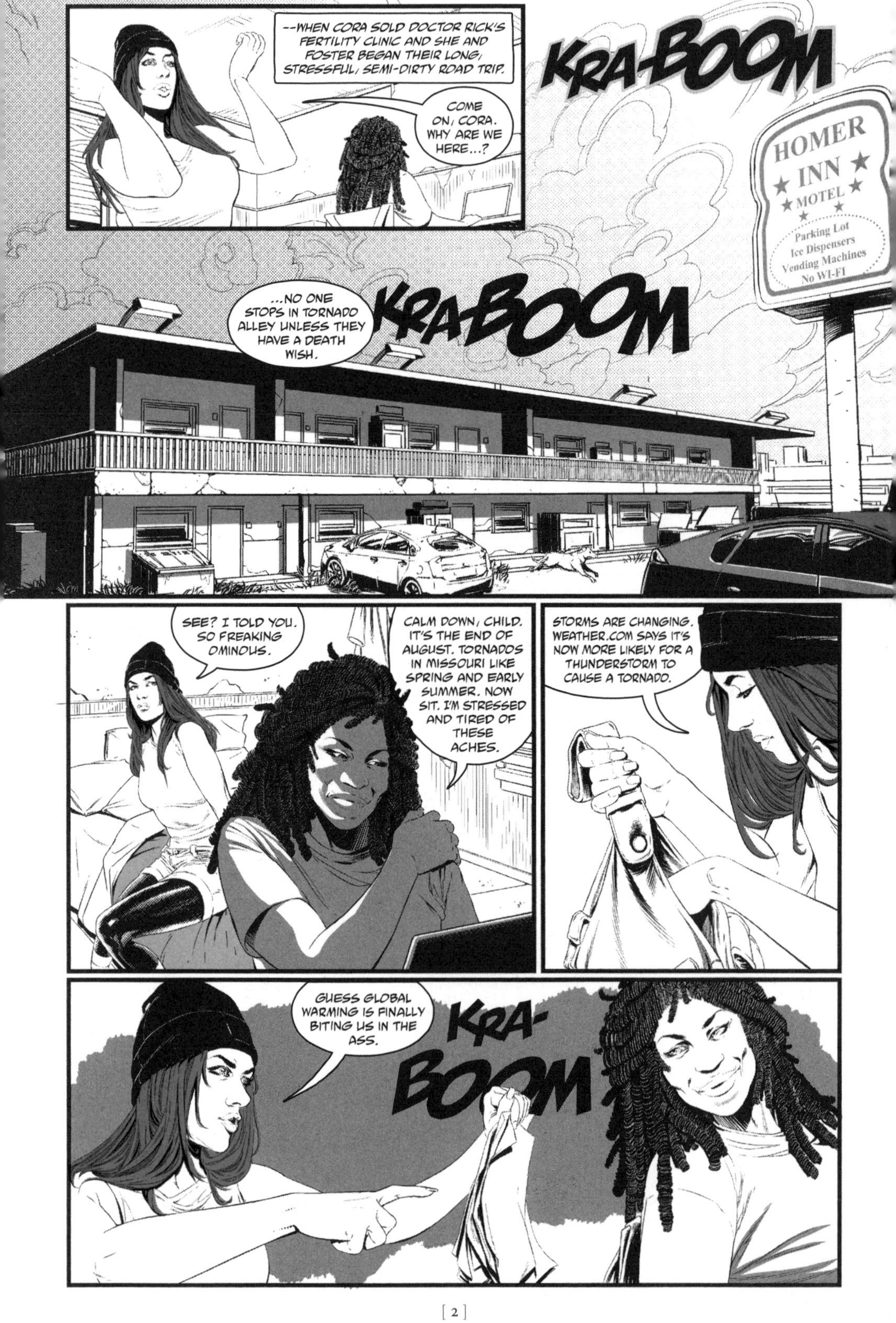
--WHEN CORA SOLD DOCTOR RICK'S FERTILITY CLINIC AND SHE AND FOSTER BEGAN THEIR LONG, STRESSFUL, SEMI-DIRTY ROAD TRIP.
COME ON, CORA. WHY ARE WE HERE...?
KRA-BOOM
HOMER INN MOTEL
Parking Lot
Ice Dispensers
Vending Machines
No WI-FI
...NO ONE STOPS IN TORNADO ALLEY UNLESS THEY HAVE A DEATH WISH.
KRA-BOOM
SEE? I TOLD YOU. SO FREAKING OMINOUS.
CALM DOWN, CHILD. IT'S THE END OF AUGUST. TORNADOS IN MISSOURI LIKE SPRING AND EARLY SUMMER. NOW SIT. I'M STRESSED AND TIRED OF THESE ACHES.
STORMS ARE CHANGING. WEATHER.COM SAYS IT'S NOW MORE LIKELY FOR A THUNDERSTORM TO CAUSE A TORNADO.
GUESS GLOBAL WARMING IS FINALLY BITING US IN THE ASS.
KRA-BOOM

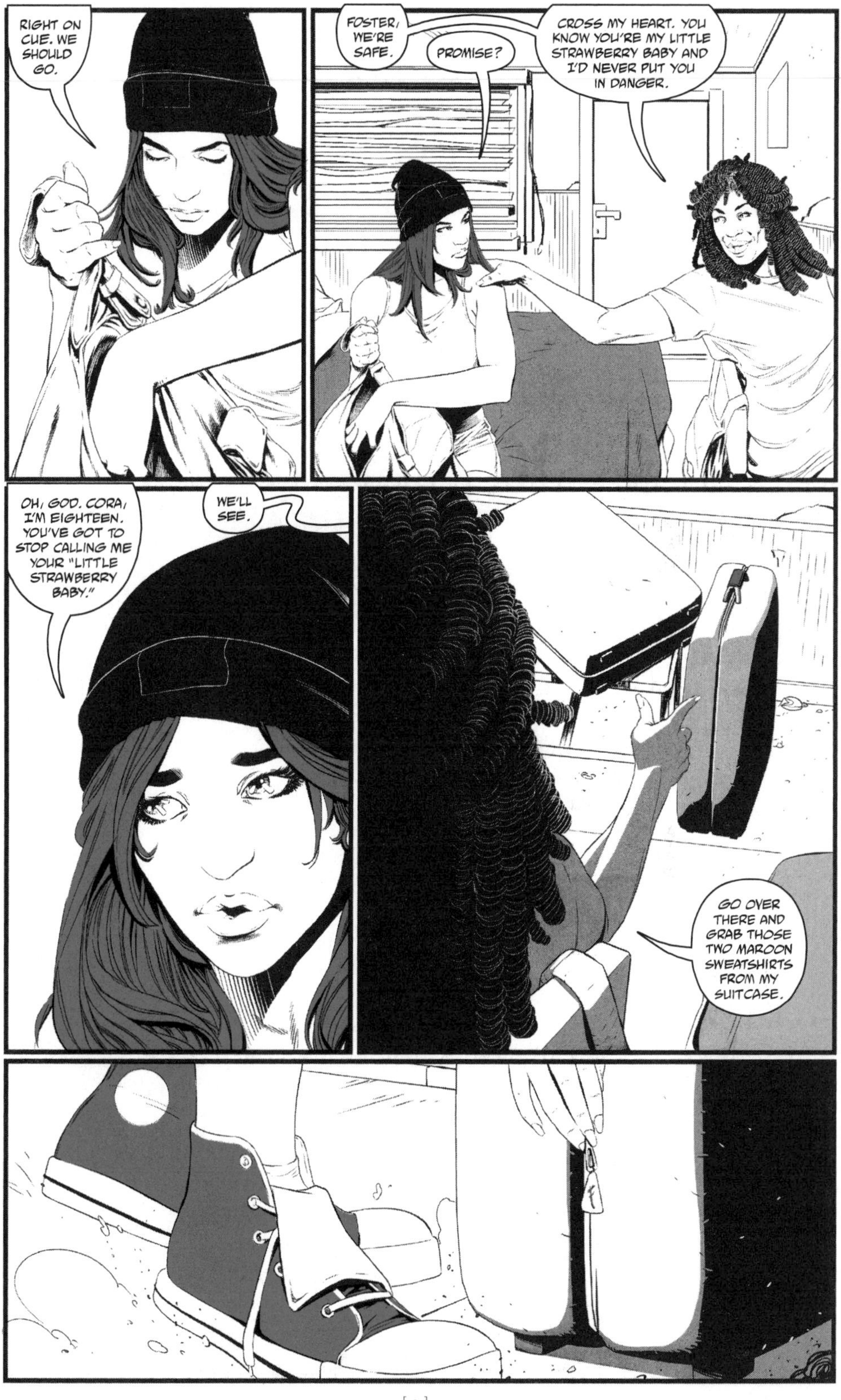
RIGHT ON CUE. WE SHOULD GO.
FOSTER, WE'RE SAFE.
PROMISE?
CROSS MY HEART. YOU KNOW YOU'RE MY LITTLE STRAWBERRY BABY AND I'D NEVER PUT YOU IN DANGER.
OH, GOD. CORA, I'M EIGHTEEN. YOU'VE GOT TO STOP CALLING ME YOUR "LITTLE STRAWBERRY BABY."
WE'LL SEE.
GO OVER THERE AND GRAB THOSE TWO MAROON SWEATSHIRTS FROM MY SUITCASE.

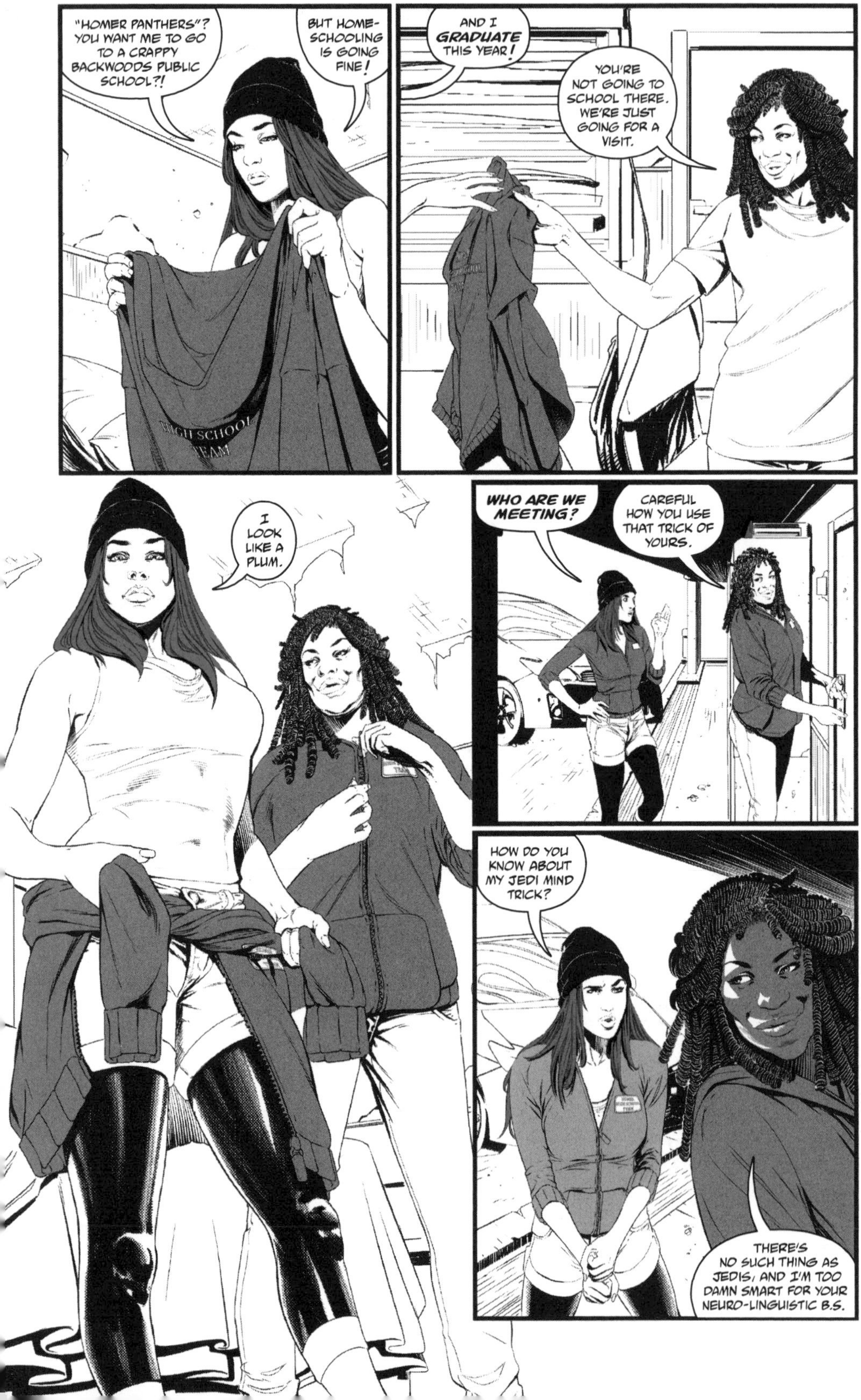
"HOMER PANTHERS"? YOU WANT ME TO GO TO A CRAPPY BACKWOODS PUBLIC SCHOOL?!
BUT HOME-SCHOOLING IS GOING FINE!
AND I GRADUATE THIS YEAR!
YOU'RE NOT GOING TO SCHOOL THERE. WE'RE JUST GOING FOR A VISIT.
HIGH SCHOOL TEAM
I LOOK LIKE A PLUM.
WHO ARE WE MEETING?
CAREFUL HOW YOU USE THAT TRICK OF YOURS.
HOW DO YOU KNOW ABOUT MY JEDI MIND TRICK?
THERE'S NO SUCH THING AS JEDIS, AND I'M TOO DAMN SMART FOR YOUR NEURO-LINGUISTIC B.S.

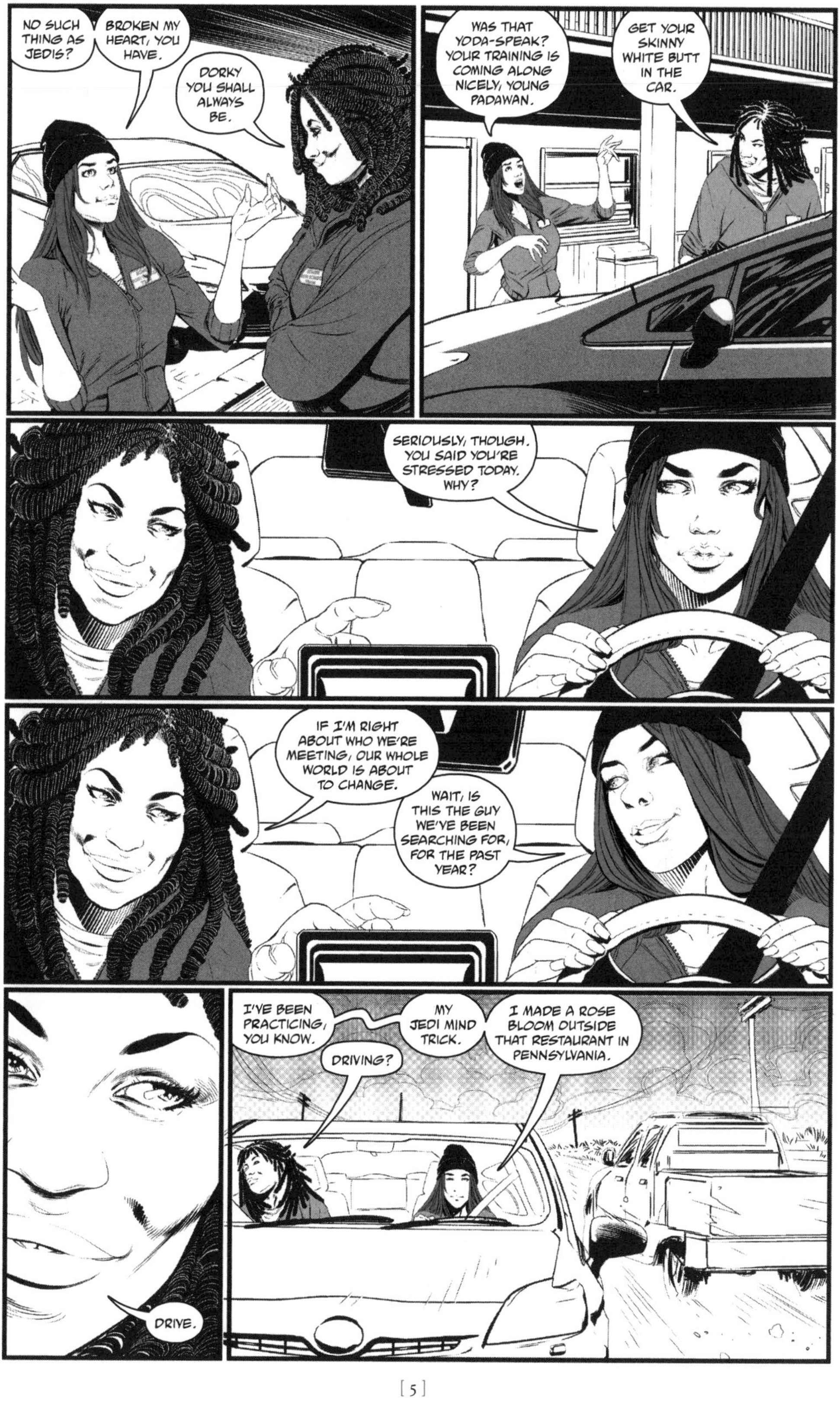
NO SUCH THING AS JEDIS?
BROKEN MY HEART, YOU HAVE.
DORKY YOU SHALL ALWAYS BE.
WAS THAT YODA-SPEAK? YOUR TRAINING IS COMING ALONG NICELY, YOUNG PADAWAN.
GET YOUR SKINNY WHITE BUTT IN THE CAR.
SERIOUSLY, THOUGH. YOU SAID YOU'RE STRESSED TODAY. WHY?
IF I'M RIGHT ABOUT WHO WE'RE MEETING, OUR WHOLE WORLD IS ABOUT TO CHANGE.
WAIT, IS THIS THE GUY WE'VE BEEN SEARCHING FOR, FOR THE PAST YEAR?
DRIVE.
I'VE BEEN PRACTICING, YOU KNOW.
DRIVING?
MY JEDI MIND TRICK.
I MADE A ROSE BLOOM OUTSIDE THAT RESTAURANT IN PENNSYLVANIA.

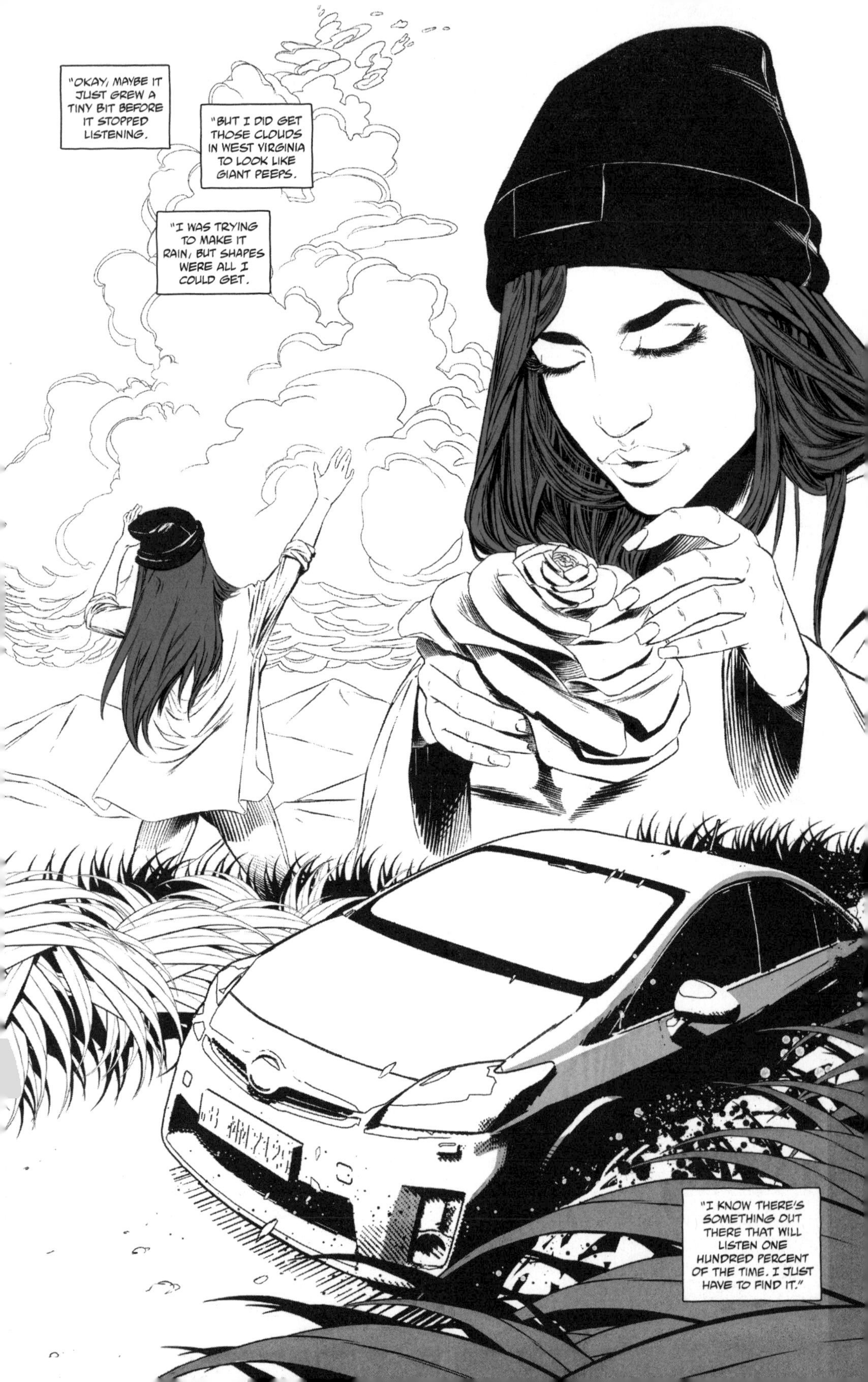
"OKAY, MAYBE IT JUST GREW A TINY BIT BEFORE IT STOPPED LISTENING.
"BUT I DID GET THOSE CLOUDS IN WEST VIRGINIA TO LOOK LIKE GIANT PEEPS.
"I WAS TRYING TO MAKE IT RAIN, BUT SHAPES WERE ALL I COULD GET.
"I KNOW THERE'S SOMETHING OUT THERE THAT WILL LISTEN ONE HUNDRED PERCENT OF THE TIME. I JUST HAVE TO FIND IT."

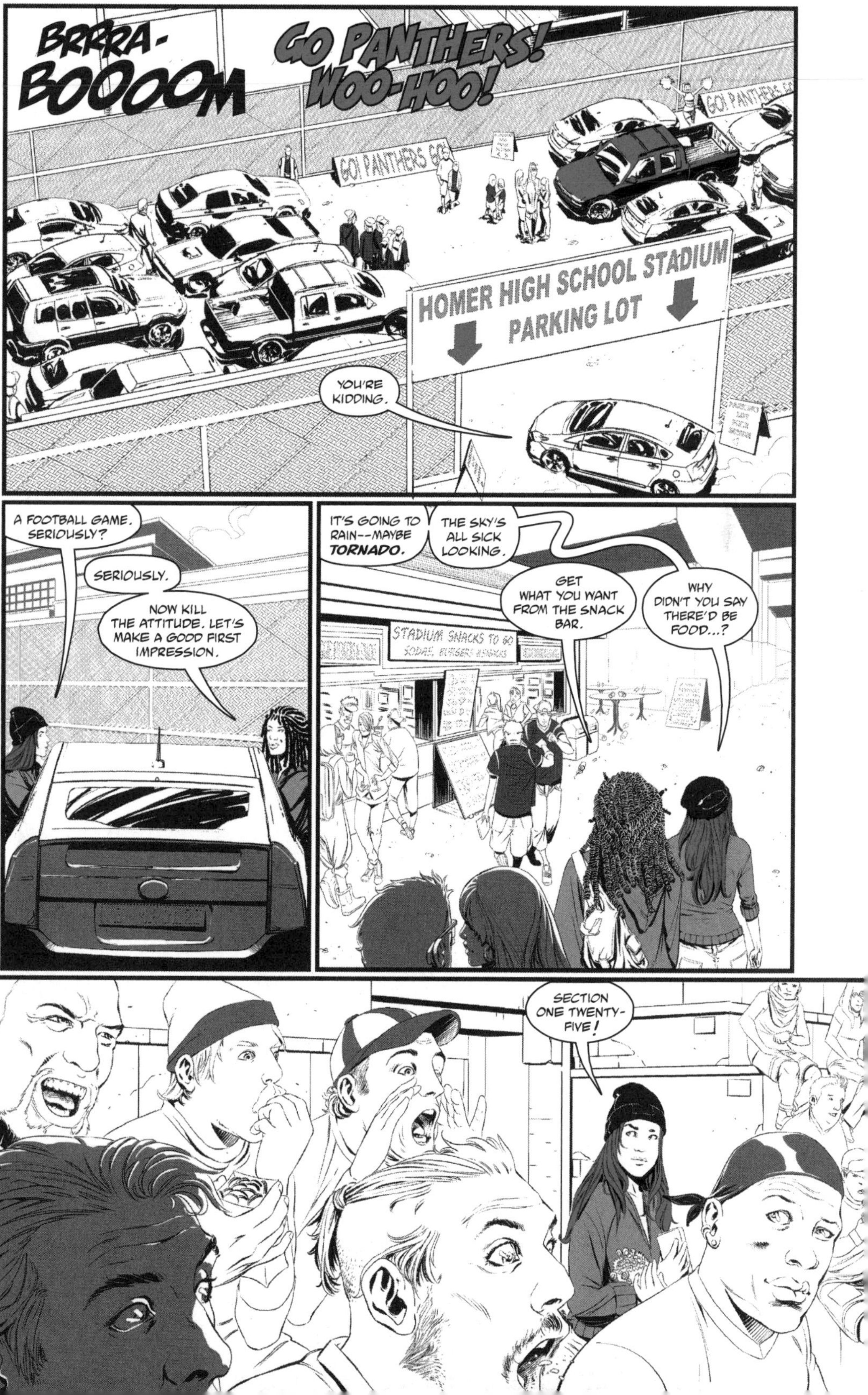
BRRRA-BOOOOOM
GO PANTHERS! WOO-HOO!
GO! PANTHERS GO
HOMER HIGH SCHOOL STADIUM
PARKING LOT
YOU'RE KIDDING.
A FOOTBALL GAME. SERIOUSLY?
SERIOUSLY.
NOW KILL THE ATTITUDE. LET'S MAKE A GOOD FIRST IMPRESSION.
IT'S GOING TO RAIN--MAYBE *TORNADO.*
THE SKY'S ALL SICK LOOKING.
GET WHAT YOU WANT FROM THE SNACK BAR.
WHY DIDN'T YOU SAY THERE'D BE FOOD...?
STADIUM SNACKS TO GO
SODAS, BURGERS & SNACKS
SECTION ONE TWENTY-FIVE!

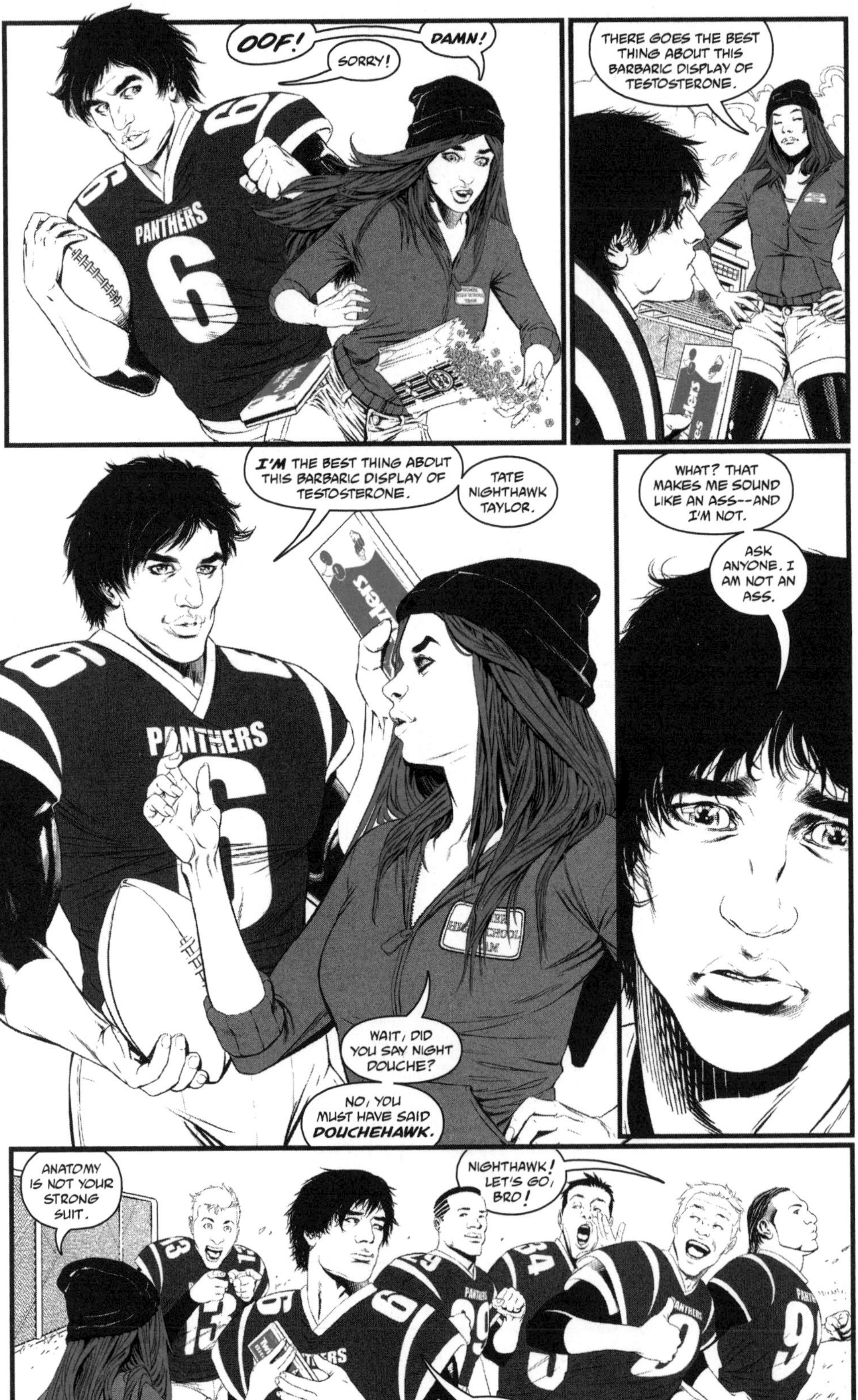
OOF!
SORRY!
DAMN!
THERE GOES THE BEST THING ABOUT THIS BARBARIC DISPLAY OF TESTOSTERONE.
I'M THE BEST THING ABOUT THIS BARBARIC DISPLAY OF TESTOSTERONE.
TATE NIGHTHAWK TAYLOR.
WAIT, DID YOU SAY NIGHT DOUCHE?
NO, YOU MUST HAVE SAID DOUCHEHAWK.
WHAT? THAT MAKES ME SOUND LIKE AN ASS--AND I'M NOT.
ASK ANYONE. I AM NOT AN ASS.
ANATOMY IS NOT YOUR STRONG SUIT.
NIGHTHAWK! LET'S GO, BRO!
COMING!

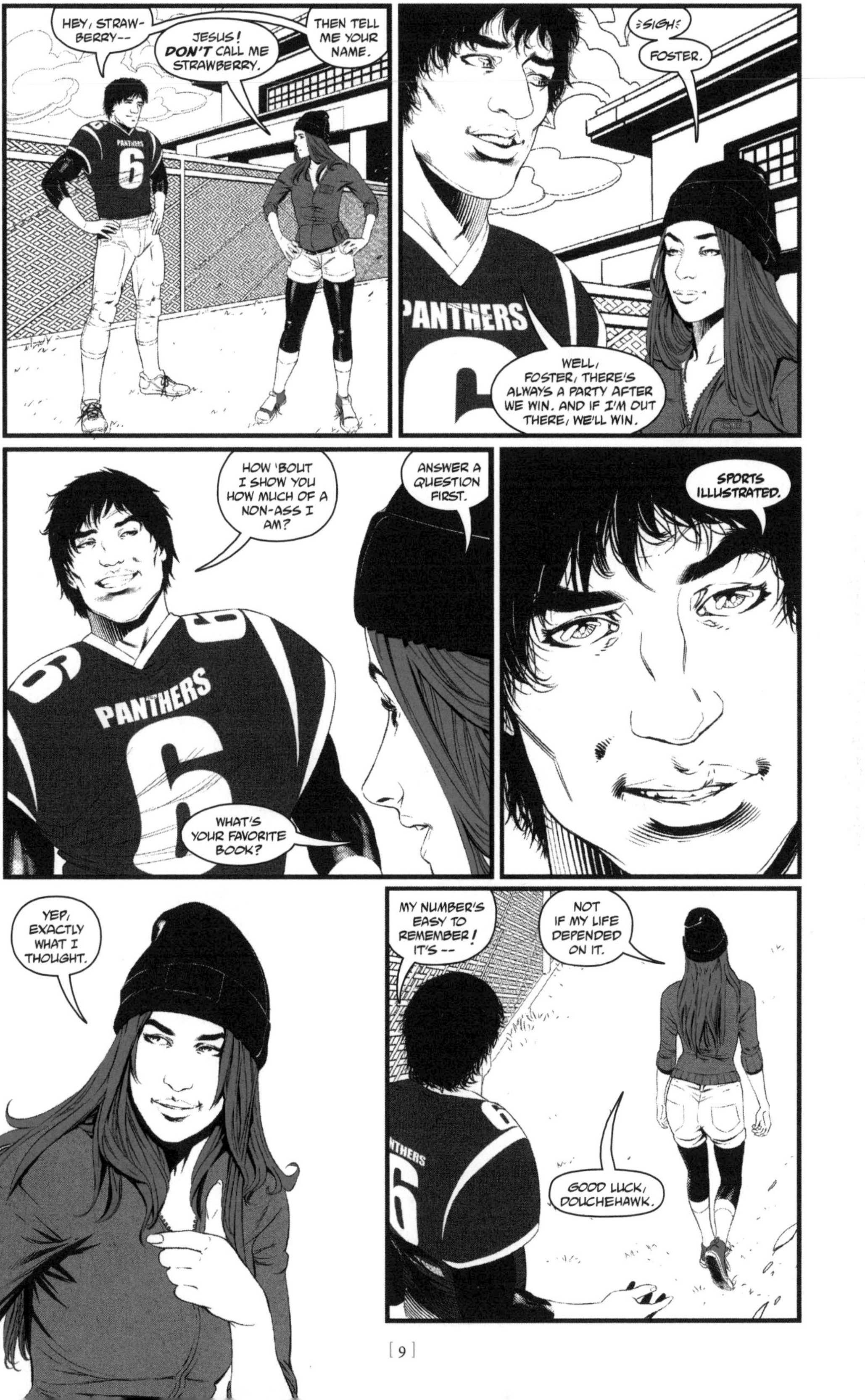
HEY, STRAW-BERRY--
JESUS! DON'T CALL ME STRAWBERRY.
THEN TELL ME YOUR NAME.
PANTHERS
6
SIGH
FOSTER.
PANTHERS
WELL, FOSTER, THERE'S ALWAYS A PARTY AFTER WE WIN. AND IF I'M OUT THERE, WE'LL WIN.
HOW 'BOUT I SHOW YOU HOW MUCH OF A NON-ASS I AM?
ANSWER A QUESTION FIRST.
PANTHERS
6
WHAT'S YOUR FAVORITE BOOK?
SPORTS ILLUSTRATED.
YEP, EXACTLY WHAT I THOUGHT.
MY NUMBER'S EASY TO REMEMBER! IT'S --
NOT IF MY LIFE DEPENDED ON IT.
GOOD LUCK, DOUCHEHAWK.

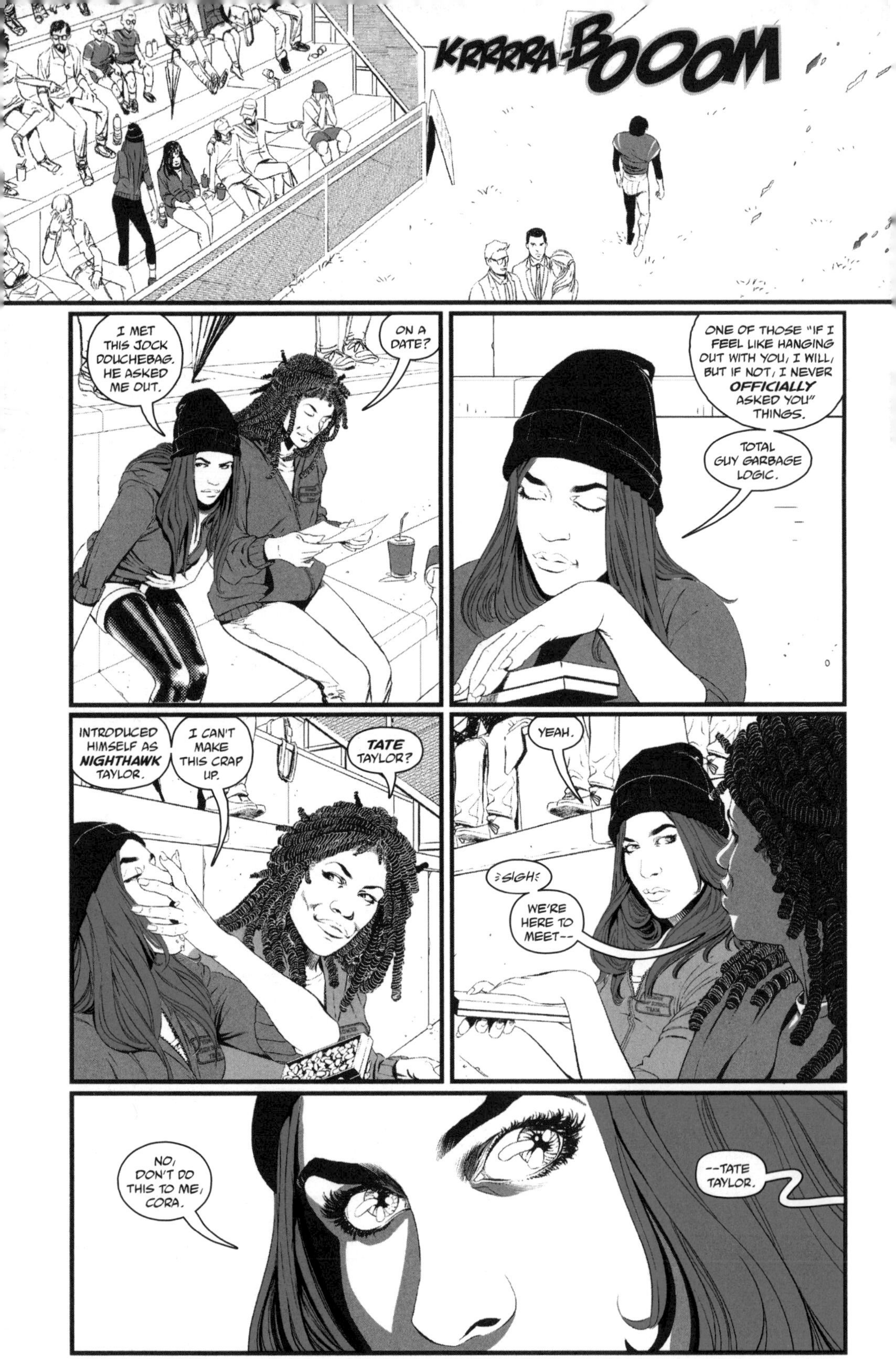
KRRRRA-BOOOM
I MET THIS JOCK DOUCHEBAG. HE ASKED ME OUT.
ON A DATE?
ONE OF THOSE "IF I FEEL LIKE HANGING OUT WITH YOU, I WILL, BUT IF NOT, I NEVER OFFICIALLY ASKED YOU" THINGS.
TOTAL GUY GARBAGE LOGIC.
INTRODUCED HIMSELF AS NIGHTHAWK TAYLOR.
I CAN'T MAKE THIS CRAP UP.
TATE TAYLOR?
YEAH.
SIGH
WE'RE HERE TO MEET--
--TATE TAYLOR.
NO, DON'T DO THIS TO ME, CORA.

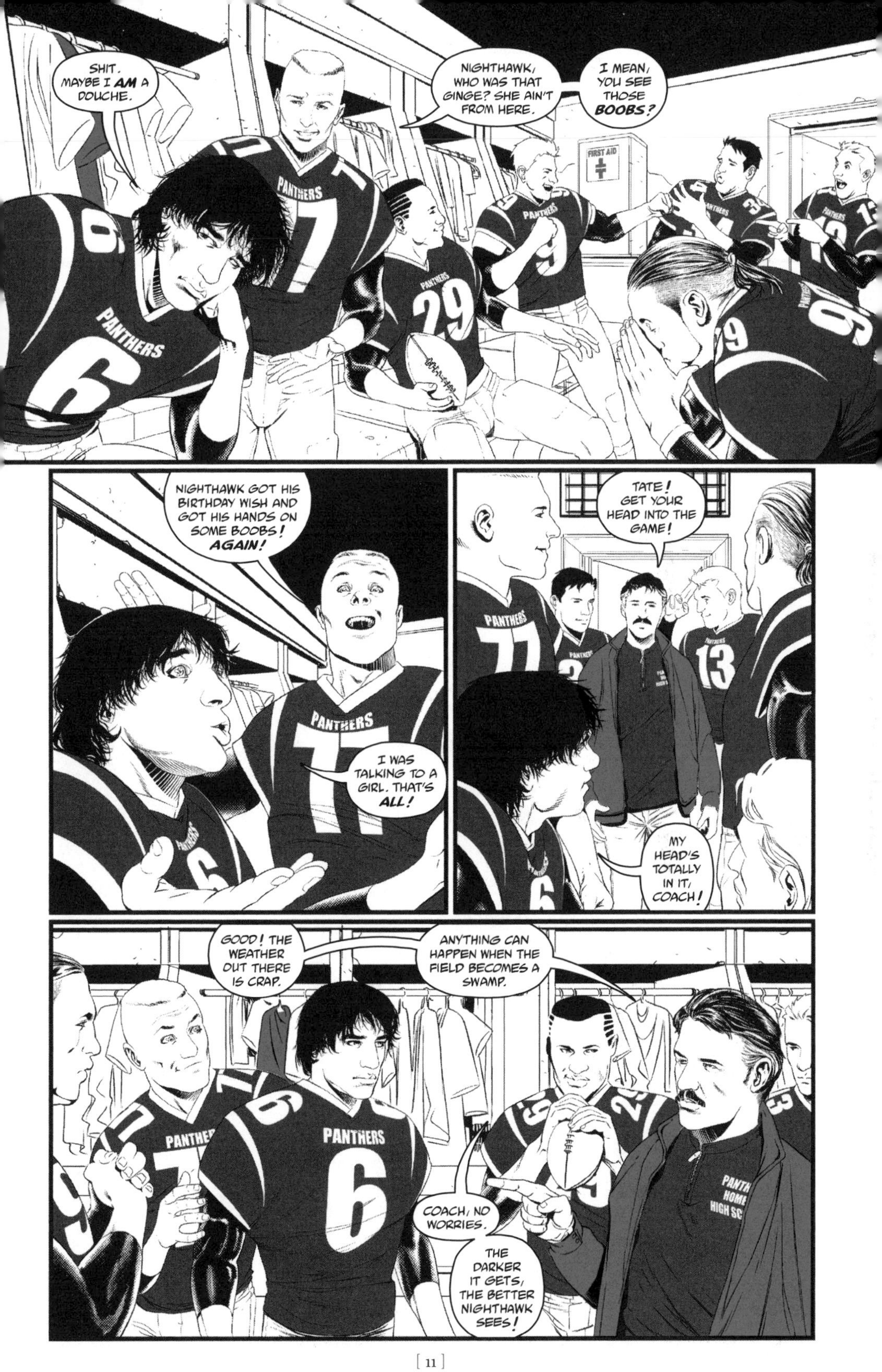
SHIT. MAYBE I **AM** A DOUCHE.
NIGHTHAWK, WHO WAS THAT GINGE? SHE AIN'T FROM HERE.
I MEAN, YOU SEE THOSE **BOOBS?**
FIRST AID
PANTHERS
NIGHTHAWK GOT HIS BIRTHDAY WISH AND GOT HIS HANDS ON SOME BOOBS! **AGAIN!**
I WAS TALKING TO A GIRL. THAT'S **ALL!**
TATE! GET YOUR HEAD INTO THE GAME!
MY HEAD'S TOTALLY IN IT, COACH!
GOOD! THE WEATHER OUT THERE IS CRAP.
ANYTHING CAN HAPPEN WHEN THE FIELD BECOMES A SWAMP.
COACH, NO WORRIES.
THE DARKER IT GETS, THE BETTER NIGHTHAWK SEES!

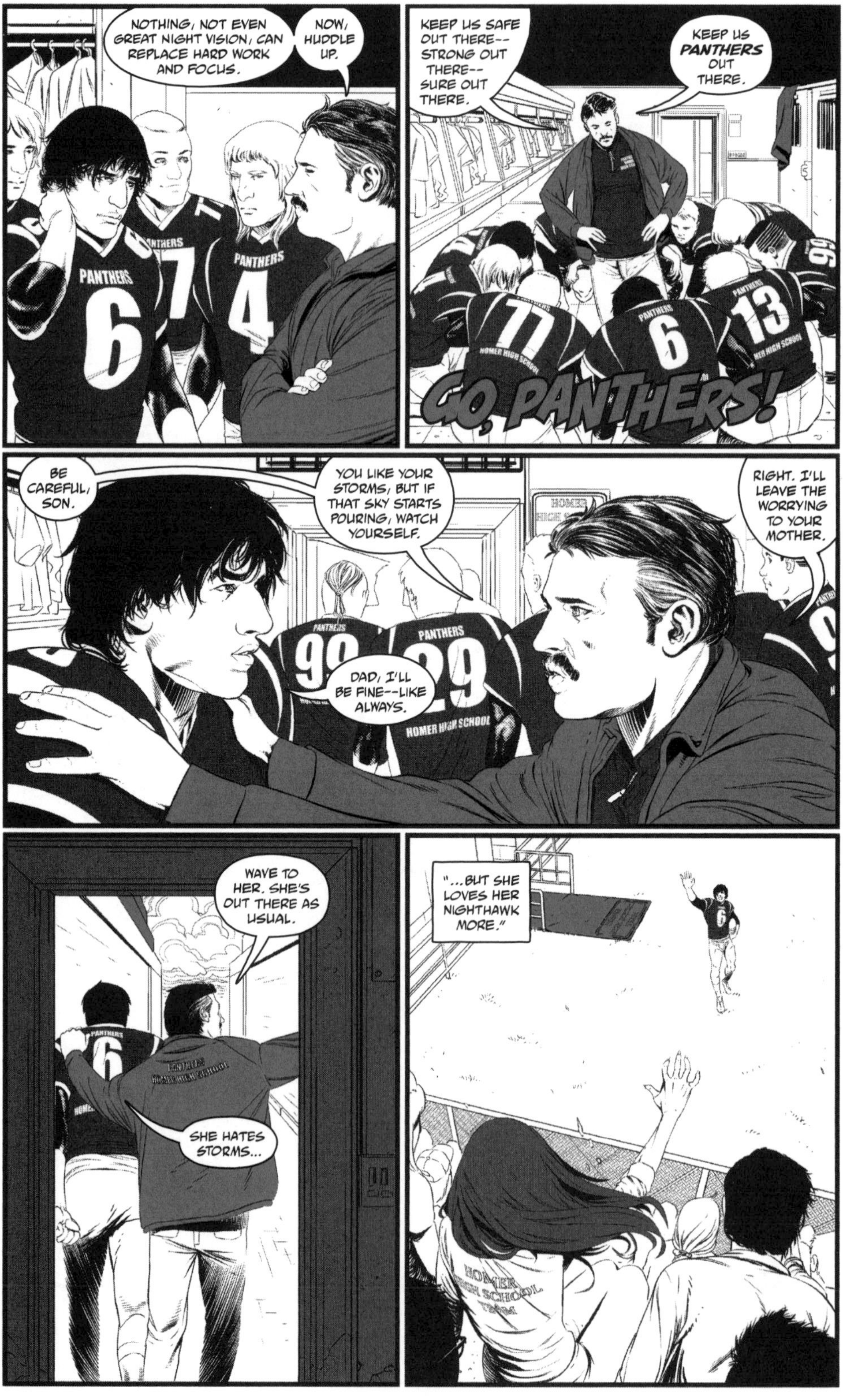
NOTHING, NOT EVEN GREAT NIGHT VISION, CAN REPLACE HARD WORK AND FOCUS.
NOW, HUDDLE UP.
KEEP US SAFE OUT THERE-- STRONG OUT THERE-- SURE OUT THERE.
KEEP US PANTHERS OUT THERE.
GO, PANTHERS!
BE CAREFUL, SON.
YOU LIKE YOUR STORMS, BUT IF THAT SKY STARTS POURING, WATCH YOURSELF.
DAD, I'LL BE FINE--LIKE ALWAYS.
RIGHT. I'LL LEAVE THE WORRYING TO YOUR MOTHER.
WAVE TO HER. SHE'S OUT THERE AS USUAL.
SHE HATES STORMS...
"...BUT SHE LOVES HER NIGHTHAWK MORE."

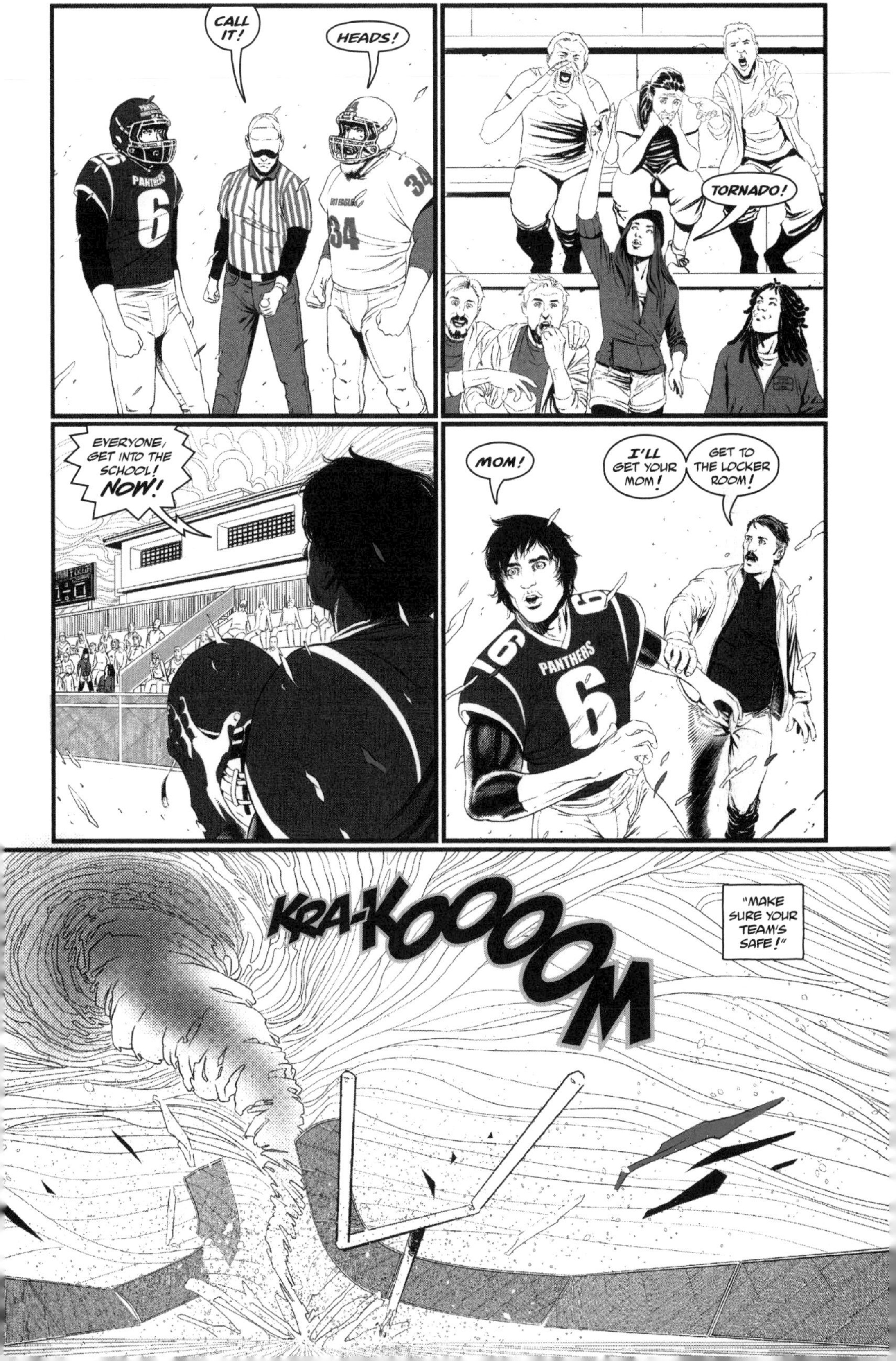
CALL IT!
HEADS!
TORNADO!
EVERYONE, GET INTO THE SCHOOL! NOW!
MOM!
I'LL GET YOUR MOM!
GET TO THE LOCKER ROOM!
KRA-KOOOOOM
"MAKE SURE YOUR TEAM'S SAFE!"

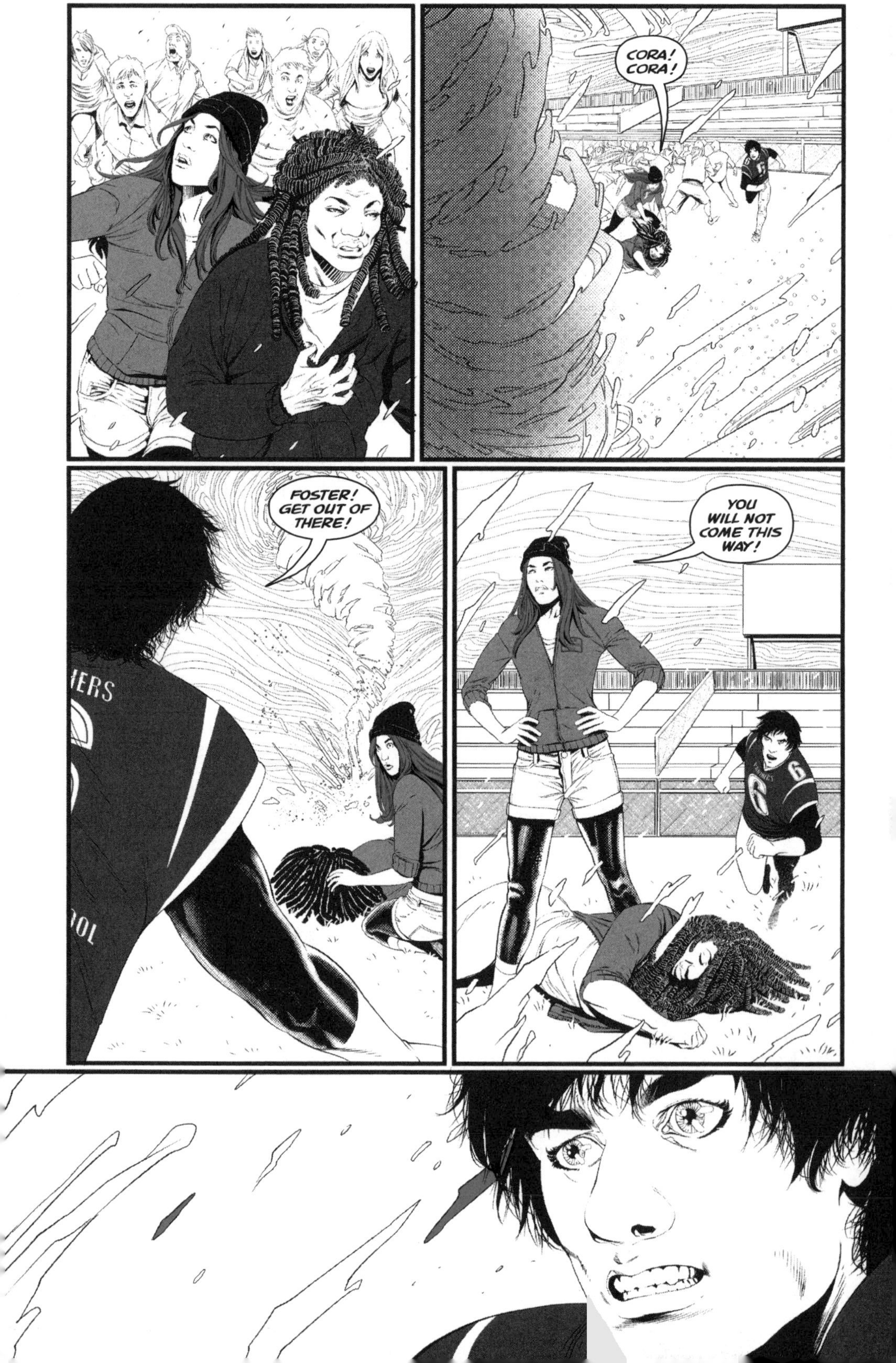
CORA! CORA!
FOSTER! GET OUT OF THERE!
YOU WILL NOT COME THIS WAY!

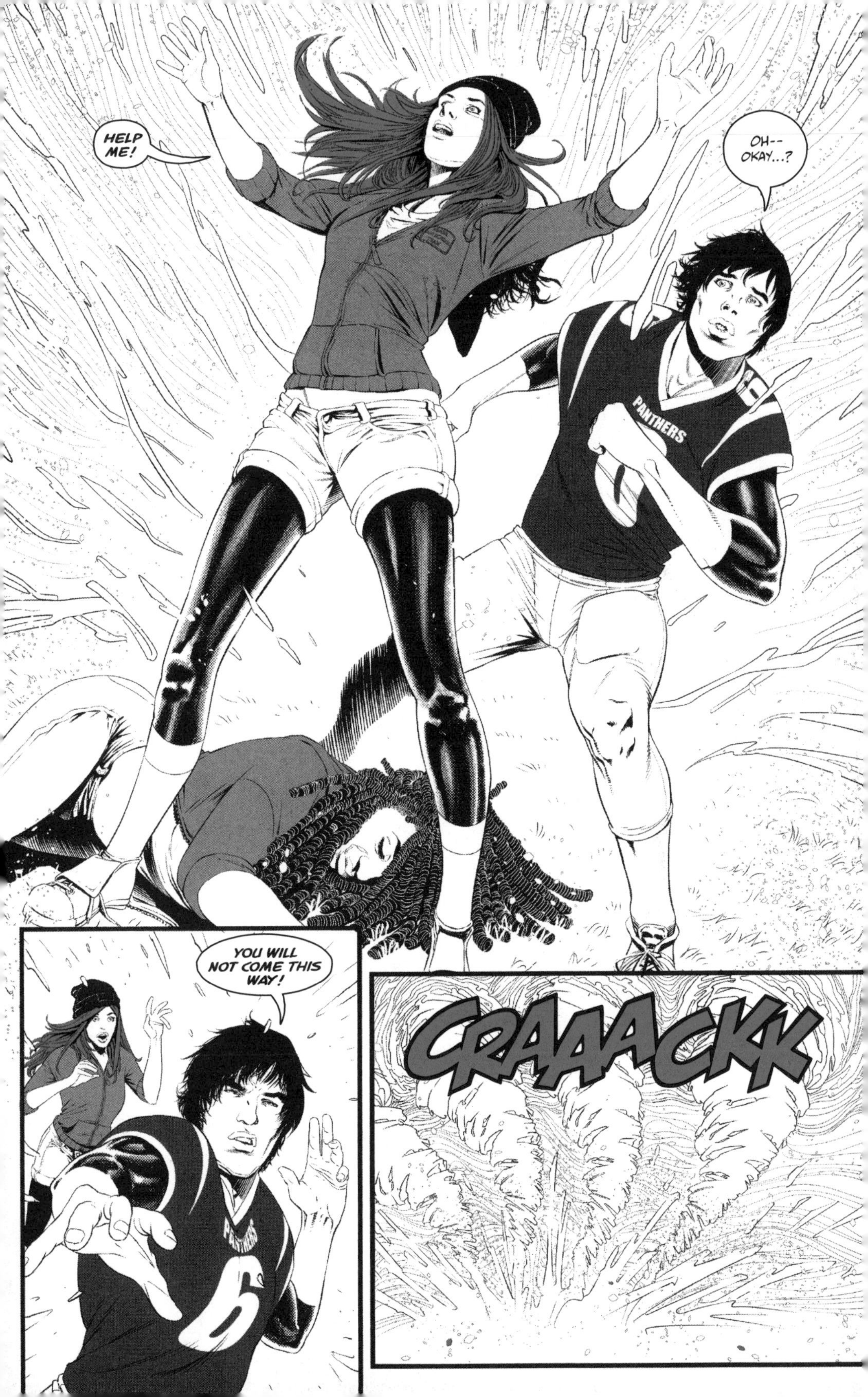
HELP ME!
OH-- OKAY...?
PANTHERS
YOU WILL NOT COME THIS WAY!
CRAAACKK

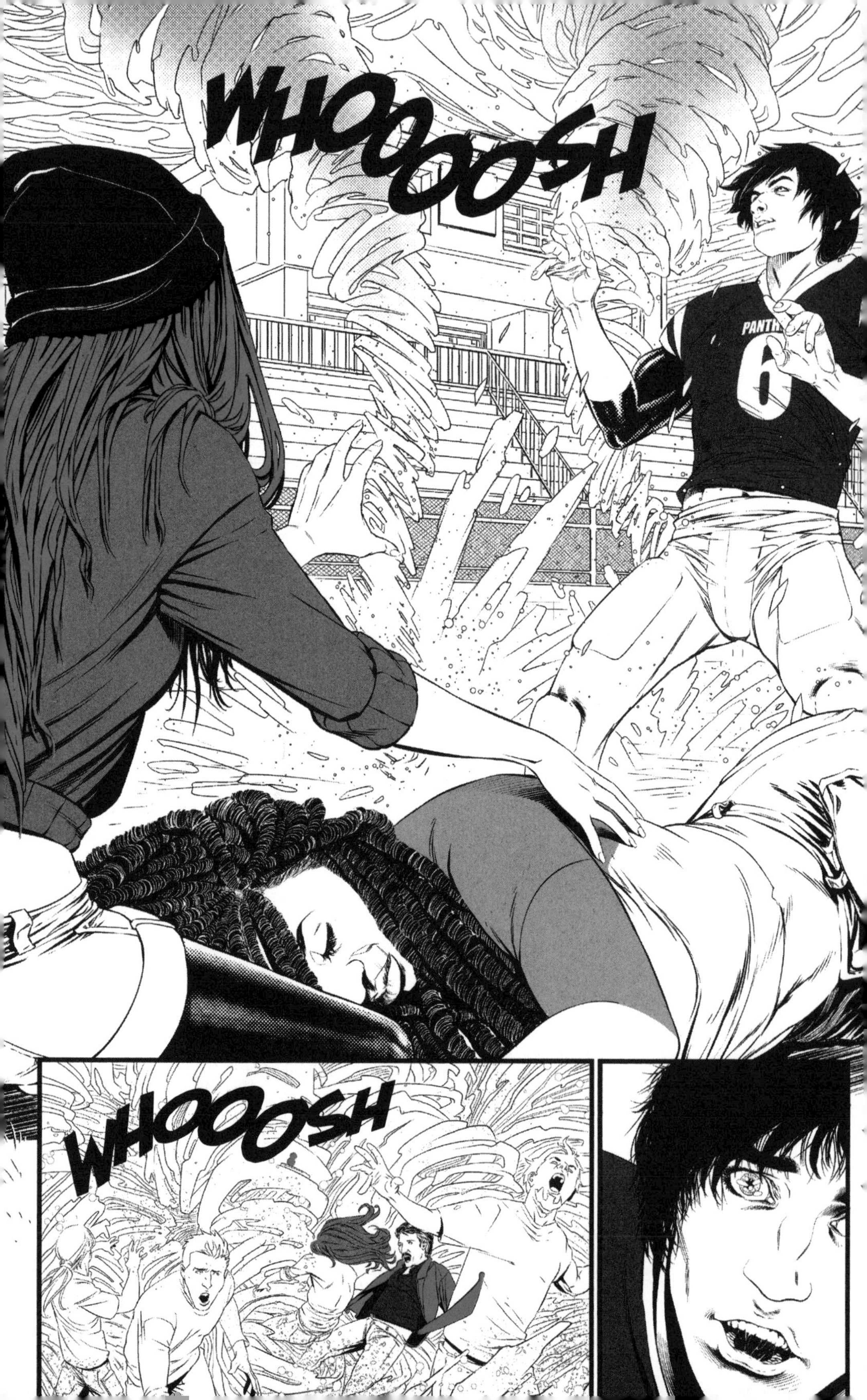
WHOOOOSH
PANTH
6
WHOOOSH

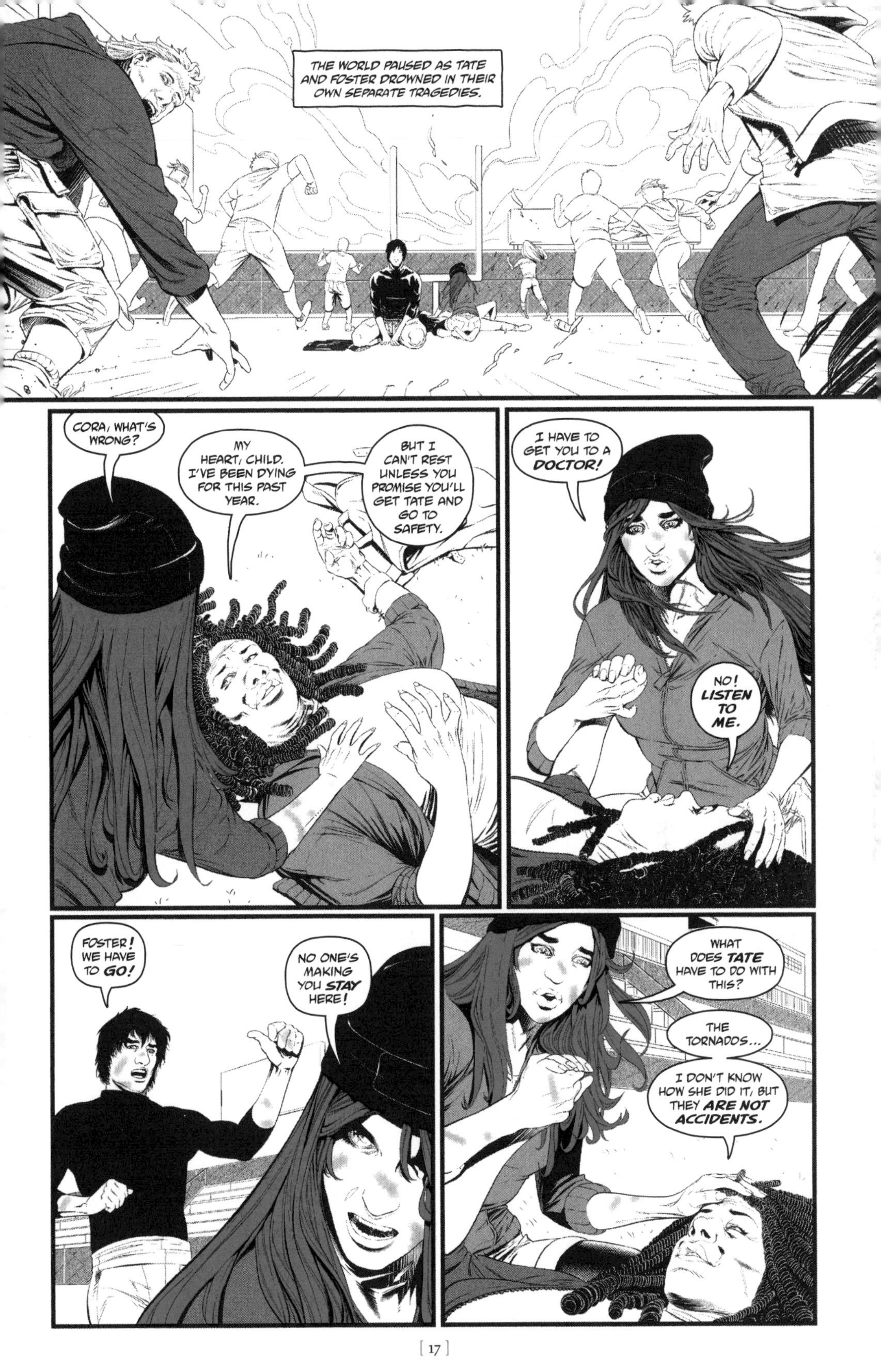
THE WORLD PAUSED AS TATE AND FOSTER DROWNED IN THEIR OWN SEPARATE TRAGEDIES.
CORA, WHAT'S WRONG?
MY HEART, CHILD. I'VE BEEN DYING FOR THIS PAST YEAR.
BUT I CAN'T REST UNLESS YOU PROMISE YOU'LL GET TATE AND GO TO SAFETY.
I HAVE TO GET YOU TO A DOCTOR!
NO! LISTEN TO ME.
FOSTER! WE HAVE TO GO!
NO ONE'S MAKING YOU STAY HERE!
WHAT DOES TATE HAVE TO DO WITH THIS?
THE TORNADOS...
I DON'T KNOW HOW SHE DID IT, BUT THEY ARE NOT ACCIDENTS.

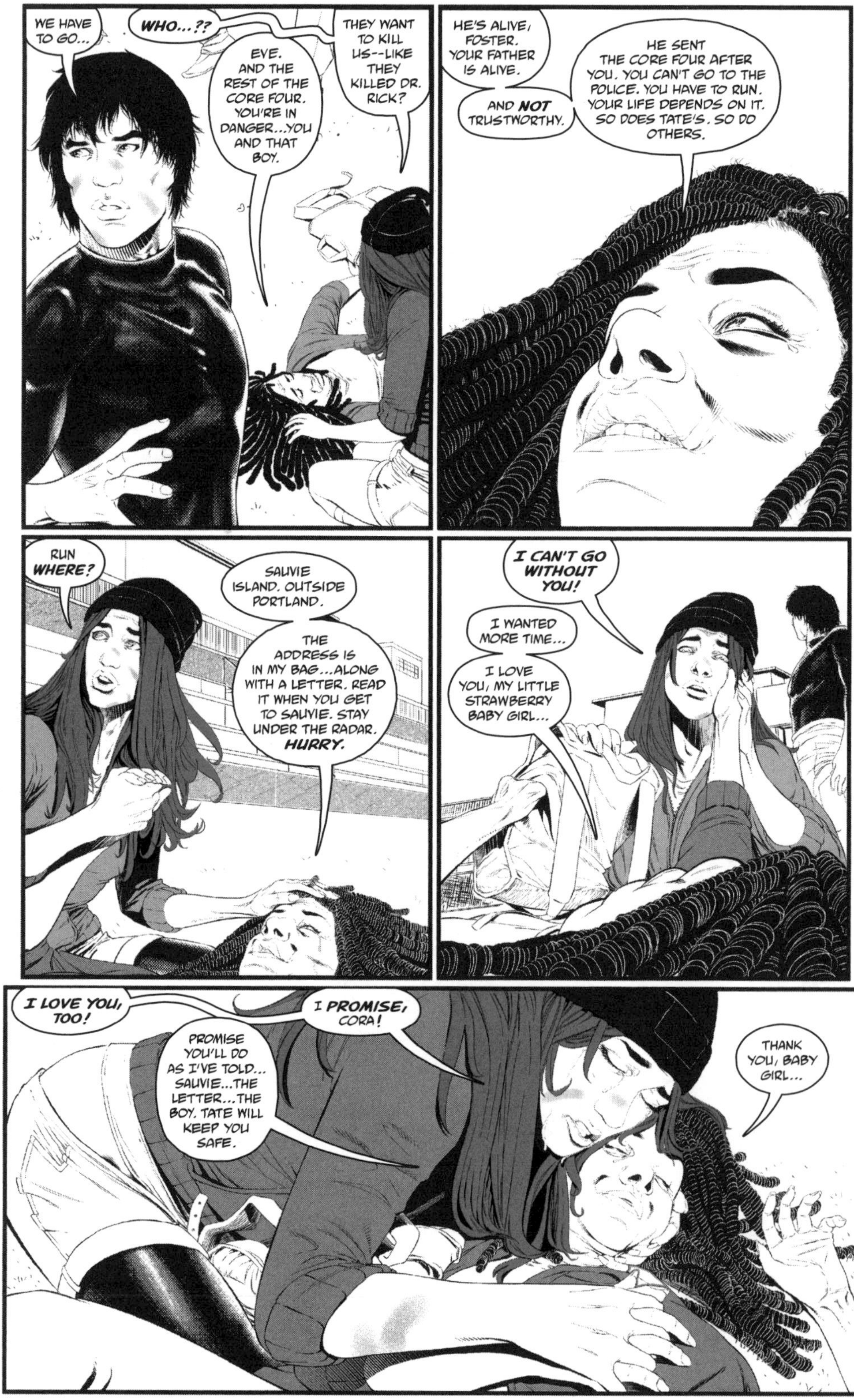
WE HAVE TO GO...
WHO...??
EVE. AND THE REST OF THE CORE FOUR. YOU'RE IN DANGER...YOU AND THAT BOY.
THEY WANT TO KILL US--LIKE THEY KILLED DR. RICK?
HE'S ALIVE, FOSTER. YOUR FATHER IS ALIVE.
AND NOT TRUSTWORTHY.
HE SENT THE CORE FOUR AFTER YOU. YOU CAN'T GO TO THE POLICE. YOU HAVE TO RUN. YOUR LIFE DEPENDS ON IT. SO DOES TATE'S. SO DO OTHERS.
RUN WHERE?
SAUVIE ISLAND. OUTSIDE PORTLAND.
THE ADDRESS IS IN MY BAG...ALONG WITH A LETTER. READ IT WHEN YOU GET TO SAUVIE. STAY UNDER THE RADAR. HURRY.
I CAN'T GO WITHOUT YOU!
I WANTED MORE TIME...
I LOVE YOU, MY LITTLE STRAWBERRY BABY GIRL...
I LOVE YOU, TOO!
PROMISE YOU'LL DO AS I'VE TOLD... SAUVIE...THE LETTER...THE BOY. TATE WILL KEEP YOU SAFE.
I PROMISE, CORA!
THANK YOU, BABY GIRL...

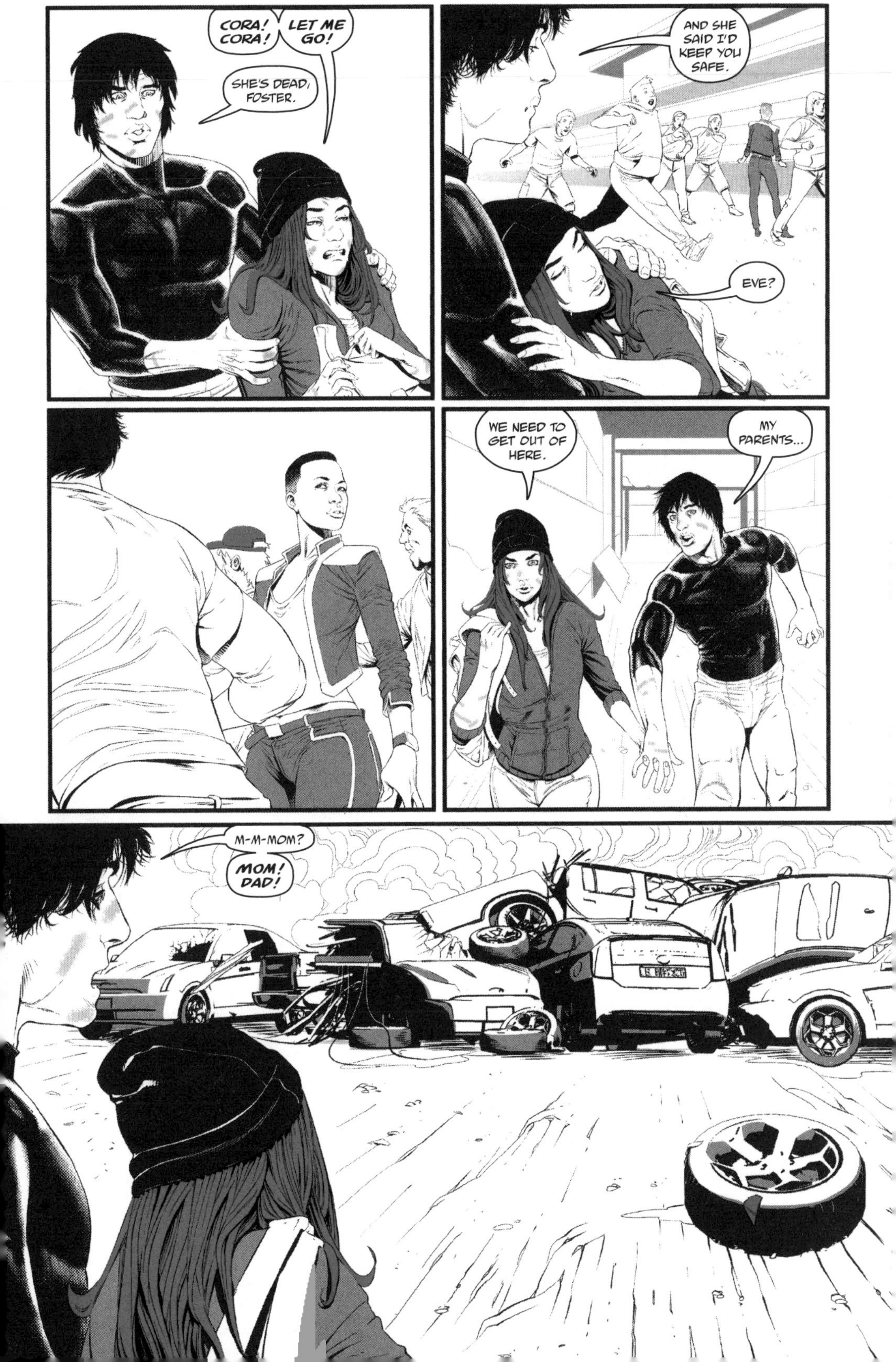
CORA! CORA!
LET ME GO!
SHE'S DEAD, FOSTER.
AND SHE SAID I'D KEEP YOU SAFE.
EVE?
WE NEED TO GET OUT OF HERE.
MY PARENTS...
M-M-MOM?
MOM! DAD!

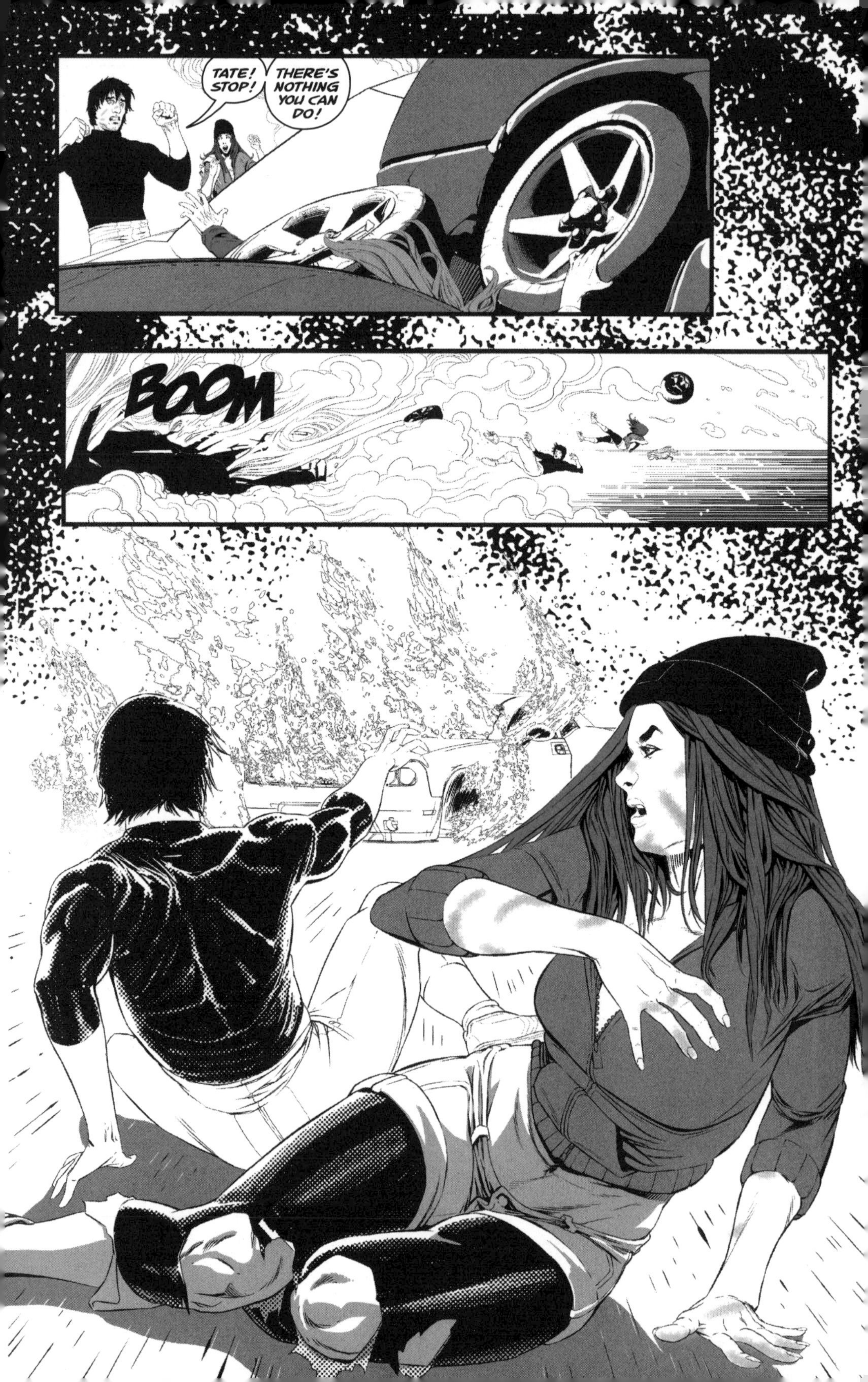
TATE! STOP!
THERE'S NOTHING YOU CAN DO!
BOOM

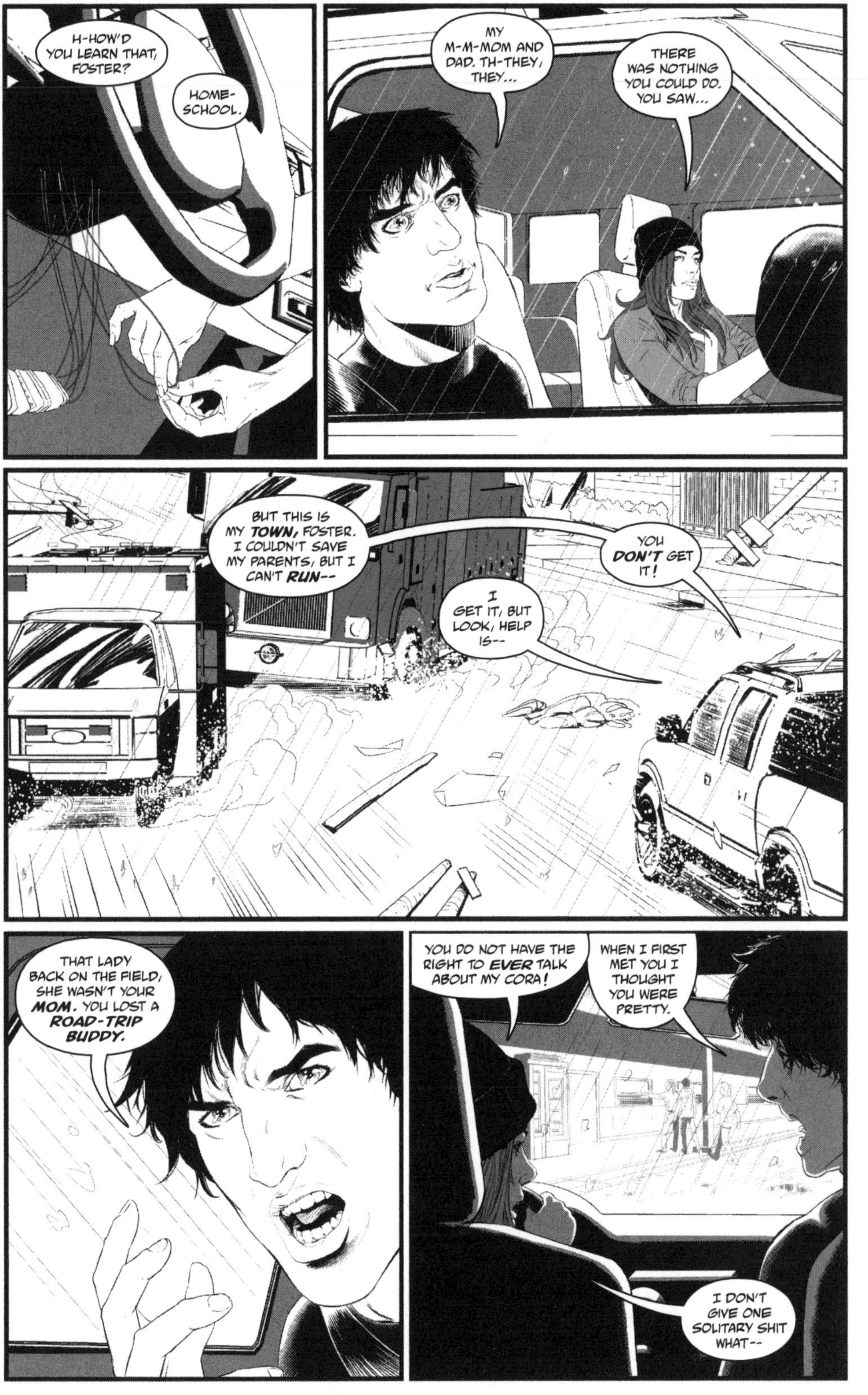
H-HOW'D YOU LEARN THAT, FOSTER?
HOME-SCHOOL.
MY M-M-MOM AND DAD. TH-THEY, THEY...
THERE WAS NOTHING YOU COULD DO. YOU SAW...
BUT THIS IS MY TOWN, FOSTER. I COULDN'T SAVE MY PARENTS, BUT I CAN'T RUN--
YOU DON'T GET IT!
I GET IT, BUT LOOK, HELP IS--
THAT LADY BACK ON THE FIELD, SHE WASN'T YOUR MOM. YOU LOST A ROAD-TRIP BUDDY.
YOU DO NOT HAVE THE RIGHT TO EVER TALK ABOUT MY CORA!
WHEN I FIRST MET YOU I THOUGHT YOU WERE PRETTY.
I DON'T GIVE ONE SOLITARY SHIT WHAT--

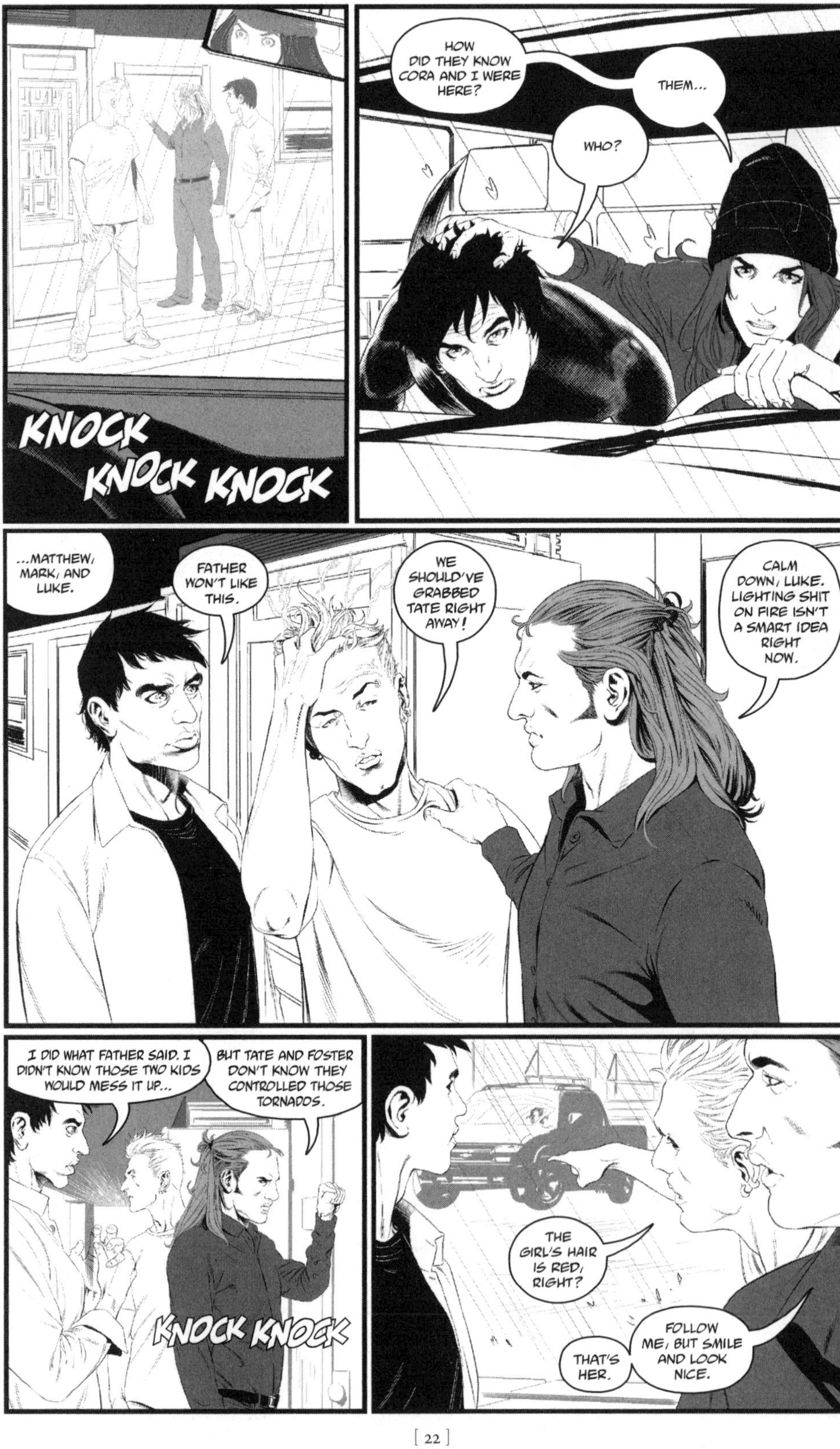
KNOCK
KNOCK KNOCK
HOW DID THEY KNOW CORA AND I WERE HERE?
THEM...
WHO?
...MATTHEW, MARK, AND LUKE.
FATHER WON'T LIKE THIS.
WE SHOULD'VE GRABBED TATE RIGHT AWAY!
CALM DOWN, LUKE. LIGHTING SHIT ON FIRE ISN'T A SMART IDEA RIGHT NOW.
I DID WHAT FATHER SAID. I DIDN'T KNOW THOSE TWO KIDS WOULD MESS IT UP...
BUT TATE AND FOSTER DON'T KNOW THEY CONTROLLED THOSE TORNADOS.
KNOCK KNOCK
THE GIRL'S HAIR IS RED, RIGHT?
THAT'S HER.
FOLLOW ME, BUT SMILE AND LOOK NICE.

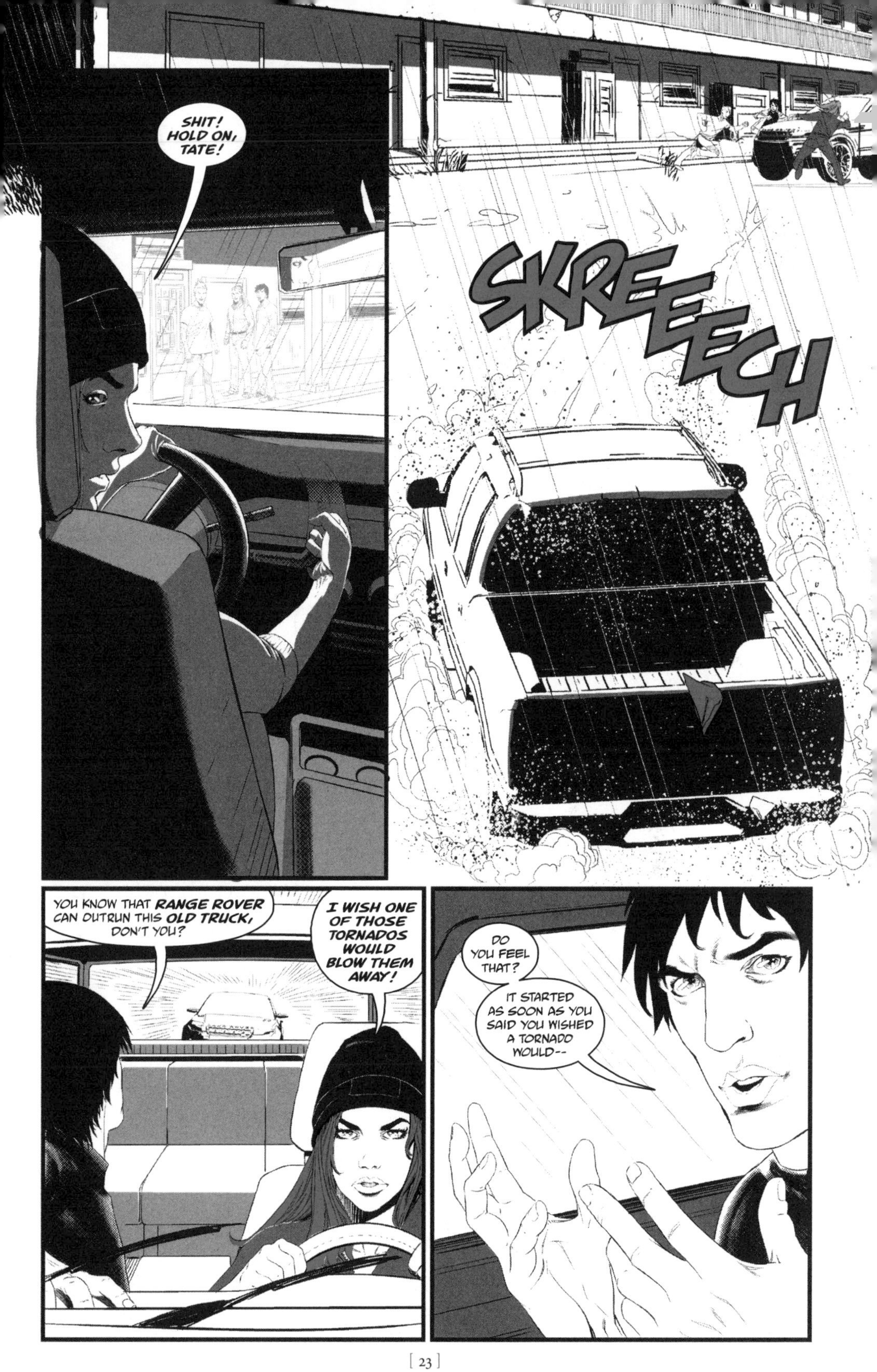
SHIT! HOLD ON, TATE!
SKREEEECH
YOU KNOW THAT RANGE ROVER CAN OUTRUN THIS OLD TRUCK, DON'T YOU?
I WISH ONE OF THOSE TORNADOS WOULD BLOW THEM AWAY!
DO YOU FEEL THAT?
IT STARTED AS SOON AS YOU SAID YOU WISHED A TORNADO WOULD--

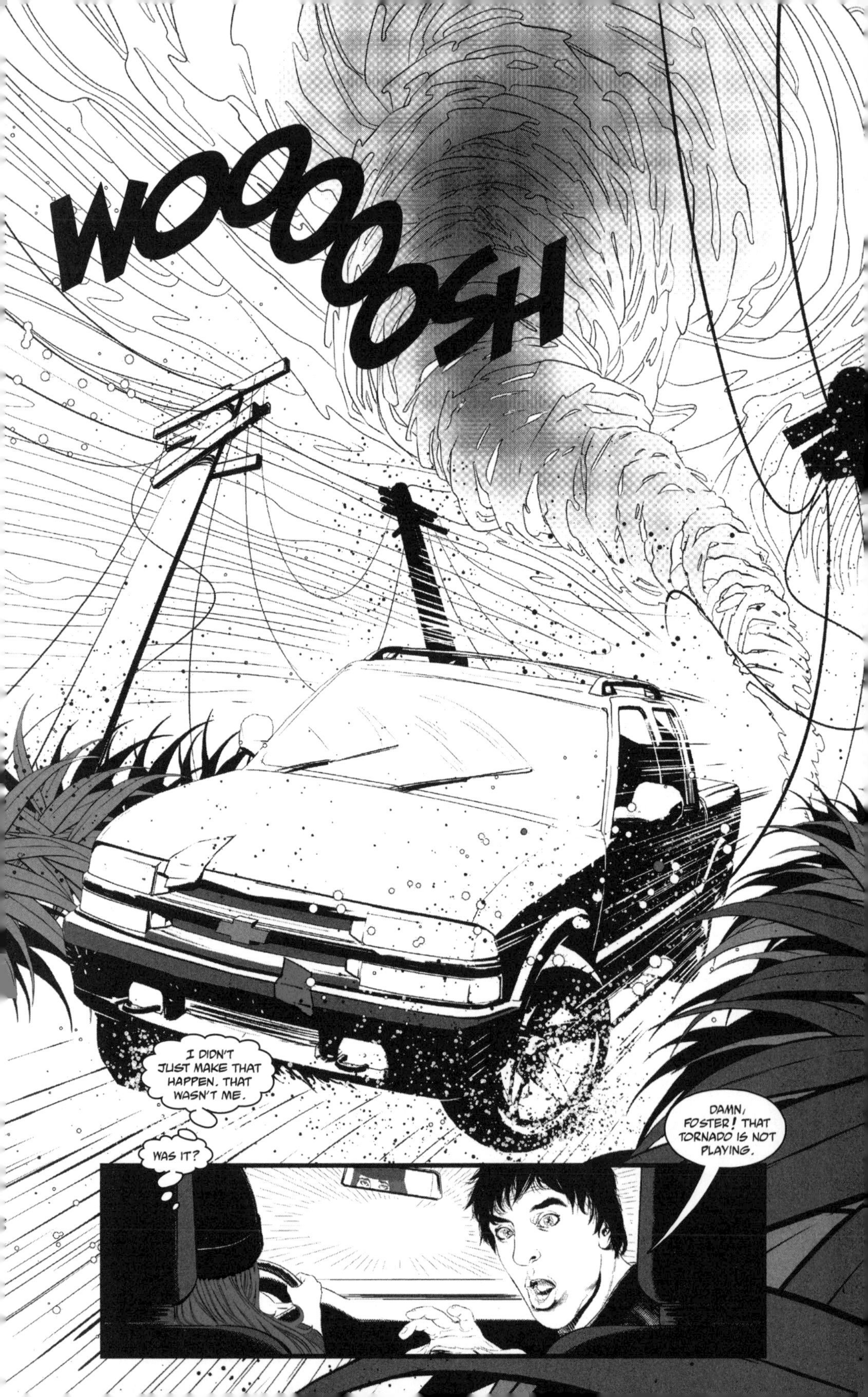
WOOOOOSH
I DIDN'T JUST MAKE THAT HAPPEN. THAT WASN'T ME.
WAS IT?
DAMN, FOSTER! THAT TORNADO IS NOT PLAYING.

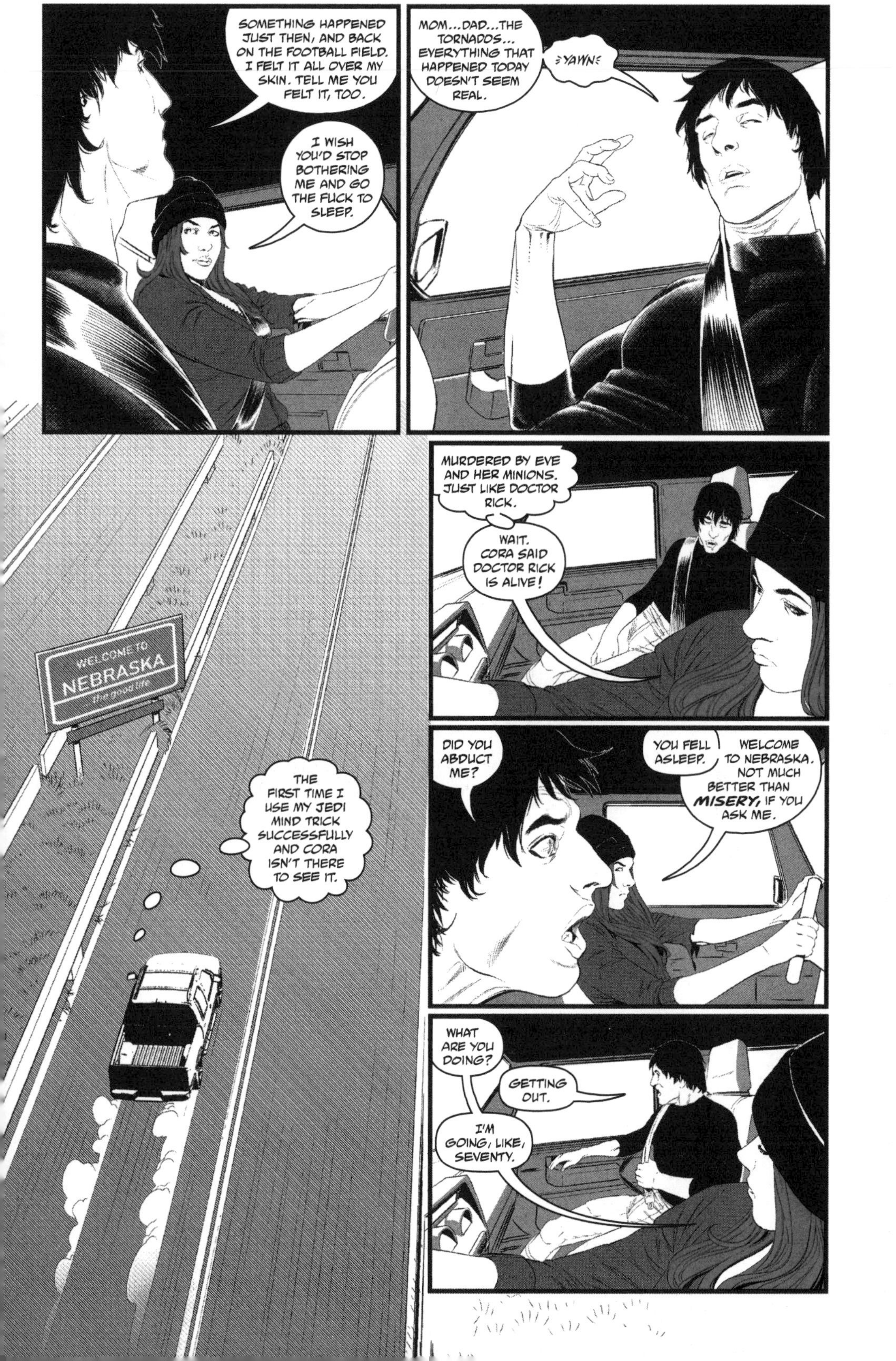
SOMETHING HAPPENED JUST THEN, AND BACK ON THE FOOTBALL FIELD. I FELT IT ALL OVER MY SKIN. TELL ME YOU FELT IT, TOO.
I WISH YOU'D STOP BOTHERING ME AND GO THE FUCK TO SLEEP.
MOM...DAD...THE TORNADOS... EVERYTHING THAT HAPPENED TODAY DOESN'T SEEM REAL.
YAWN
WELCOME TO NEBRASKA ...the good life
THE FIRST TIME I USE MY JEDI MIND TRICK SUCCESSFULLY AND CORA ISN'T THERE TO SEE IT.
MURDERED BY EVE AND HER MINIONS. JUST LIKE DOCTOR RICK.
WAIT. CORA SAID DOCTOR RICK IS ALIVE!
DID YOU ABDUCT ME?
YOU FELL ASLEEP.
WELCOME TO NEBRASKA. NOT MUCH BETTER THAN MISERY, IF YOU ASK ME.
WHAT ARE YOU DOING?
GETTING OUT.
I'M GOING, LIKE, SEVENTY.

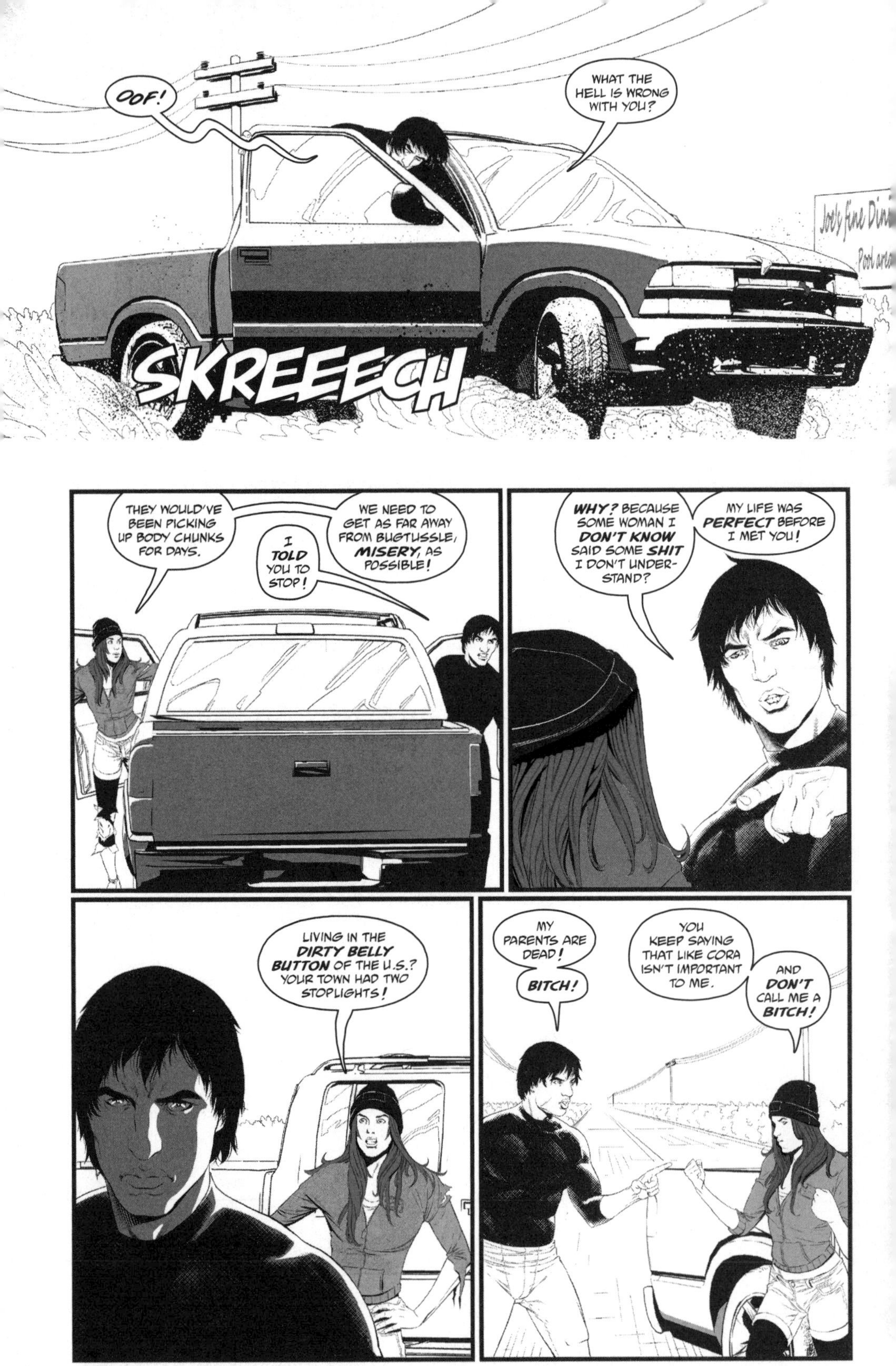
OOF!
WHAT THE HELL IS WRONG WITH YOU?
SKREEECH
THEY WOULD'VE BEEN PICKING UP BODY CHUNKS FOR DAYS.
WE NEED TO GET AS FAR AWAY FROM BUGTUSSLE, MISERY, AS POSSIBLE!
I TOLD YOU TO STOP!
WHY? BECAUSE SOME WOMAN I DON'T KNOW SAID SOME SHIT I DON'T UNDERSTAND?
MY LIFE WAS PERFECT BEFORE I MET YOU!
LIVING IN THE DIRTY BELLY BUTTON OF THE U.S.? YOUR TOWN HAD TWO STOPLIGHTS!
MY PARENTS ARE DEAD!
BITCH!
YOU KEEP SAYING THAT LIKE CORA ISN'T IMPORTANT TO ME.
AND DON'T CALL ME A BITCH!

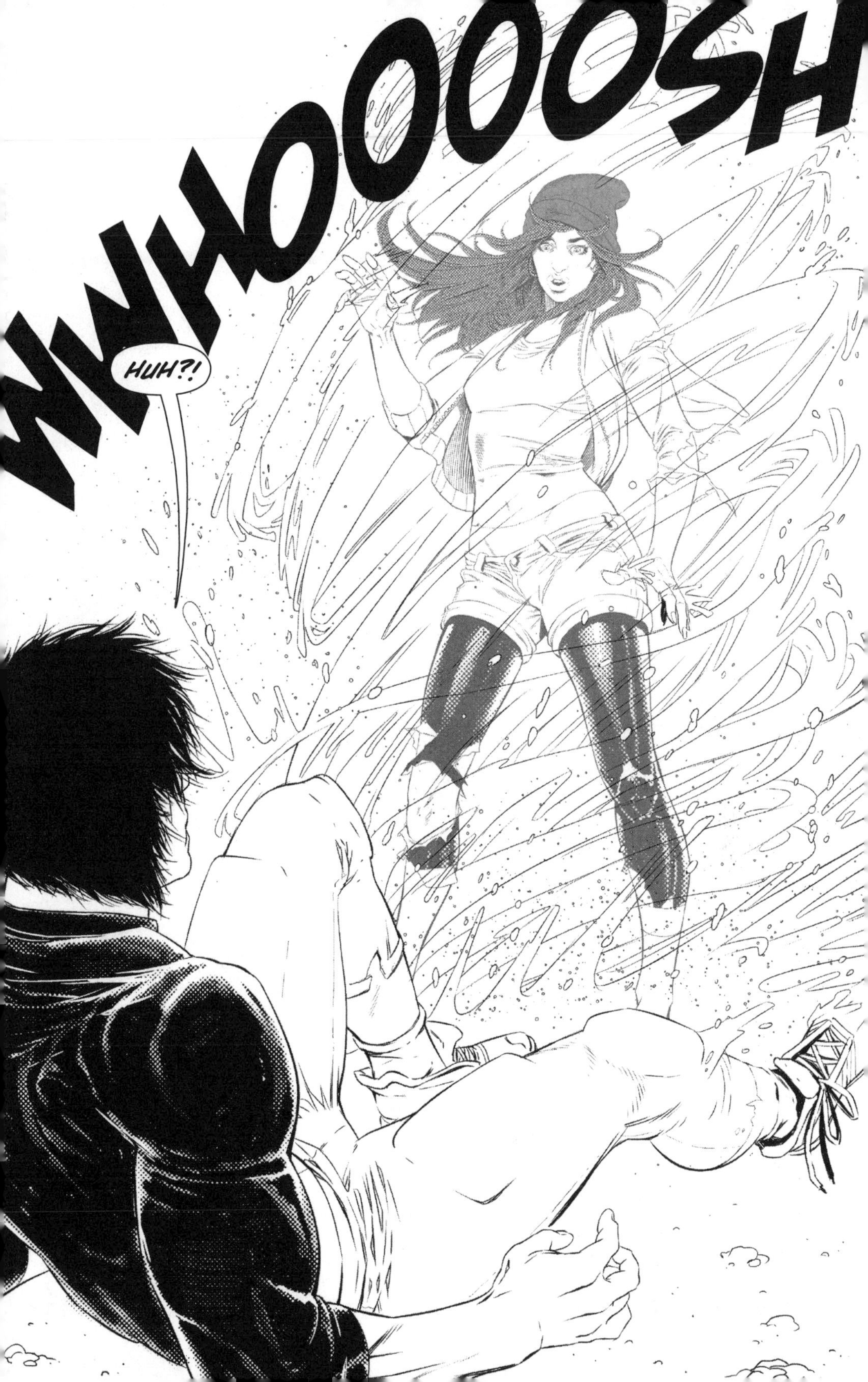
WWHOOOOOSH
HUH?!

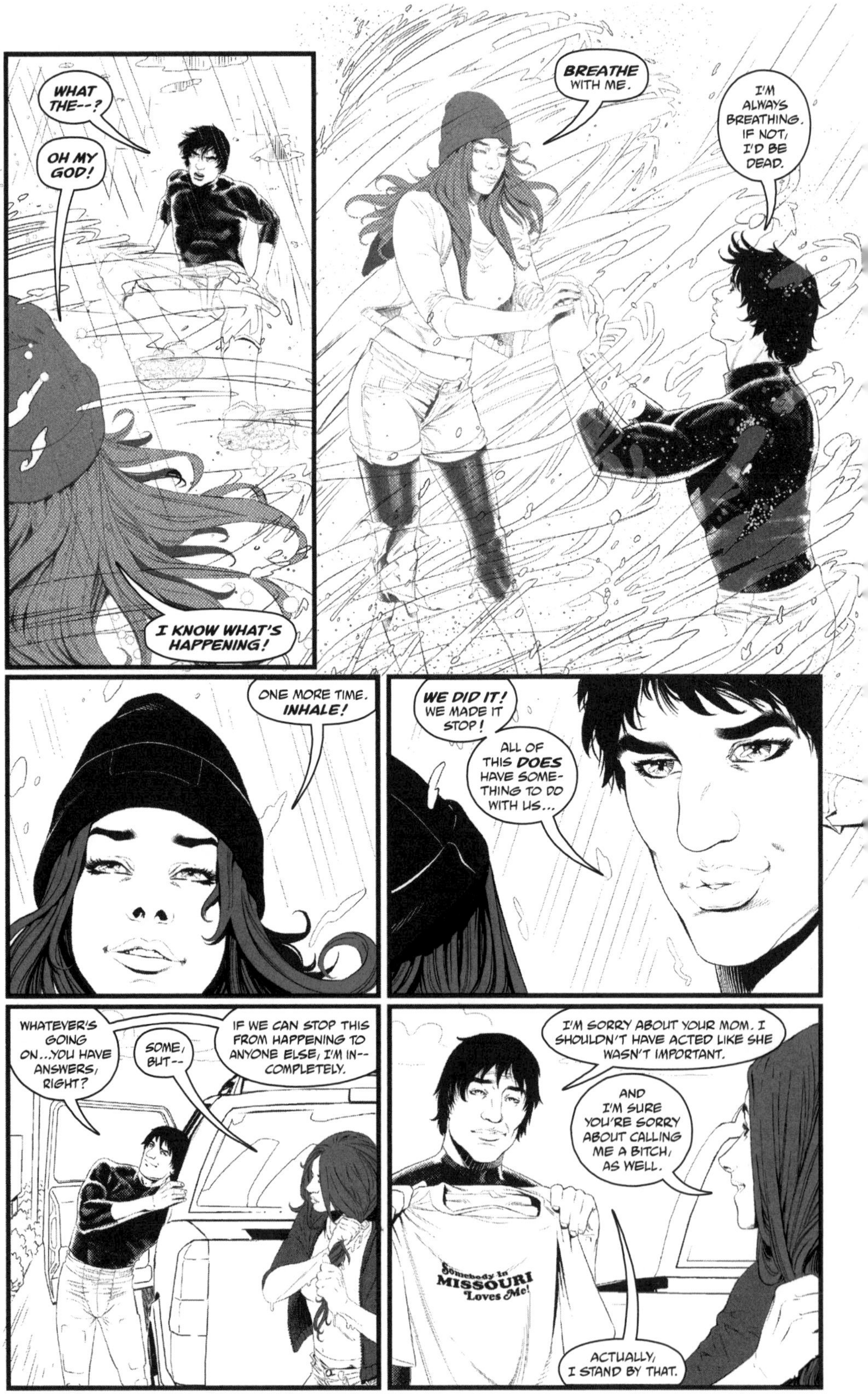
WHAT THE--?
OH MY GOD!
I KNOW WHAT'S HAPPENING!
BREATHE WITH ME.
I'M ALWAYS BREATHING. IF NOT, I'D BE DEAD.
ONE MORE TIME. INHALE!
WE DID IT! WE MADE IT STOP!
ALL OF THIS DOES HAVE SOME-THING TO DO WITH US...
WHATEVER'S GOING ON...YOU HAVE ANSWERS, RIGHT?
SOME, BUT--
IF WE CAN STOP THIS FROM HAPPENING TO ANYONE ELSE, I'M IN-- COMPLETELY.
I'M SORRY ABOUT YOUR MOM. I SHOULDN'T HAVE ACTED LIKE SHE WASN'T IMPORTANT.
AND I'M SURE YOU'RE SORRY ABOUT CALLING ME A BITCH, AS WELL.
Somebody In MISSOURI Loves Me!
ACTUALLY, I STAND BY THAT.

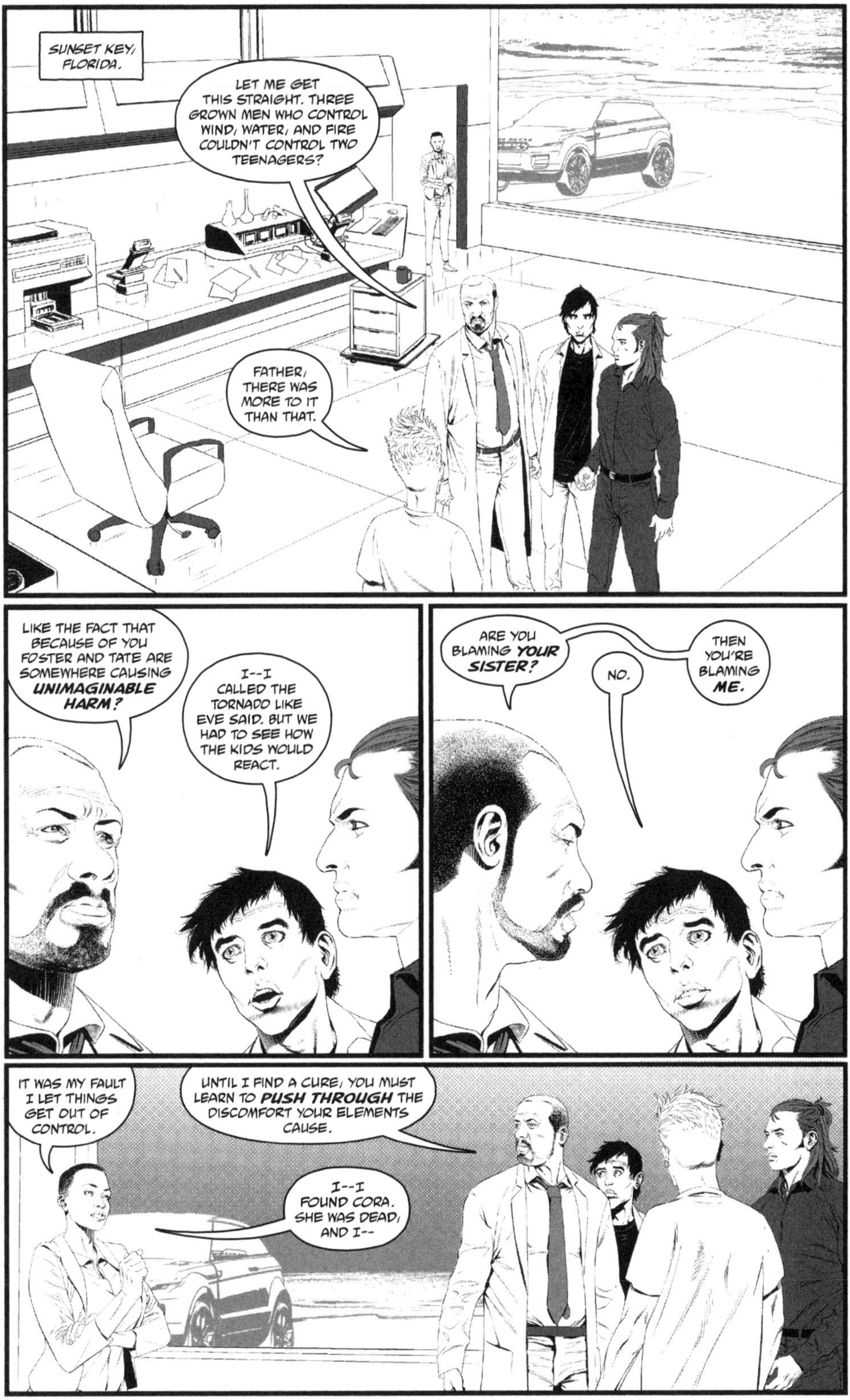
SUNSET KEY, FLORIDA.
LET ME GET THIS STRAIGHT. THREE GROWN MEN WHO CONTROL WIND, WATER, AND FIRE COULDN'T CONTROL TWO TEENAGERS?
FATHER, THERE WAS MORE TO IT THAN THAT.
LIKE THE FACT THAT BECAUSE OF YOU FOSTER AND TATE ARE SOMEWHERE CAUSING UNIMAGINABLE HARM?
I--I CALLED THE TORNADO LIKE EVE SAID. BUT WE HAD TO SEE HOW THE KIDS WOULD REACT.
ARE YOU BLAMING YOUR SISTER?
NO.
THEN YOU'RE BLAMING ME.
IT WAS MY FAULT I LET THINGS GET OUT OF CONTROL.
UNTIL I FIND A CURE, YOU MUST LEARN TO PUSH THROUGH THE DISCOMFORT YOUR ELEMENTS CAUSE.
I--I FOUND CORA. SHE WAS DEAD, AND I--

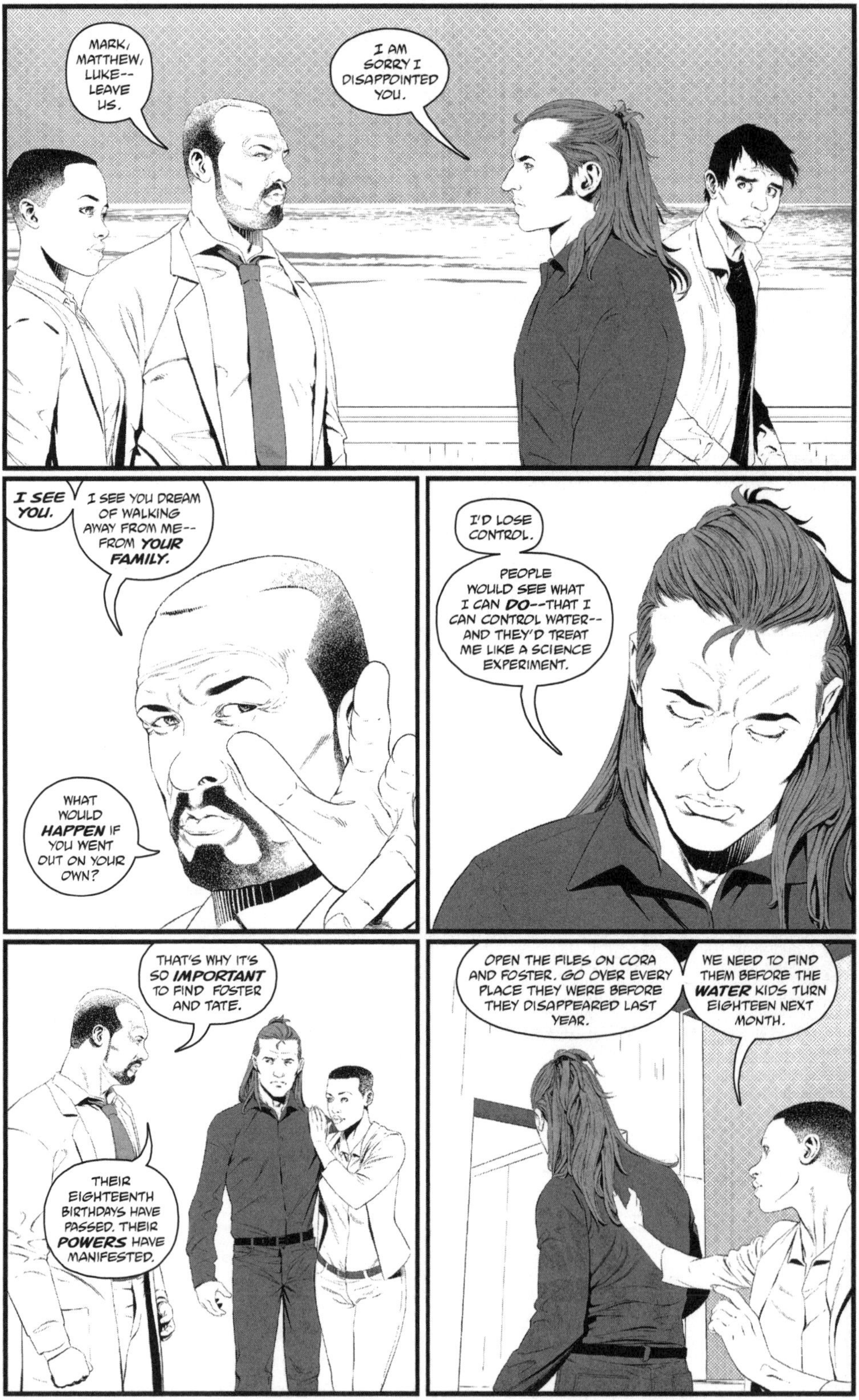
MARK, MATTHEW, LUKE-- LEAVE US.
I AM SORRY I DISAPPOINTED YOU.
I SEE YOU.
I SEE YOU DREAM OF WALKING AWAY FROM ME-- FROM YOUR FAMILY.
WHAT WOULD HAPPEN IF YOU WENT OUT ON YOUR OWN?
I'D LOSE CONTROL.
PEOPLE WOULD SEE WHAT I CAN DO--THAT I CAN CONTROL WATER-- AND THEY'D TREAT ME LIKE A SCIENCE EXPERIMENT.
THAT'S WHY IT'S SO IMPORTANT TO FIND FOSTER AND TATE.
THEIR EIGHTEENTH BIRTHDAYS HAVE PASSED. THEIR POWERS HAVE MANIFESTED.
OPEN THE FILES ON CORA AND FOSTER. GO OVER EVERY PLACE THEY WERE BEFORE THEY DISAPPEARED LAST YEAR.
WE NEED TO FIND THEM BEFORE THE WATER KIDS TURN EIGHTEEN NEXT MONTH.

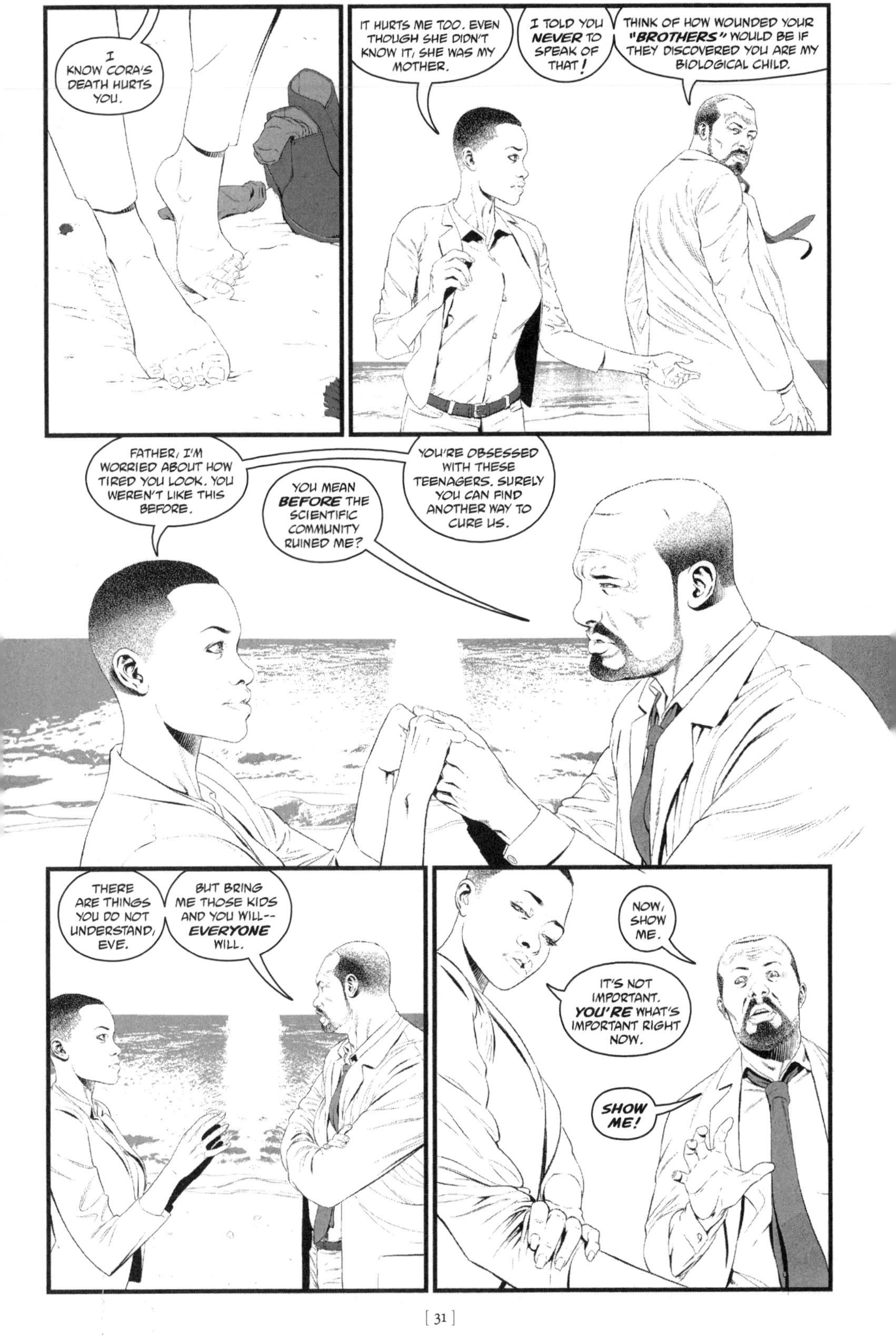
I KNOW CORA'S DEATH HURTS YOU.
IT HURTS ME TOO. EVEN THOUGH SHE DIDN'T KNOW IT, SHE WAS MY MOTHER.
I TOLD YOU NEVER TO SPEAK OF THAT!
THINK OF HOW WOUNDED YOUR "BROTHERS" WOULD BE IF THEY DISCOVERED YOU ARE MY BIOLOGICAL CHILD.
FATHER, I'M WORRIED ABOUT HOW TIRED YOU LOOK. YOU WEREN'T LIKE THIS BEFORE.
YOU MEAN BEFORE THE SCIENTIFIC COMMUNITY RUINED ME?
YOU'RE OBSESSED WITH THESE TEENAGERS. SURELY YOU CAN FIND ANOTHER WAY TO CURE US.
THERE ARE THINGS YOU DO NOT UNDERSTAND, EVE.
BUT BRING ME THOSE KIDS AND YOU WILL-- EVERYONE WILL.
NOW, SHOW ME.
IT'S NOT IMPORTANT. YOU'RE WHAT'S IMPORTANT RIGHT NOW.
SHOW ME!

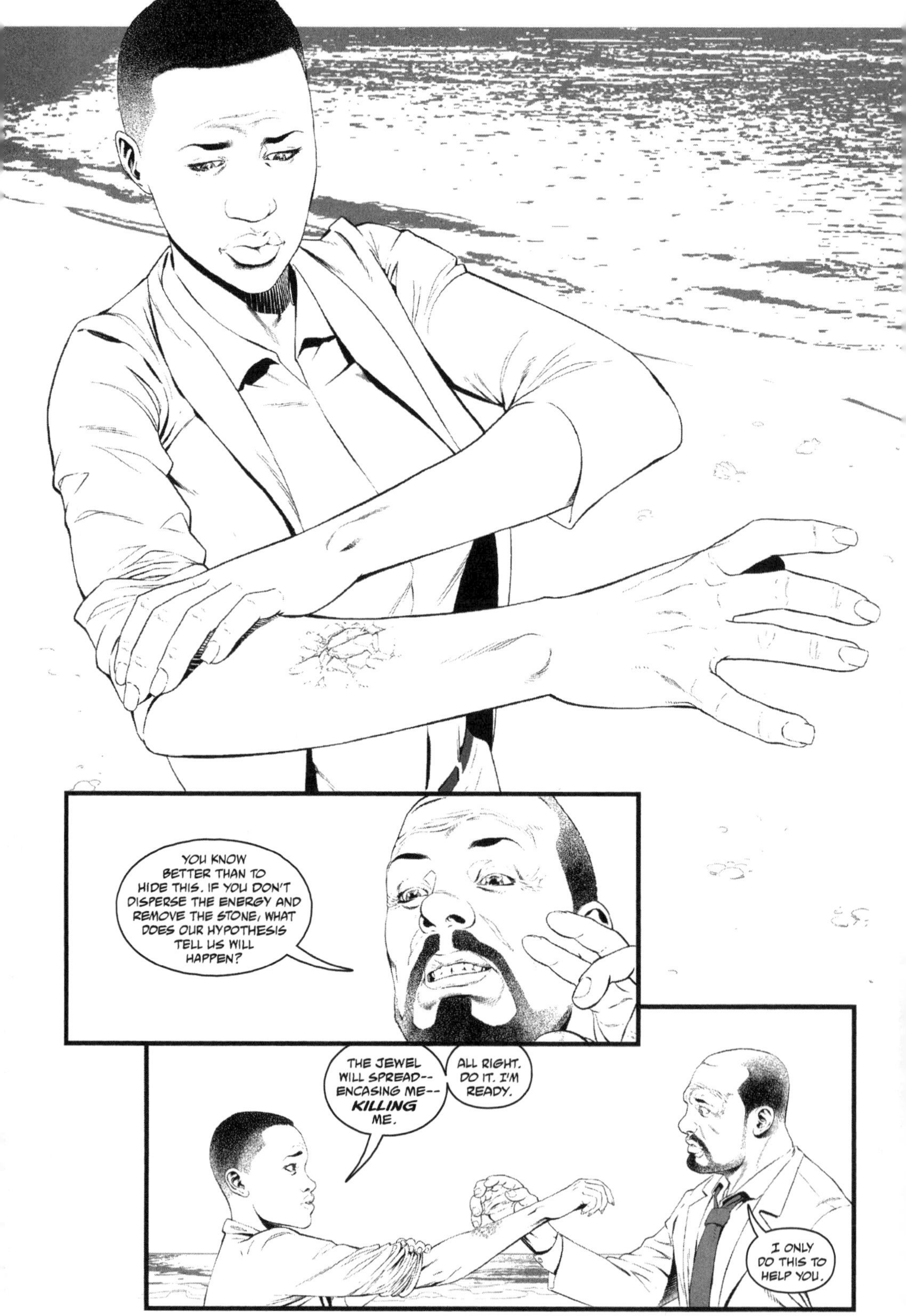
YOU KNOW BETTER THAN TO HIDE THIS. IF YOU DON'T DISPERSE THE ENERGY AND REMOVE THE STONE, WHAT DOES OUR HYPOTHESIS TELL US WILL HAPPEN?
THE JEWEL WILL SPREAD-- ENCASING ME-- **KILLING** ME.
ALL RIGHT. DO IT. I'M READY.
I ONLY DO THIS TO HELP YOU.

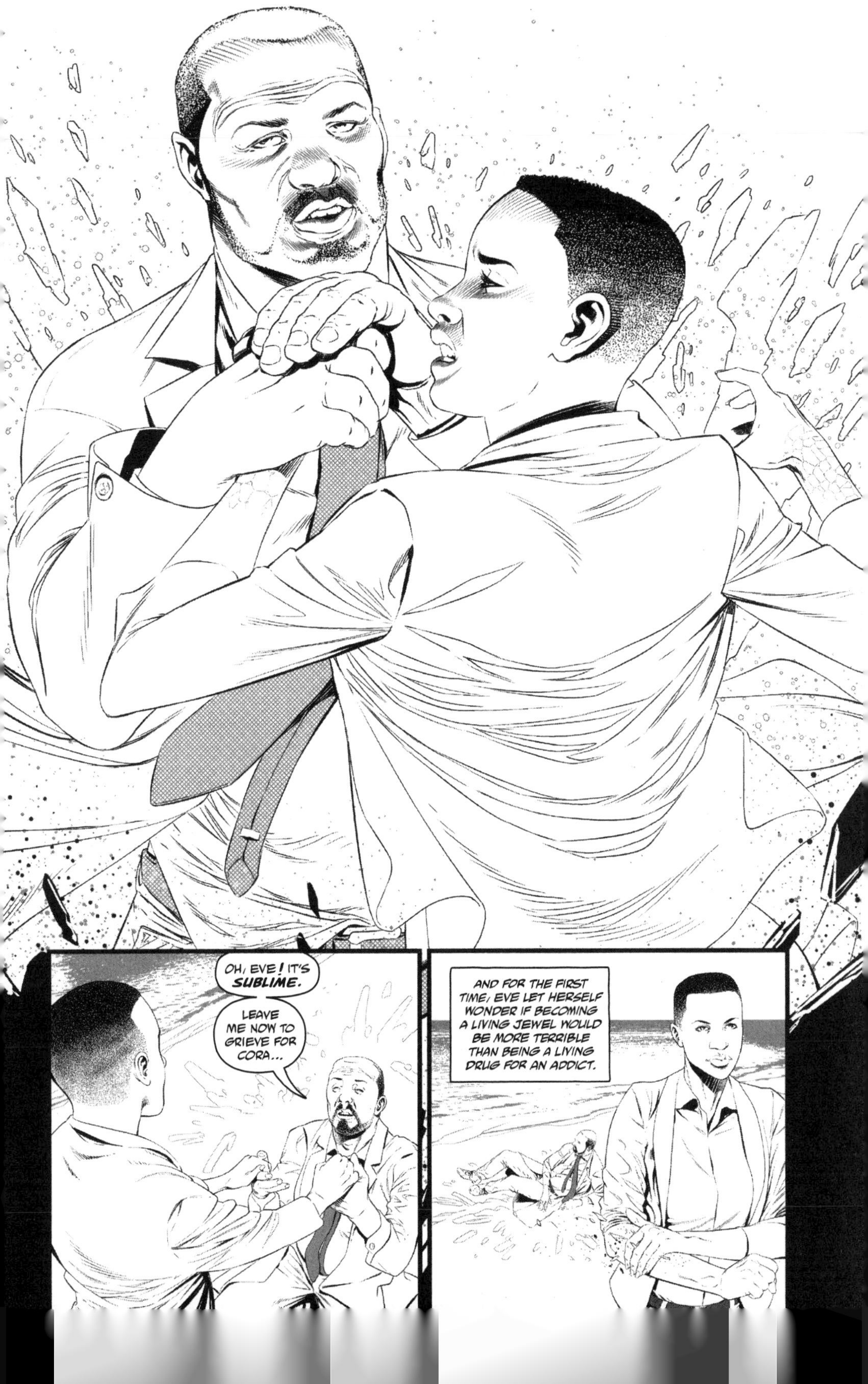
OH, EVE! IT'S SUBLIME.
LEAVE ME NOW TO GRIEVE FOR CORA...
AND FOR THE FIRST TIME, EVE LET HERSELF WONDER IF BECOMING A LIVING JEWEL WOULD BE MORE TERRIBLE THAN BEING A LIVING DRUG FOR AN ADDICT.

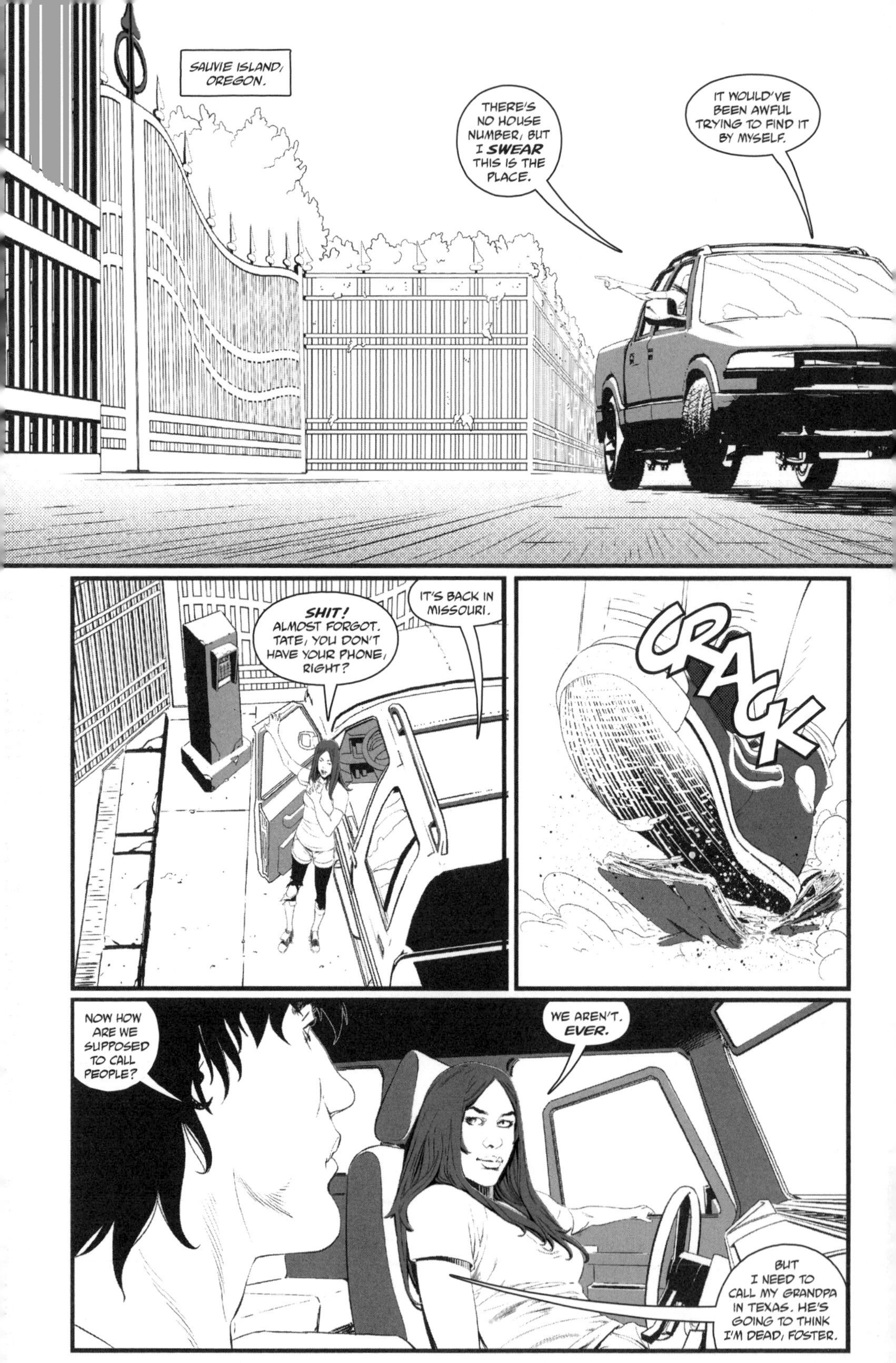
SAUVIE ISLAND, OREGON.
THERE'S NO HOUSE NUMBER, BUT I SWEAR THIS IS THE PLACE.
IT WOULD'VE BEEN AWFUL TRYING TO FIND IT BY MYSELF.
SHIT! ALMOST FORGOT. TATE, YOU DON'T HAVE YOUR PHONE, RIGHT?
IT'S BACK IN MISSOURI.
CRACK
NOW HOW ARE WE SUPPOSED TO CALL PEOPLE?
WE AREN'T. EVER.
BUT I NEED TO CALL MY GRANDPA IN TEXAS. HE'S GOING TO THINK I'M DEAD, FOSTER.

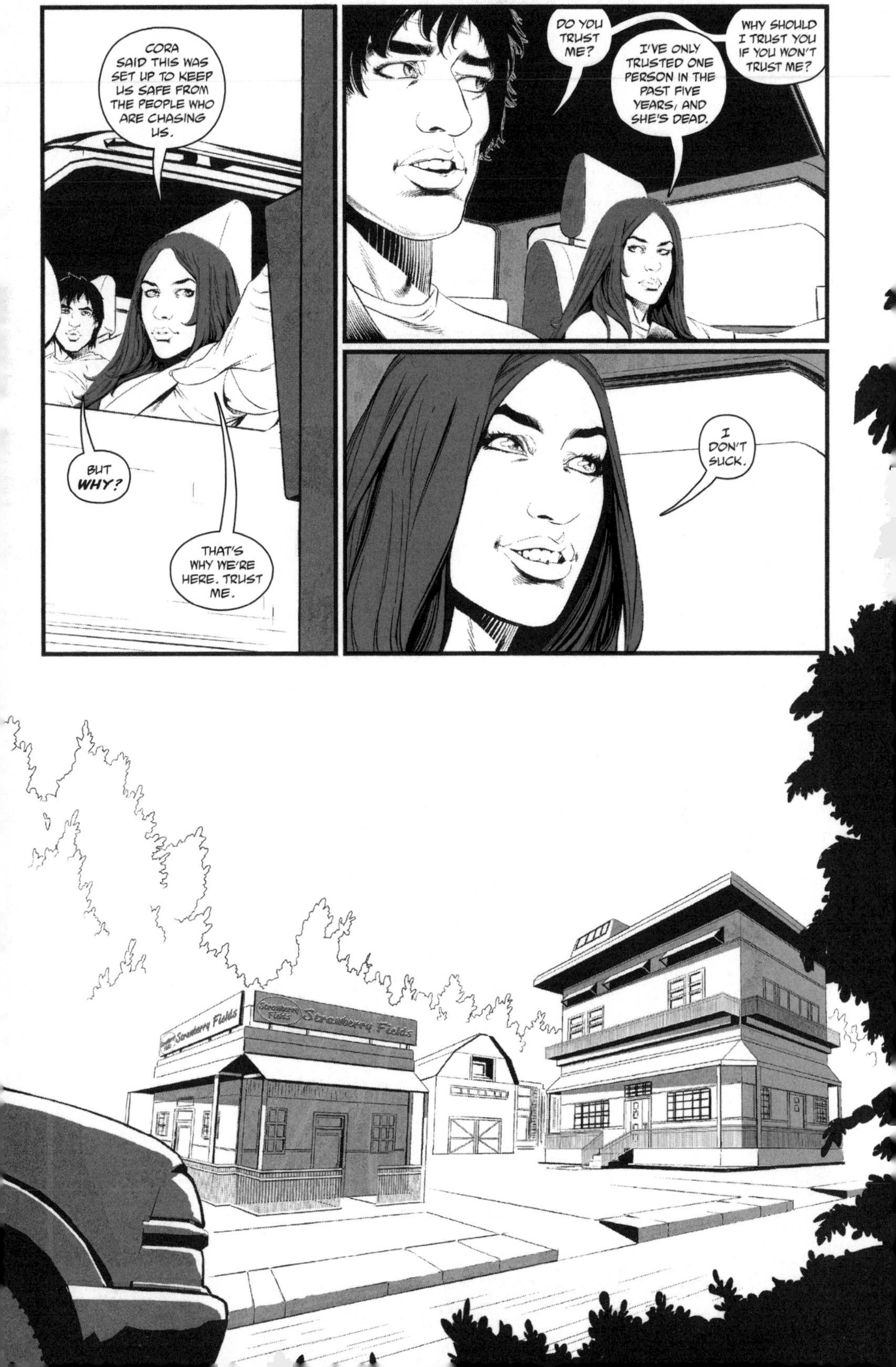
CORA SAID THIS WAS SET UP TO KEEP US SAFE FROM THE PEOPLE WHO ARE CHASING US.
BUT *WHY?*
THAT'S WHY WE'RE HERE. TRUST ME.
DO YOU TRUST ME?
I'VE ONLY TRUSTED ONE PERSON IN THE PAST FIVE YEARS, AND SHE'S DEAD.
WHY SHOULD I TRUST YOU IF YOU WON'T TRUST ME?
I DON'T SUCK.
Strawberry Fields
Strawberry Fields
Strawberry Fields

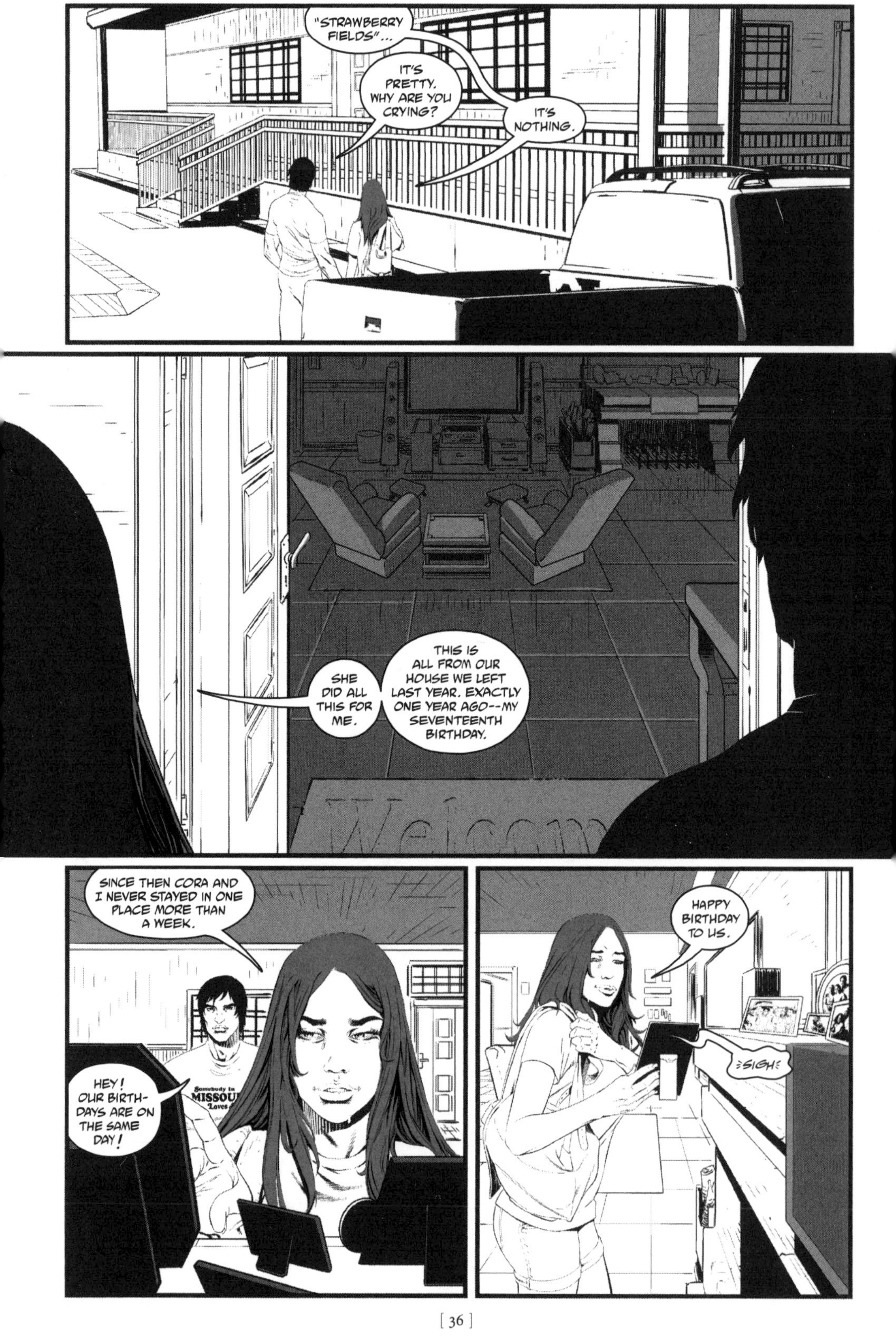
"STRAWBERRY FIELDS"...
IT'S PRETTY. WHY ARE YOU CRYING?
IT'S NOTHING.
SHE DID ALL THIS FOR ME.
THIS IS ALL FROM OUR HOUSE WE LEFT LAST YEAR. EXACTLY ONE YEAR AGO--MY SEVENTEENTH BIRTHDAY.
SINCE THEN CORA AND I NEVER STAYED IN ONE PLACE MORE THAN A WEEK.
HEY! OUR BIRTH-DAYS ARE ON THE SAME DAY!
HAPPY BIRTHDAY TO US.
SIGH

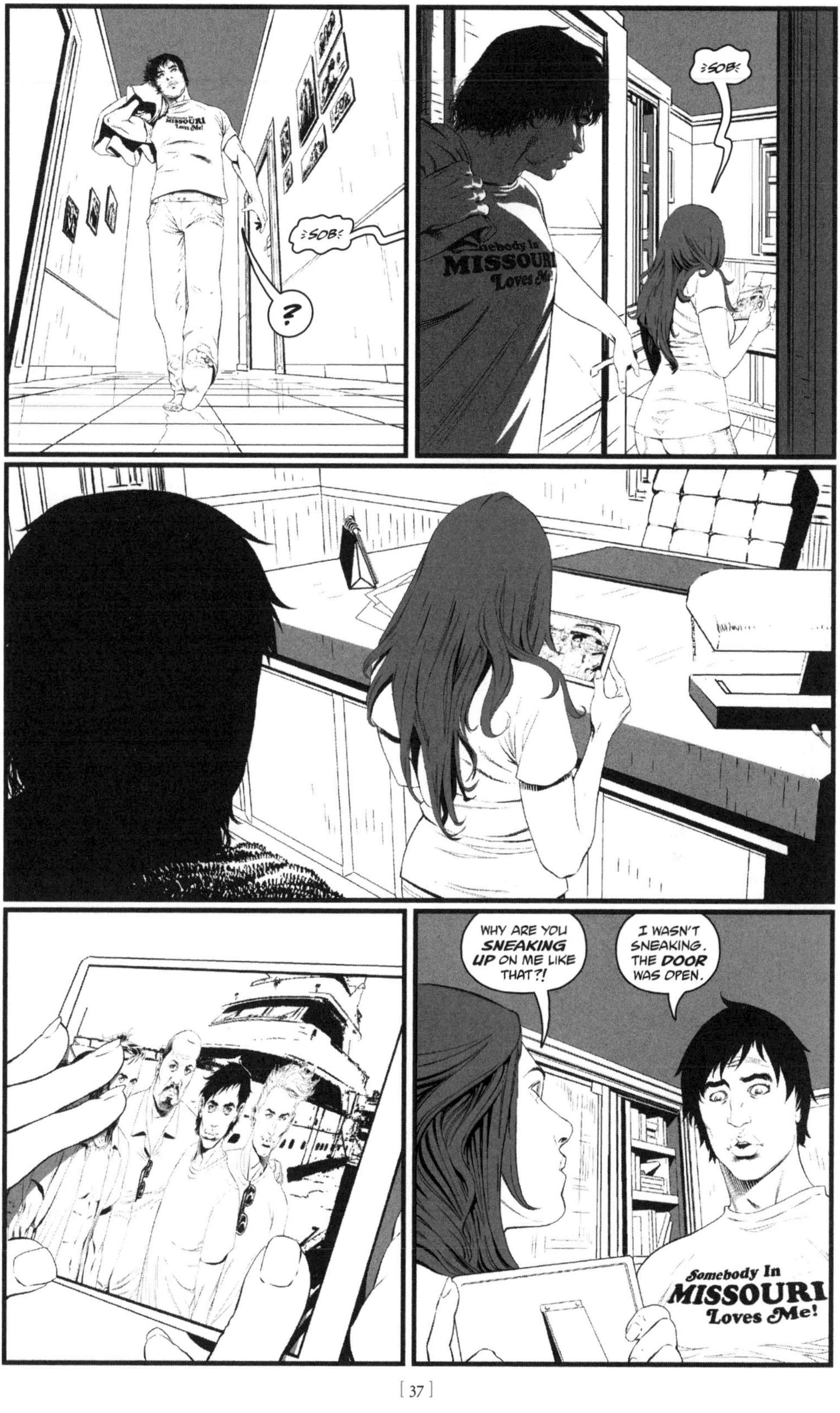
Somebody In
MISSOURI
Loves Me!
SOB
?
SOB
Somebody In
MISSOURI
Loves Me!
WHY ARE YOU SNEAKING UP ON ME LIKE THAT?!
I WASN'T SNEAKING. THE DOOR WAS OPEN.
Somebody In
MISSOURI
Loves Me!

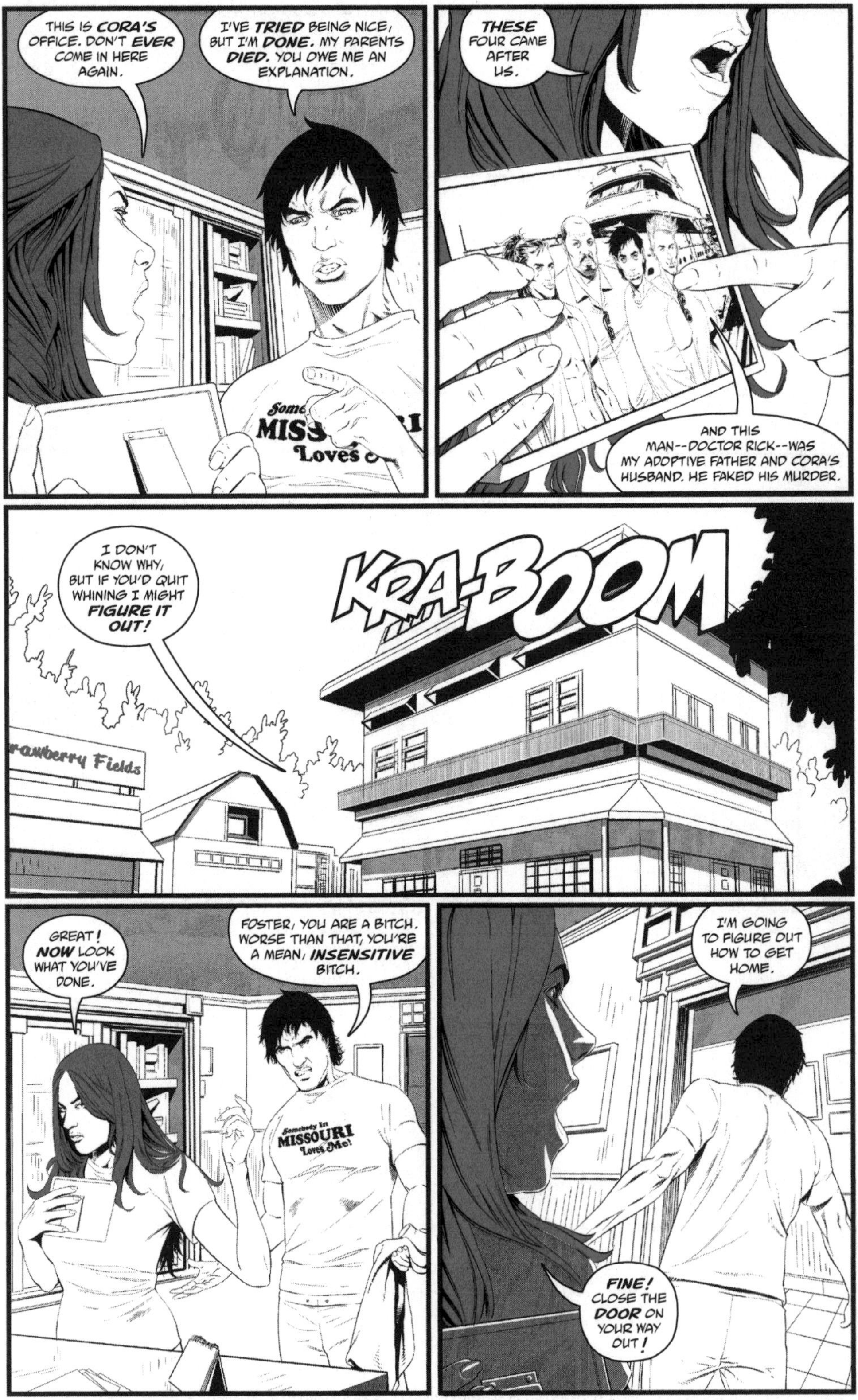
THIS IS CORA'S OFFICE. DON'T EVER COME IN HERE AGAIN.
I'VE TRIED BEING NICE, BUT I'M DONE. MY PARENTS DIED. YOU OWE ME AN EXPLANATION.
MISSOURI
Loves
THESE FOUR CAME AFTER US.
AND THIS MAN--DOCTOR RICK--WAS MY ADOPTIVE FATHER AND CORA'S HUSBAND. HE FAKED HIS MURDER.
I DON'T KNOW WHY, BUT IF YOU'D QUIT WHINING I MIGHT FIGURE IT OUT!
KRA-BOOM
rawberry Fields
GREAT! NOW LOOK WHAT YOU'VE DONE.
FOSTER, YOU ARE A BITCH. WORSE THAN THAT, YOU'RE A MEAN, INSENSITIVE BITCH.
Somebody In MISSOURI Loves Me!
I'M GOING TO FIGURE OUT HOW TO GET HOME.
FINE! CLOSE THE DOOR ON YOUR WAY OUT!

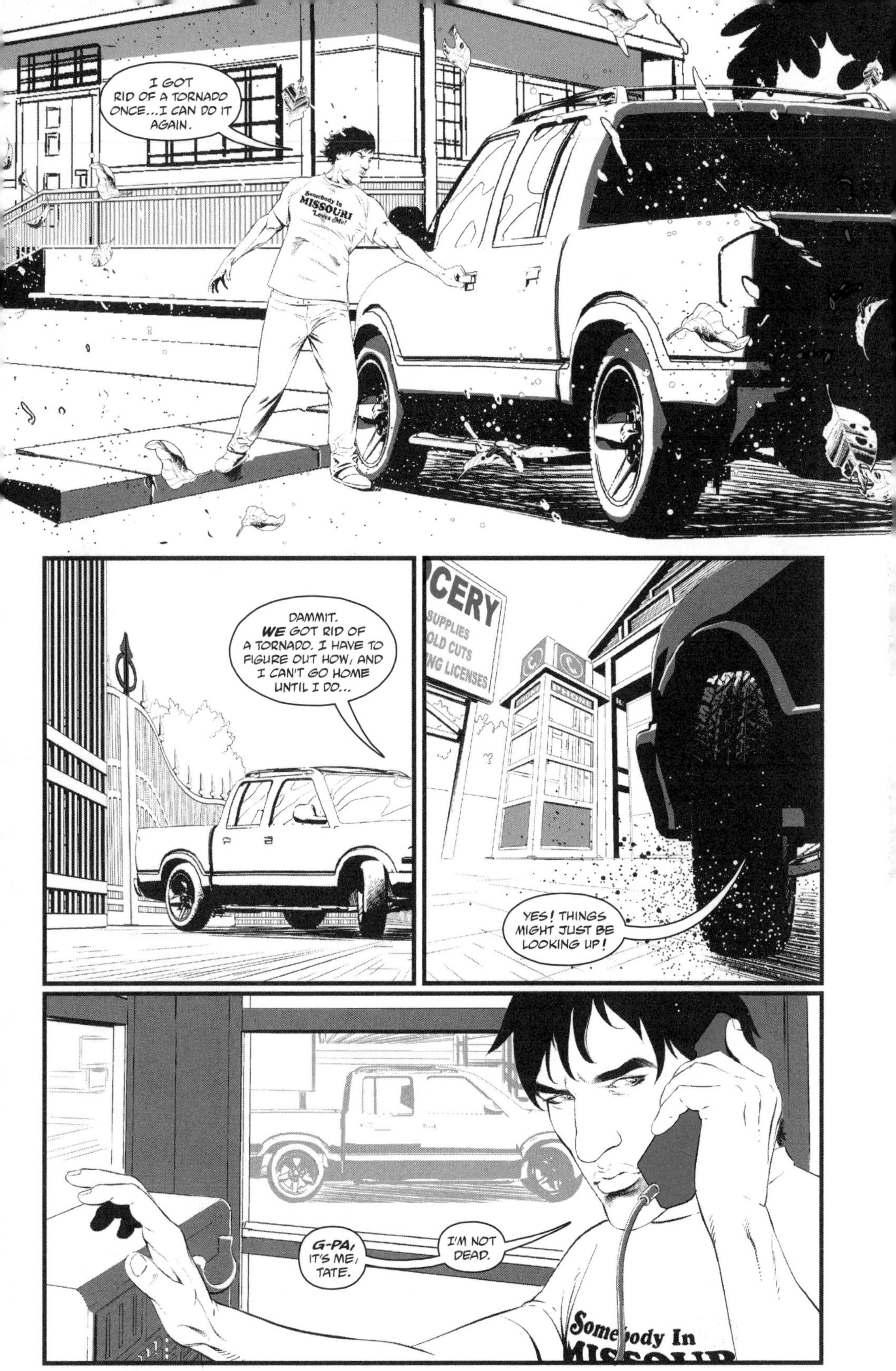
I GOT RID OF A TORNADO ONCE...I CAN DO IT AGAIN.
Somebody In MISSOURI Loves Me!
DAMMIT. WE GOT RID OF A TORNADO. I HAVE TO FIGURE OUT HOW, AND I CAN'T GO HOME UNTIL I DO...
CERY
SUPPLIES
OLD CUTS
NG LICENSES
YES! THINGS MIGHT JUST BE LOOKING UP!
G-PA, IT'S ME, TATE.
I'M NOT DEAD.
Somebody In

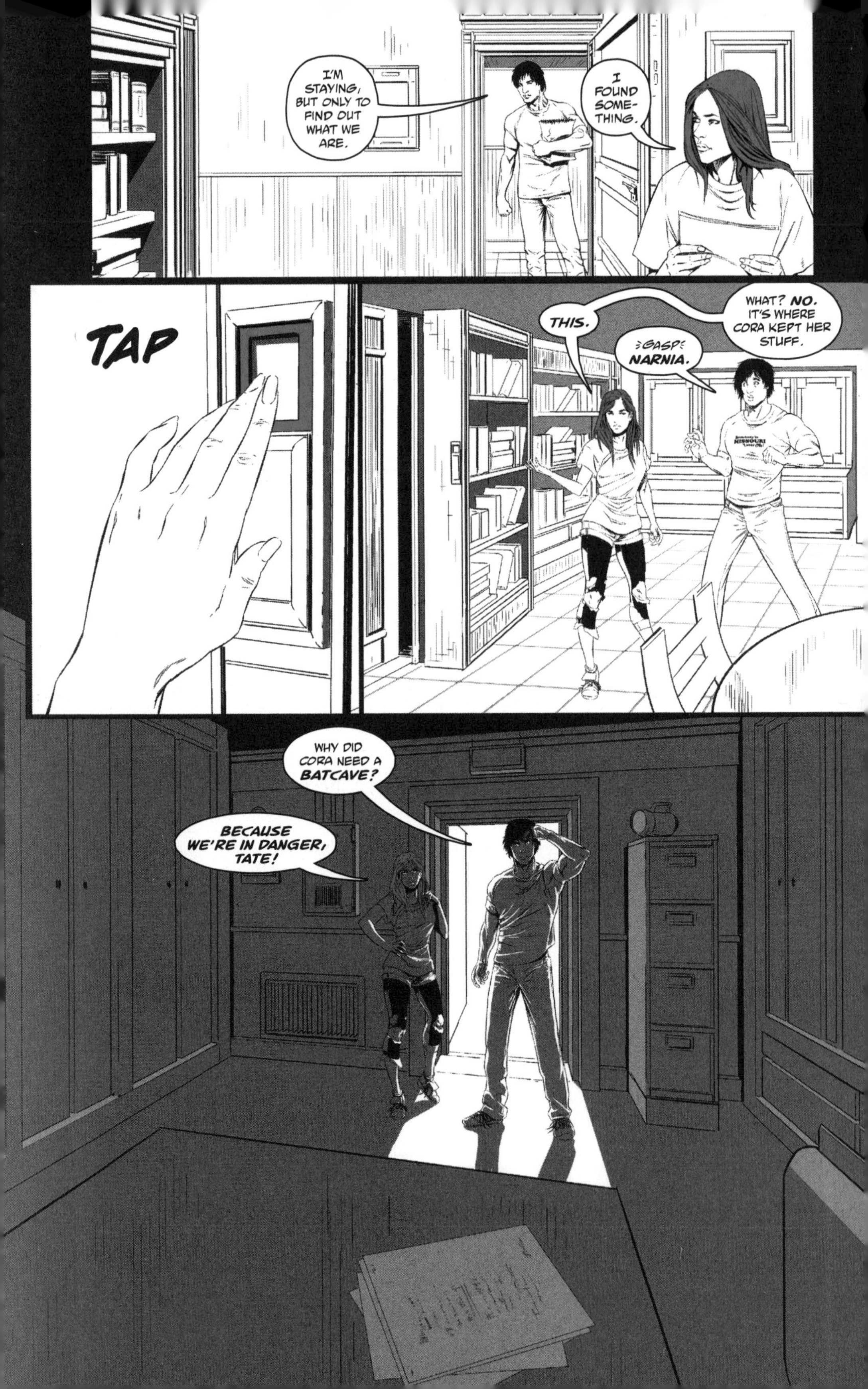

I'M STAYING, BUT ONLY TO FIND OUT WHAT WE ARE.
I FOUND SOME-THING.
TAP
THIS.
WHAT? NO. IT'S WHERE CORA KEPT HER STUFF.
GASP NARNIA.
WHY DID CORA NEED A BATCAVE?
BECAUSE WE'RE IN DANGER, TATE!

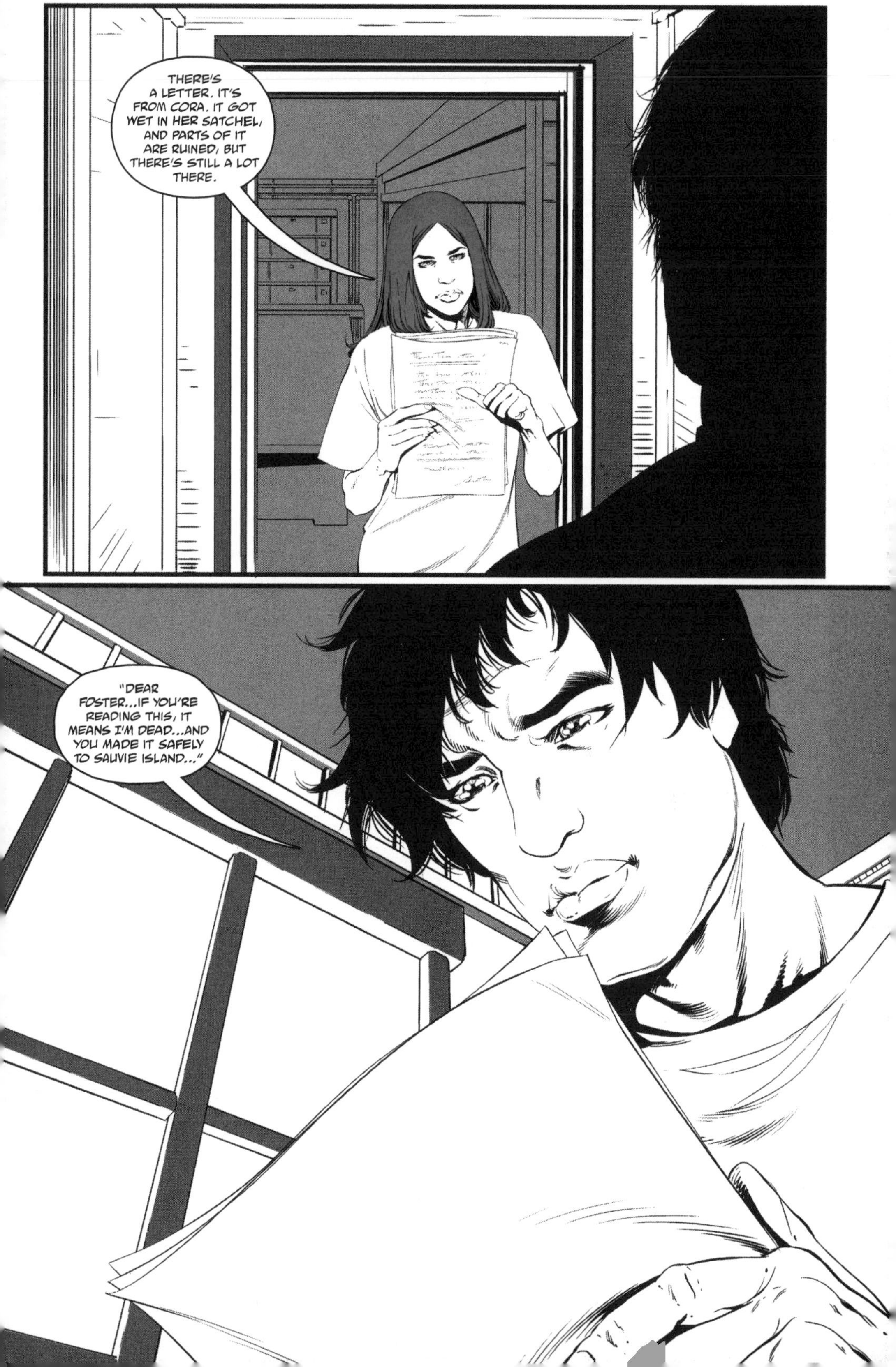
THERE'S A LETTER. IT'S FROM CORA. IT GOT WET IN HER SATCHEL, AND PARTS OF IT ARE RUINED, BUT THERE'S STILL A LOT THERE.
"DEAR FOSTER...IF YOU'RE READING THIS, IT MEANS I'M DEAD...AND YOU MADE IT SAFELY TO SAUVIE ISLAND..."

Dear Foster,

If you're reading this it means that Im dead and you made it safely to Sauvie Island.. First, I'm so sorry I didn't tell you I was sick, but baby girl, that was my choice. My heart disease was bad. Terminal. I chose to spend my remaining time with you and not in a hospital. It was my choice, Foster, and I don't regret it – so don't you blame yourself. Not for one instant. I won't have it.

Next – Molly you in danger girl!

Go ahead, Strawberry. Let yourself laugh like you and I would if we were reading this together. Don't ever forget to smile that beautiful smile and have fun. And then get to work. I know how you like your bulleted points, so to begin:

- You're already in my office at Strawberry Fields (Named after you, my little strawberry baby girl!). If you're sitting at my desk look to your left. Go to the bookshelf where it meets the wall. Run your fingers under the edge of the middle shelf to find the hidden button. Press it and then step back. It's going to swing open to reveal a safe room. Yes, it's very Kingsman-like. No, I'm not hiding Colin Firth in there, though girl, I know you know I wish!

  Look around the safe room. Be sure you keep the supplies current,

- In the rear left corner a square of the wood floor can be lifted if you use the letter opener on my desk. It's another trap door. You can drop down into the crawl space under the house and get out. The safe is important. The combo is the same as the front gate. Change that ASAP. Inside the safe you'll find:
- Documents for your new identity, Foster Fields, as well as documents for Tate's new identity, Tate Johnson.

  You have money. Quite a lot of it, actually. Spend it, but be careful. Foster, the plastic is there for emergencies. Try not to use it. You know how to stay off the grid. We've been practicing for the past year. Keep it up.
- Oh, yes, I was sure Tate was the kid you and I have been looking for. I should have told you sooner. I thought you and I would have more time. Forgive me, baby girl.
-

  Study them. You must know your enemy.

You know your stepfather used to believe he could halt climate change and save the earth by genetically engineering fetuses so that

experimented on four fetuses, born about thirty-six years ago.   the Core Four: Eve, Mark, Matthew, and Luke. You also remember that they were why your father's experiments on Sunset Island were shut down. He told me that the Core Four were complete failures and that they were living normal lives on their own after the island facility was closed five years ago, just before his "death." I didn't question him. I wanted to believe him. Then he died in that boating accident, and I thought the subject moot.

Until I sold his Portland clinic four years ago. I was cleaning out the basement and I found a stash of hidden files – the twelve in the safe. As I read through them I realized I had been wrong

wrong to believe he died five years ago. Most importantly, I had been wrong to believe he did not experiment on you.

Okay, now, don't you be scared. This is all going to be okay. There is nothing wrong with you. You are perfect exactly as you are. Oh, baby girl, I wish I could be with you now, but I want you to know that my strength is still with you – my love is still with you – my heart will always be with you. You can do this, but you're going to have to open yourself to help.

Sorry. I digress. This is more difficult than I thought it would be.

Read the files. Look through the newspaper clippings and internet stories I collected. You'll see what I did. Those Core Four – they've popped up in the news over the past five years whenever there were major natural disasters. Study the pictures. Do you see him in the crowd?

Doctor Rick Stewart is not dead.

Foster, we talked about that final picture – the one he took with the Core Four right before his fatal "accident." We thought they had something to do with his death, but the more research I did, the more I've come to believe Rick faked his death with the help of the Core Four and he's waiting until turn eighteen. That's when the Core Four began to manifest their abilities. I believe that's when you

abilities

Core Four are going to come after you.

find the others.

I do not know why he created eight of you this time instead of four. I do not know who the other six kids are; I only know their birthdates   I found Tate

his unusually good night vision – the same as your night vision.

connect the dots to the others. You always have been good at puzzles. I have faith in that beautiful, unique brain of yours.

? I'll tell you Strawberry:

- You and Tate are linked
- Your stepfather needs you and the other children t

- Rick Stewart and the Core Four cannot be trusted

se the man who was my husband for thirty years – the man who was your father – he couldn't have done these terrible things. He couldn't have faked his death. He couldn't be trying to manipulate the earth's climate. He couldn't be after my sweet strawberry girl. But, Foster, I truly believe he is, and if you see any of the Core Four you will know he is.

Do not ever underestimate him. And if he has become as ruthless as he is brilliant, it isn't just you and seven other kids who are in danger - the world is in danger.

You can't risk going to the authorities, They'd make you science experiments – or worse. And they can't keep you safe. Rick's a lot smarter than they are.

I have to close this now, baby girl. Strawberry Fields is your future - you can be safe on that fertile little island, I truly believe it. create a sanctuary for you and the others, and this was the best I could do. I planned on being there with you. Forgive me for dying too soon - but you know how I like to be early rather than late.

I want you to understand one thing beyond everything else. The greatest joy in my life has been being your mother. You brought love and light, laughter and happiness to me, and you have made me so, so proud. Trust your heart. It's beautiful. I know I've taught you to hold tight to your feelings. I did that to keep you safe, but now that I'm gone you're going to have to allow yourself to trust others. You'll be smart about it. I know you will.

I love you, Strawberry, more than I've ever loved anyone. Be kind to yourself, baby. You're doing the best you can, and that's all I've ever asked of you.

Your Mama,
Cora

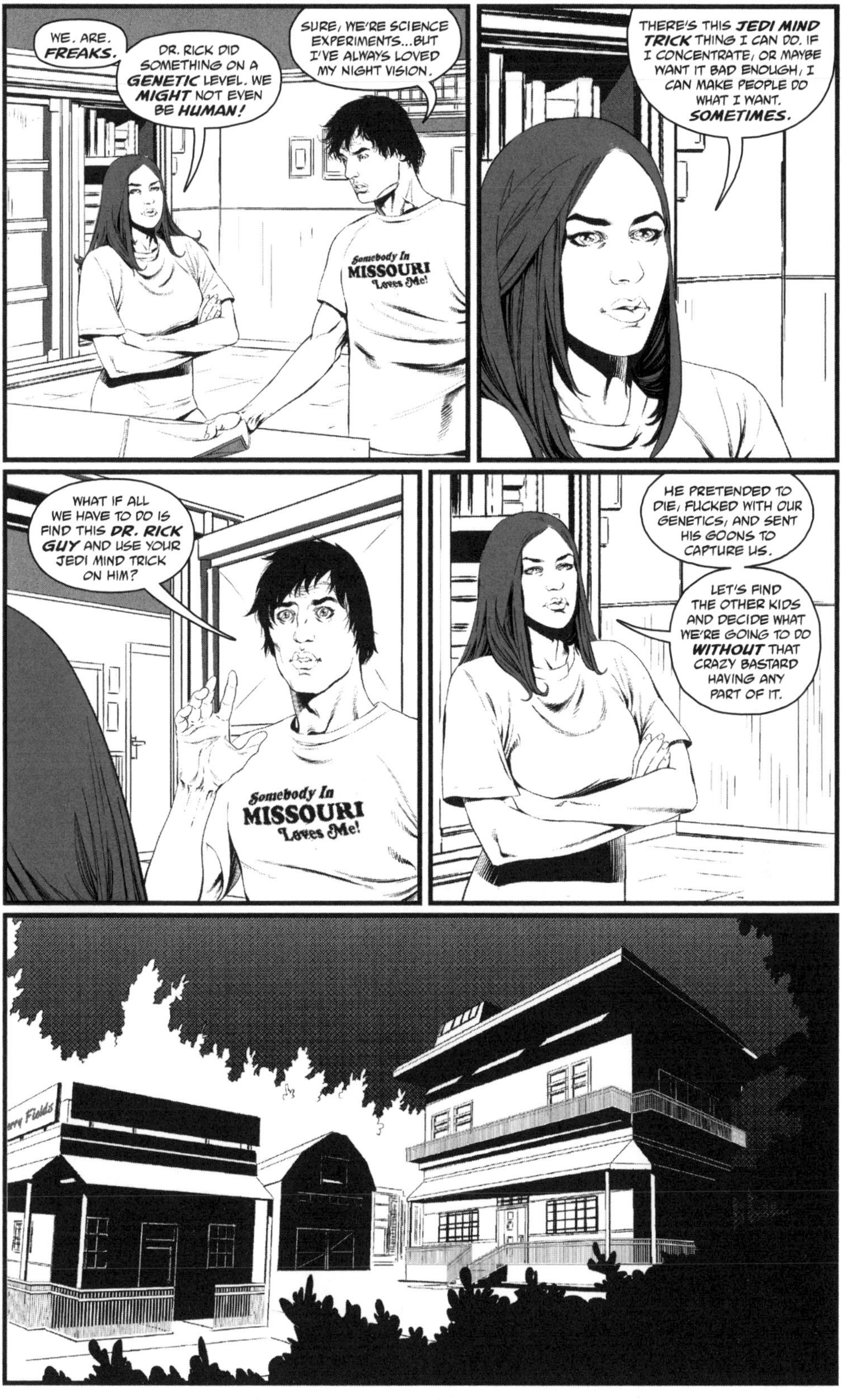
WE. ARE. FREAKS.
DR. RICK DID SOMETHING ON A GENETIC LEVEL. WE MIGHT NOT EVEN BE HUMAN!
SURE, WE'RE SCIENCE EXPERIMENTS...BUT I'VE ALWAYS LOVED MY NIGHT VISION.
Somebody In MISSOURI Loves Me!
THERE'S THIS JEDI MIND TRICK THING I CAN DO. IF I CONCENTRATE, OR MAYBE WANT IT BAD ENOUGH, I CAN MAKE PEOPLE DO WHAT I WANT. SOMETIMES.
WHAT IF ALL WE HAVE TO DO IS FIND THIS DR. RICK GUY AND USE YOUR JEDI MIND TRICK ON HIM?
Somebody In MISSOURI Loves Me!
HE PRETENDED TO DIE, FUCKED WITH OUR GENETICS, AND SENT HIS GOONS TO CAPTURE US.
LET'S FIND THE OTHER KIDS AND DECIDE WHAT WE'RE GOING TO DO WITHOUT THAT CRAZY BASTARD HAVING ANY PART OF IT.

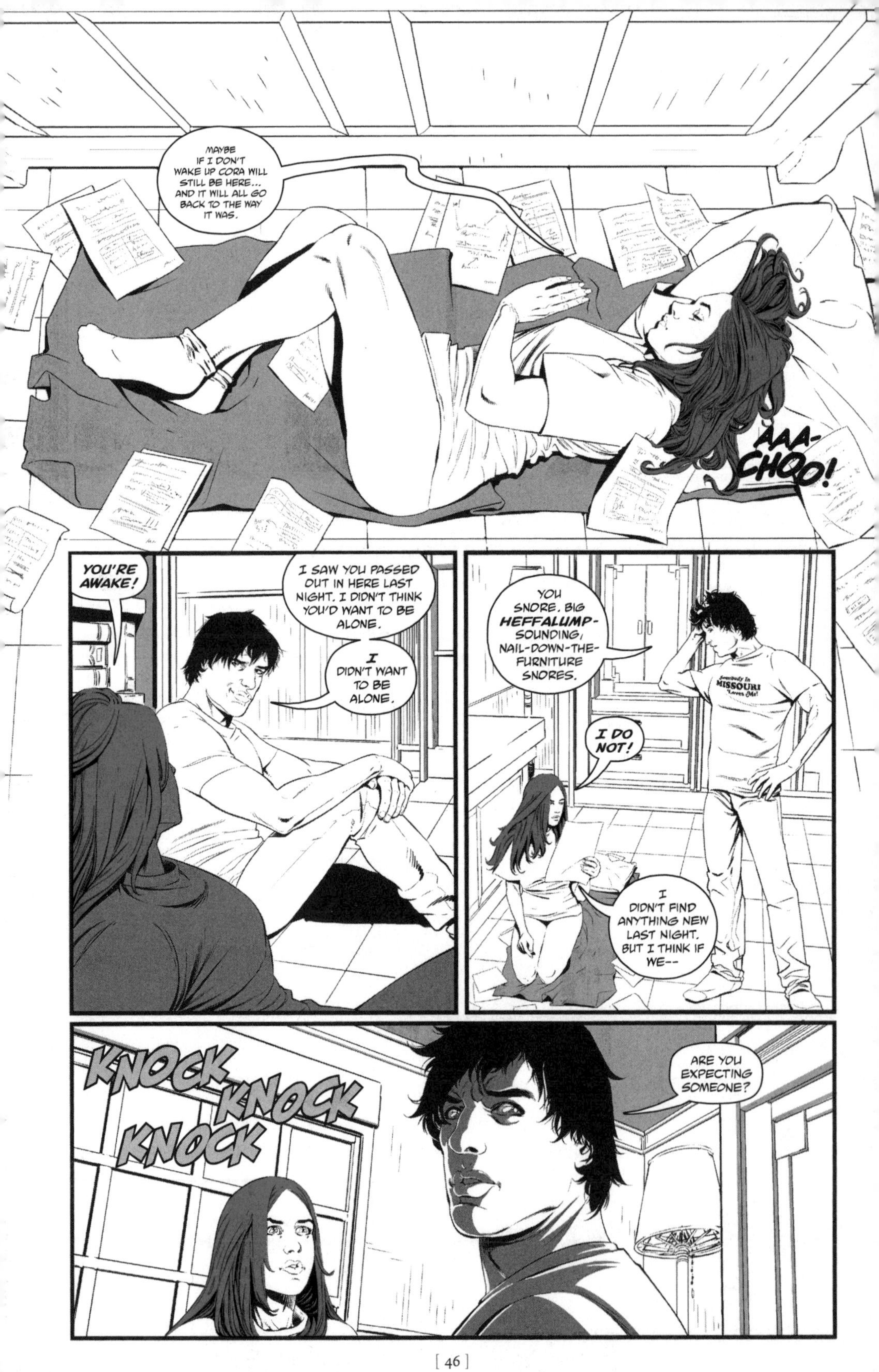
MAYBE IF I DON'T WAKE UP CORA WILL STILL BE HERE... AND IT WILL ALL GO BACK TO THE WAY IT WAS.
AAA-CHOO!
YOU'RE AWAKE!
I SAW YOU PASSED OUT IN HERE LAST NIGHT. I DIDN'T THINK YOU'D WANT TO BE ALONE.
I DIDN'T WANT TO BE ALONE.
YOU SNORE. BIG HEFFALUMP-SOUNDING, NAIL-DOWN-THE-FURNITURE SNORES.
Somebody In MISSOURI Loves Me!
I DO NOT!
I DIDN'T FIND ANYTHING NEW LAST NIGHT. BUT I THINK IF WE--
KNOCK KNOCK KNOCK
ARE YOU EXPECTING SOMEONE?

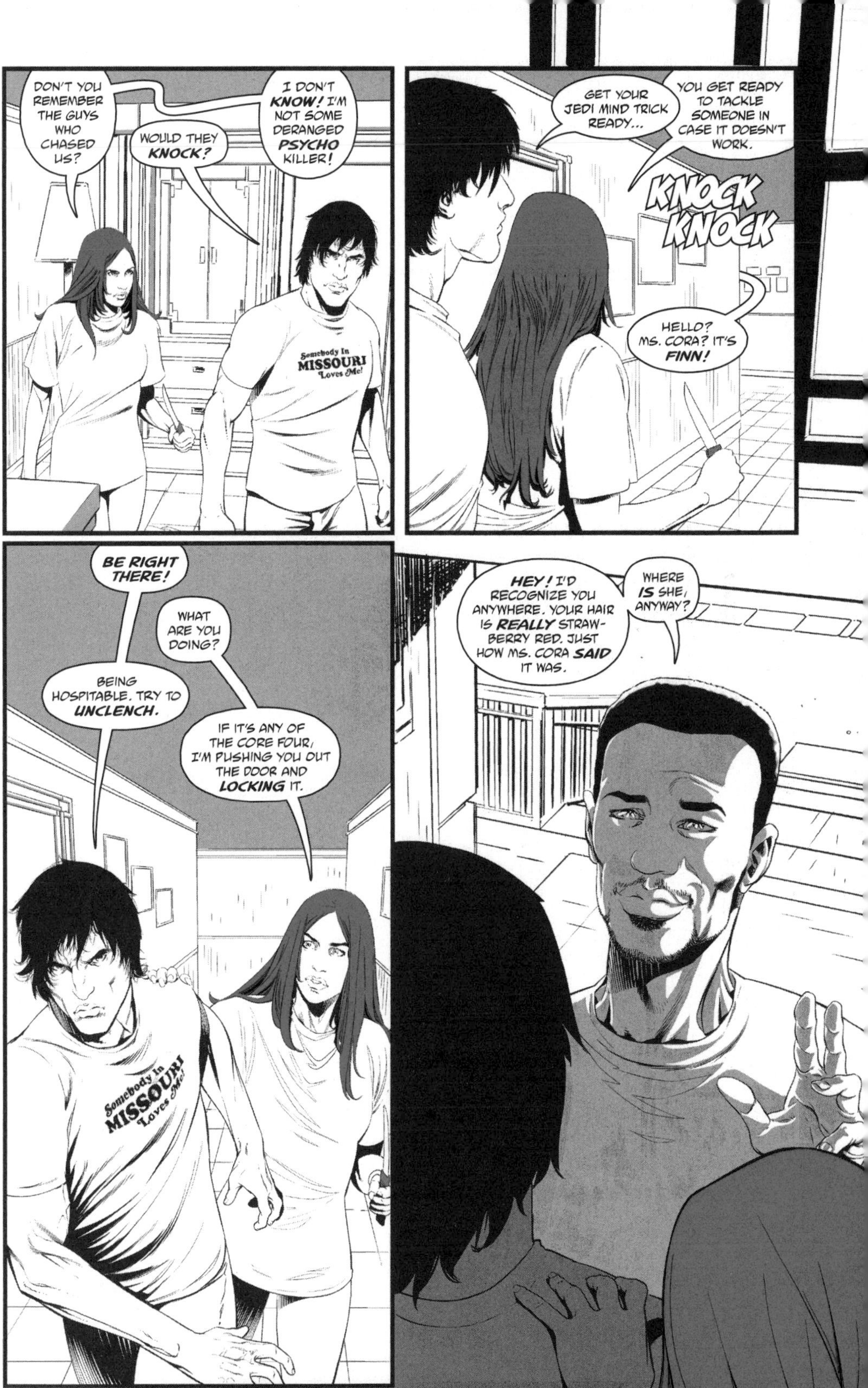
DON'T YOU REMEMBER THE GUYS WHO CHASED US?
WOULD THEY KNOCK?
I DON'T KNOW! I'M NOT SOME DERANGED PSYCHO KILLER!
Somebody In MISSOURI Loves Me!
GET YOUR JEDI MIND TRICK READY...
YOU GET READY TO TACKLE SOMEONE IN CASE IT DOESN'T WORK.
KNOCK KNOCK
HELLO? MS. CORA? IT'S FINN!
BE RIGHT THERE!
WHAT ARE YOU DOING?
BEING HOSPITABLE. TRY TO UNCLENCH.
IF IT'S ANY OF THE CORE FOUR, I'M PUSHING YOU OUT THE DOOR AND LOCKING IT.
Somebody In MISSOURI Loves Me!
HEY! I'D RECOGNIZE YOU ANYWHERE. YOUR HAIR IS REALLY STRAWBERRY RED. JUST HOW MS. CORA SAID IT WAS.
WHERE IS SHE, ANYWAY?

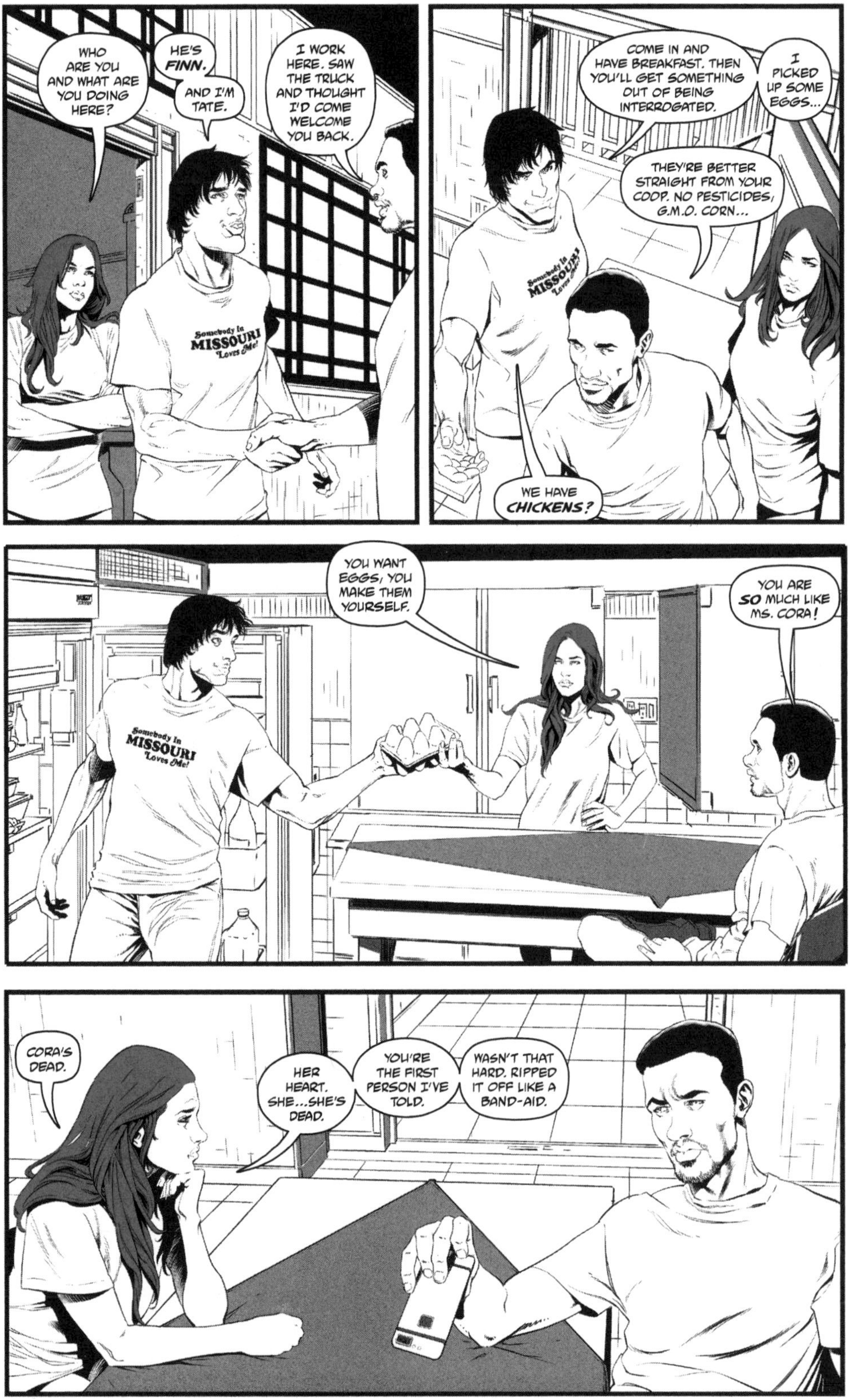
WHO ARE YOU AND WHAT ARE YOU DOING HERE?
HE'S **FINN.**
AND I'M TATE.
I WORK HERE. SAW THE TRUCK AND THOUGHT I'D COME WELCOME YOU BACK.
COME IN AND HAVE BREAKFAST. THEN YOU'LL GET SOMETHING OUT OF BEING INTERROGATED.
I PICKED UP SOME EGGS...
THEY'RE BETTER STRAIGHT FROM YOUR COOP. NO PESTICIDES, G.M.O. CORN...
WE HAVE **CHICKENS?**
Somebody In MISSOURI Loves Me!
YOU WANT EGGS, YOU MAKE THEM YOURSELF.
YOU ARE **SO** MUCH LIKE MS. CORA!
CORA'S DEAD.
HER HEART. SHE...SHE'S DEAD.
YOU'RE THE FIRST PERSON I'VE TOLD.
WASN'T THAT HARD. RIPPED IT OFF LIKE A BAND-AID.

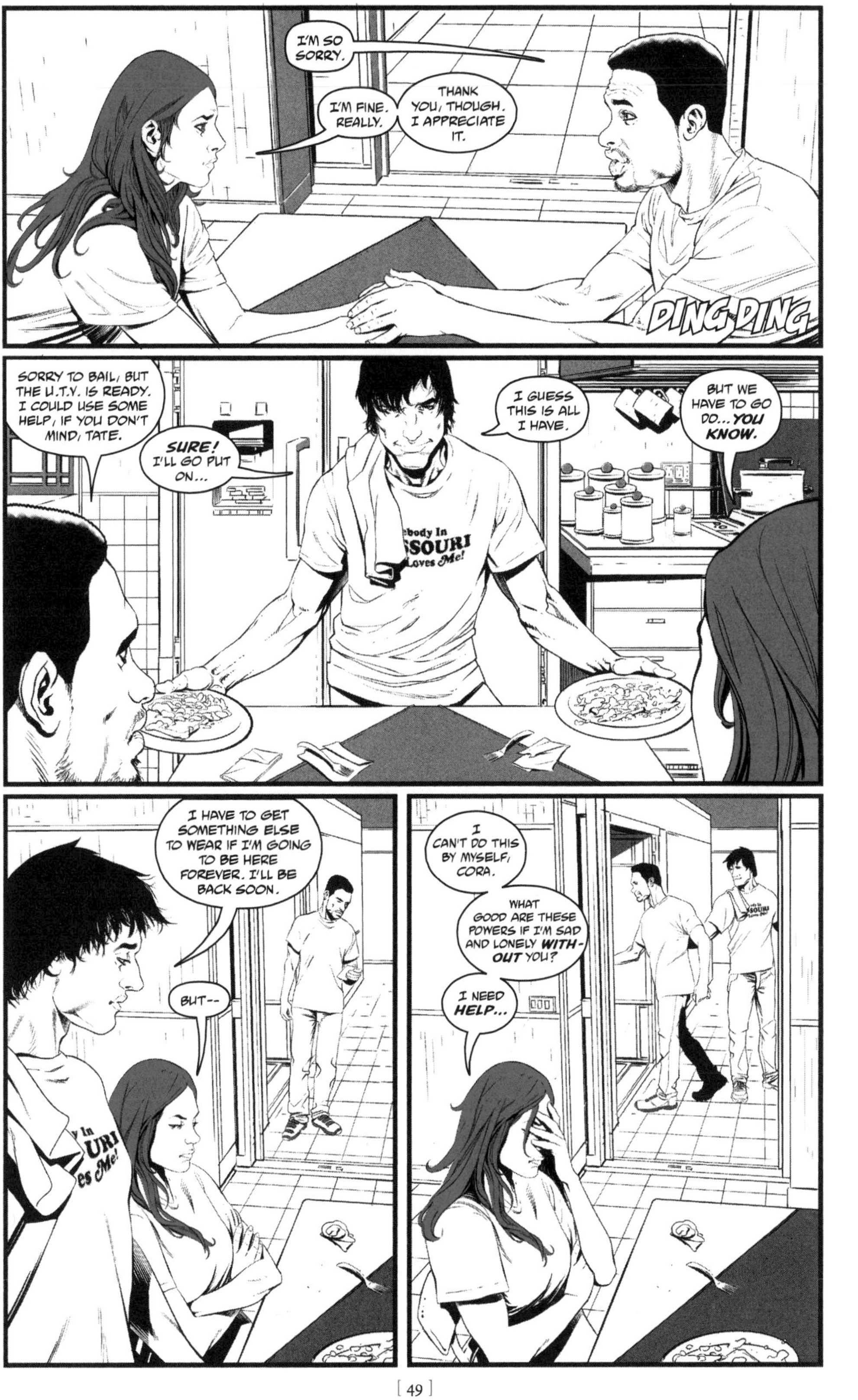
I'M SO SORRY.
I'M FINE. REALLY.
THANK YOU, THOUGH. I APPRECIATE IT.
DING DING
SORRY TO BAIL, BUT THE U.T.V. IS READY. I COULD USE SOME HELP, IF YOU DON'T MIND, TATE.
SURE! I'LL GO PUT ON...
I GUESS THIS IS ALL I HAVE.
BUT WE HAVE TO GO DO... **YOU KNOW.**
I HAVE TO GET SOMETHING ELSE TO WEAR IF I'M GOING TO BE HERE FOREVER. I'LL BE BACK SOON.
BUT--
I CAN'T DO THIS BY MYSELF, CORA.
WHAT GOOD ARE THESE POWERS IF I'M SAD AND LONELY **WITHOUT** YOU?
I NEED **HELP...**

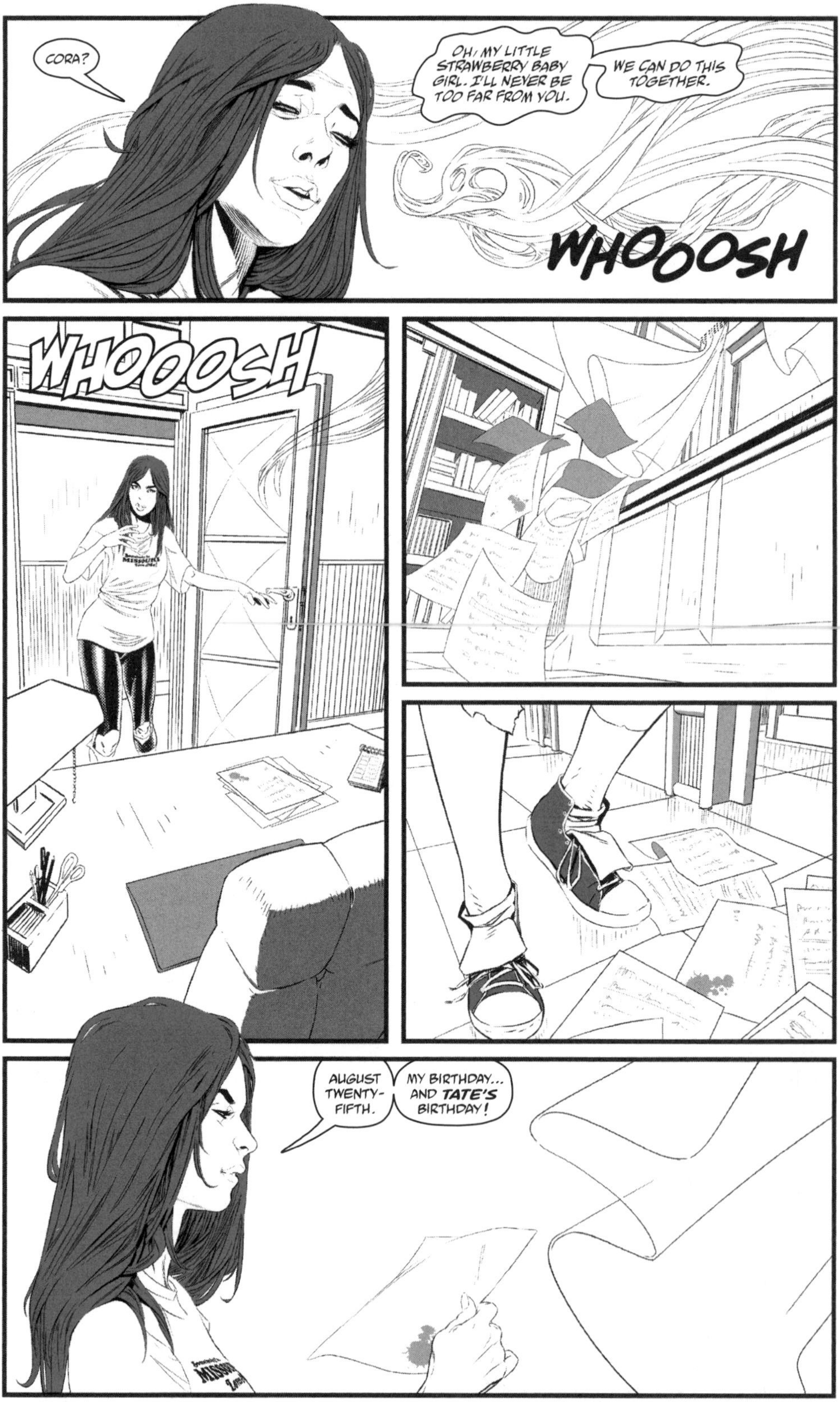
CORA?
OH, MY LITTLE STRAWBERRY BABY GIRL. I'LL NEVER BE TOO FAR FROM YOU.
WE CAN DO THIS TOGETHER.
WHOOOSH
WHOOOSH
AUGUST TWENTY-FIFTH.
MY BIRTHDAY... AND *TATE'S* BIRTHDAY!

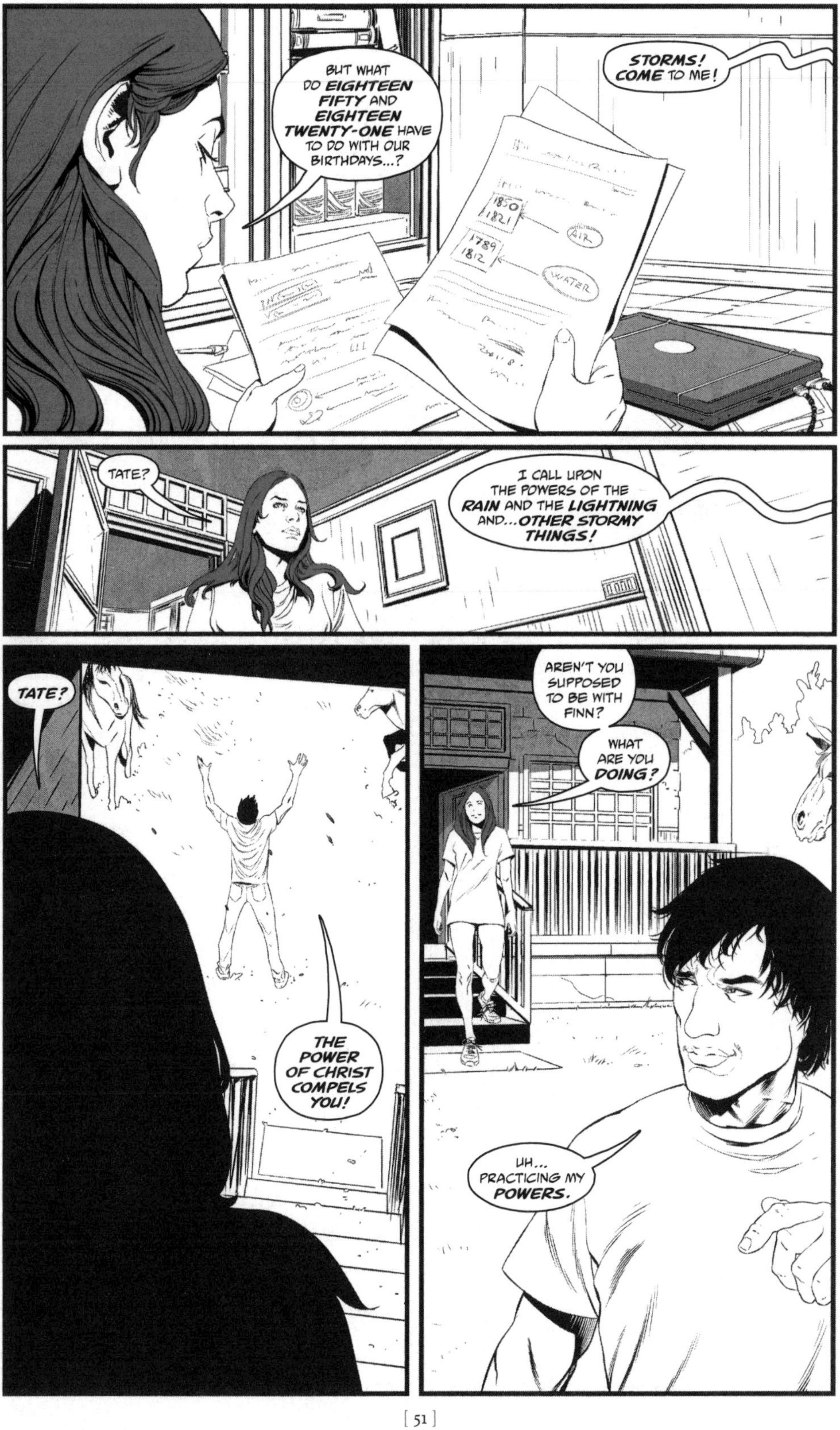
BUT WHAT DO EIGHTEEN FIFTY AND EIGHTEEN TWENTY-ONE HAVE TO DO WITH OUR BIRTHDAYS...?
STORMS! COME TO ME!
1850
1821
AIR
1789
1812
WATER
TATE?
I CALL UPON THE POWERS OF THE RAIN AND THE LIGHTNING AND...OTHER STORMY THINGS!
TATE?
THE POWER OF CHRIST COMPELS YOU!
AREN'T YOU SUPPOSED TO BE WITH FINN?
WHAT ARE YOU DOING?
UH... PRACTICING MY POWERS.

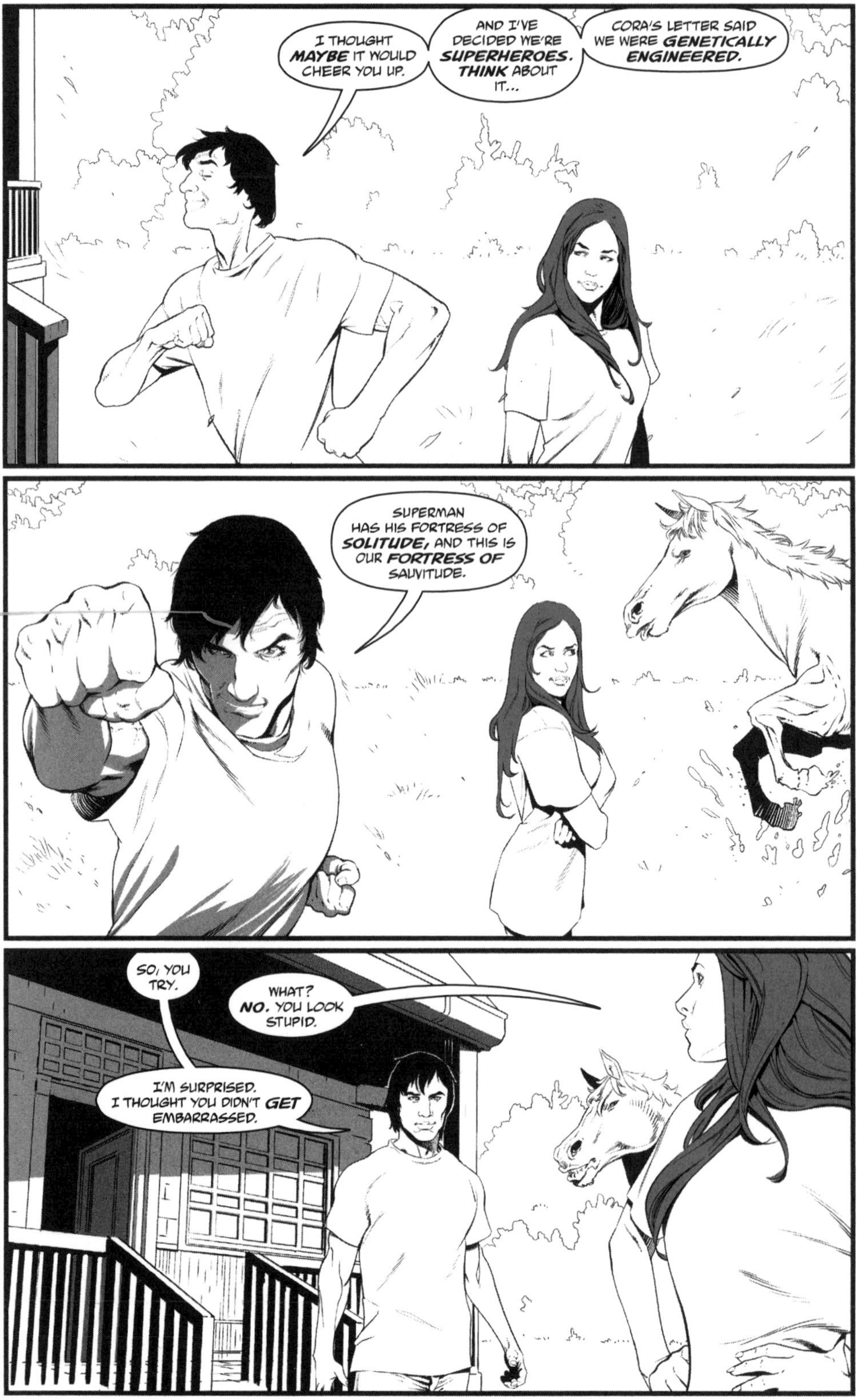
I THOUGHT MAYBE IT WOULD CHEER YOU UP.
AND I'VE DECIDED WE'RE SUPERHEROES. THINK ABOUT IT...
CORA'S LETTER SAID WE WERE GENETICALLY ENGINEERED.
SUPERMAN HAS HIS FORTRESS OF SOLITUDE, AND THIS IS OUR FORTRESS OF SAUVITUDE.
SO, YOU TRY.
WHAT? NO. YOU LOOK STUPID.
I'M SURPRISED. I THOUGHT YOU DIDN'T GET EMBARRASSED.

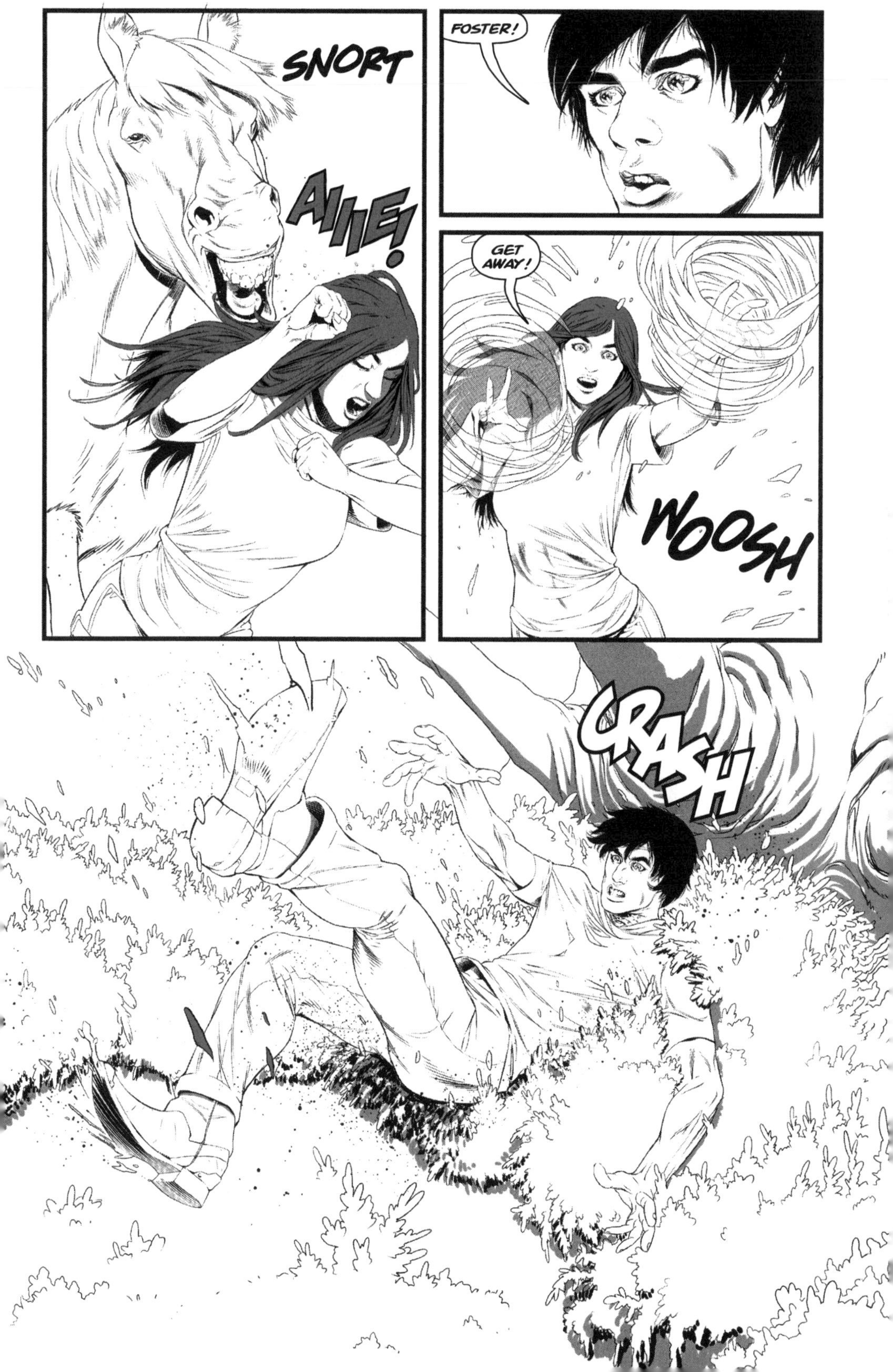
SNORT
AIIIE!
FOSTER!
GET AWAY!
WOOSH
CRASH

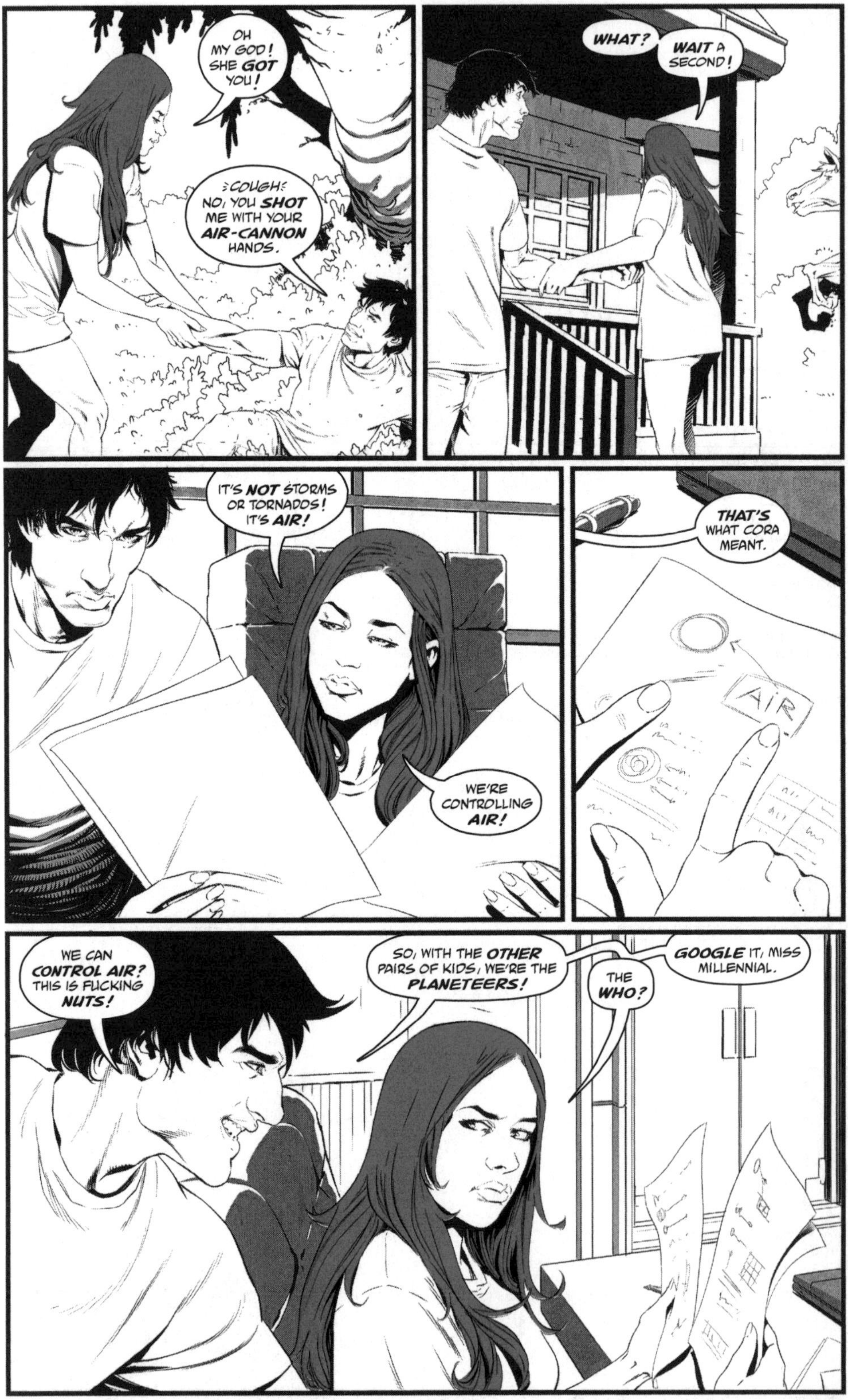
OH MY GOD! SHE GOT YOU!
≈COUGH≈ NO, YOU SHOT ME WITH YOUR AIR-CANNON HANDS.
WHAT?
WAIT A SECOND!
IT'S NOT STORMS OR TORNADOS! IT'S AIR!
WE'RE CONTROLLING AIR!
THAT'S WHAT CORA MEANT.
AIR
WE CAN CONTROL AIR? THIS IS FUCKING NUTS!
SO, WITH THE OTHER PAIRS OF KIDS, WE'RE THE PLANETEERS!
THE WHO?
GOOGLE IT, MISS MILLENNIAL.

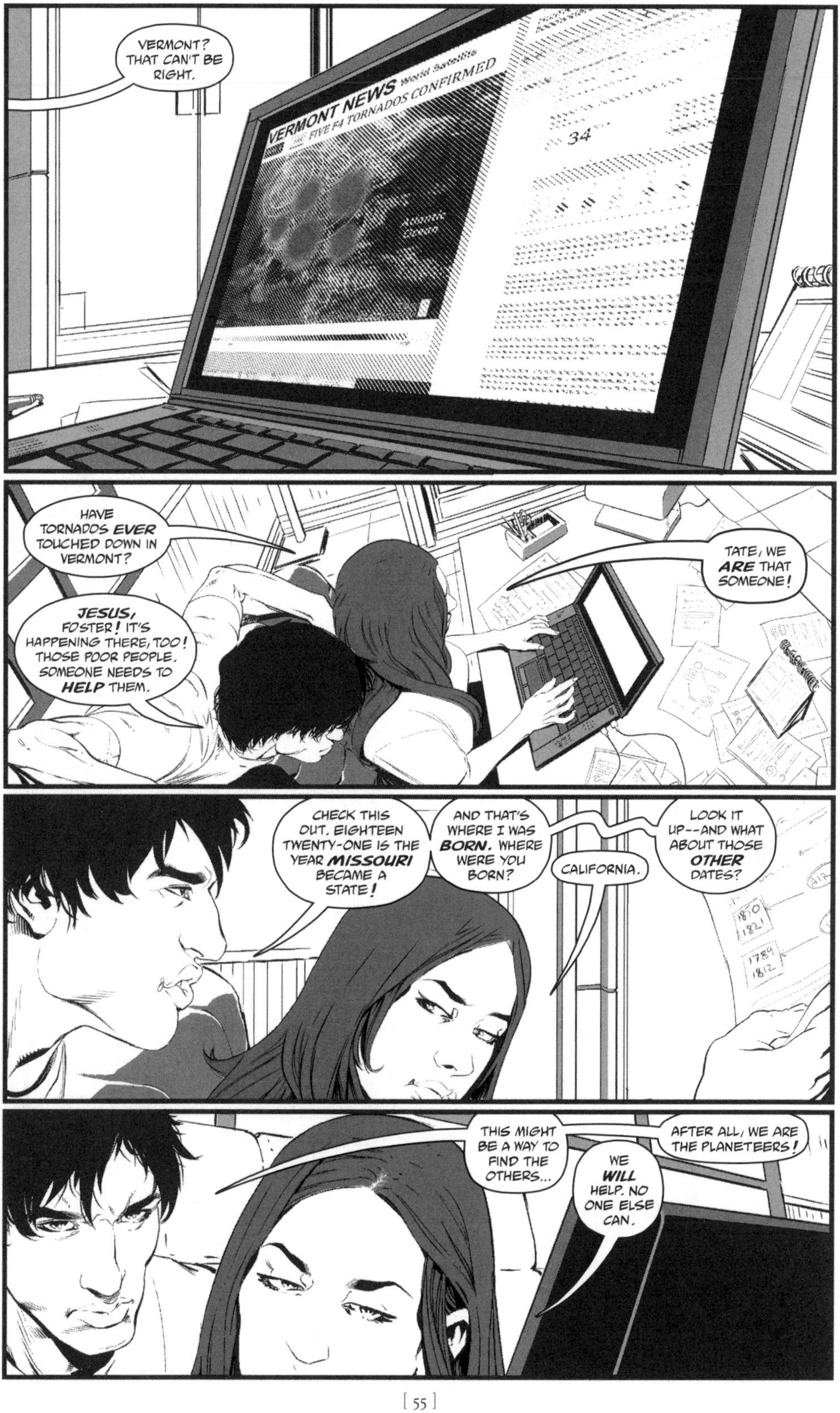
VERMONT? THAT CAN'T BE RIGHT.
VERMONT NEWS World Satellite
FIVE F4 TORNADOS CONFIRMED
34
HAVE TORNADOS EVER TOUCHED DOWN IN VERMONT?
JESUS, FOSTER! IT'S HAPPENING THERE, TOO! THOSE POOR PEOPLE. SOMEONE NEEDS TO HELP THEM.
TATE, WE ARE THAT SOMEONE!
CHECK THIS OUT. EIGHTEEN TWENTY-ONE IS THE YEAR MISSOURI BECAME A STATE!
AND THAT'S WHERE I WAS BORN. WHERE WERE YOU BORN?
CALIFORNIA.
LOOK IT UP--AND WHAT ABOUT THOSE OTHER DATES?
1850
1821
1789
1812
THIS MIGHT BE A WAY TO FIND THE OTHERS...
WE WILL HELP. NO ONE ELSE CAN.
AFTER ALL, WE ARE THE PLANETEERS!

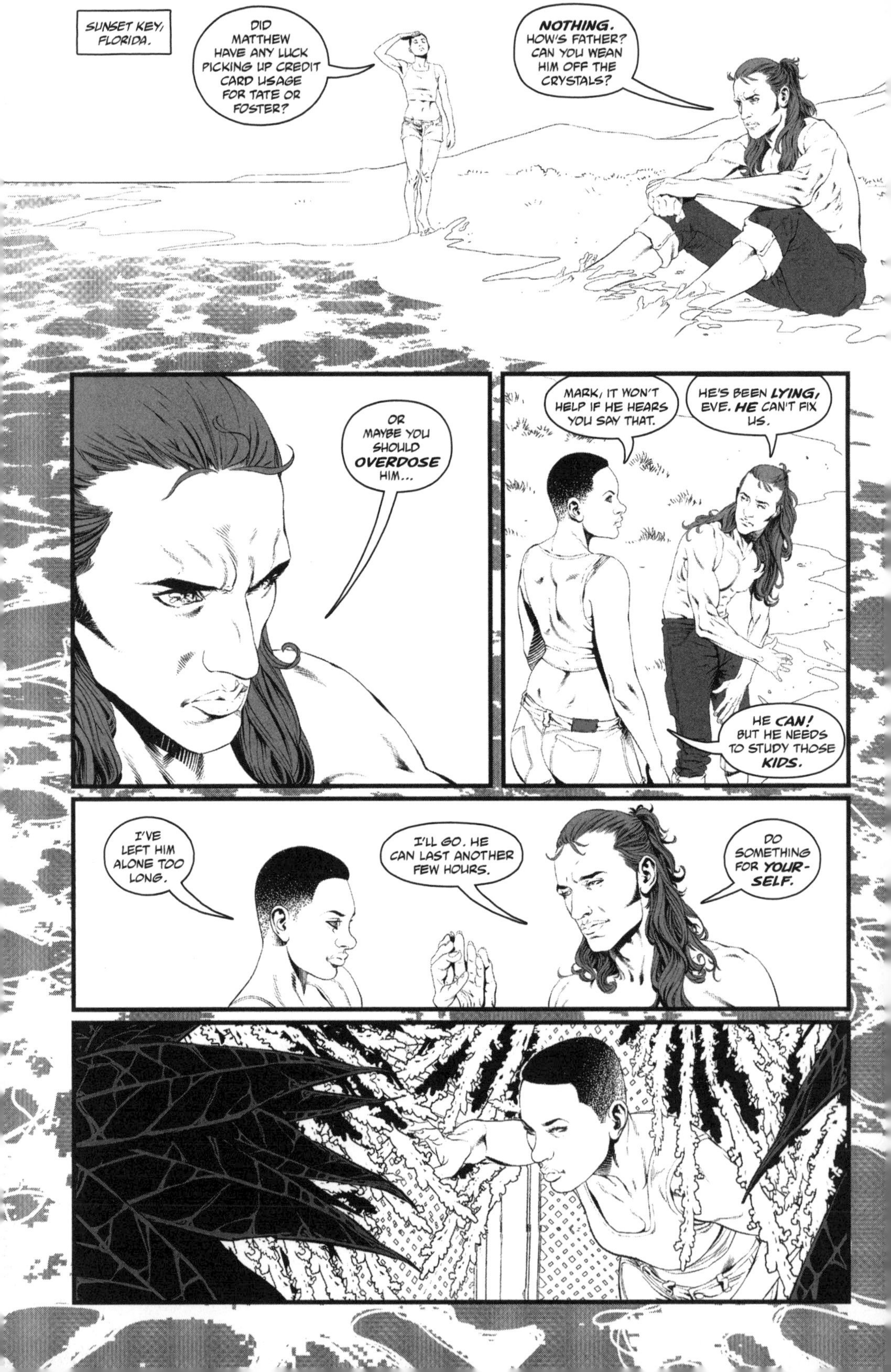
SUNSET KEY, FLORIDA.
DID MATTHEW HAVE ANY LUCK PICKING UP CREDIT CARD USAGE FOR TATE OR FOSTER?
NOTHING. HOW'S FATHER? CAN YOU WEAN HIM OFF THE CRYSTALS?
OR MAYBE YOU SHOULD OVERDOSE HIM...
MARK, IT WON'T HELP IF HE HEARS YOU SAY THAT.
HE'S BEEN LYING, EVE. HE CAN'T FIX US.
HE CAN! BUT HE NEEDS TO STUDY THOSE KIDS.
I'VE LEFT HIM ALONE TOO LONG.
I'LL GO. HE CAN LAST ANOTHER FEW HOURS.
DO SOMETHING FOR YOURSELF.

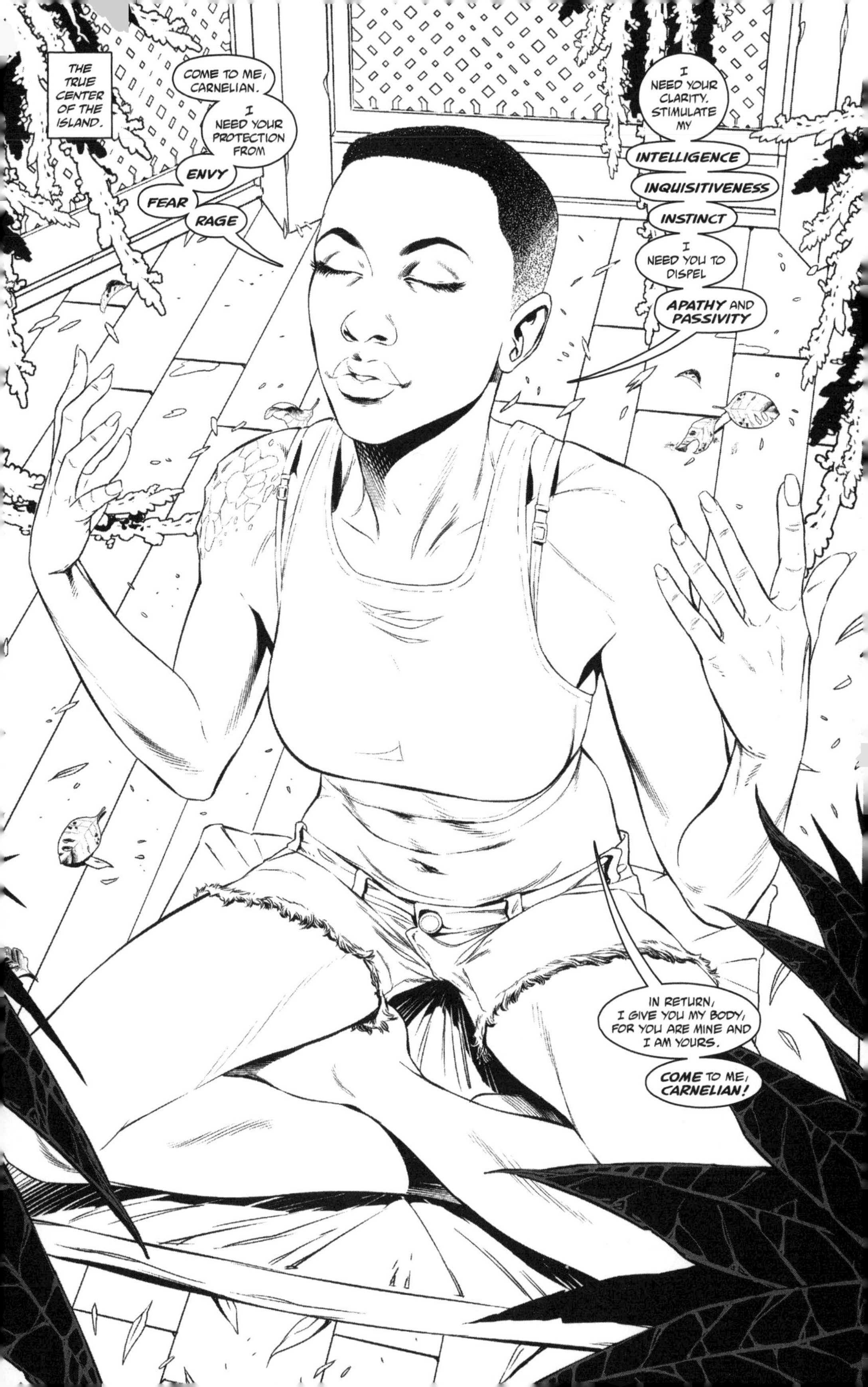
THE TRUE CENTER OF THE ISLAND.
COME TO ME, CARNELIAN.
I NEED YOUR PROTECTION FROM
ENVY
FEAR
RAGE
I NEED YOUR CLARITY. STIMULATE MY
INTELLIGENCE
INQUISITIVENESS
INSTINCT
I NEED YOU TO DISPEL
APATHY AND PASSIVITY
IN RETURN, I GIVE YOU MY BODY, FOR YOU ARE MINE AND I AM YOURS.
COME TO ME, CARNELIAN!

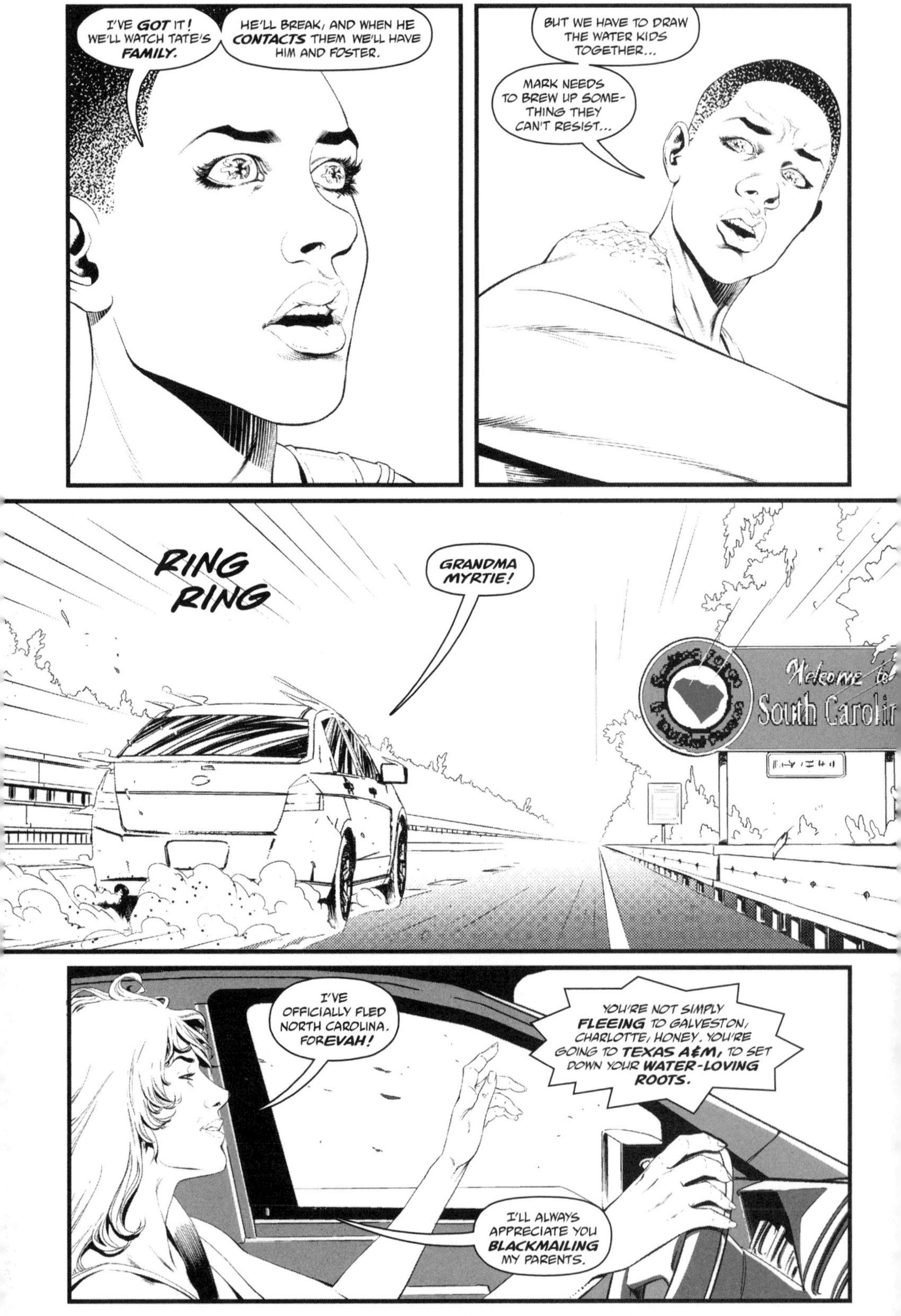
I'VE GOT IT! WE'LL WATCH TATE'S FAMILY.
HE'LL BREAK, AND WHEN HE CONTACTS THEM WE'LL HAVE HIM AND FOSTER.
BUT WE HAVE TO DRAW THE WATER KIDS TOGETHER...
MARK NEEDS TO BREW UP SOMETHING THEY CAN'T RESIST...
RING RING
GRANDMA MYRTIE!
Welcome to
South Carolin
I'VE OFFICIALLY FLED NORTH CAROLINA. FOREVAH!
YOU'RE NOT SIMPLY FLEEING TO GALVESTON, CHARLOTTE, HONEY. YOU'RE GOING TO TEXAS A&M, TO SET DOWN YOUR WATER-LOVING ROOTS.
I'LL ALWAYS APPRECIATE YOU BLACKMAILING MY PARENTS.

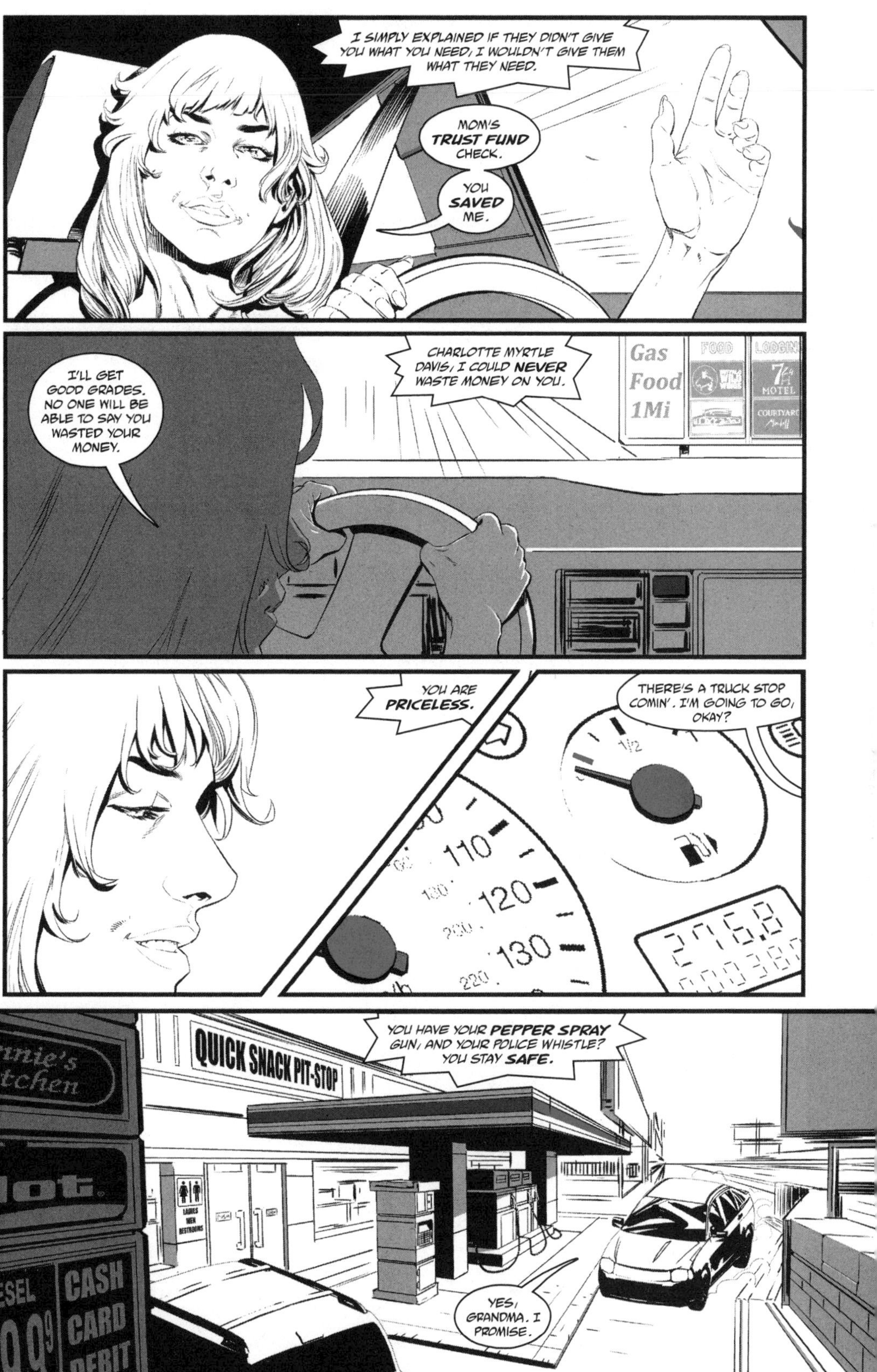
I SIMPLY EXPLAINED IF THEY DIDN'T GIVE YOU WHAT YOU NEED, I WOULDN'T GIVE THEM WHAT THEY NEED.
MOM'S **TRUST FUND** CHECK.
YOU **SAVED** ME.
Gas Food 1Mi
FOOD
MOTEL
CHARLOTTE MYRTLE DAVIS, I COULD **NEVER** WASTE MONEY ON YOU.
I'LL GET GOOD GRADES. NO ONE WILL BE ABLE TO SAY YOU WASTED YOUR MONEY.
YOU ARE **PRICELESS.**
THERE'S A TRUCK STOP COMIN'. I'M GOING TO GO, OKAY?
QUICK SNACK PIT-STOP
Bonnie's Kitchen
DIESEL
1.99 9
CASH
CARD
DEBIT
YOU HAVE YOUR **PEPPER SPRAY** GUN, AND YOUR POLICE WHISTLE? YOU STAY **SAFE.**
YES, GRANDMA. I PROMISE.

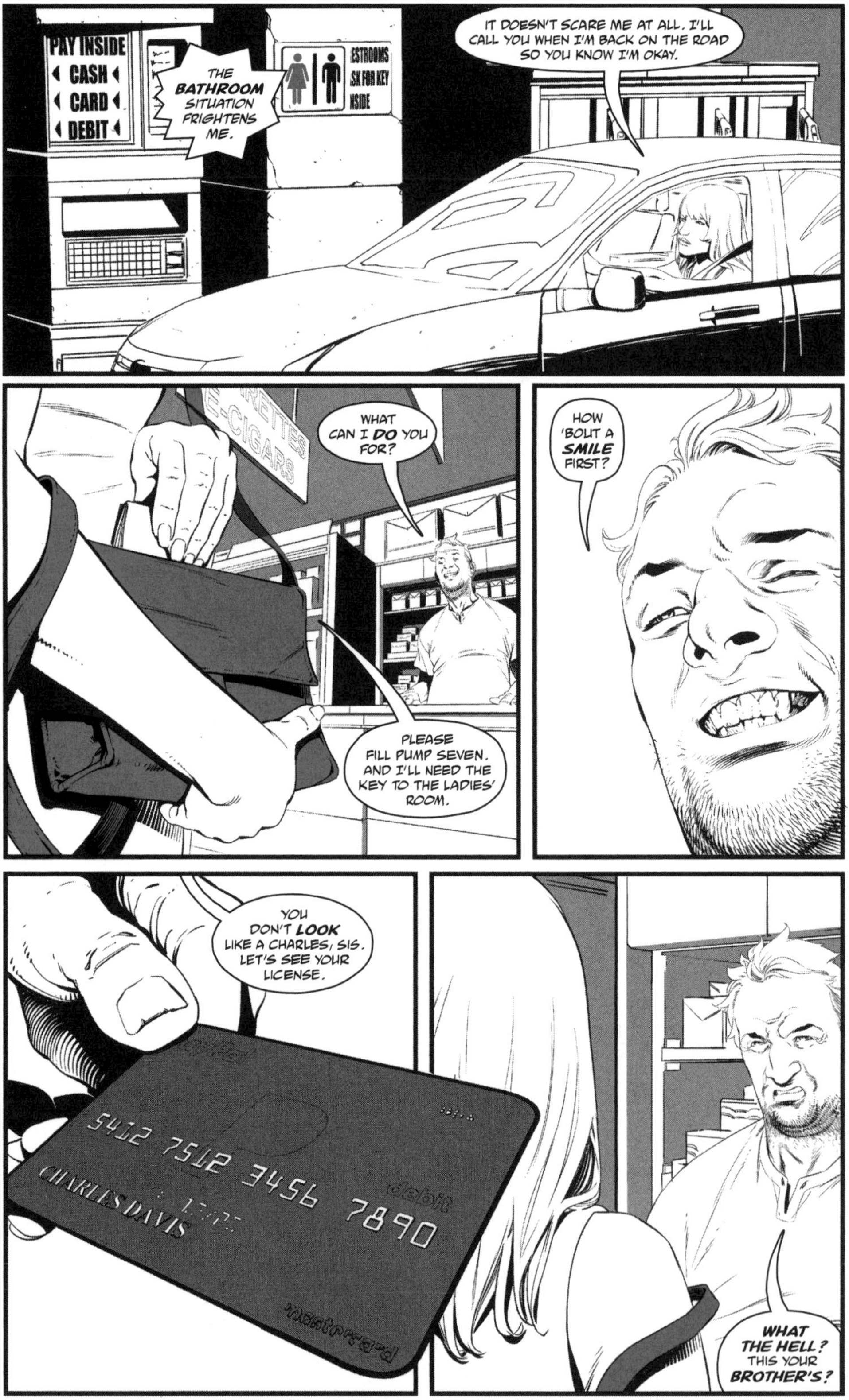
PAY INSIDE
CASH
CARD
DEBIT
THE BATHROOM SITUATION FRIGHTENS ME.
IT DOESN'T SCARE ME AT ALL. I'LL CALL YOU WHEN I'M BACK ON THE ROAD SO YOU KNOW I'M OKAY.
E-CIGARS
WHAT CAN I DO YOU FOR?
PLEASE FILL PUMP SEVEN. AND I'LL NEED THE KEY TO THE LADIES' ROOM.
HOW 'BOUT A SMILE FIRST?
YOU DON'T LOOK LIKE A CHARLES, SIS. LET'S SEE YOUR LICENSE.
5412 7512 3456 7890
CHARLES DAVIS
debit
WHAT THE HELL? THIS YOUR BROTHER'S?

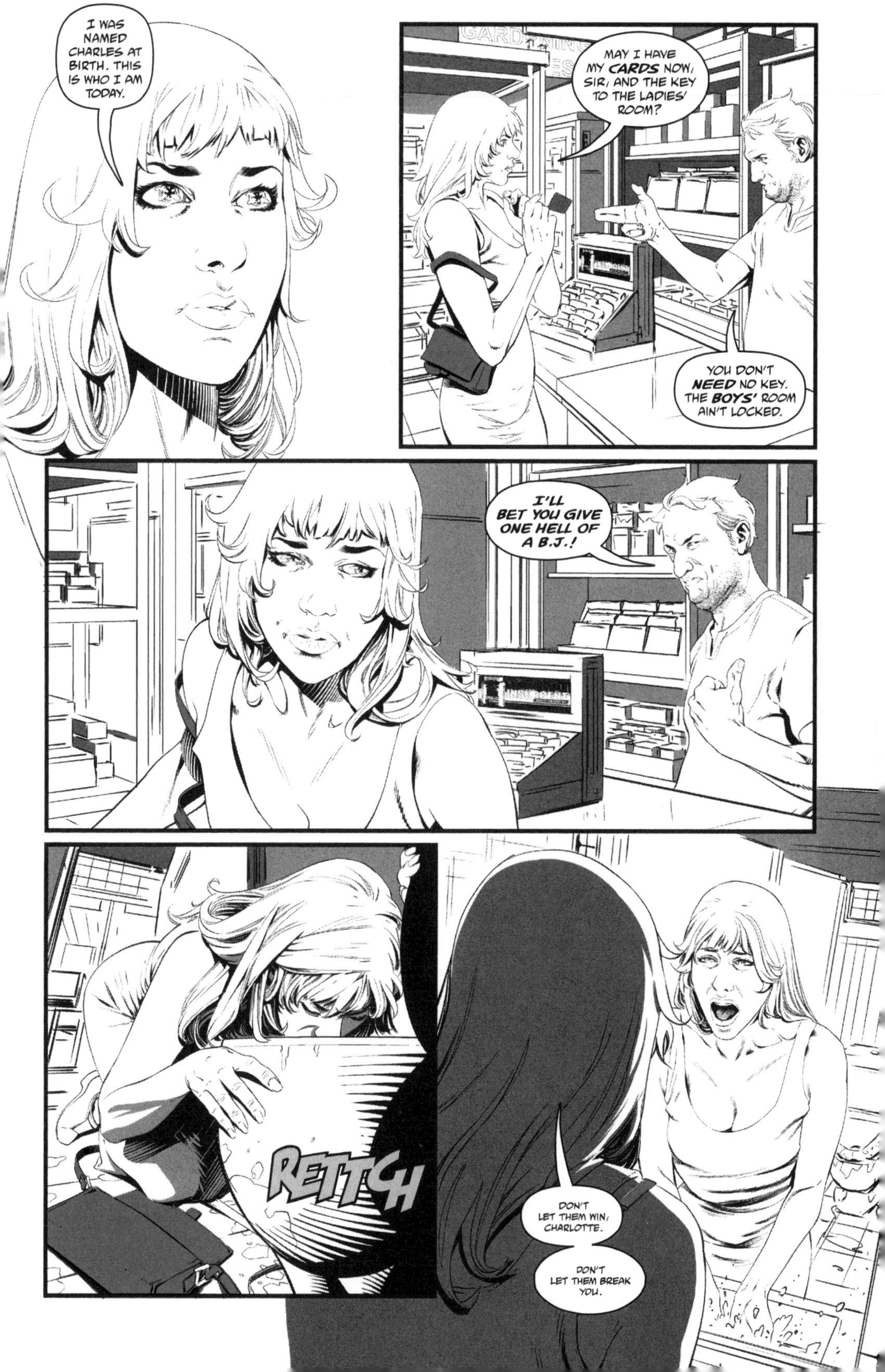
I WAS NAMED CHARLES AT BIRTH. THIS IS WHO I AM TODAY.
MAY I HAVE MY CARDS NOW, SIR, AND THE KEY TO THE LADIES' ROOM?
YOU DON'T NEED NO KEY. THE BOYS' ROOM AIN'T LOCKED.
I'LL BET YOU GIVE ONE HELL OF A B.J.!
RETTCH
DON'T LET THEM WIN, CHARLOTTE.
DON'T LET THEM BREAK YOU.

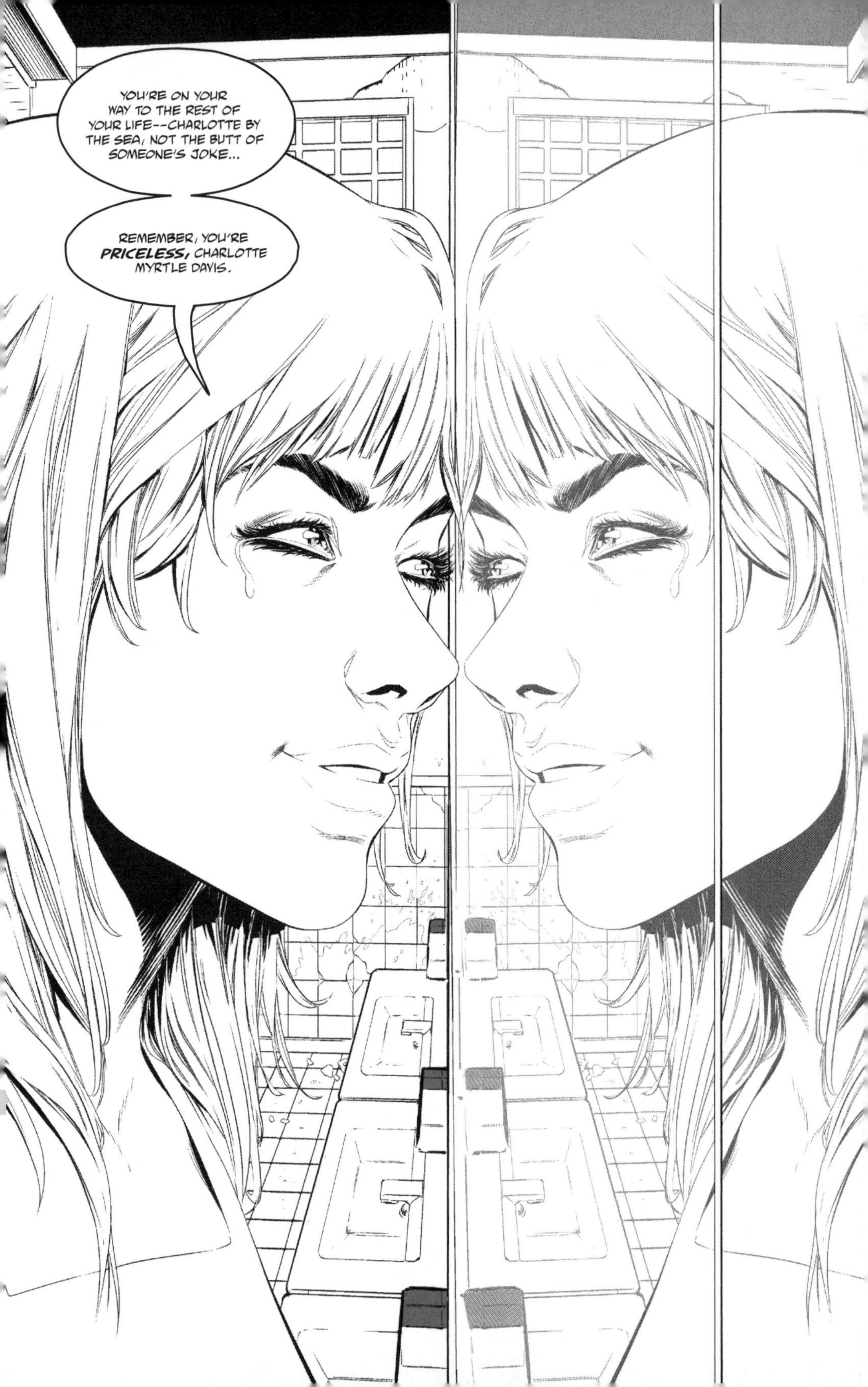
YOU'RE ON YOUR WAY TO THE REST OF YOUR LIFE--CHARLOTTE BY THE SEA, NOT THE BUTT OF SOMEONE'S JOKE...
REMEMBER, YOU'RE **PRICELESS,** CHARLOTTE MYRTLE DAVIS.

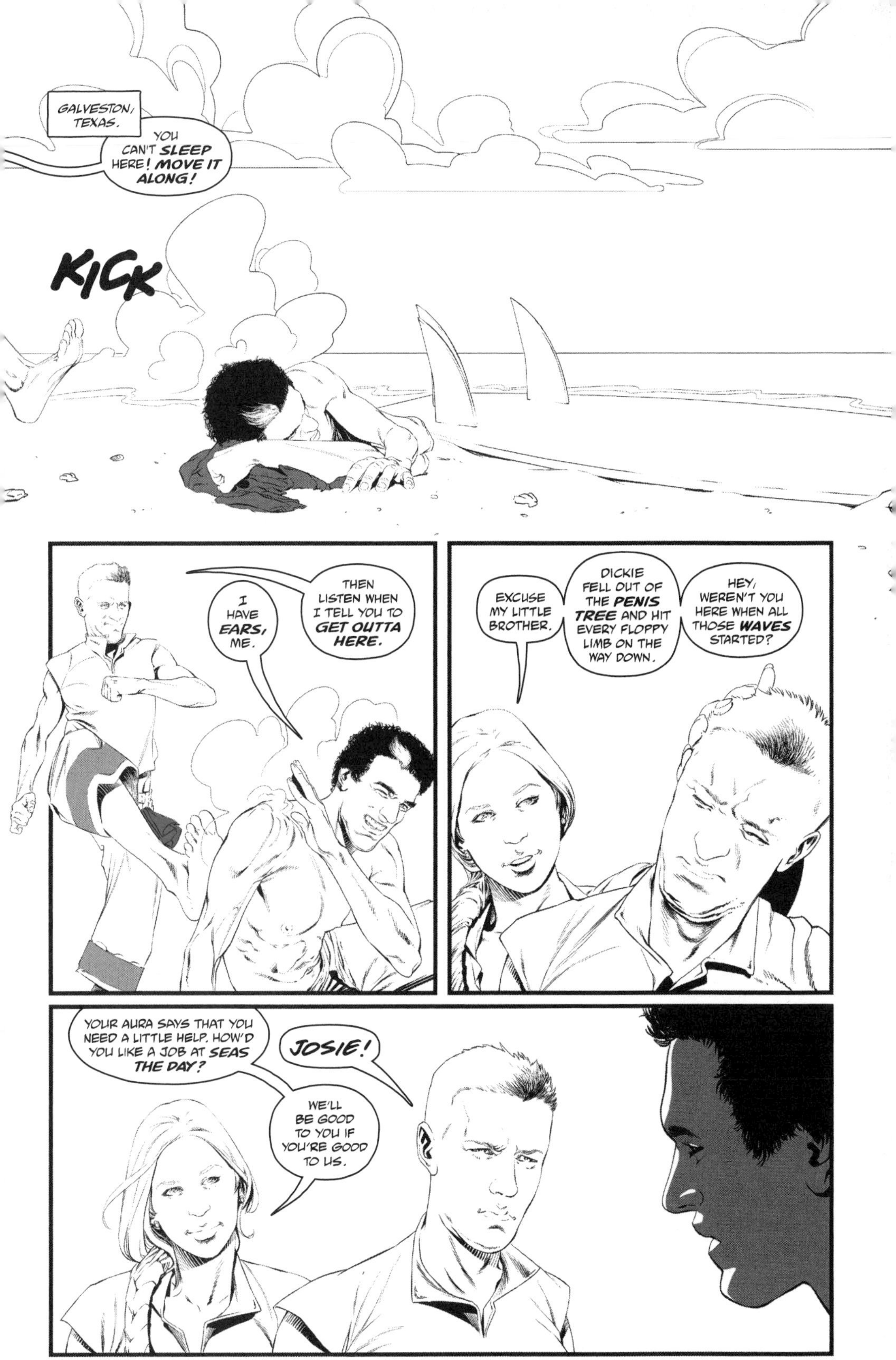
GALVESTON, TEXAS.
YOU CAN'T SLEEP HERE! MOVE IT ALONG!
KICK
I HAVE EARS, ME.
THEN LISTEN WHEN I TELL YOU TO GET OUTTA HERE.
EXCUSE MY LITTLE BROTHER.
DICKIE FELL OUT OF THE PENIS TREE AND HIT EVERY FLOPPY LIMB ON THE WAY DOWN.
HEY, WEREN'T YOU HERE WHEN ALL THOSE WAVES STARTED?
YOUR AURA SAYS THAT YOU NEED A LITTLE HELP. HOW'D YOU LIKE A JOB AT SEAS THE DAY?
JOSIE!
WE'LL BE GOOD TO YOU IF YOU'RE GOOD TO US.

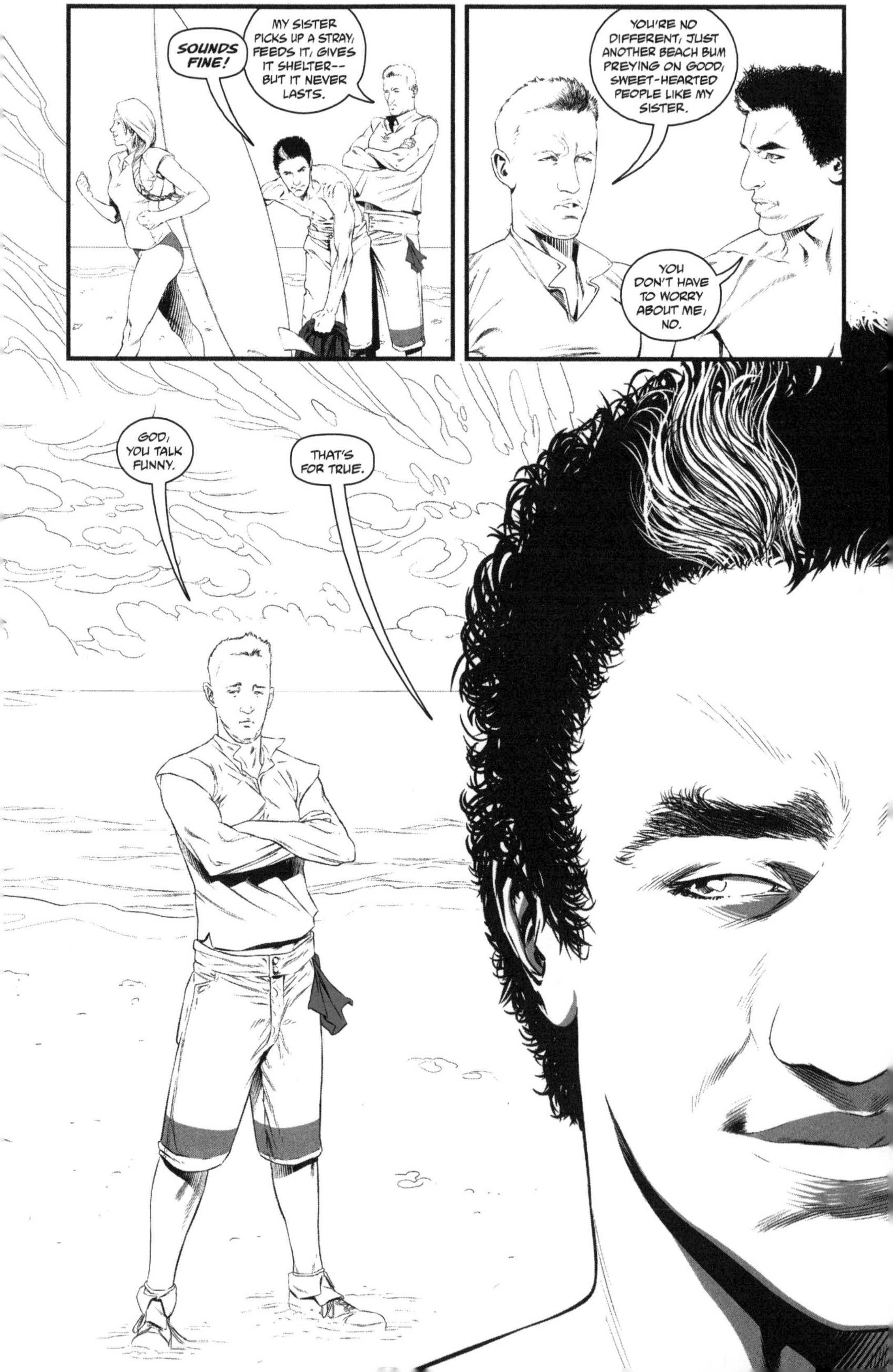
SOUNDS FINE!
MY SISTER PICKS UP A STRAY, FEEDS IT, GIVES IT SHELTER-- BUT IT NEVER LASTS.
YOU'RE NO DIFFERENT, JUST ANOTHER BEACH BUM PREYING ON GOOD, SWEET-HEARTED PEOPLE LIKE MY SISTER.
YOU DON'T HAVE TO WORRY ABOUT ME, NO.
GOD, YOU TALK FUNNY.
THAT'S FOR TRUE.

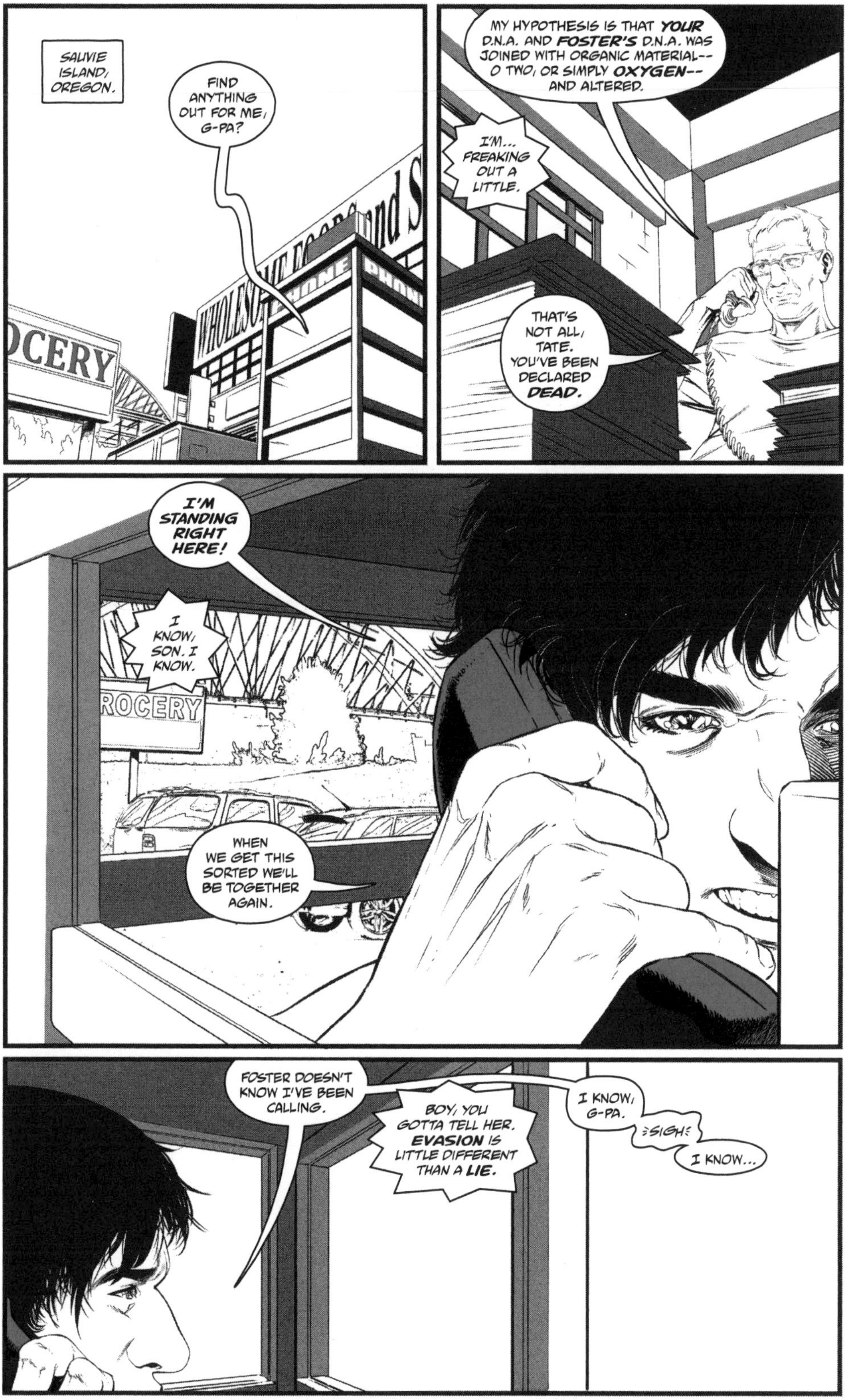
SAUVIE ISLAND, OREGON.
FIND ANYTHING OUT FOR ME, G-PA?
MY HYPOTHESIS IS THAT YOUR D.N.A. AND FOSTER'S D.N.A. WAS JOINED WITH ORGANIC MATERIAL-- O TWO, OR SIMPLY OXYGEN-- AND ALTERED.
I'M... FREAKING OUT A LITTLE.
THAT'S NOT ALL, TATE. YOU'VE BEEN DECLARED DEAD.
I'M STANDING RIGHT HERE!
I KNOW, SON. I KNOW.
ROCERY
WHEN WE GET THIS SORTED WE'LL BE TOGETHER AGAIN.
FOSTER DOESN'T KNOW I'VE BEEN CALLING.
BOY, YOU GOTTA TELL HER. EVASION IS LITTLE DIFFERENT THAN A LIE.
I KNOW, G-PA.
SIGH
I KNOW...

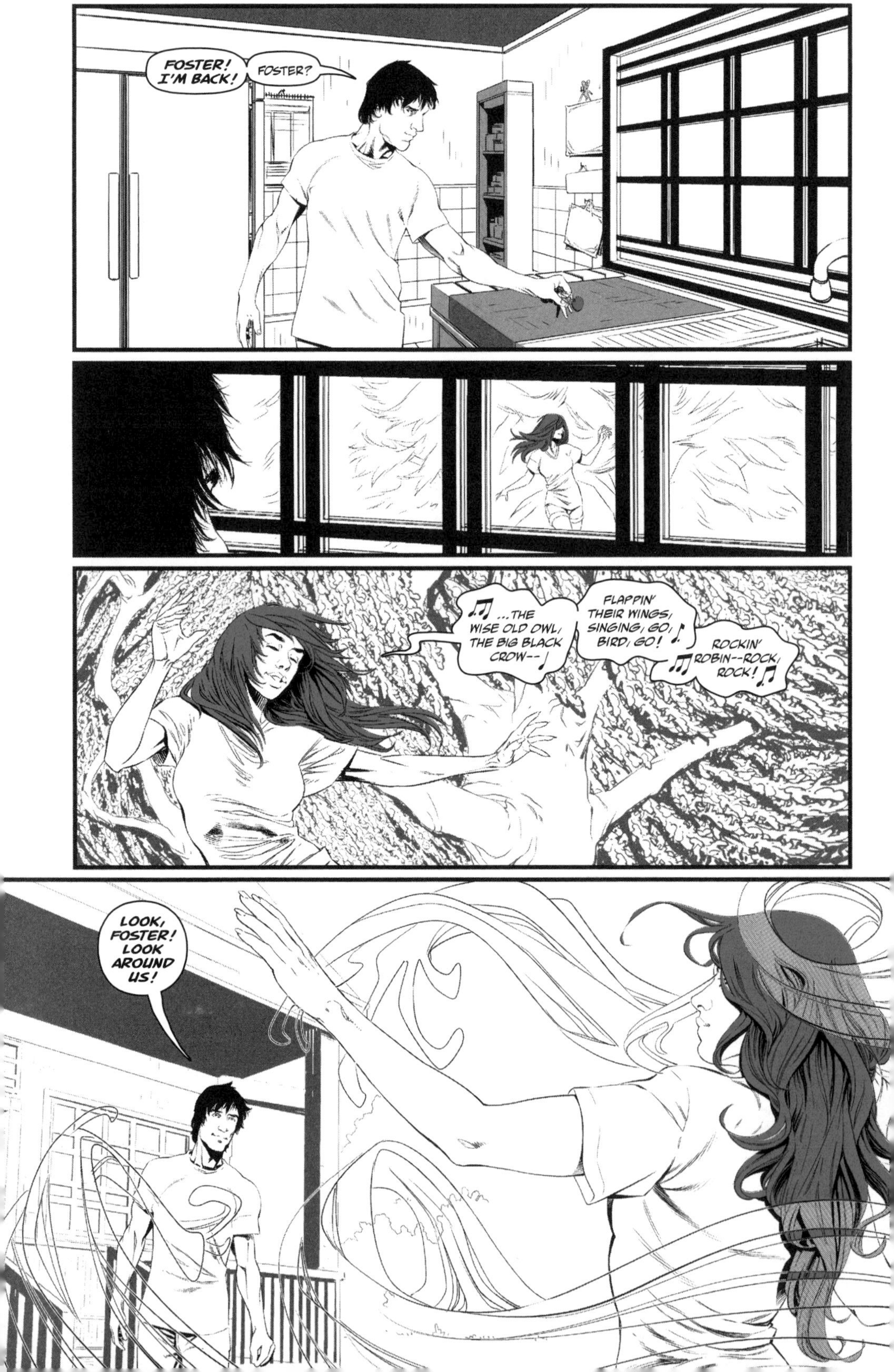
FOSTER! I'M BACK!
FOSTER?
♫ ...THE WISE OLD OWL, THE BIG BLACK CROW--♪
FLAPPIN' THEIR WINGS, SINGING, GO, BIRD, GO! ♪
♫ ROCKIN' ROBIN--ROCK, ROCK! ♫
LOOK, FOSTER! LOOK AROUND US!

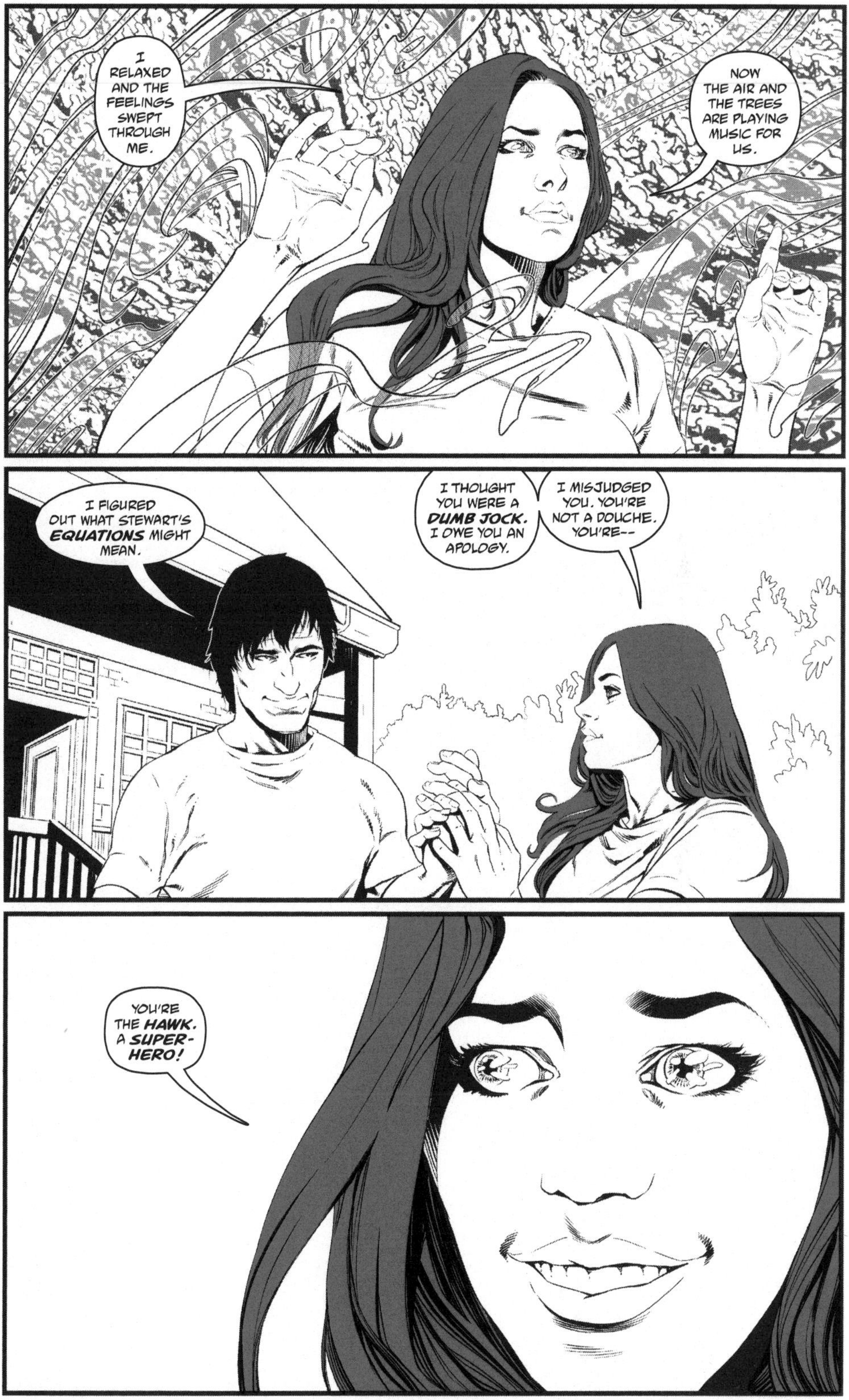
I RELAXED AND THE FEELINGS SWEPT THROUGH ME.
NOW THE AIR AND THE TREES ARE PLAYING MUSIC FOR US.
I FIGURED OUT WHAT STEWART'S **EQUATIONS** MIGHT MEAN.
I THOUGHT YOU WERE A **DUMB JOCK**. I OWE YOU AN APOLOGY.
I MISJUDGED YOU. YOU'RE NOT A DOUCHE. YOU'RE--
YOU'RE THE **HAWK**. A **SUPER-HERO!**

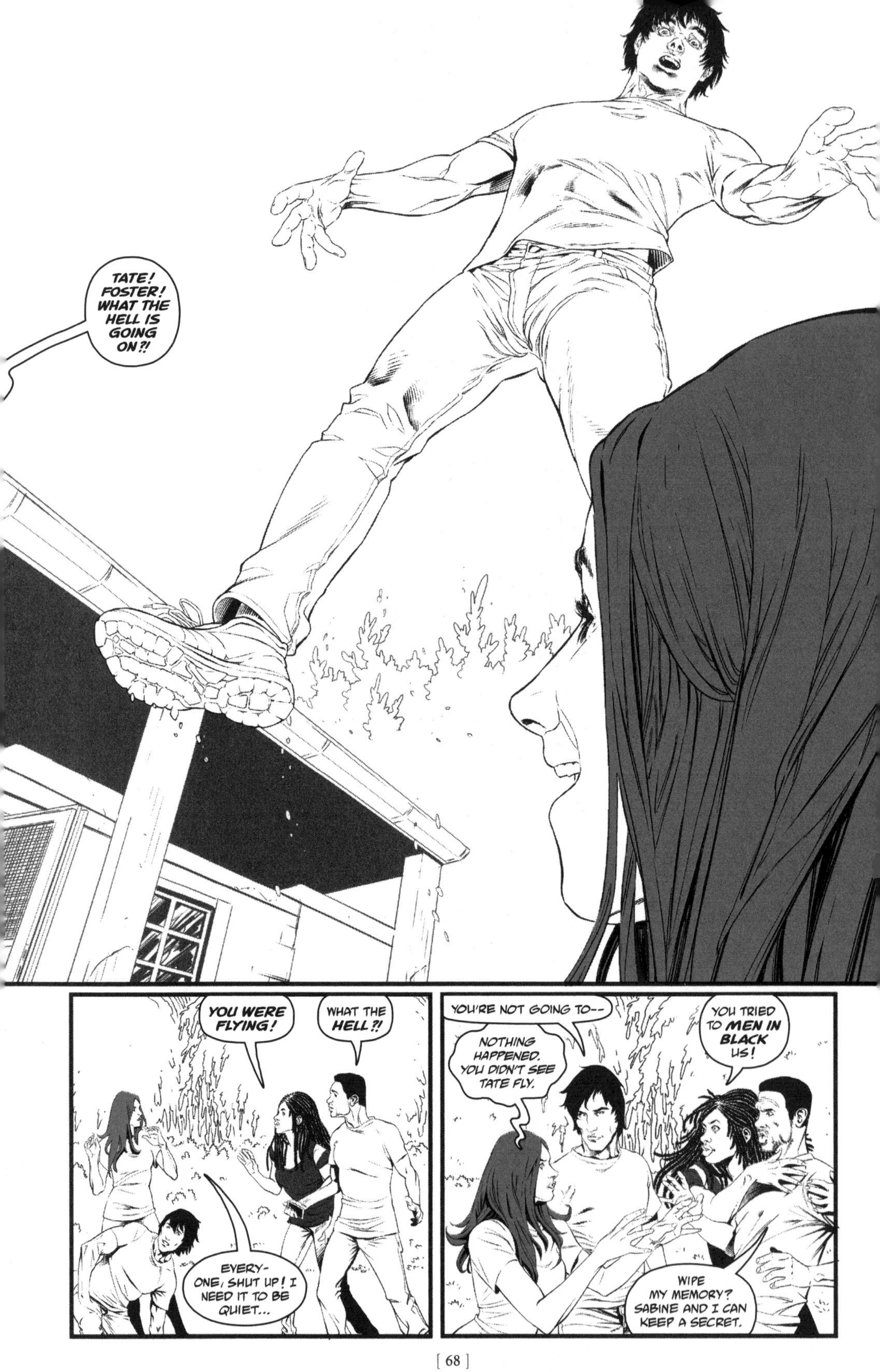
TATE! FOSTER! WHAT THE HELL IS GOING ON?!
YOU WERE FLYING!
WHAT THE HELL?!
EVERY-ONE, SHUT UP! I NEED IT TO BE QUIET...
YOU'RE NOT GOING TO--
NOTHING HAPPENED. YOU DIDN'T SEE TATE FLY.
YOU TRIED TO MEN IN BLACK US!
WIPE MY MEMORY? SABINE AND I CAN KEEP A SECRET.

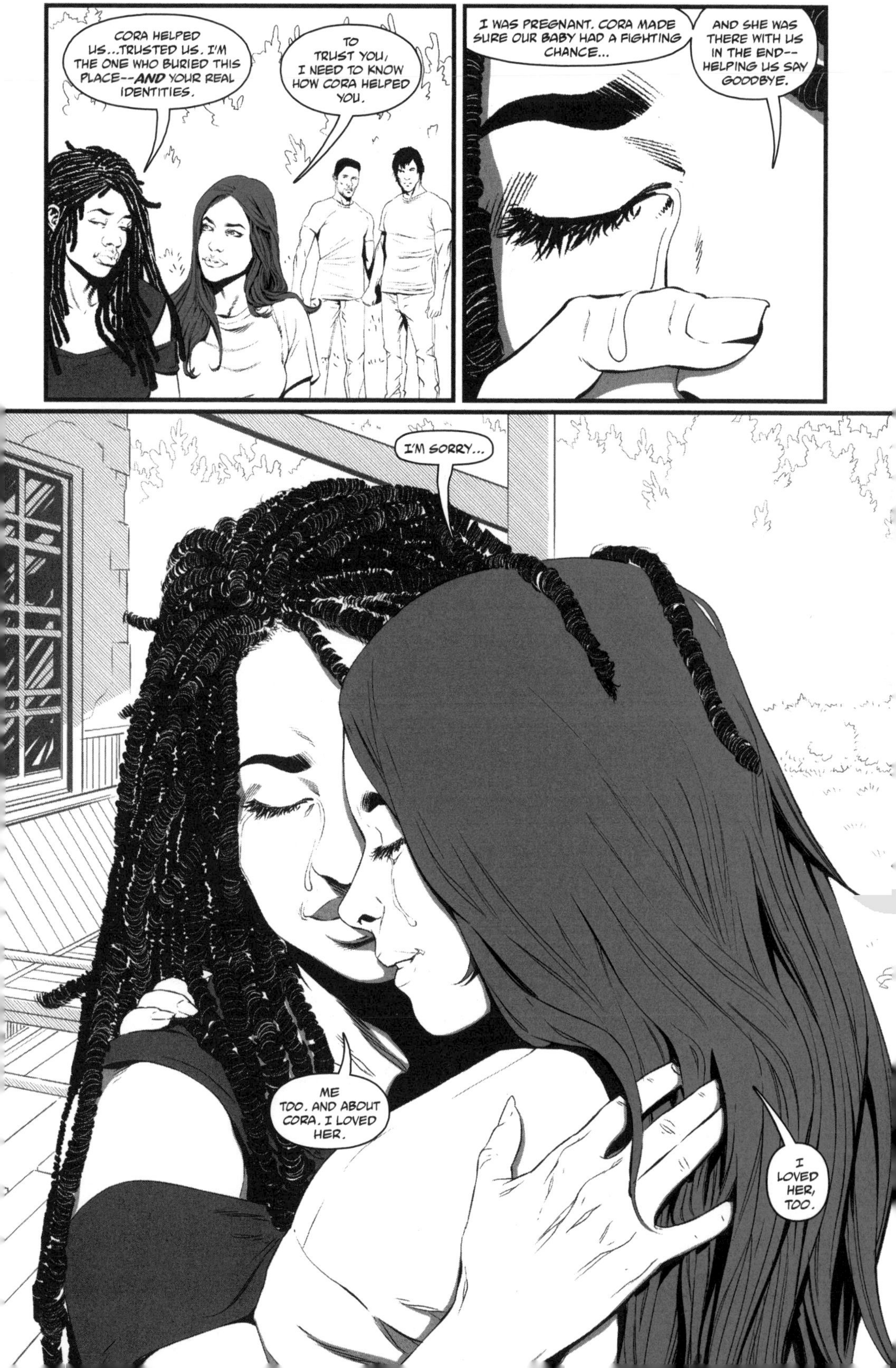
CORA HELPED US...TRUSTED US. I'M THE ONE WHO BURIED THIS PLACE--AND YOUR REAL IDENTITIES.
TO TRUST YOU, I NEED TO KNOW HOW CORA HELPED YOU.
I WAS PREGNANT. CORA MADE SURE OUR BABY HAD A FIGHTING CHANCE...
AND SHE WAS THERE WITH US IN THE END--HELPING US SAY GOODBYE.
I'M SORRY...
ME TOO. AND ABOUT CORA. I LOVED HER.
I LOVED HER, TOO.

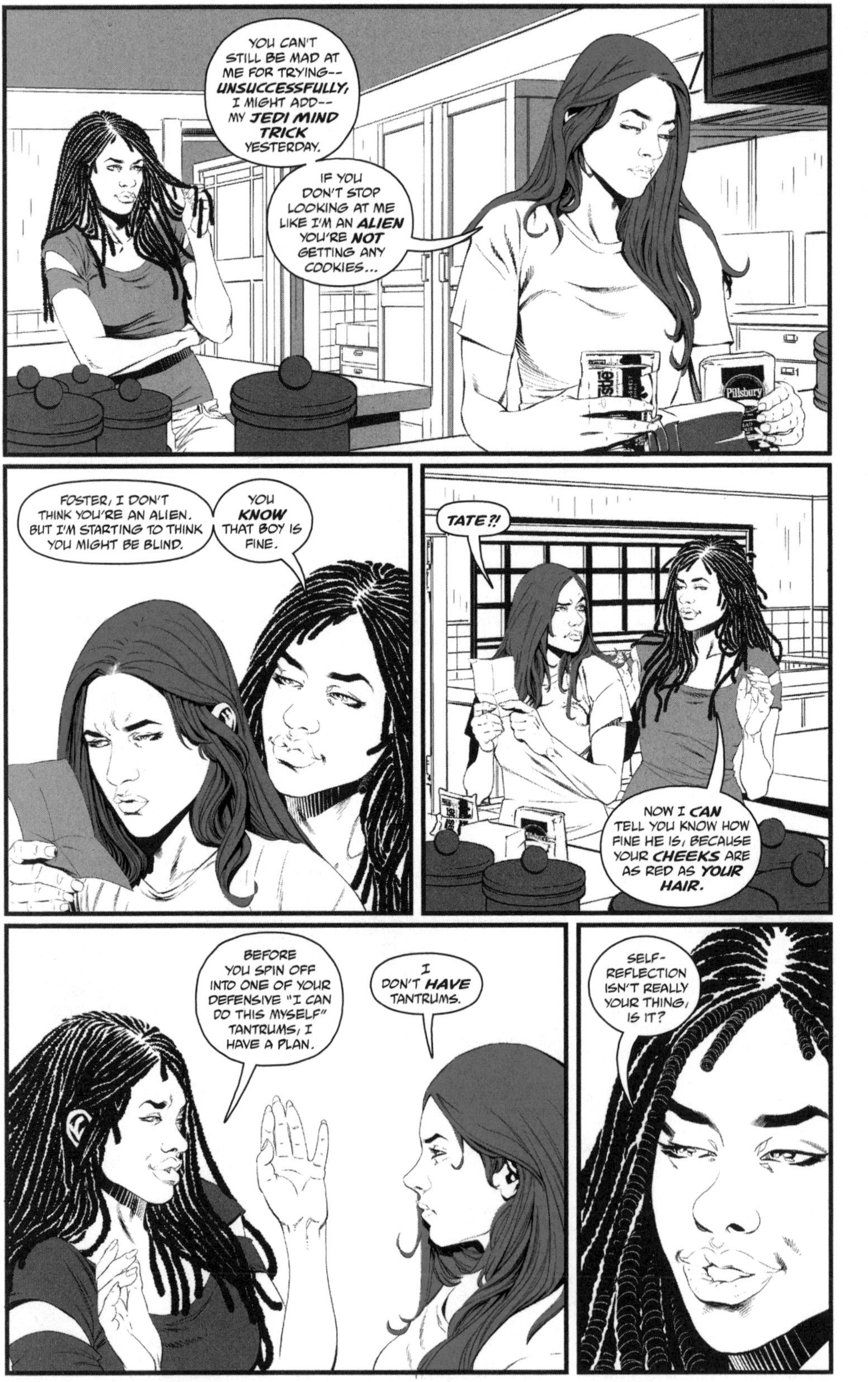
YOU CAN'T STILL BE MAD AT ME FOR TRYING-- UNSUCCESSFULLY, I MIGHT ADD-- MY JEDI MIND TRICK YESTERDAY.
IF YOU DON'T STOP LOOKING AT ME LIKE I'M AN ALIEN YOU'RE NOT GETTING ANY COOKIES...
FOSTER, I DON'T THINK YOU'RE AN ALIEN. BUT I'M STARTING TO THINK YOU MIGHT BE BLIND.
YOU KNOW THAT BOY IS FINE.
TATE?!
NOW I CAN TELL YOU KNOW HOW FINE HE IS, BECAUSE YOUR CHEEKS ARE AS RED AS YOUR HAIR.
BEFORE YOU SPIN OFF INTO ONE OF YOUR DEFENSIVE "I CAN DO THIS MYSELF" TANTRUMS, I HAVE A PLAN.
I DON'T HAVE TANTRUMS.
SELF-REFLECTION ISN'T REALLY YOUR THING, IS IT?

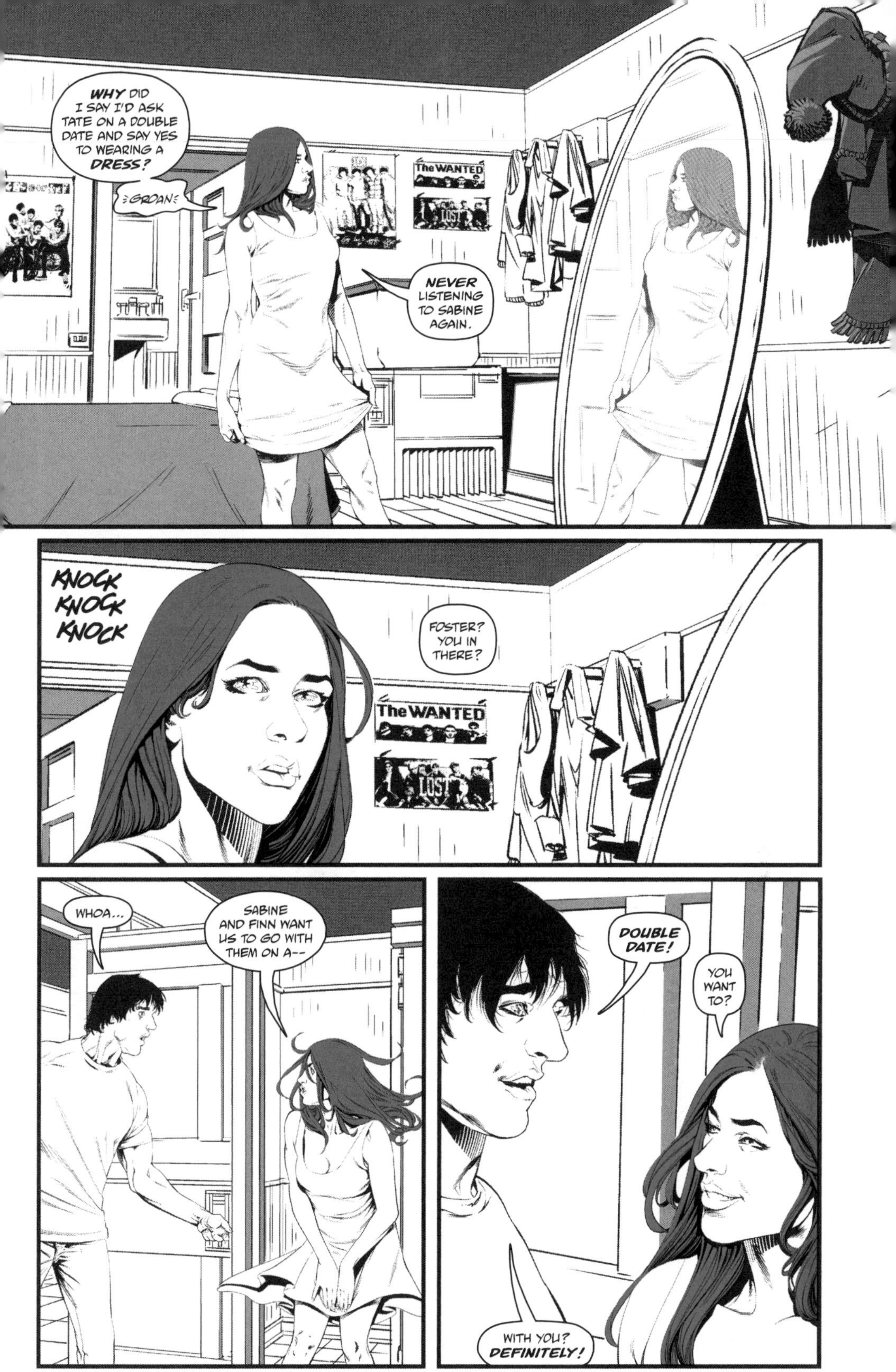
WHY DID I SAY I'D ASK TATE ON A DOUBLE DATE AND SAY YES TO WEARING A DRESS?
GROAN
The WANTED
LOST
NEVER LISTENING TO SABINE AGAIN.
KNOCK KNOCK KNOCK
FOSTER? YOU IN THERE?
The WANTED
LOST
WHOA...
SABINE AND FINN WANT US TO GO WITH THEM ON A--
DOUBLE DATE!
YOU WANT TO?
WITH YOU? DEFINITELY!

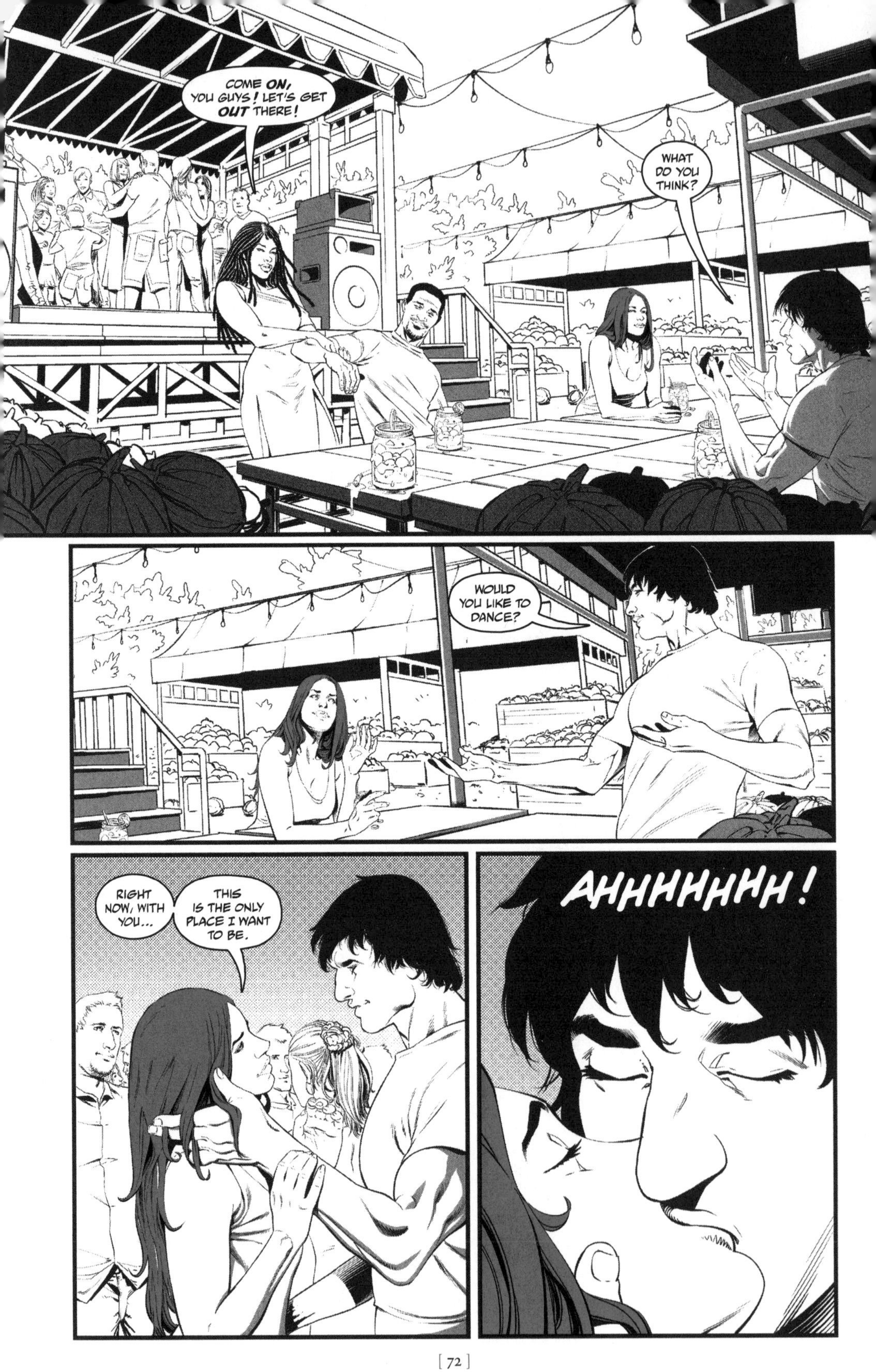
COME ON, YOU GUYS! LET'S GET OUT THERE!
WHAT DO YOU THINK?
WOULD YOU LIKE TO DANCE?
RIGHT NOW, WITH YOU...
THIS IS THE ONLY PLACE I WANT TO BE.
AHHHHHHH!

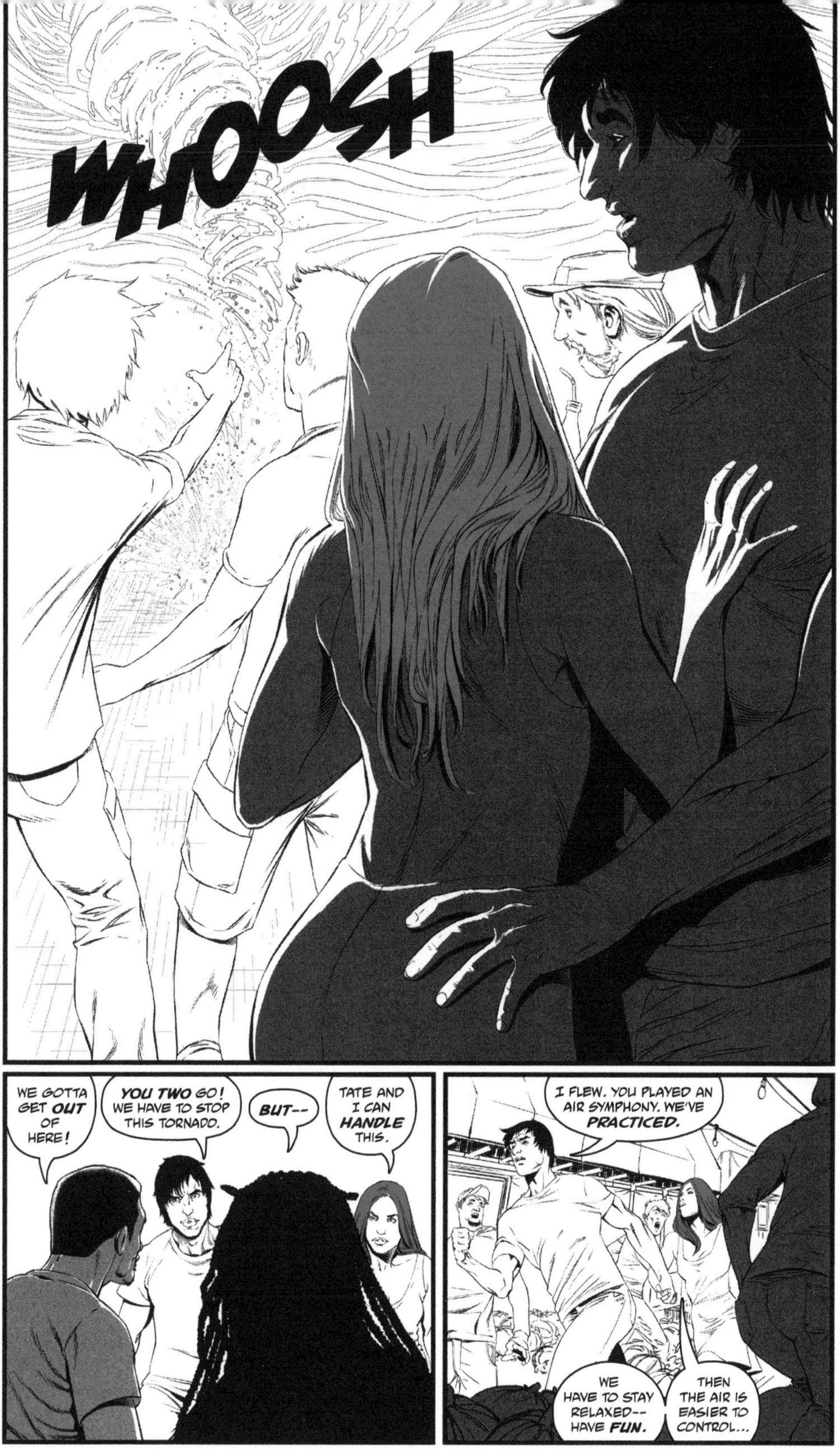
WHOOSH
WE GOTTA GET OUT OF HERE!
YOU TWO GO! WE HAVE TO STOP THIS TORNADO.
BUT--
TATE AND I CAN HANDLE THIS.
I FLEW. YOU PLAYED AN AIR SYMPHONY. WE'VE PRACTICED.
WE HAVE TO STAY RELAXED-- HAVE FUN.
THEN THE AIR IS EASIER TO CONTROL...

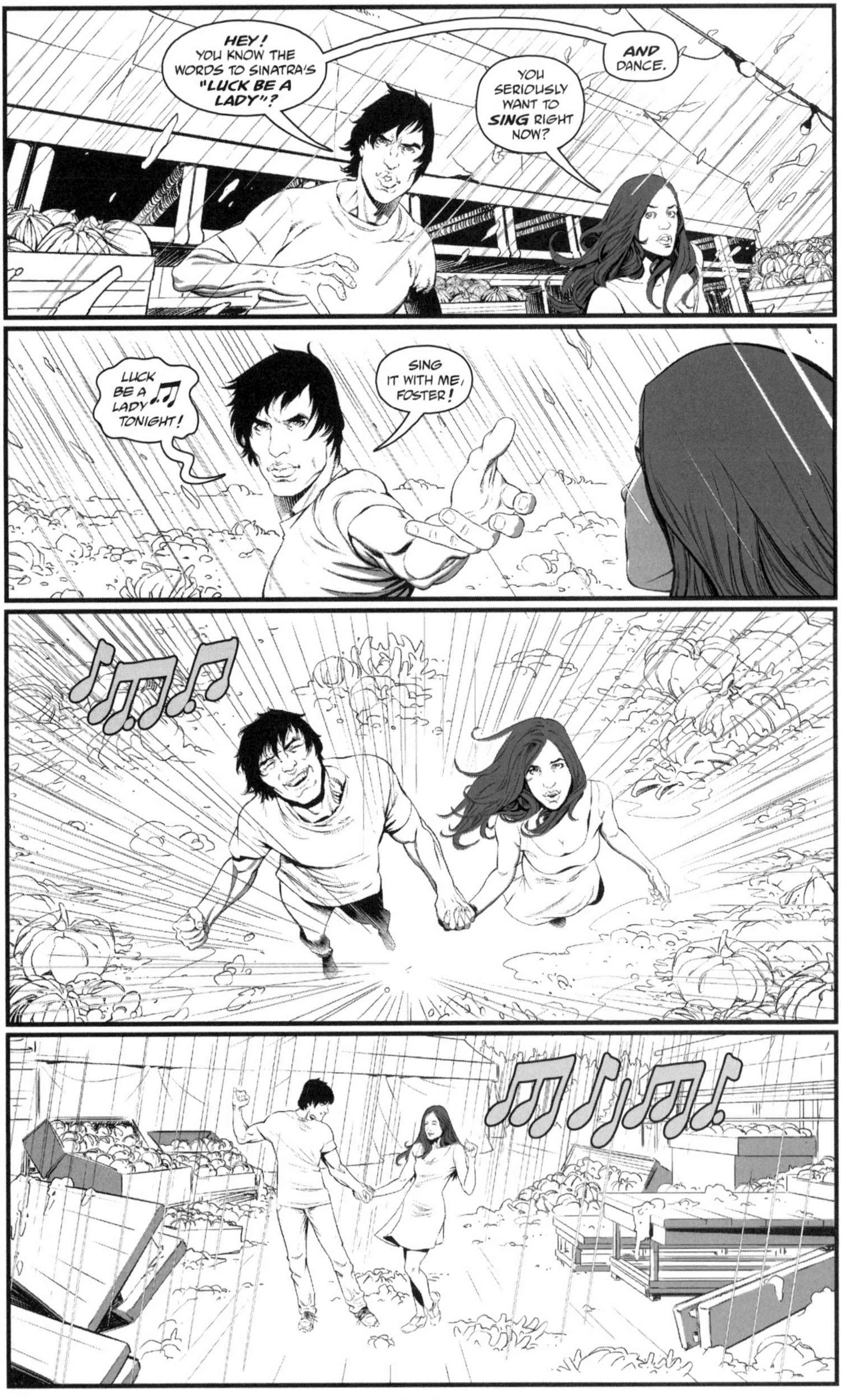
HEY! YOU KNOW THE WORDS TO SINATRA'S "LUCK BE A LADY"?
YOU SERIOUSLY WANT TO SING RIGHT NOW?
AND DANCE.
LUCK BE A LADY TONIGHT!
SING IT WITH ME, FOSTER!

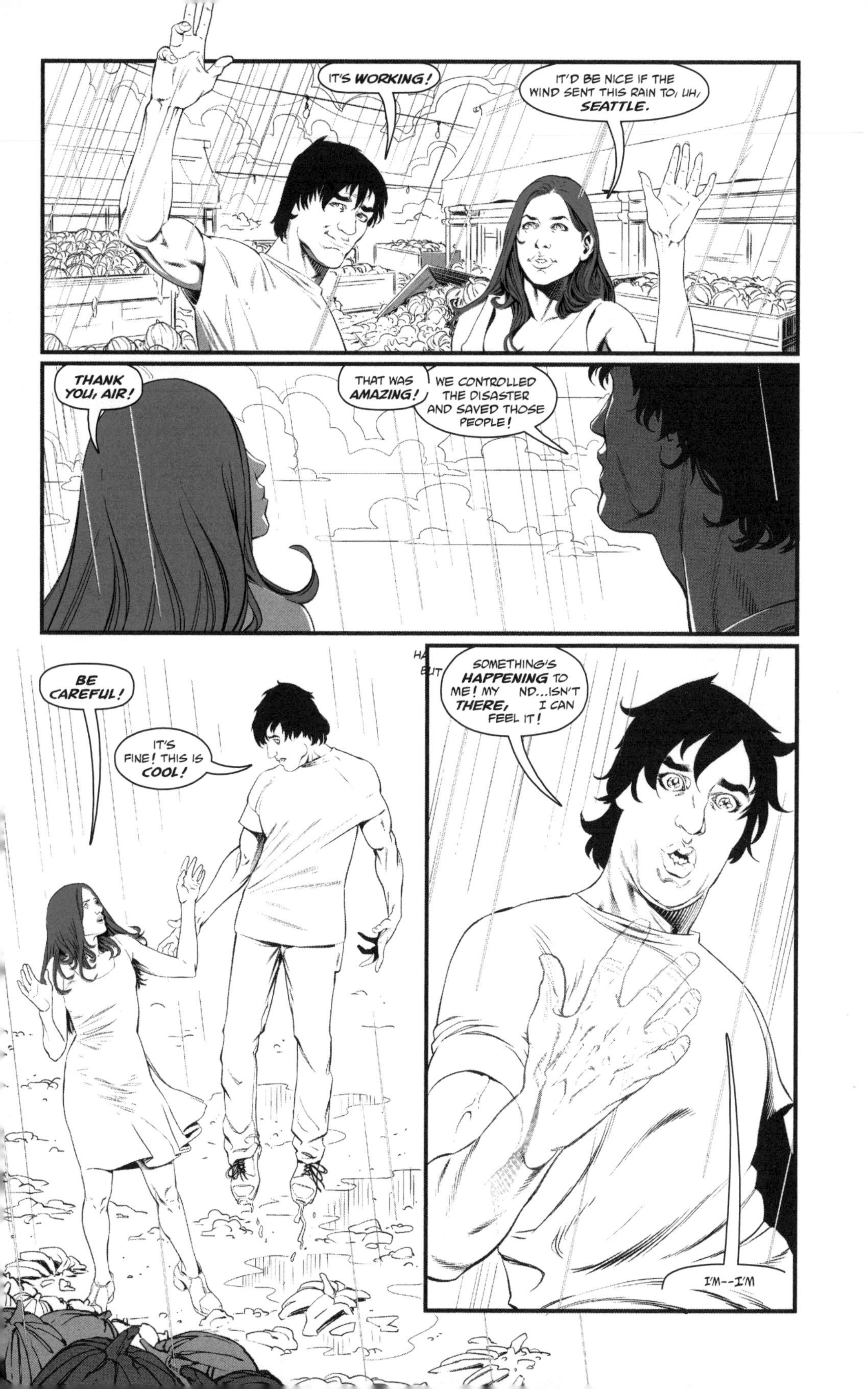
IT'S **WORKING!**
IT'D BE NICE IF THE WIND SENT THIS RAIN TO, UH, **SEATTLE.**
THANK YOU, AIR!
THAT WAS **AMAZING!**
WE CONTROLLED THE DISASTER AND SAVED THOSE PEOPLE!
BE CAREFUL!
IT'S FINE! THIS IS **COOL!**
SOMETHING'S **HAPPENING** TO ME! MY ND...ISN'T **THERE,** I CAN FEEL IT!
I'M--I'M

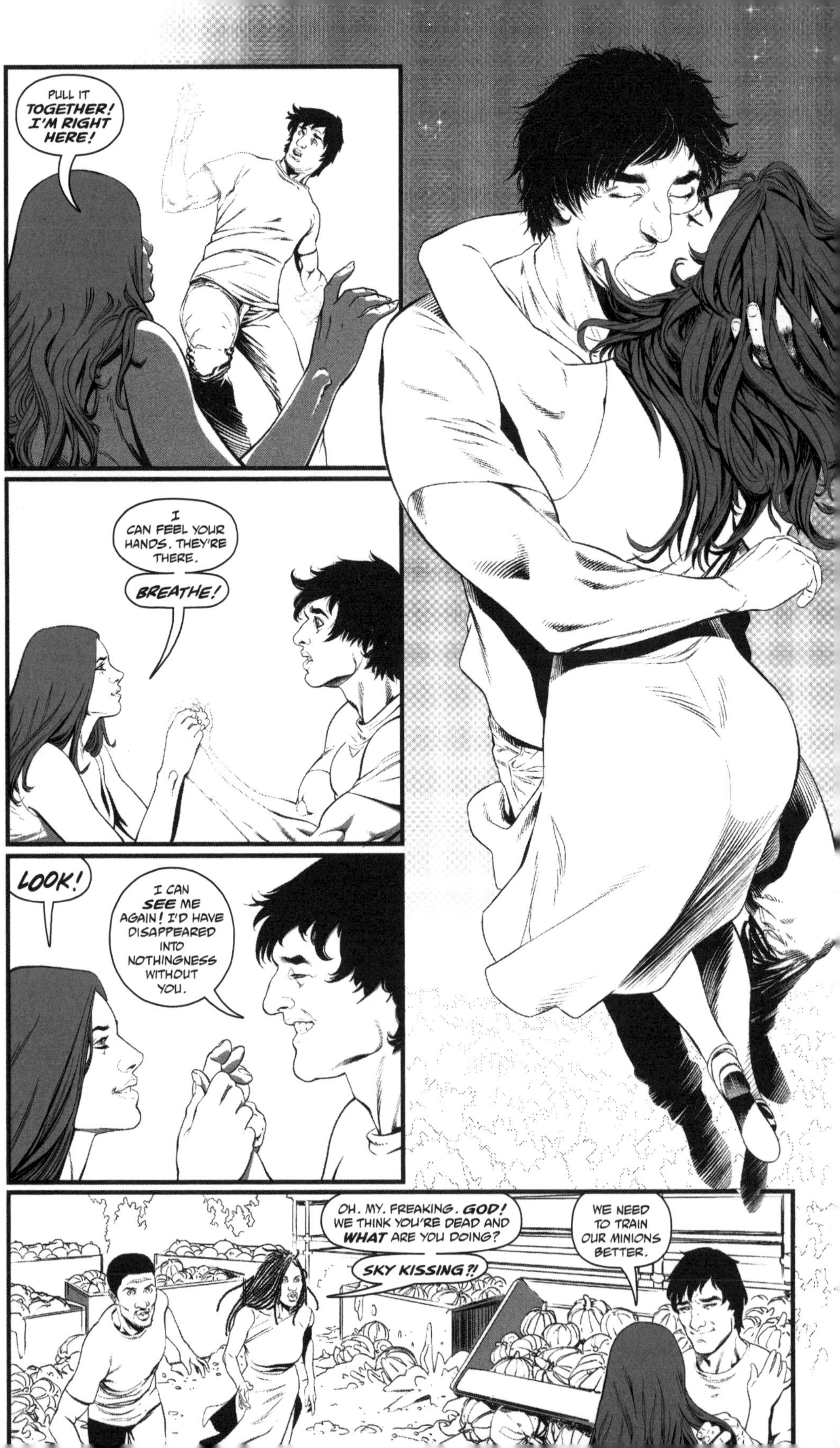
PULL IT TOGETHER! I'M RIGHT HERE!
I CAN FEEL YOUR HANDS. THEY'RE THERE.
BREATHE!
LOOK!
I CAN SEE ME AGAIN! I'D HAVE DISAPPEARED INTO NOTHINGNESS WITHOUT YOU.
OH. MY. FREAKING. GOD! WE THINK YOU'RE DEAD AND WHAT ARE YOU DOING?
SKY KISSING?!
WE NEED TO TRAIN OUR MINIONS BETTER.

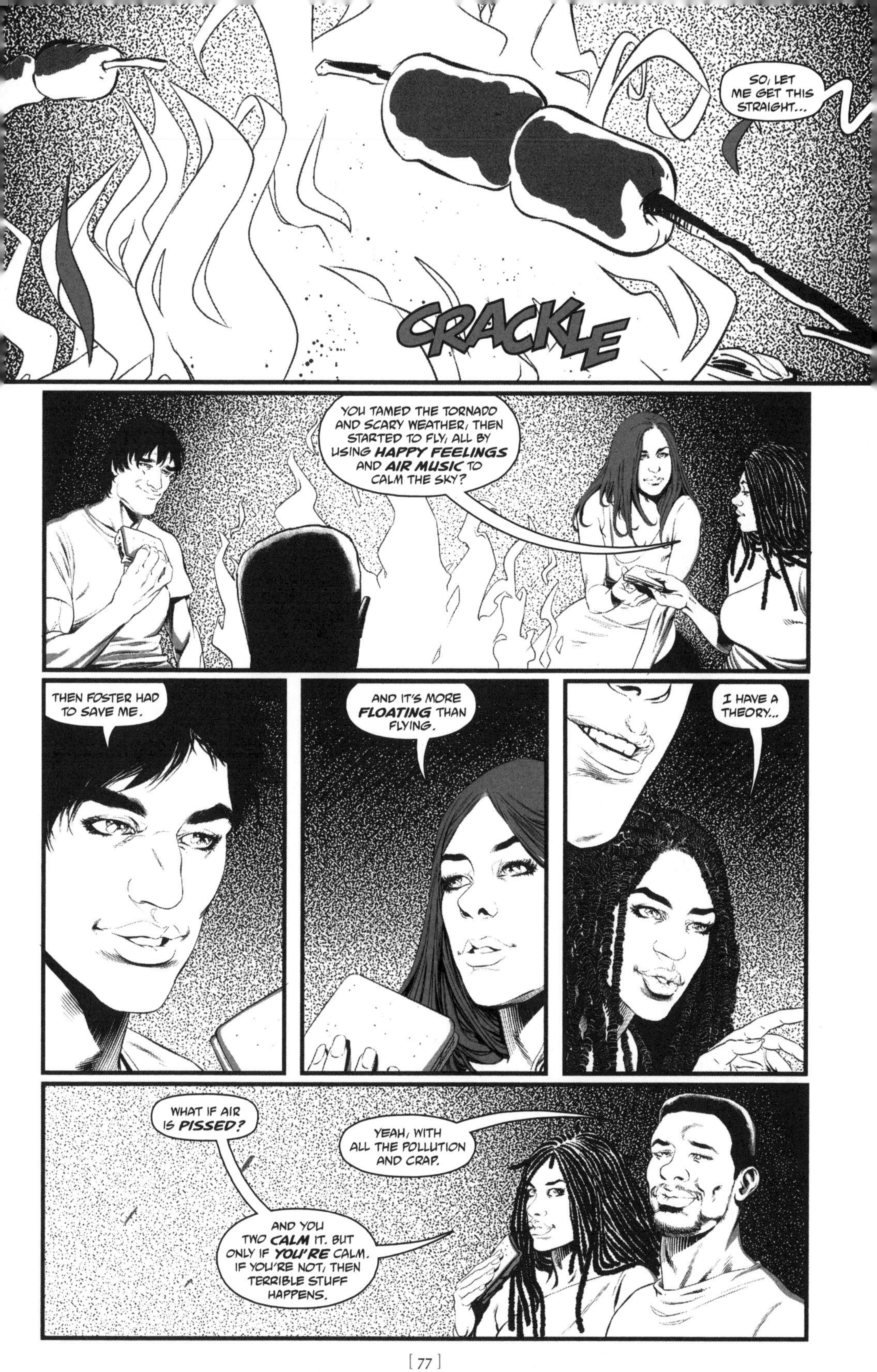
SO, LET ME GET THIS STRAIGHT...
CRACKLE
YOU TAMED THE TORNADO AND SCARY WEATHER, THEN STARTED TO FLY, ALL BY USING HAPPY FEELINGS AND AIR MUSIC TO CALM THE SKY?
THEN FOSTER HAD TO SAVE ME.
AND IT'S MORE FLOATING THAN FLYING.
I HAVE A THEORY...
WHAT IF AIR IS PISSED?
YEAH, WITH ALL THE POLLUTION AND CRAP.
AND YOU TWO CALM IT. BUT ONLY IF YOU'RE CALM. IF YOU'RE NOT, THEN TERRIBLE STUFF HAPPENS.

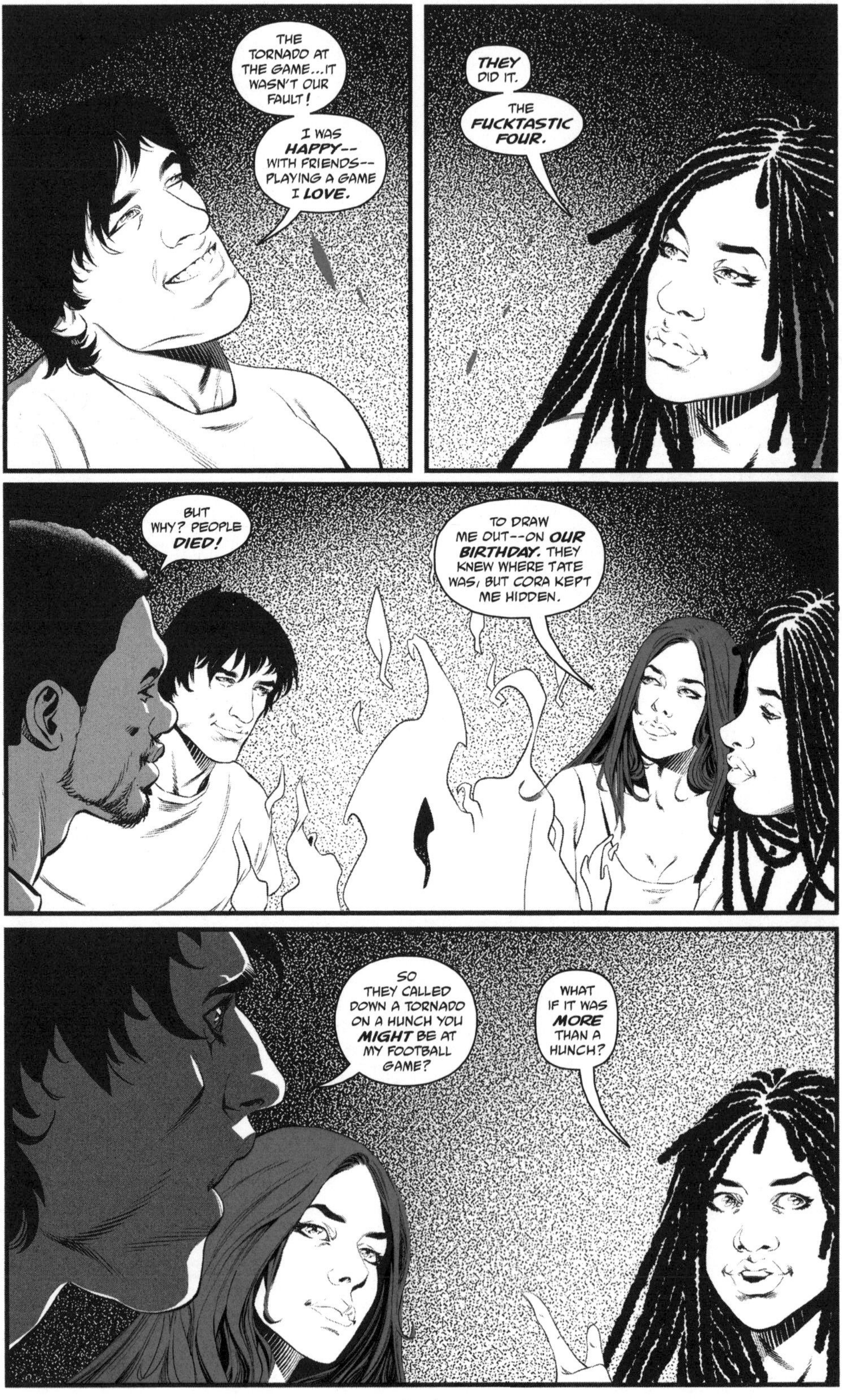
THE TORNADO AT THE GAME...IT WASN'T OUR FAULT!
I WAS HAPPY-- WITH FRIENDS-- PLAYING A GAME I LOVE.
THEY DID IT.
THE FUCKTASTIC FOUR.
BUT WHY? PEOPLE DIED!
TO DRAW ME OUT--ON OUR BIRTHDAY. THEY KNEW WHERE TATE WAS, BUT CORA KEPT ME HIDDEN.
SO THEY CALLED DOWN A TORNADO ON A HUNCH YOU MIGHT BE AT MY FOOTBALL GAME?
WHAT IF IT WAS MORE THAN A HUNCH?

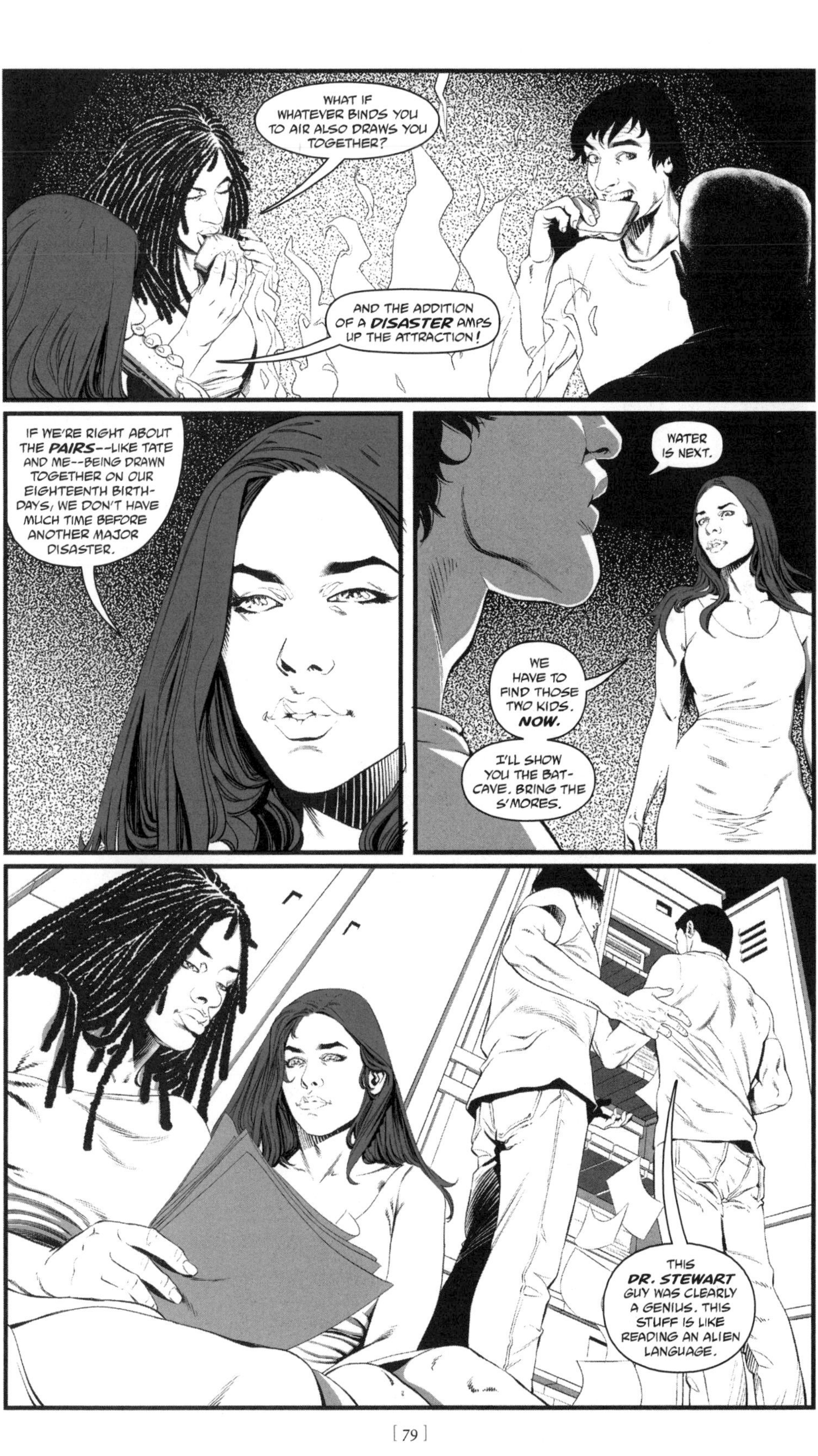
WHAT IF WHATEVER BINDS YOU TO AIR ALSO DRAWS YOU TOGETHER?
AND THE ADDITION OF A DISASTER AMPS UP THE ATTRACTION!
IF WE'RE RIGHT ABOUT THE PAIRS--LIKE TATE AND ME--BEING DRAWN TOGETHER ON OUR EIGHTEENTH BIRTHDAYS, WE DON'T HAVE MUCH TIME BEFORE ANOTHER MAJOR DISASTER.
WATER IS NEXT.
WE HAVE TO FIND THOSE TWO KIDS. NOW.
I'LL SHOW YOU THE BAT-CAVE. BRING THE S'MORES.
THIS DR. STEWART GUY WAS CLEARLY A GENIUS. THIS STUFF IS LIKE READING AN ALIEN LANGUAGE.

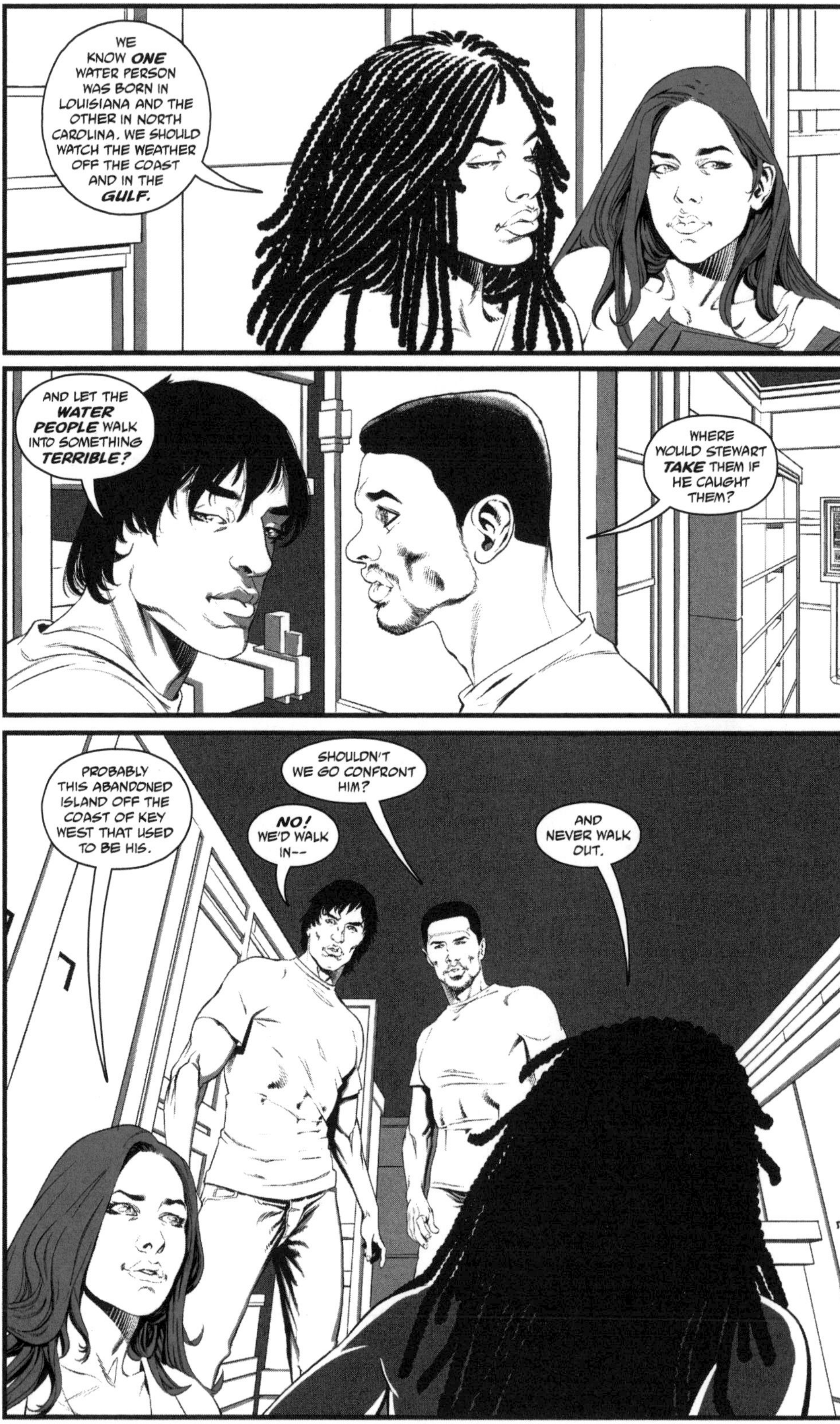
WE KNOW ONE WATER PERSON WAS BORN IN LOUISIANA AND THE OTHER IN NORTH CAROLINA. WE SHOULD WATCH THE WEATHER OFF THE COAST AND IN THE GULF.
AND LET THE WATER PEOPLE WALK INTO SOMETHING TERRIBLE?
WHERE WOULD STEWART TAKE THEM IF HE CAUGHT THEM?
PROBABLY THIS ABANDONED ISLAND OFF THE COAST OF KEY WEST THAT USED TO BE HIS.
SHOULDN'T WE GO CONFRONT HIM?
NO! WE'D WALK IN--
AND NEVER WALK OUT.

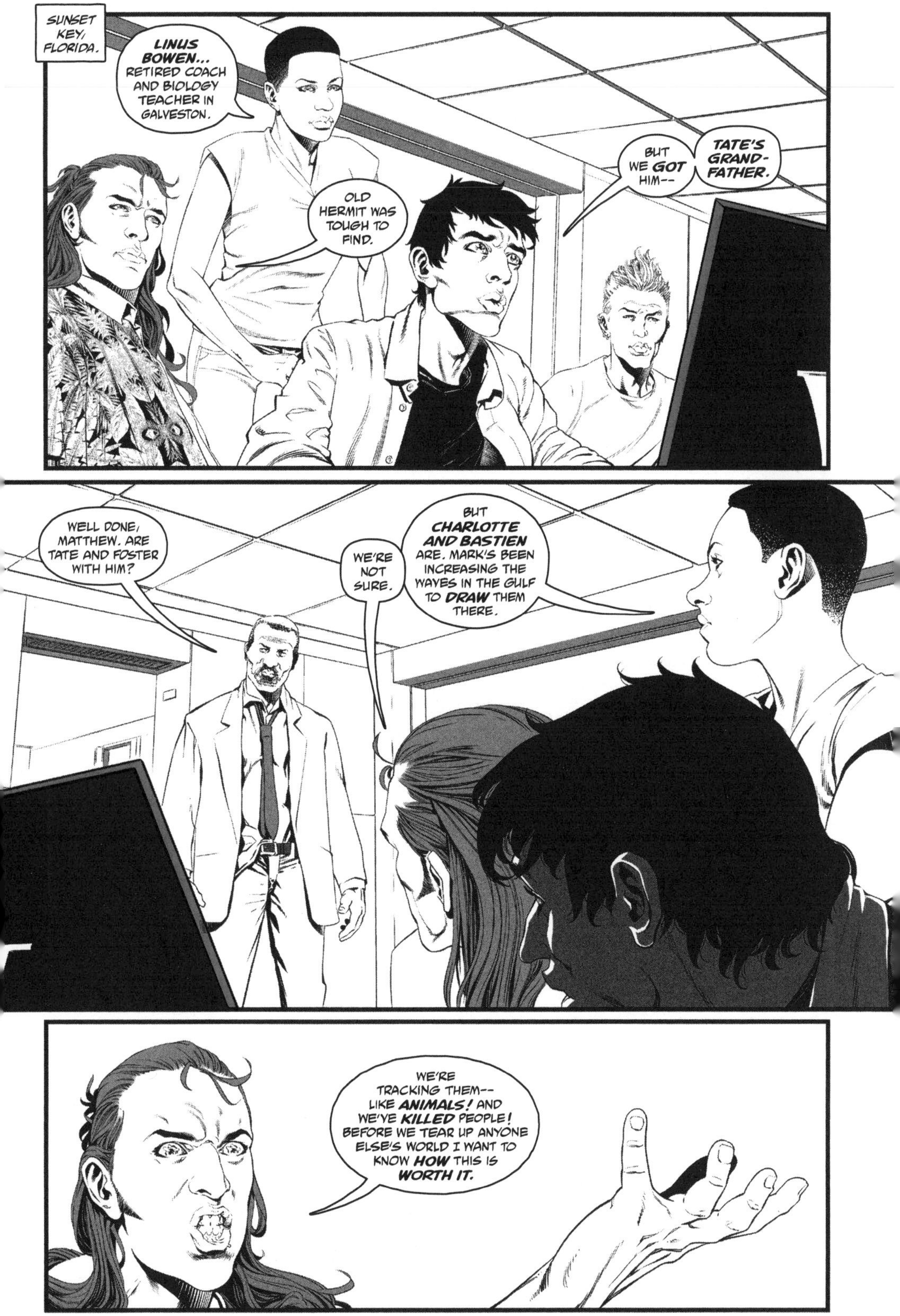
SUNSET KEY, FLORIDA.
LINUS BOWEN... RETIRED COACH AND BIOLOGY TEACHER IN GALVESTON.
OLD HERMIT WAS TOUGH TO FIND.
BUT WE GOT HIM--
TATE'S GRANDFATHER.
WELL DONE, MATTHEW. ARE TATE AND FOSTER WITH HIM?
WE'RE NOT SURE.
BUT CHARLOTTE AND BASTIEN ARE. MARK'S BEEN INCREASING THE WAVES IN THE GULF TO DRAW THEM THERE.
WE'RE TRACKING THEM-- LIKE ANIMALS! AND WE'VE KILLED PEOPLE! BEFORE WE TEAR UP ANYONE ELSE'S WORLD I WANT TO KNOW HOW THIS IS WORTH IT.

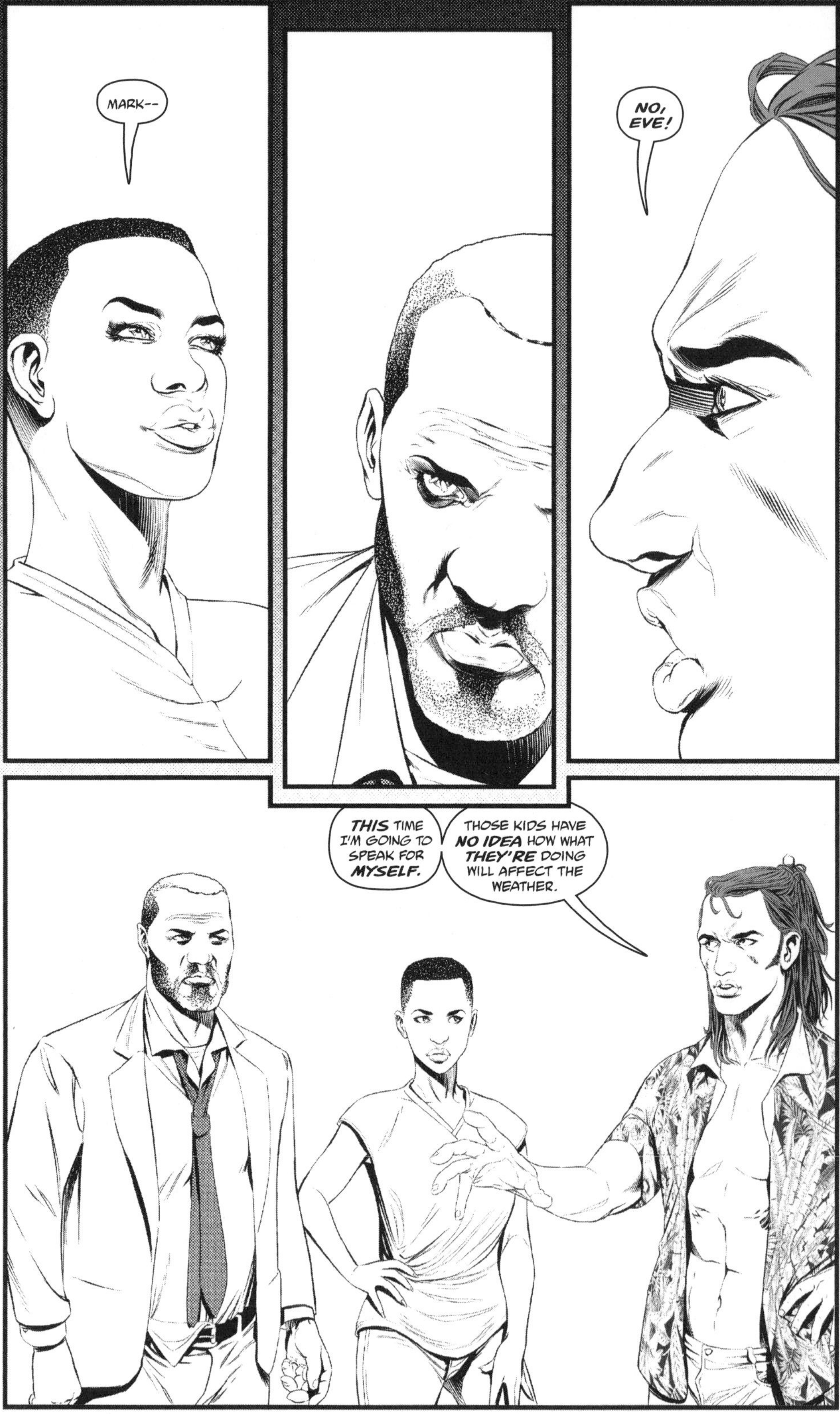
MARK--
NO, EVE!
THIS TIME I'M GOING TO SPEAK FOR MYSELF.
THOSE KIDS HAVE NO IDEA HOW WHAT THEY'RE DOING WILL AFFECT THE WEATHER.

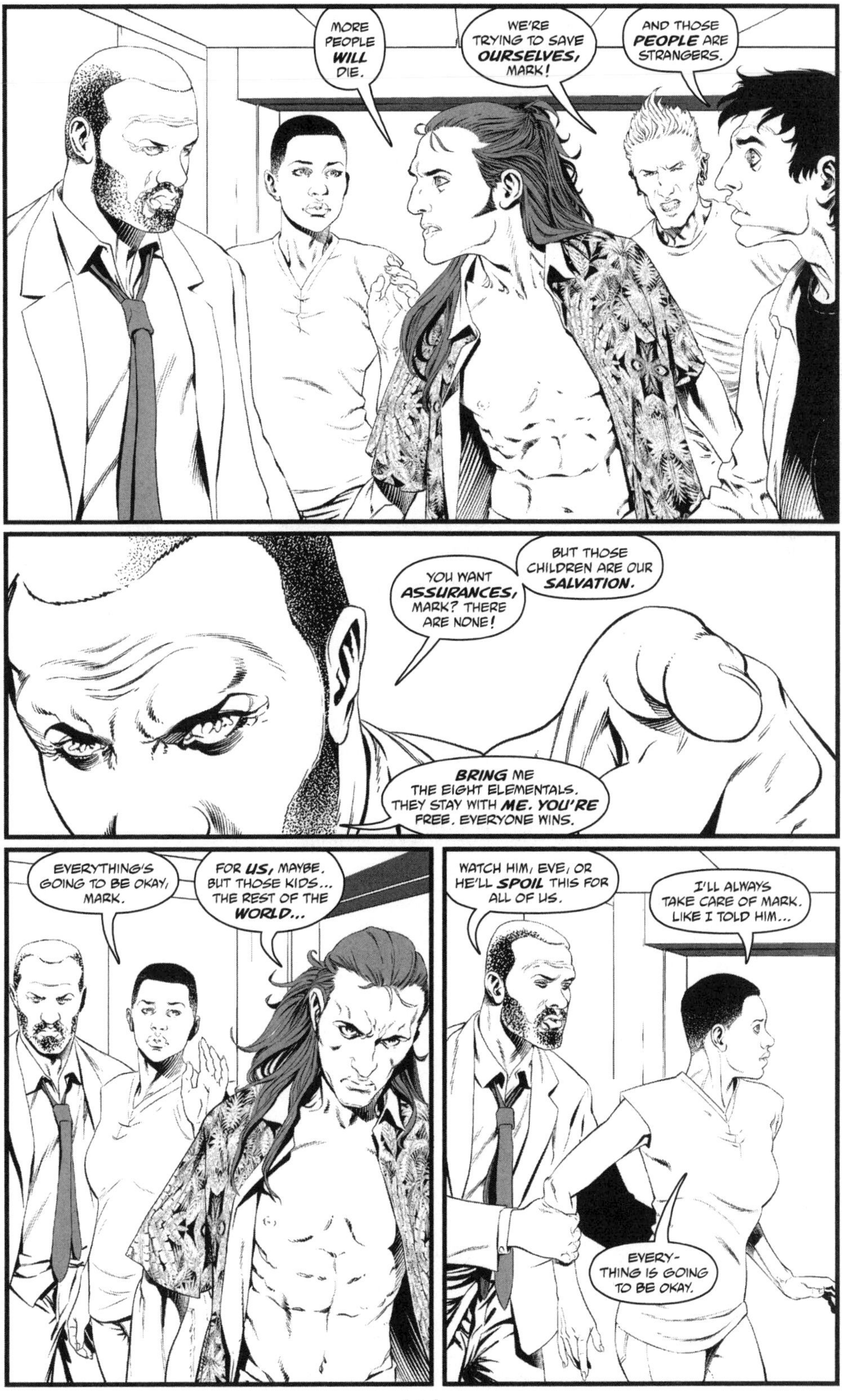
MORE PEOPLE WILL DIE.
WE'RE TRYING TO SAVE OURSELVES, MARK!
AND THOSE PEOPLE ARE STRANGERS.
YOU WANT ASSURANCES, MARK? THERE ARE NONE!
BUT THOSE CHILDREN ARE OUR SALVATION.
BRING ME THE EIGHT ELEMENTALS. THEY STAY WITH ME. YOU'RE FREE. EVERYONE WINS.
EVERYTHING'S GOING TO BE OKAY, MARK.
FOR US, MAYBE. BUT THOSE KIDS... THE REST OF THE WORLD...
WATCH HIM, EVE, OR HE'LL SPOIL THIS FOR ALL OF US.
I'LL ALWAYS TAKE CARE OF MARK. LIKE I TOLD HIM...
EVERY-THING IS GOING TO BE OKAY.

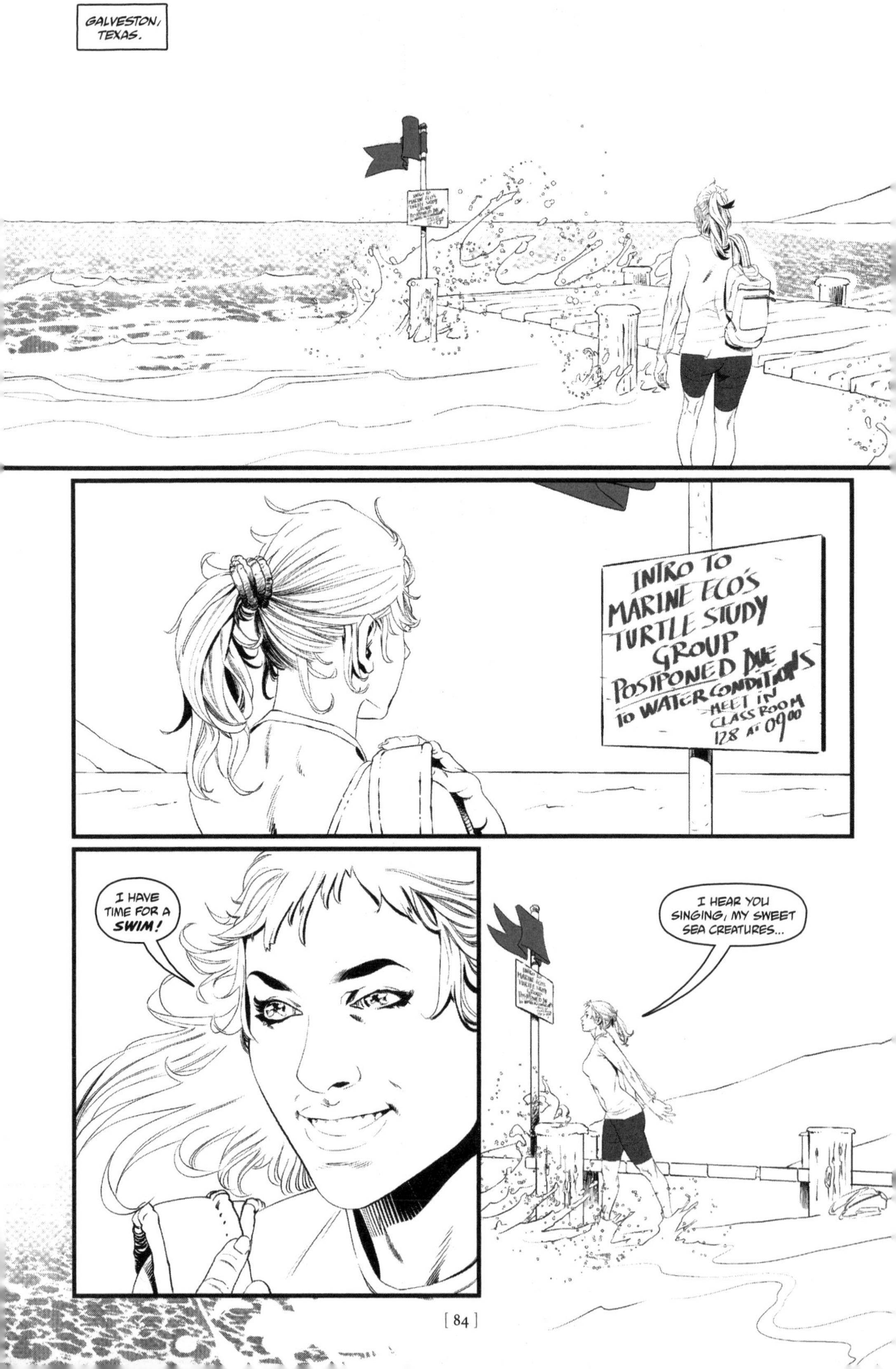
GALVESTON, TEXAS.
INTRO TO MARINE ECO'S TURTLE STUDY GROUP POSTPONED DUE TO WATER CONDITIONS
-MEET IN CLASS ROOM 128 AT 0900
I HAVE TIME FOR A SWIM!
I HEAR YOU SINGING, MY SWEET SEA CREATURES...

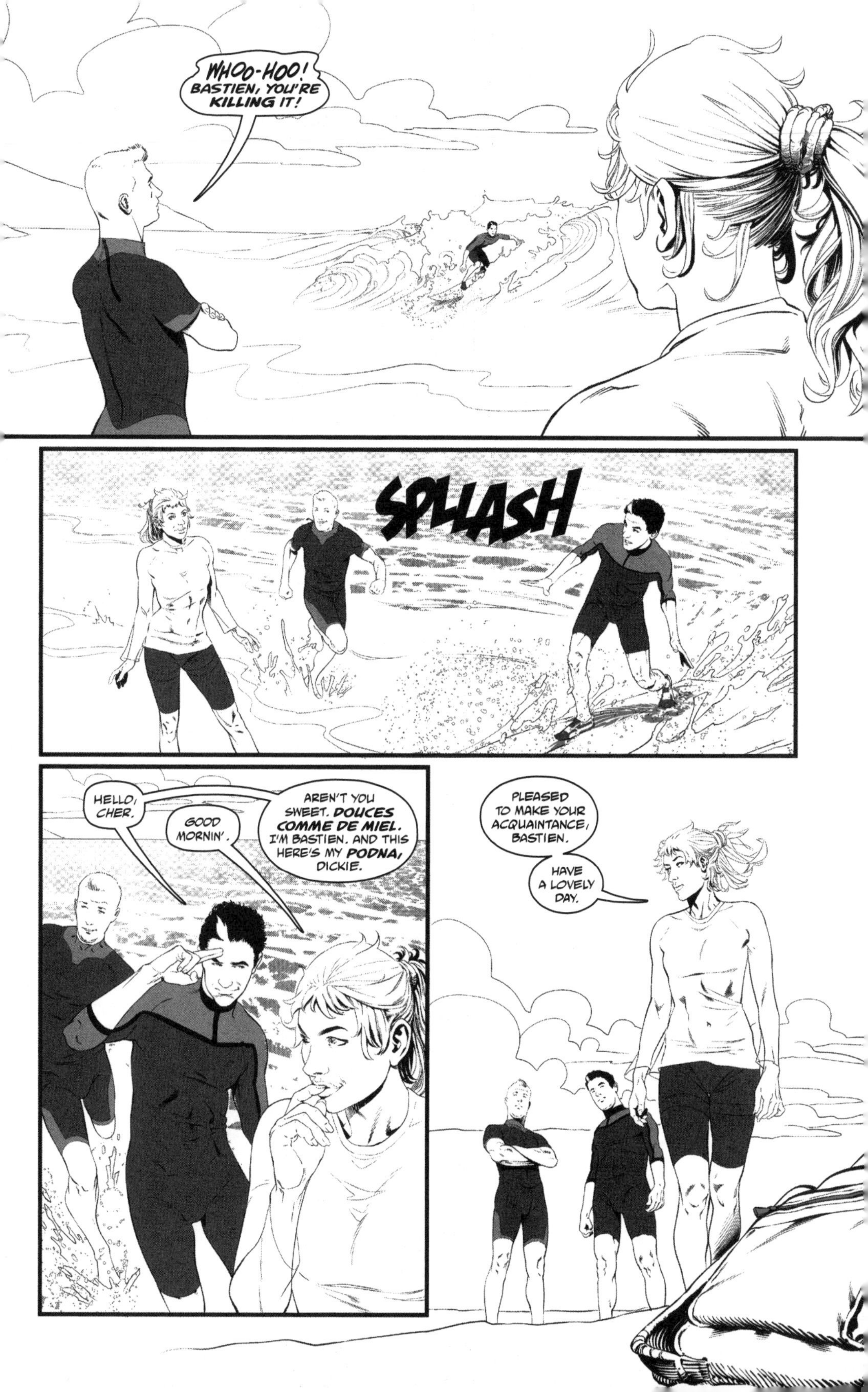
WHOO-HOO! BASTIEN, YOU'RE KILLING IT!
SPLLASH
HELLO, CHER.
GOOD MORNIN'.
AREN'T YOU SWEET. DOUCES COMME DE MIEL. I'M BASTIEN. AND THIS HERE'S MY PODNA, DICKIE.
PLEASED TO MAKE YOUR ACQUAINTANCE, BASTIEN.
HAVE A LOVELY DAY.

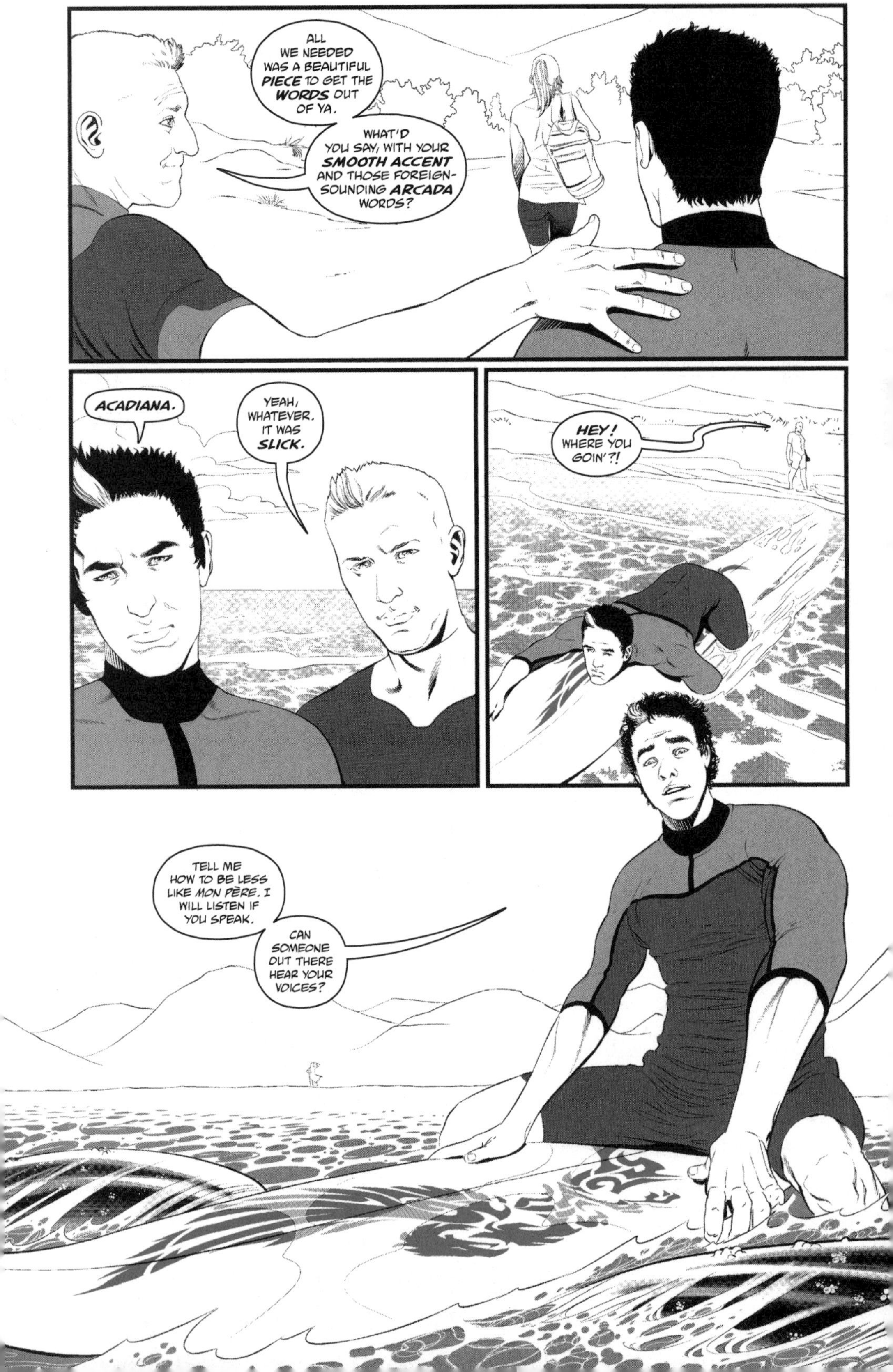
ALL WE NEEDED WAS A BEAUTIFUL PIECE TO GET THE WORDS OUT OF YA.
WHAT'D YOU SAY, WITH YOUR SMOOTH ACCENT AND THOSE FOREIGN-SOUNDING ARCADA WORDS?
ACADIANA.
YEAH, WHATEVER. IT WAS SLICK.
HEY! WHERE YOU GOIN'?!
TELL ME HOW TO BE LESS LIKE MON PÈRE. I WILL LISTEN IF YOU SPEAK.
CAN SOMEONE OUT THERE HEAR YOUR VOICES?

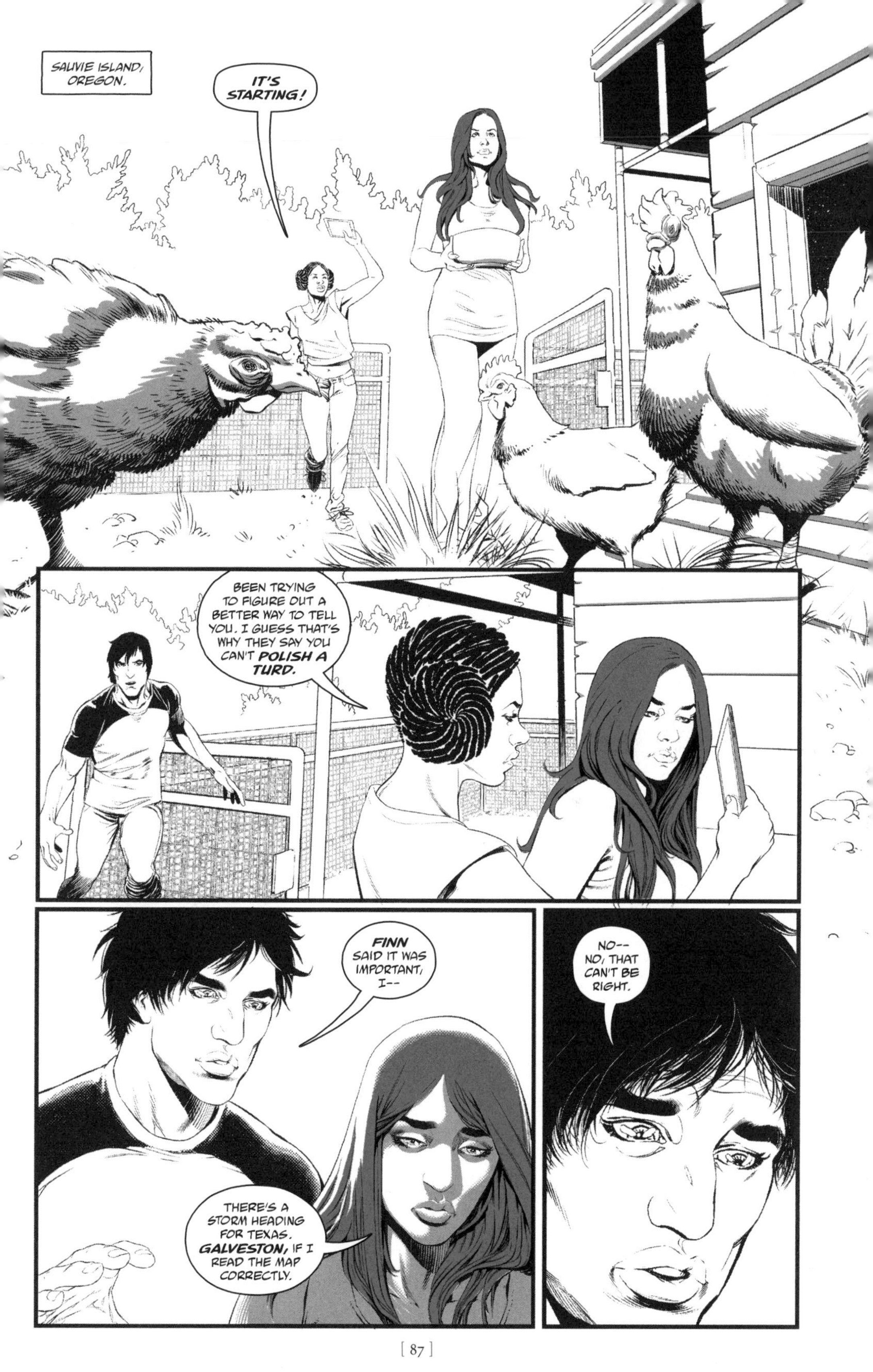
SAUVIE ISLAND, OREGON.
IT'S STARTING!
BEEN TRYING TO FIGURE OUT A BETTER WAY TO TELL YOU. I GUESS THAT'S WHY THEY SAY YOU CAN'T POLISH A TURD.
FINN SAID IT WAS IMPORTANT, I--
THERE'S A STORM HEADING FOR TEXAS. GALVESTON, IF I READ THE MAP CORRECTLY.
NO-- NO, THAT CAN'T BE RIGHT.

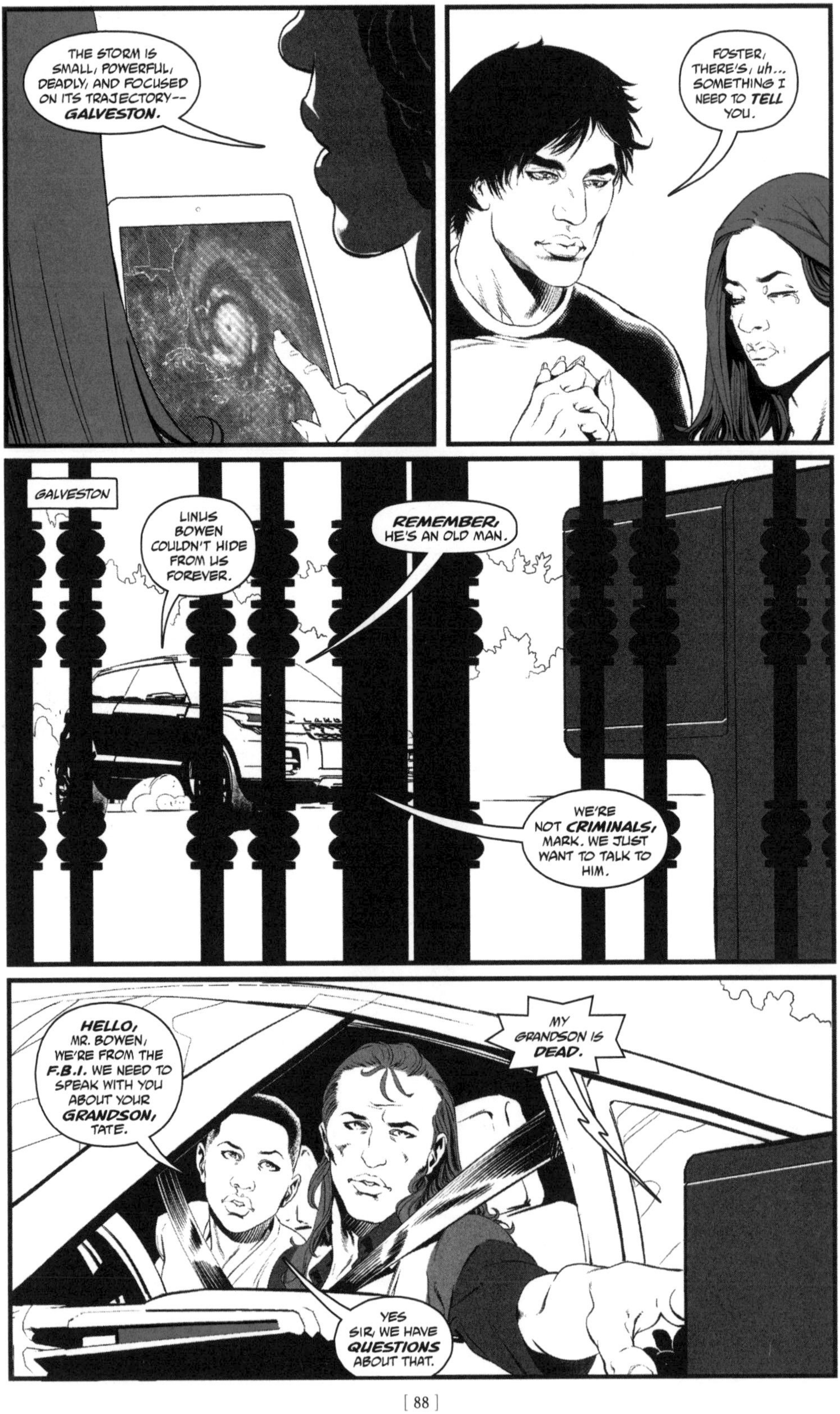
THE STORM IS SMALL, POWERFUL, DEADLY, AND FOCUSED ON ITS TRAJECTORY-- GALVESTON.
FOSTER, THERE'S, uh... SOMETHING I NEED TO TELL YOU.
GALVESTON
LINUS BOWEN COULDN'T HIDE FROM US FOREVER.
REMEMBER, HE'S AN OLD MAN.
WE'RE NOT CRIMINALS, MARK. WE JUST WANT TO TALK TO HIM.
HELLO, MR. BOWEN, WE'RE FROM THE F.B.I. WE NEED TO SPEAK WITH YOU ABOUT YOUR GRANDSON, TATE.
MY GRANDSON IS DEAD.
YES SIR, WE HAVE QUESTIONS ABOUT THAT.

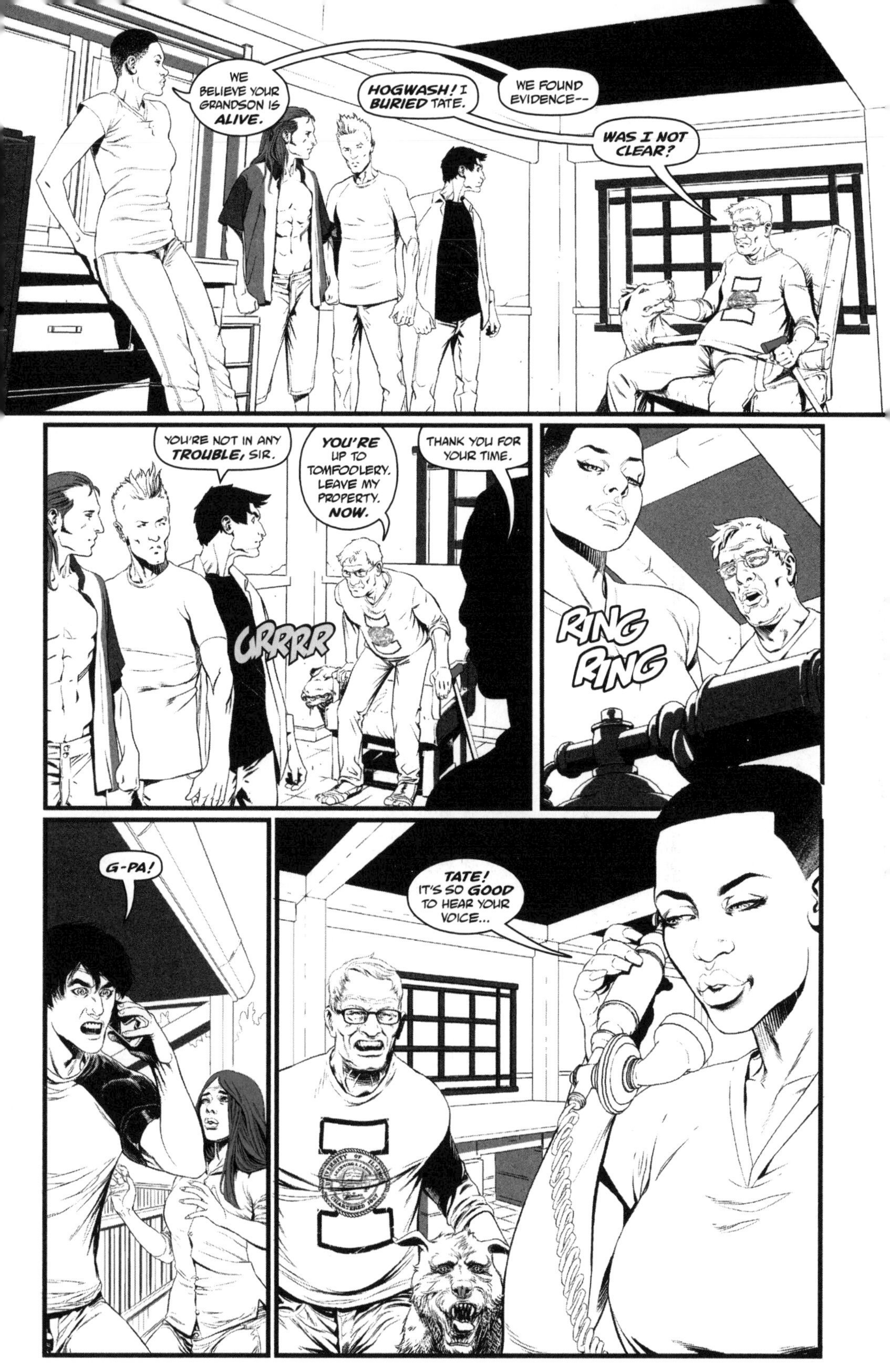

WE BELIEVE YOUR GRANDSON IS ALIVE.
HOGWASH! I BURIED TATE.
WE FOUND EVIDENCE--
WAS I NOT CLEAR?
YOU'RE NOT IN ANY TROUBLE, SIR.
YOU'RE UP TO TOMFOOLERY. LEAVE MY PROPERTY. NOW.
THANK YOU FOR YOUR TIME.
GRRRR
RING RING
G-PA!
TATE! IT'S SO GOOD TO HEAR YOUR VOICE...

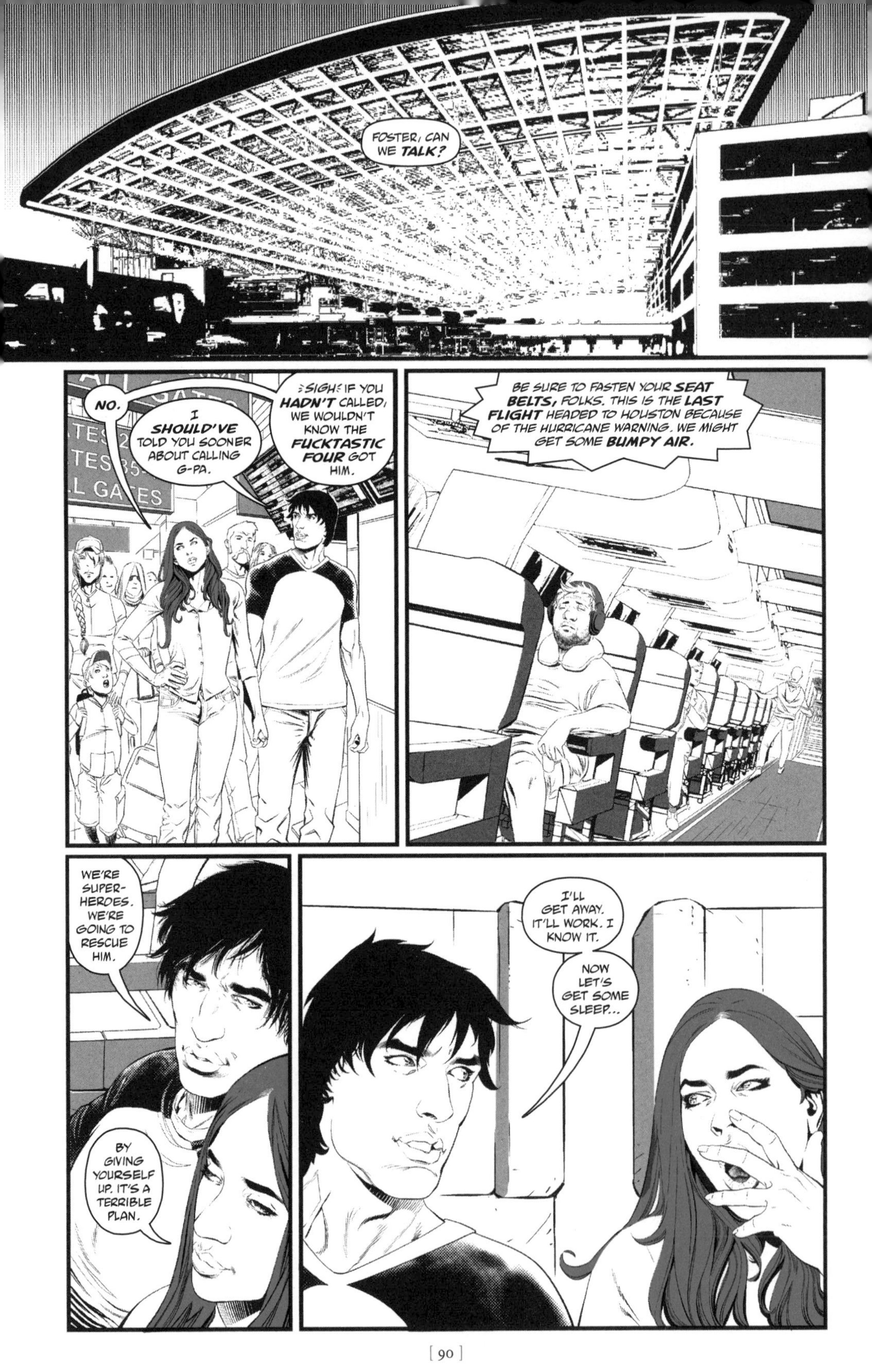
FOSTER, CAN WE TALK?
NO.
I SHOULD'VE TOLD YOU SOONER ABOUT CALLING G-PA.
SIGH IF YOU HADN'T CALLED, WE WOULDN'T KNOW THE FUCKTASTIC FOUR GOT HIM.
BE SURE TO FASTEN YOUR SEAT BELTS, FOLKS. THIS IS THE LAST FLIGHT HEADED TO HOUSTON BECAUSE OF THE HURRICANE WARNING. WE MIGHT GET SOME BUMPY AIR.
WE'RE SUPER-HEROES. WE'RE GOING TO RESCUE HIM.
BY GIVING YOURSELF UP. IT'S A TERRIBLE PLAN.
I'LL GET AWAY. IT'LL WORK. I KNOW IT.
NOW LET'S GET SOME SLEEP...

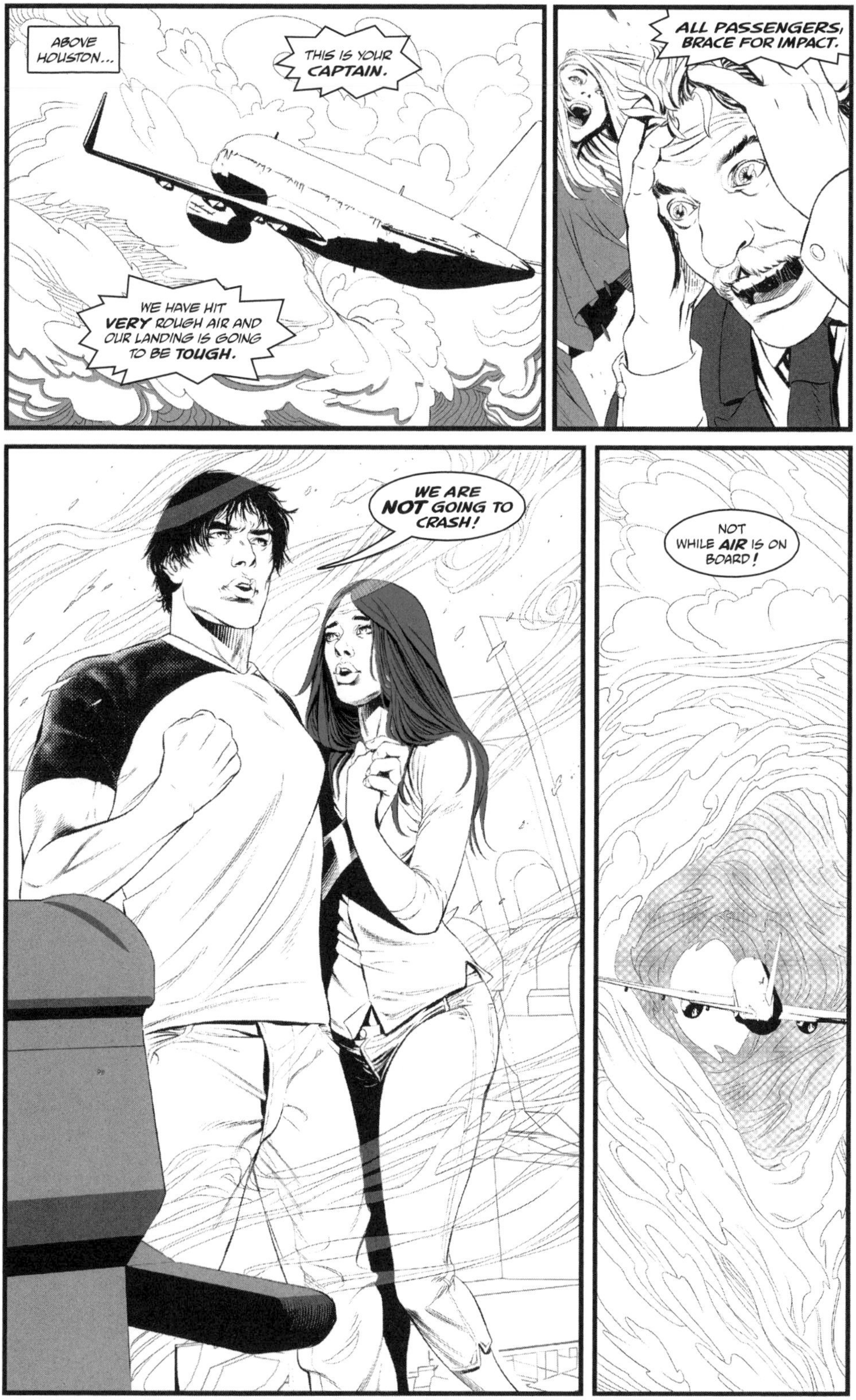
ABOVE HOUSTON...
THIS IS YOUR CAPTAIN.
WE HAVE HIT VERY ROUGH AIR AND OUR LANDING IS GOING TO BE TOUGH.
ALL PASSENGERS, BRACE FOR IMPACT.
WE ARE NOT GOING TO CRASH!
NOT WHILE AIR IS ON BOARD!

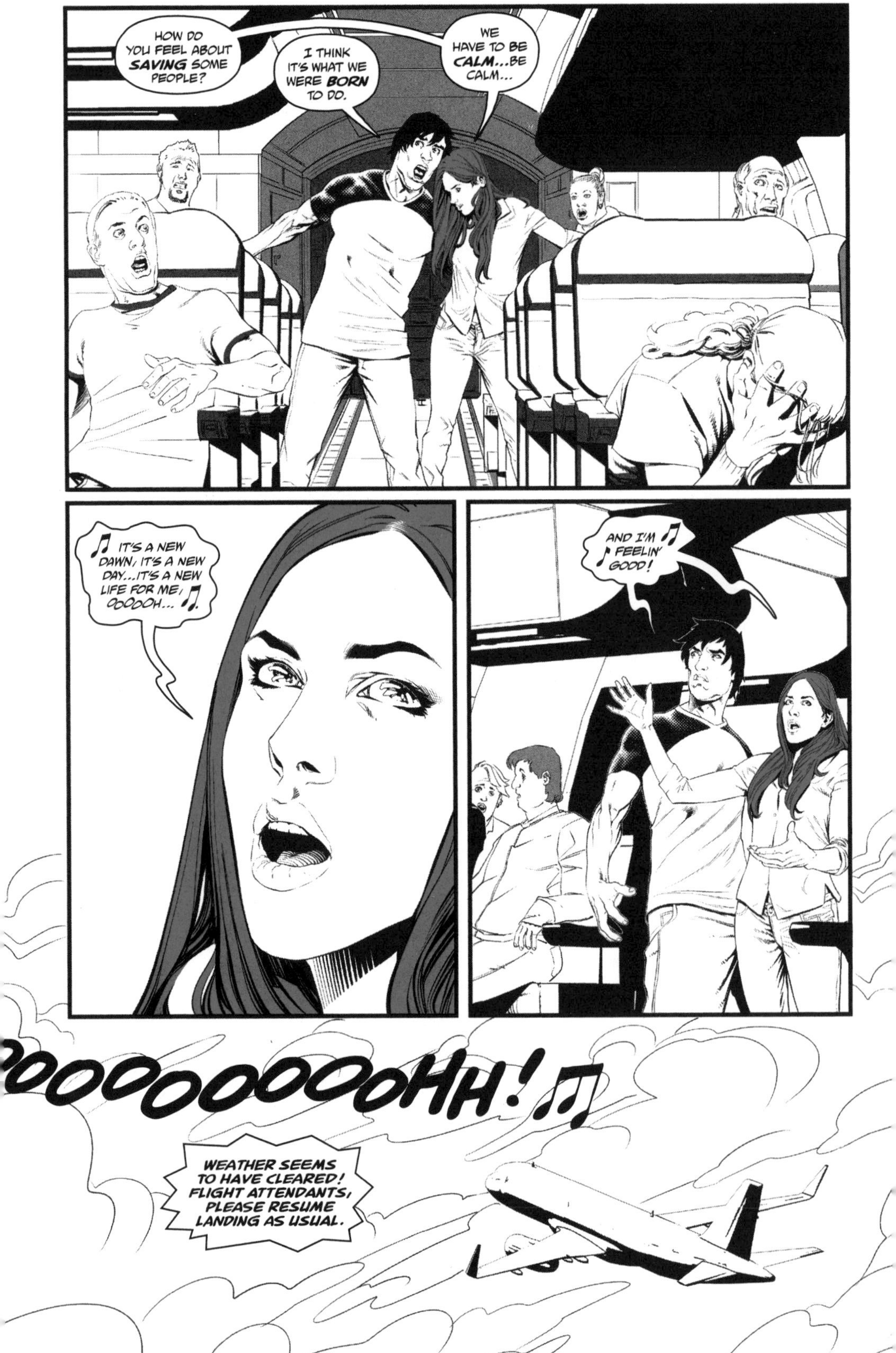
HOW DO YOU FEEL ABOUT SAVING SOME PEOPLE?
I THINK IT'S WHAT WE WERE BORN TO DO.
WE HAVE TO BE CALM...BE CALM...
♫ IT'S A NEW DAWN, IT'S A NEW DAY...IT'S A NEW LIFE FOR ME, OOOOOH... ♫
AND I'M FEELIN' GOOD! ♫
OOOOOOOOOOHH! ♫
WEATHER SEEMS TO HAVE CLEARED! FLIGHT ATTENDANTS, PLEASE RESUME LANDING AS USUAL.

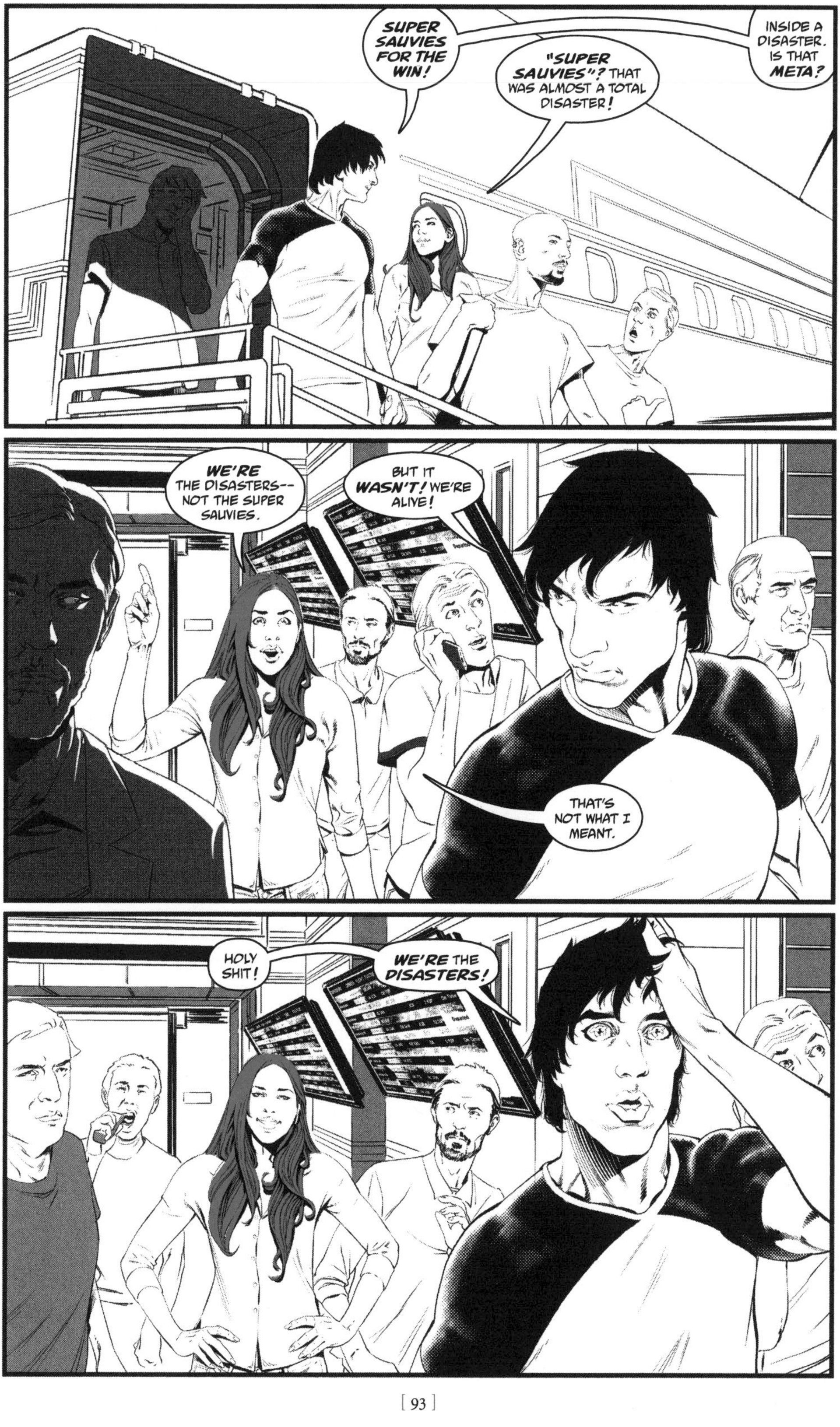
SUPER SAUVIES FOR THE WIN!
"SUPER SAUVIES"? THAT WAS ALMOST A TOTAL DISASTER!
INSIDE A DISASTER. IS THAT META?
WE'RE THE DISASTERS-- NOT THE SUPER SAUVIES.
BUT IT WASN'T! WE'RE ALIVE!
THAT'S NOT WHAT I MEANT.
HOLY SHIT!
WE'RE THE DISASTERS!

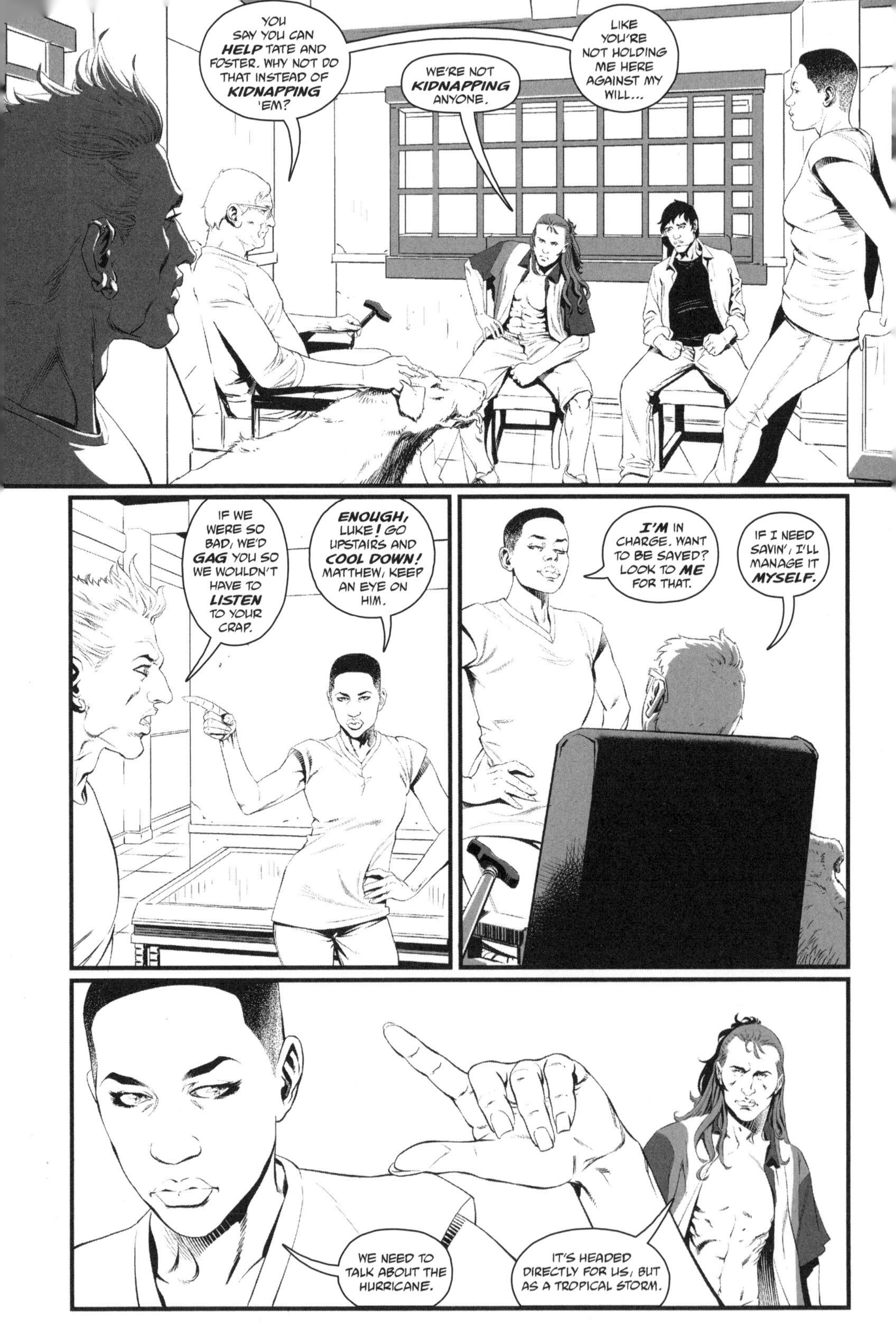
YOU SAY YOU CAN HELP TATE AND FOSTER. WHY NOT DO THAT INSTEAD OF KIDNAPPING 'EM?
WE'RE NOT KIDNAPPING ANYONE.
LIKE YOU'RE NOT HOLDING ME HERE AGAINST MY WILL...
IF WE WERE SO BAD, WE'D GAG YOU SO WE WOULDN'T HAVE TO LISTEN TO YOUR CRAP.
ENOUGH, LUKE! GO UPSTAIRS AND COOL DOWN! MATTHEW, KEEP AN EYE ON HIM.
I'M IN CHARGE. WANT TO BE SAVED? LOOK TO ME FOR THAT.
IF I NEED SAVIN', I'LL MANAGE IT MYSELF.
WE NEED TO TALK ABOUT THE HURRICANE.
IT'S HEADED DIRECTLY FOR US, BUT AS A TROPICAL STORM.

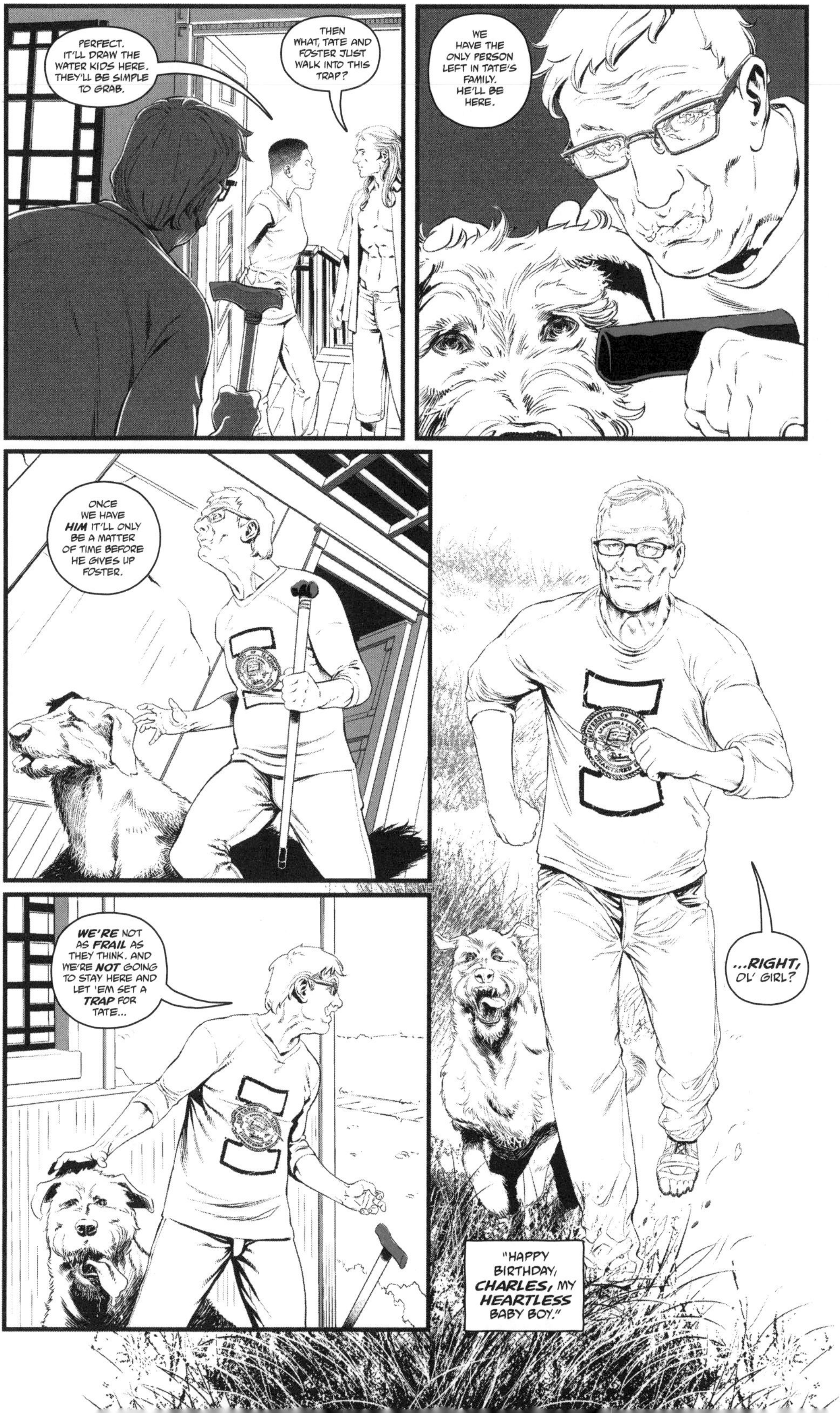
PERFECT. IT'LL DRAW THE WATER KIDS HERE. THEY'LL BE SIMPLE TO GRAB.
THEN WHAT, TATE AND FOSTER JUST WALK INTO THIS TRAP?
WE HAVE THE ONLY PERSON LEFT IN TATE'S FAMILY. HE'LL BE HERE.
ONCE WE HAVE HIM IT'LL ONLY BE A MATTER OF TIME BEFORE HE GIVES UP FOSTER.
WE'RE NOT AS FRAIL AS THEY THINK. AND WE'RE NOT GOING TO STAY HERE AND LET 'EM SET A TRAP FOR TATE...
...RIGHT, OL' GIRL?
"HAPPY BIRTHDAY, CHARLES, MY HEARTLESS BABY BOY."

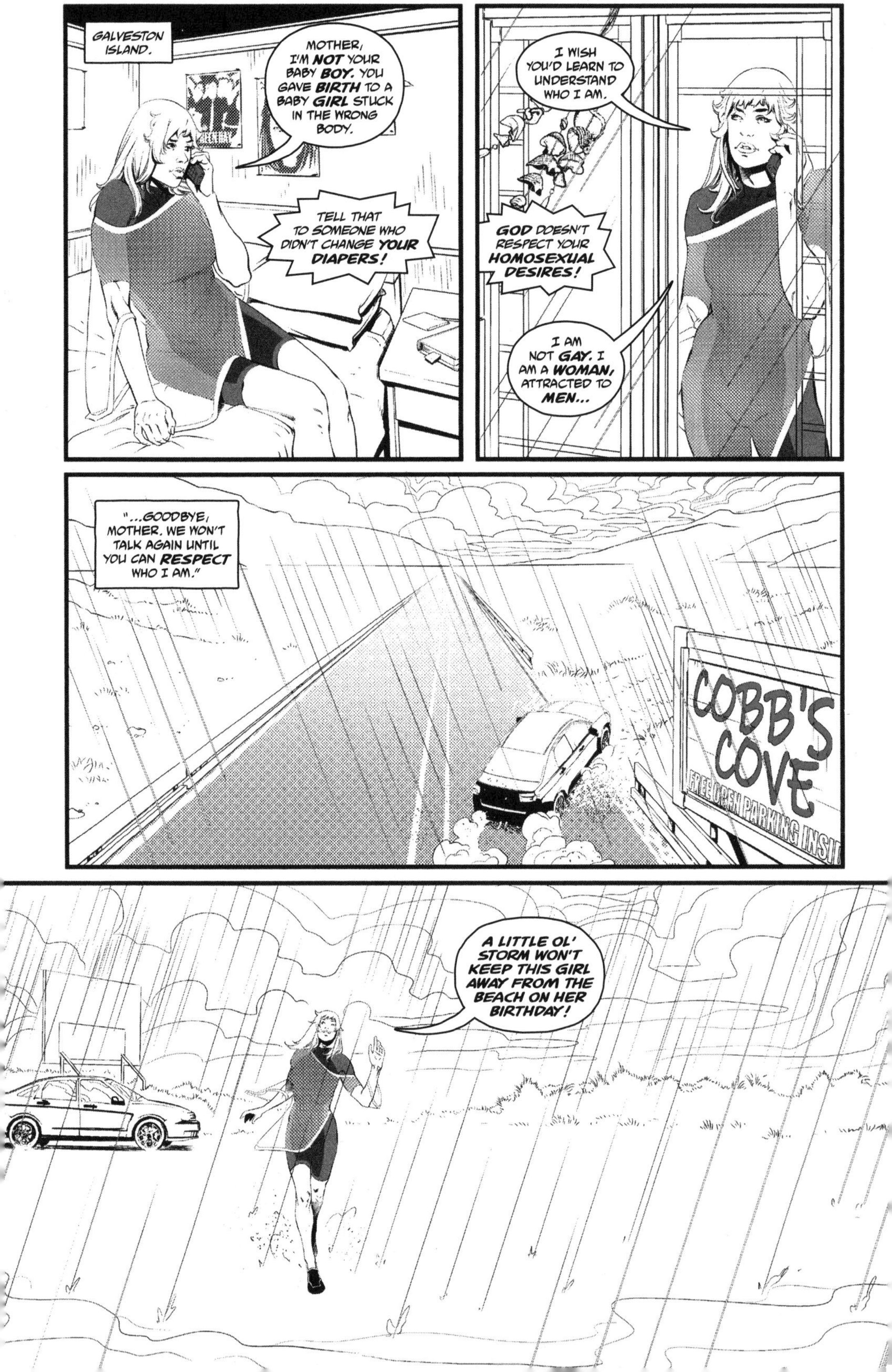
GALVESTON ISLAND.
MOTHER, I'M NOT YOUR BABY BOY. YOU GAVE BIRTH TO A BABY GIRL STUCK IN THE WRONG BODY.
TELL THAT TO SOMEONE WHO DIDN'T CHANGE YOUR DIAPERS!
I WISH YOU'D LEARN TO UNDERSTAND WHO I AM.
GOD DOESN'T RESPECT YOUR HOMOSEXUAL DESIRES!
I AM NOT GAY. I AM A WOMAN, ATTRACTED TO MEN...
"...GOODBYE, MOTHER. WE WON'T TALK AGAIN UNTIL YOU CAN RESPECT WHO I AM."
COBB'S COVE
FREE OPEN PARKING INSI
A LITTLE OL' STORM WON'T KEEP THIS GIRL AWAY FROM THE BEACH ON HER BIRTHDAY!

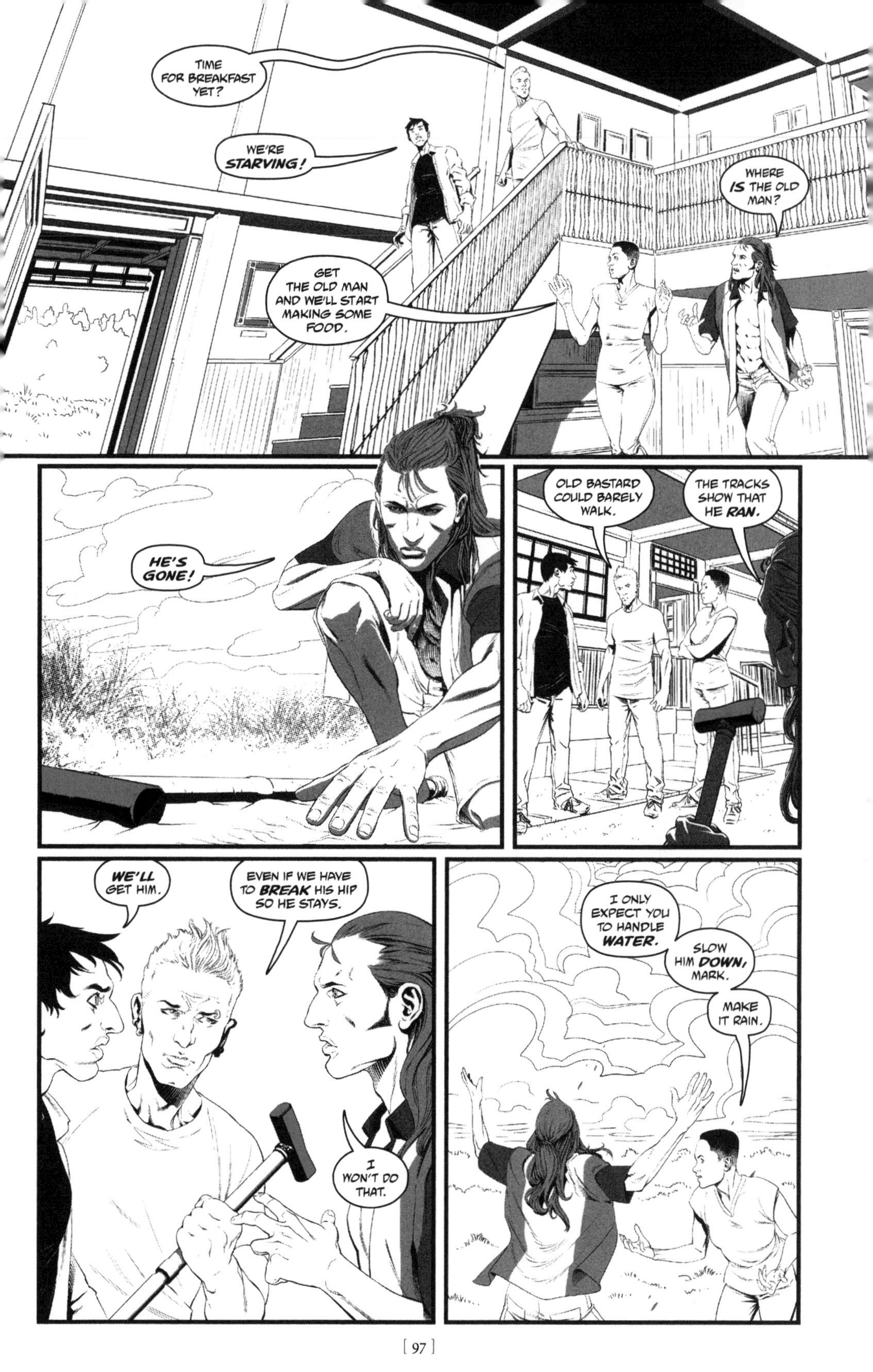
TIME FOR BREAKFAST YET?
WE'RE STARVING!
WHERE IS THE OLD MAN?
GET THE OLD MAN AND WE'LL START MAKING SOME FOOD.
HE'S GONE!
OLD BASTARD COULD BARELY WALK.
THE TRACKS SHOW THAT HE RAN.
WE'LL GET HIM.
EVEN IF WE HAVE TO BREAK HIS HIP SO HE STAYS.
I WON'T DO THAT.
I ONLY EXPECT YOU TO HANDLE WATER.
SLOW HIM DOWN, MARK.
MAKE IT RAIN.

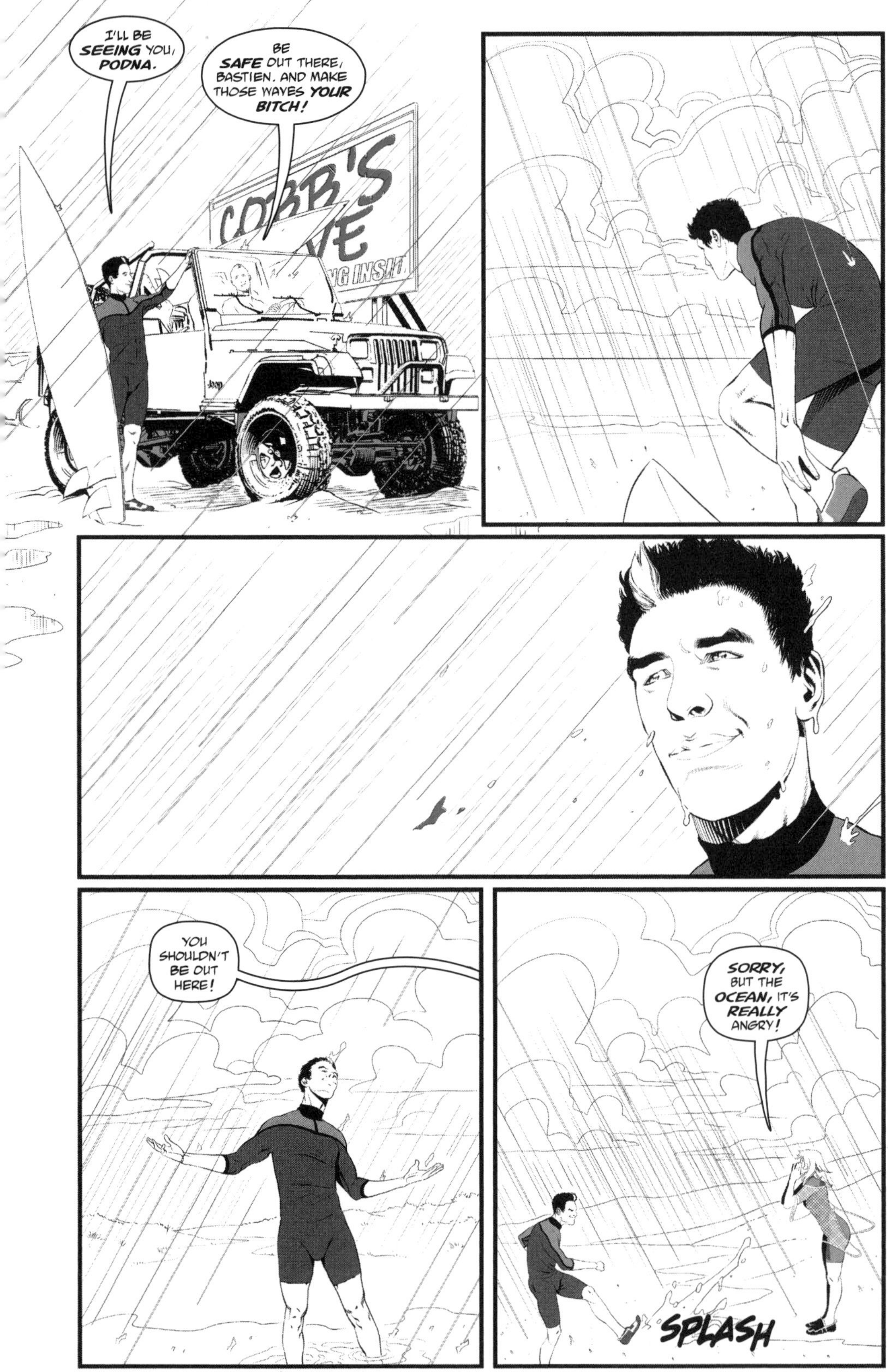
I'LL BE SEEING YOU, PODNA.
BE SAFE OUT THERE, BASTIEN. AND MAKE THOSE WAVES YOUR BITCH!
YOU SHOULDN'T BE OUT HERE!
SORRY, BUT THE OCEAN, IT'S REALLY ANGRY!
SPLASH

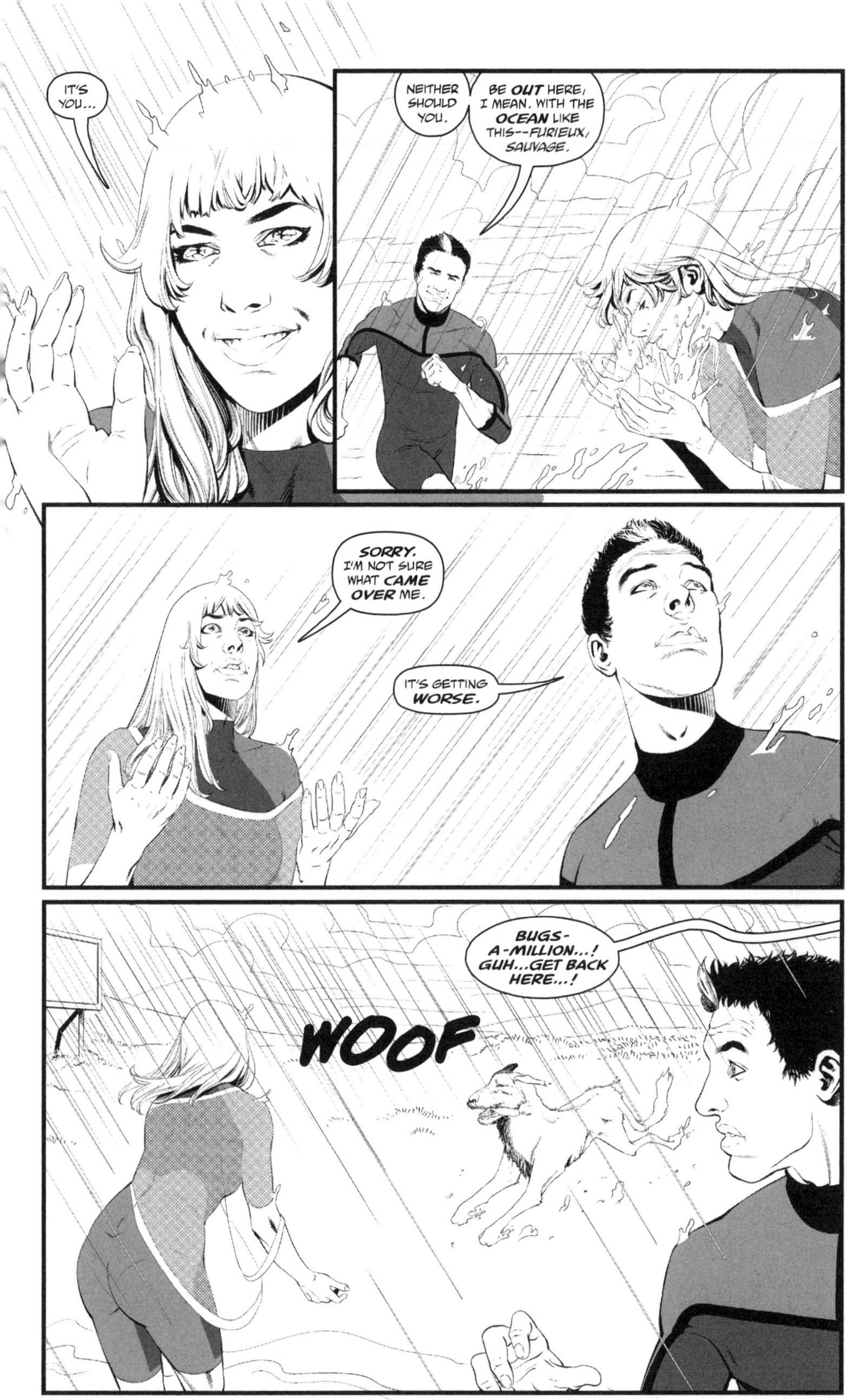
IT'S YOU...
NEITHER SHOULD YOU.
BE OUT HERE, I MEAN. WITH THE OCEAN LIKE THIS--FURIEUX, SAUVAGE.
SORRY. I'M NOT SURE WHAT CAME OVER ME.
IT'S GETTING WORSE.
BUGS-A-MILLION...! GUH...GET BACK HERE...!
WOOF

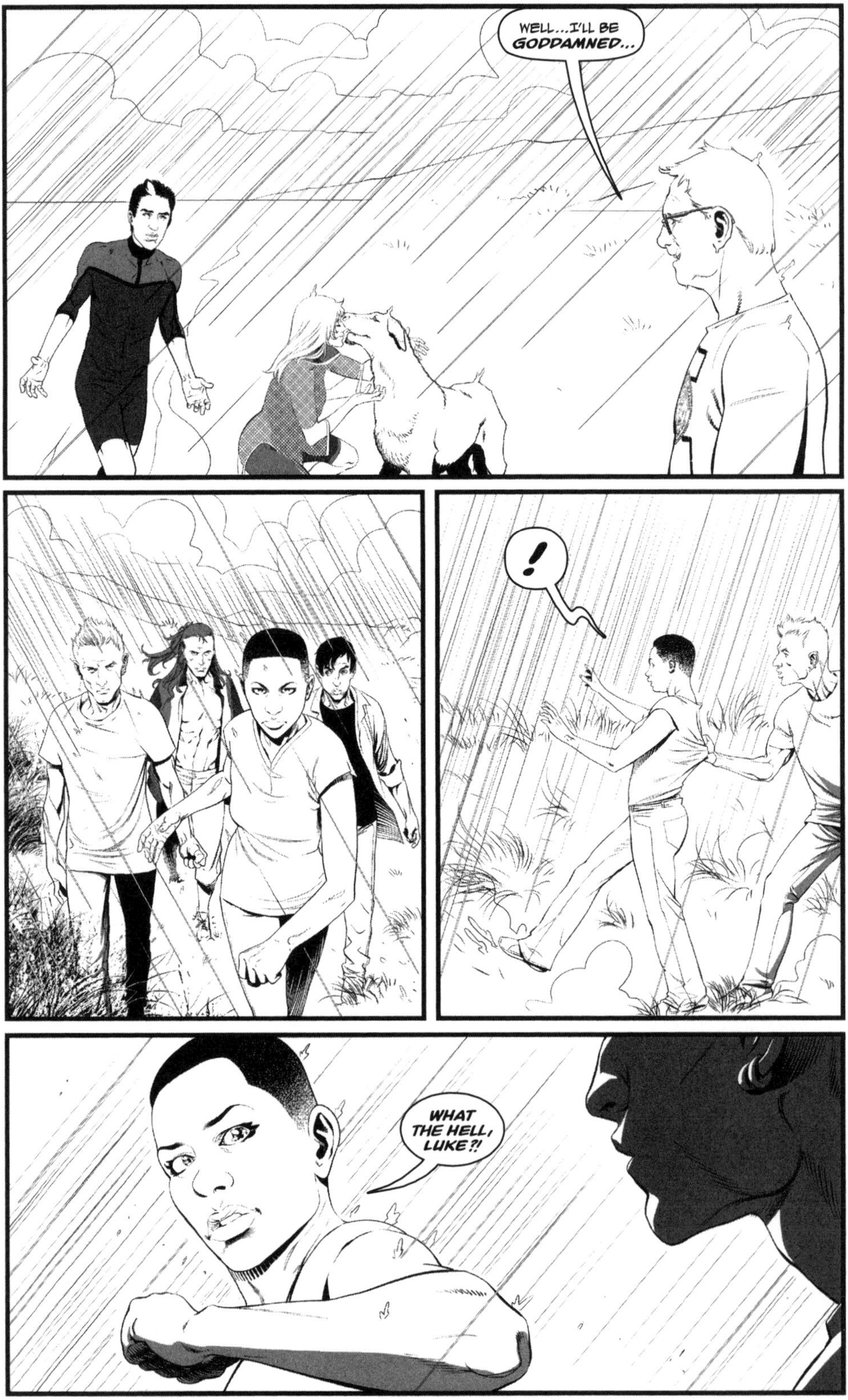
WELL...I'LL BE GODDAMNED...
!
WHAT THE HELL, LUKE?!

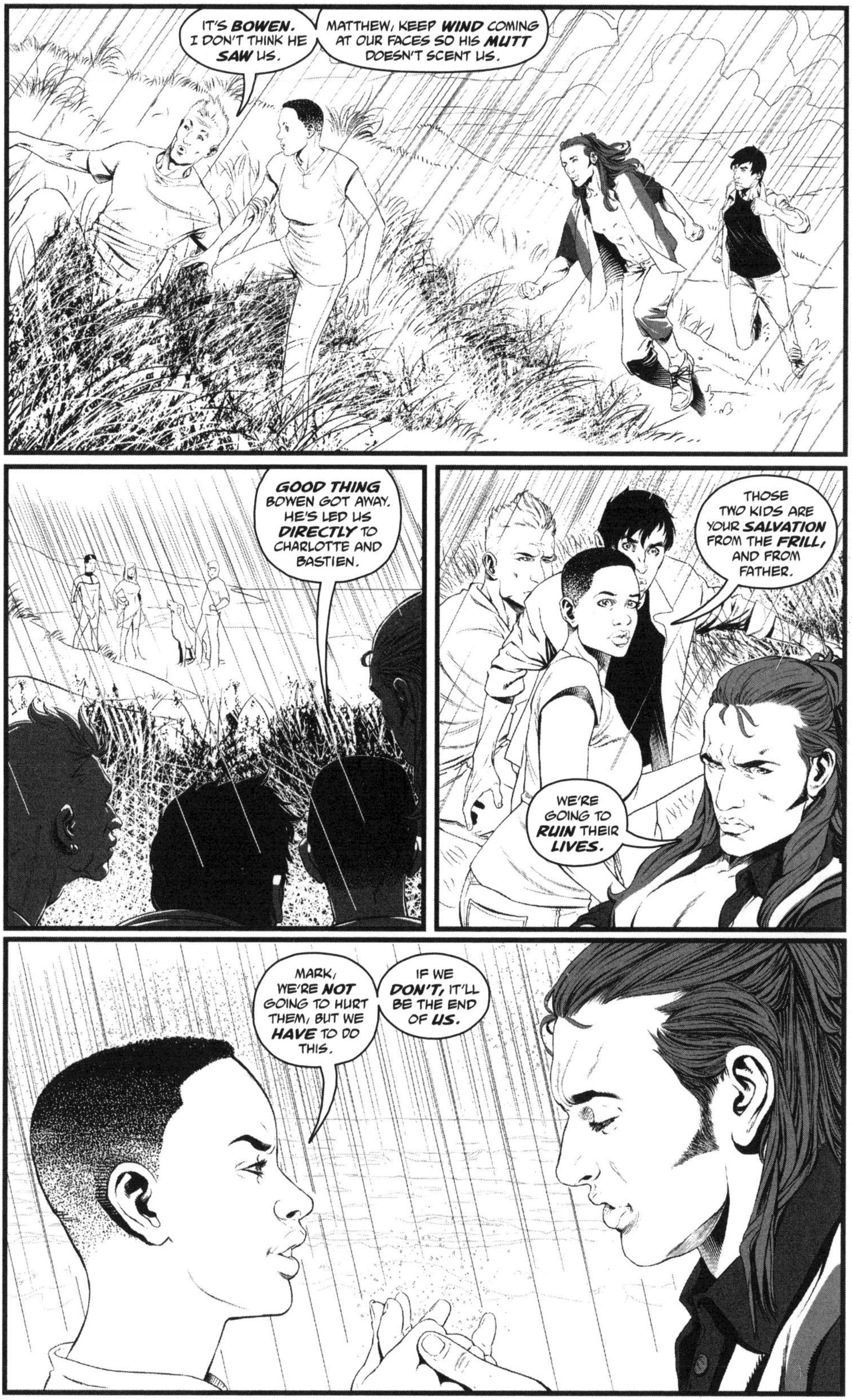
IT'S BOWEN. I DON'T THINK HE SAW US.
MATTHEW, KEEP WIND COMING AT OUR FACES SO HIS MUTT DOESN'T SCENT US.
GOOD THING BOWEN GOT AWAY. HE'S LED US DIRECTLY TO CHARLOTTE AND BASTIEN.
THOSE TWO KIDS ARE YOUR SALVATION FROM THE FRILL, AND FROM FATHER.
WE'RE GOING TO RUIN THEIR LIVES.
MARK, WE'RE NOT GOING TO HURT THEM, BUT WE HAVE TO DO THIS.
IF WE DON'T, IT'LL BE THE END OF US.

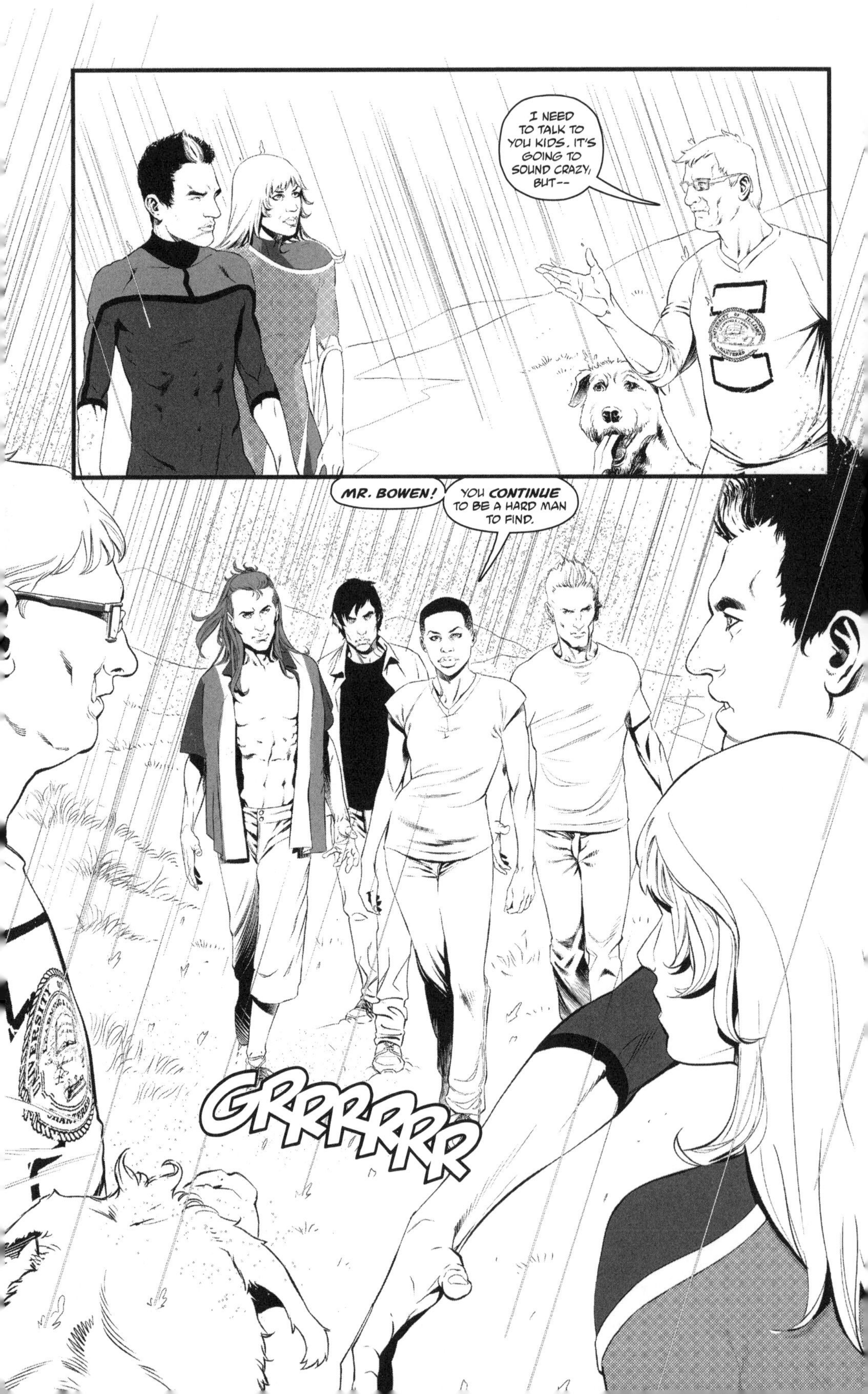

I NEED TO TALK TO YOU KIDS. IT'S GOING TO SOUND CRAZY, BUT--
MR. BOWEN!
YOU CONTINUE TO BE A HARD MAN TO FIND.
GRRRRRR

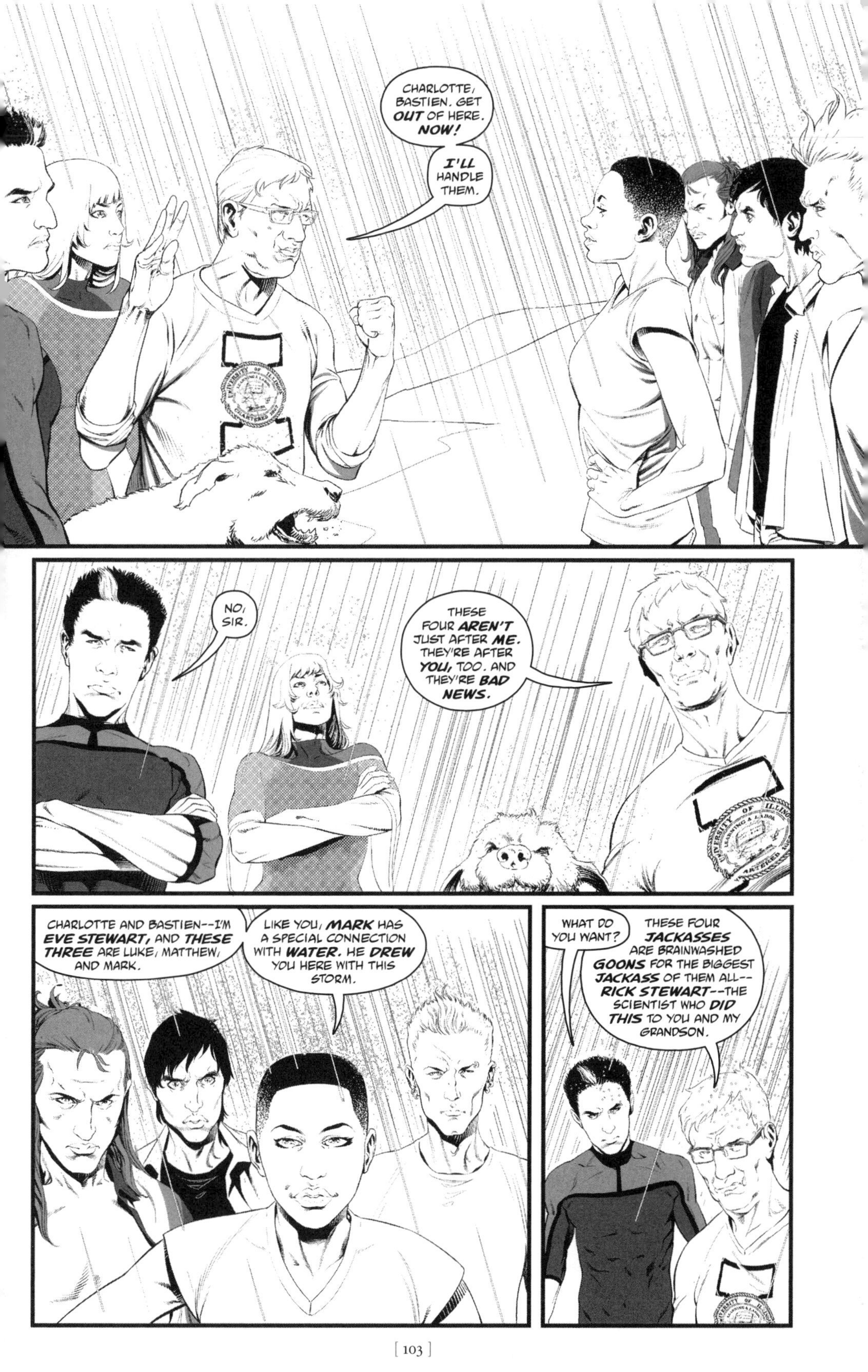

CHARLOTTE, BASTIEN. GET OUT OF HERE. NOW!
I'LL HANDLE THEM.
NO, SIR.
THESE FOUR AREN'T JUST AFTER ME. THEY'RE AFTER YOU, TOO. AND THEY'RE BAD NEWS.
CHARLOTTE AND BASTIEN--I'M EVE STEWART, AND THESE THREE ARE LUKE, MATTHEW, AND MARK.
LIKE YOU, MARK HAS A SPECIAL CONNECTION WITH WATER. HE DREW YOU HERE WITH THIS STORM.
WHAT DO YOU WANT?
THESE FOUR JACKASSES ARE BRAINWASHED GOONS FOR THE BIGGEST JACKASS OF THEM ALL--RICK STEWART--THE SCIENTIST WHO DID THIS TO YOU AND MY GRANDSON.

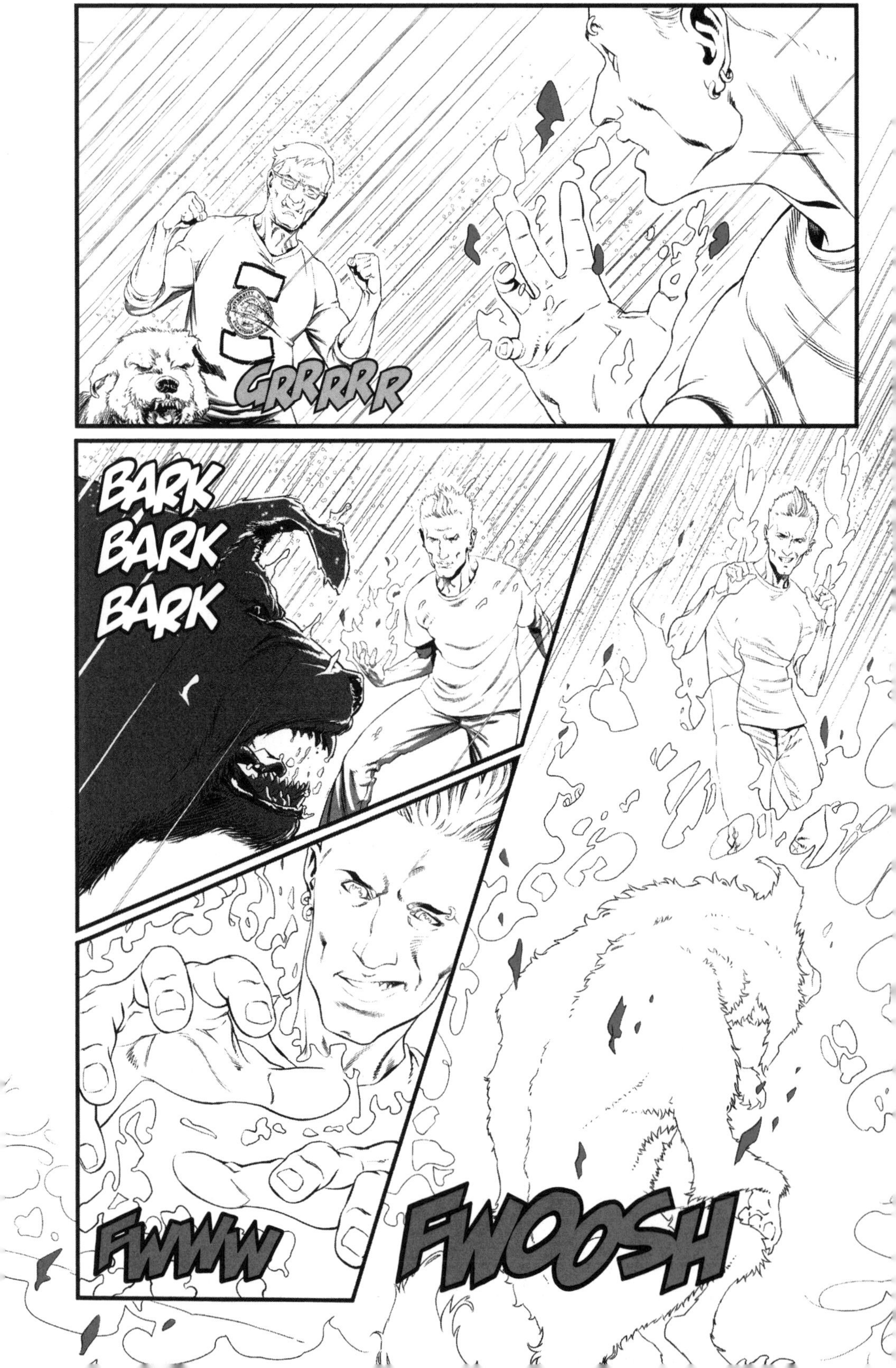
GRRRRR
BARK
BARK
BARK
FWWW
FWOOSH

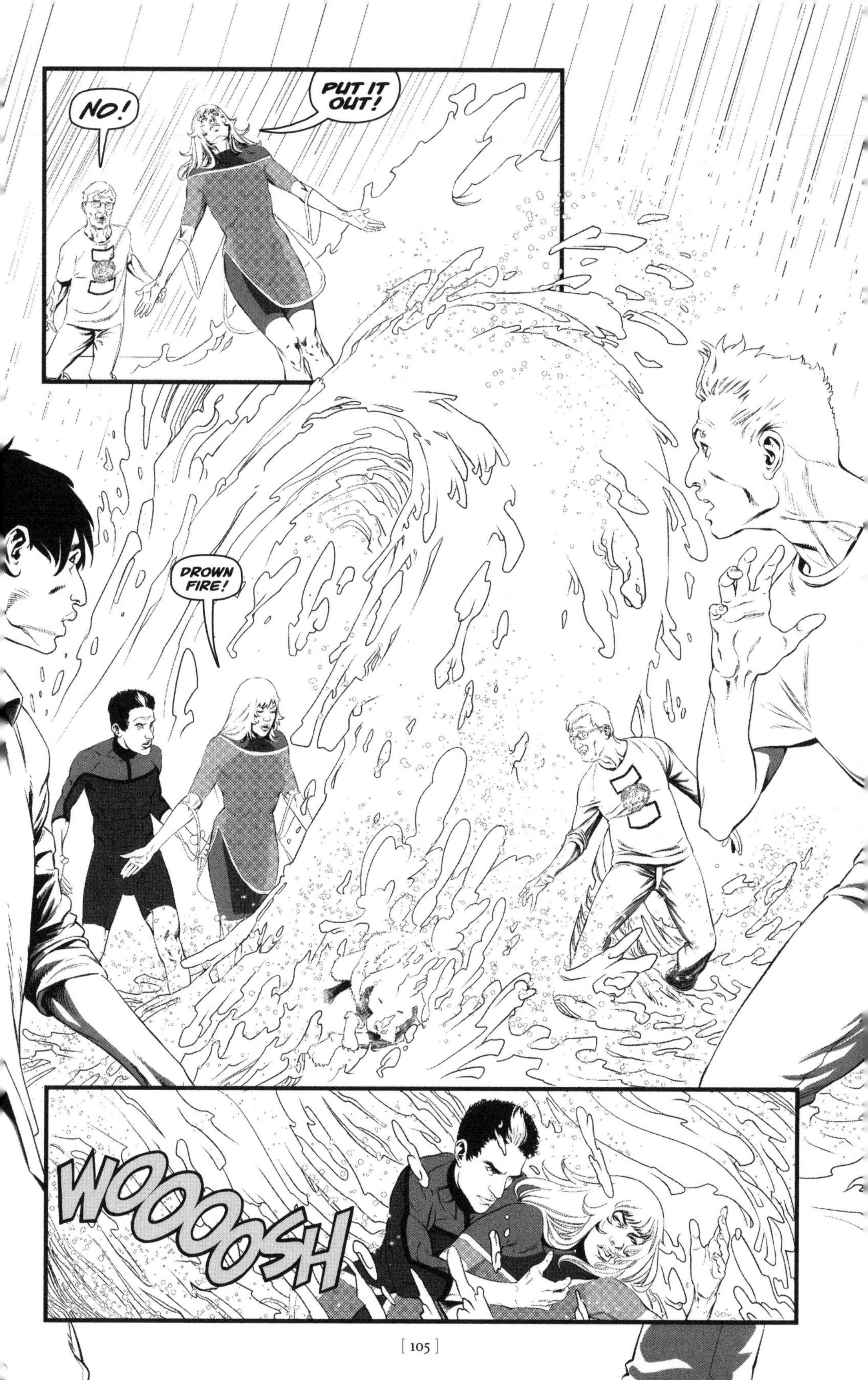
NO!
PUT IT OUT!
DROWN FIRE!
WOOOOSH

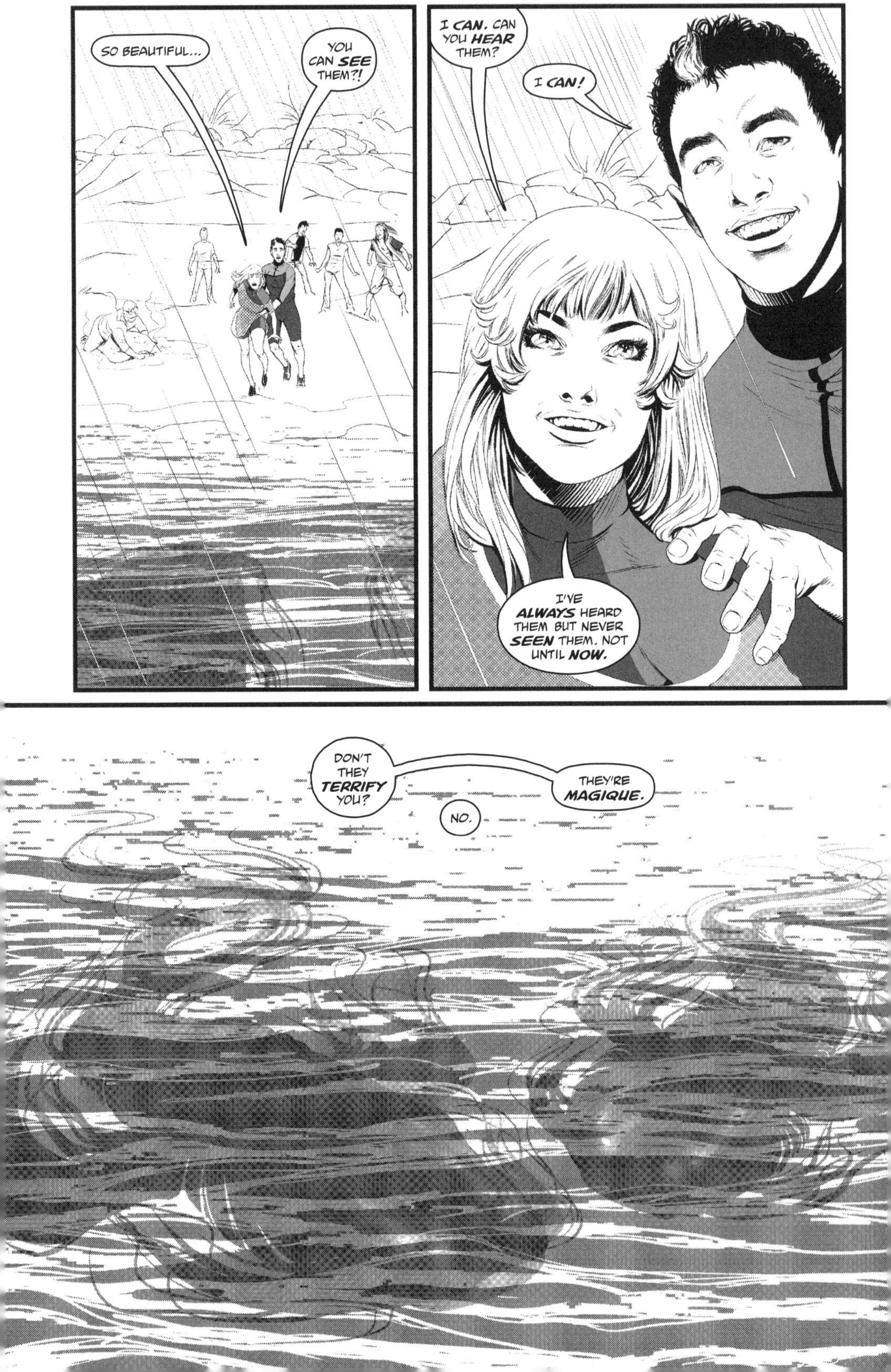
SO BEAUTIFUL...
YOU CAN SEE THEM?!
I CAN. CAN YOU HEAR THEM?
I CAN!
I'VE ALWAYS HEARD THEM BUT NEVER SEEN THEM. NOT UNTIL NOW.
DON'T THEY TERRIFY YOU?
NO.
THEY'RE MAGIQUE.

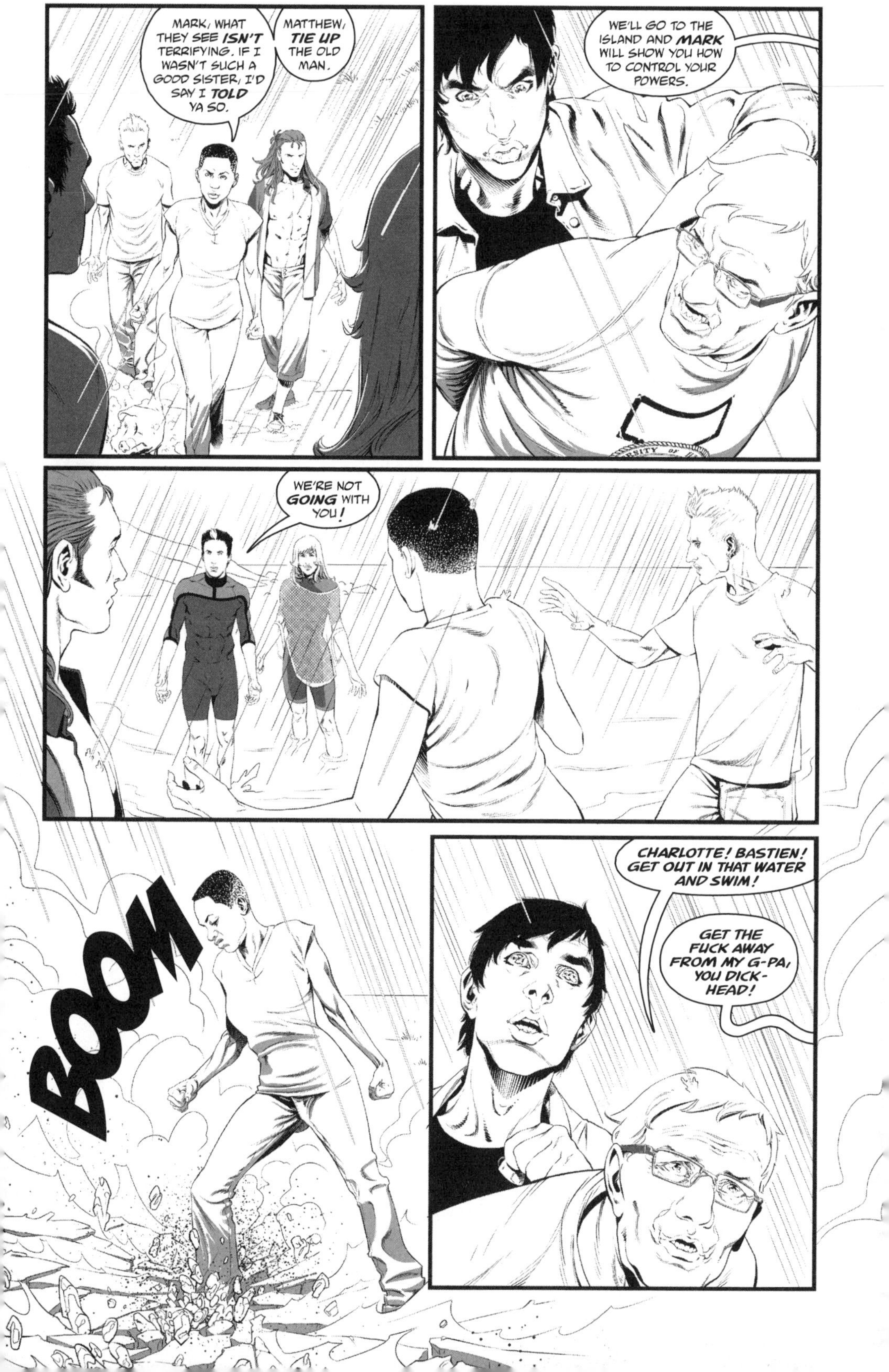
MARK, WHAT THEY SEE ISN'T TERRIFYING. IF I WASN'T SUCH A GOOD SISTER, I'D SAY I TOLD YA SO.
MATTHEW, TIE UP THE OLD MAN.
WE'LL GO TO THE ISLAND AND MARK WILL SHOW YOU HOW TO CONTROL YOUR POWERS.
WE'RE NOT GOING WITH YOU!
BOOM
CHARLOTTE! BASTIEN! GET OUT IN THAT WATER AND SWIM!
GET THE FUCK AWAY FROM MY G-PA, YOU DICK-HEAD!

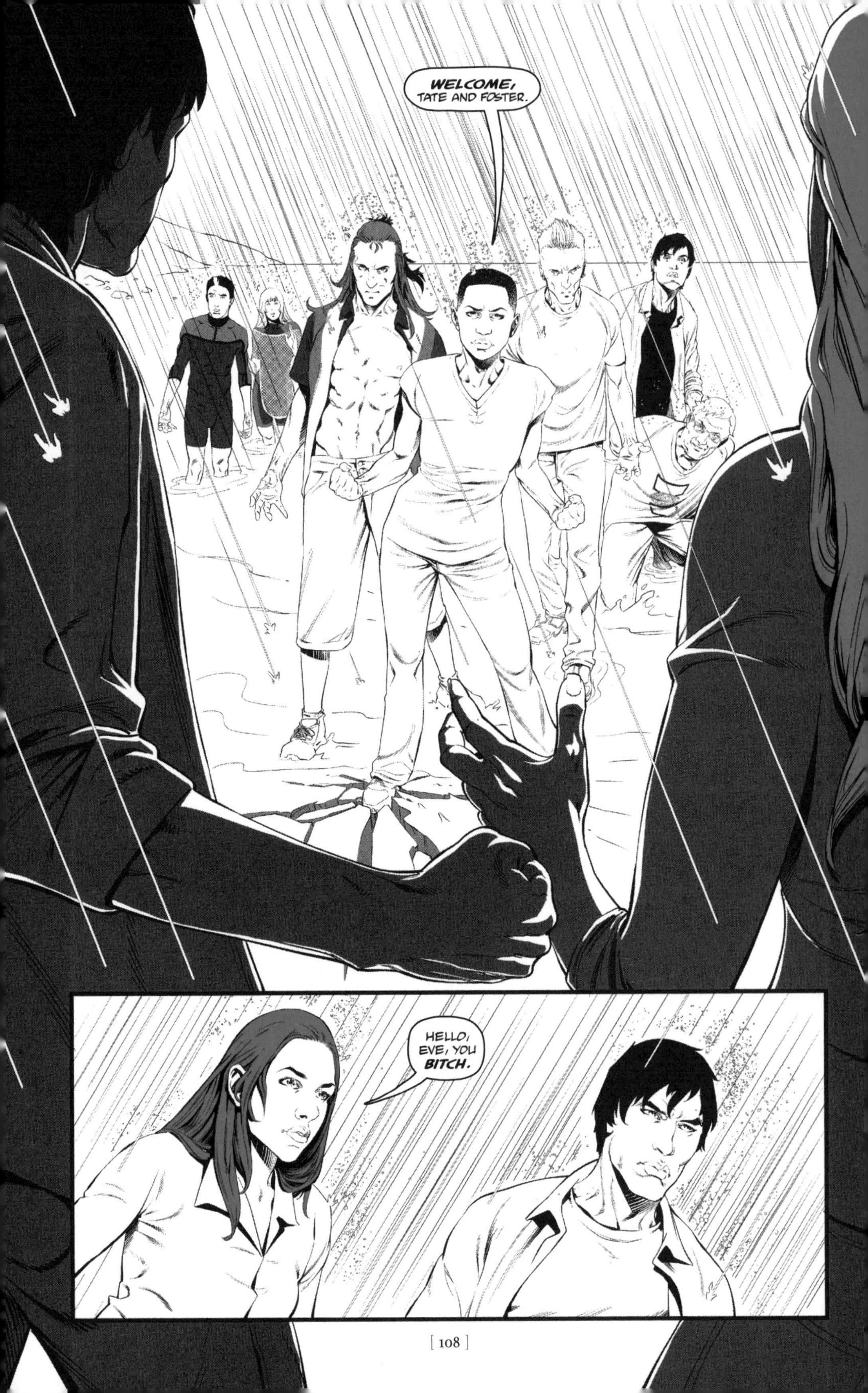
WELCOME, TATE AND FOSTER.
HELLO, EVE, YOU BITCH.

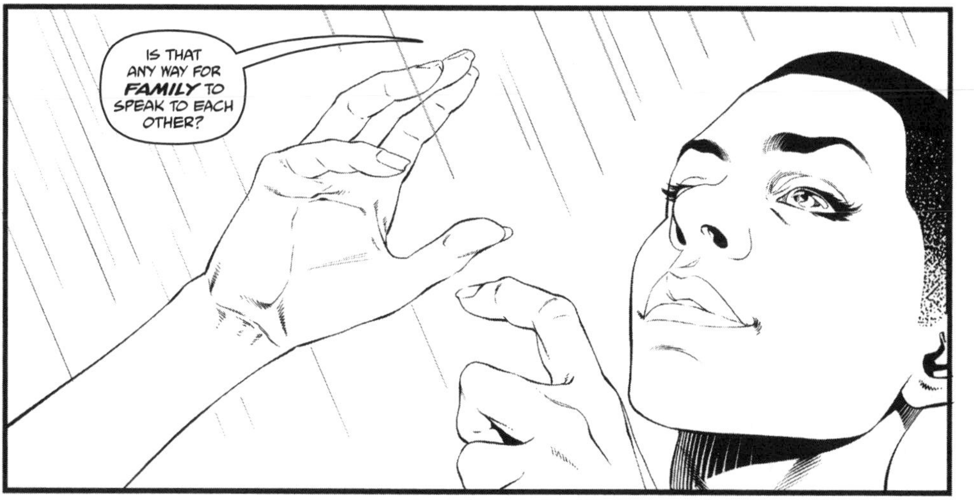
IS THAT ANY WAY FOR **FAMILY** TO SPEAK TO EACH OTHER?

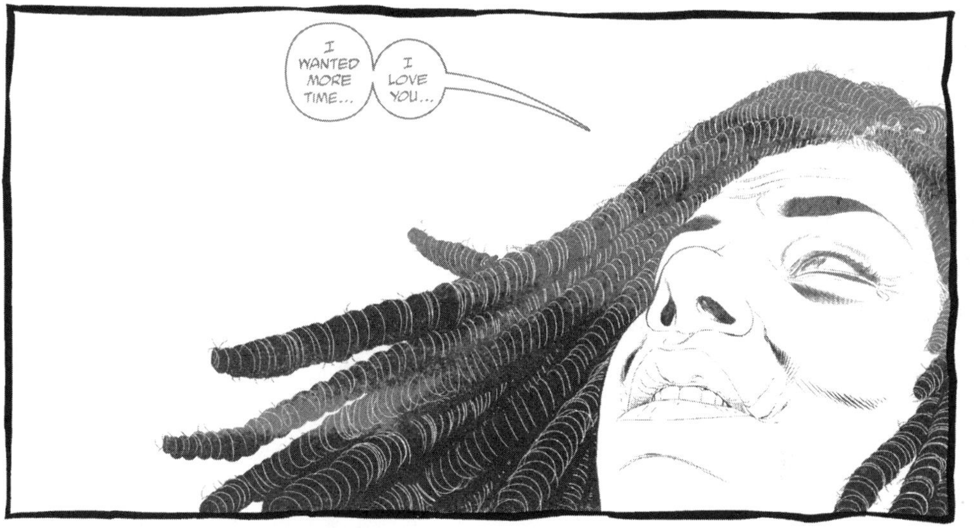
I WANTED MORE TIME...
I LOVE YOU...

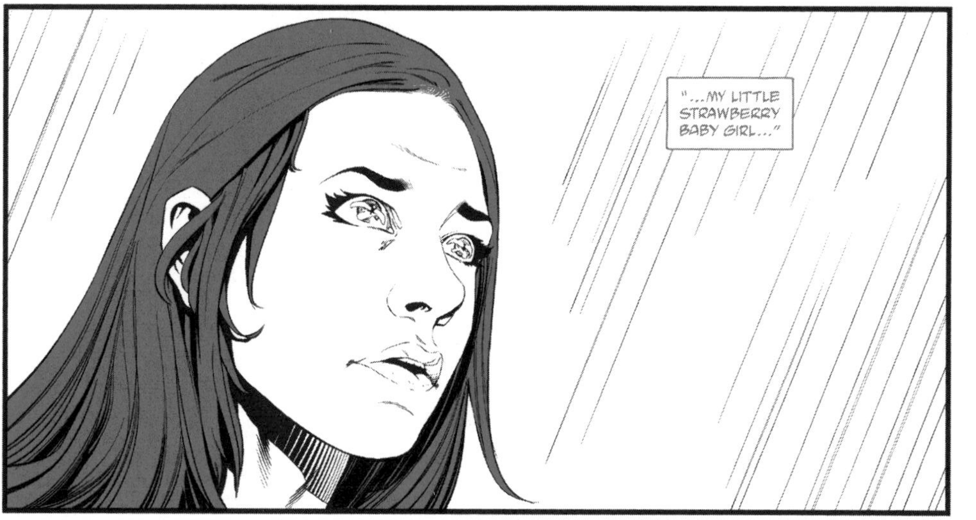
"...MY LITTLE STRAWBERRY BABY GIRL..."

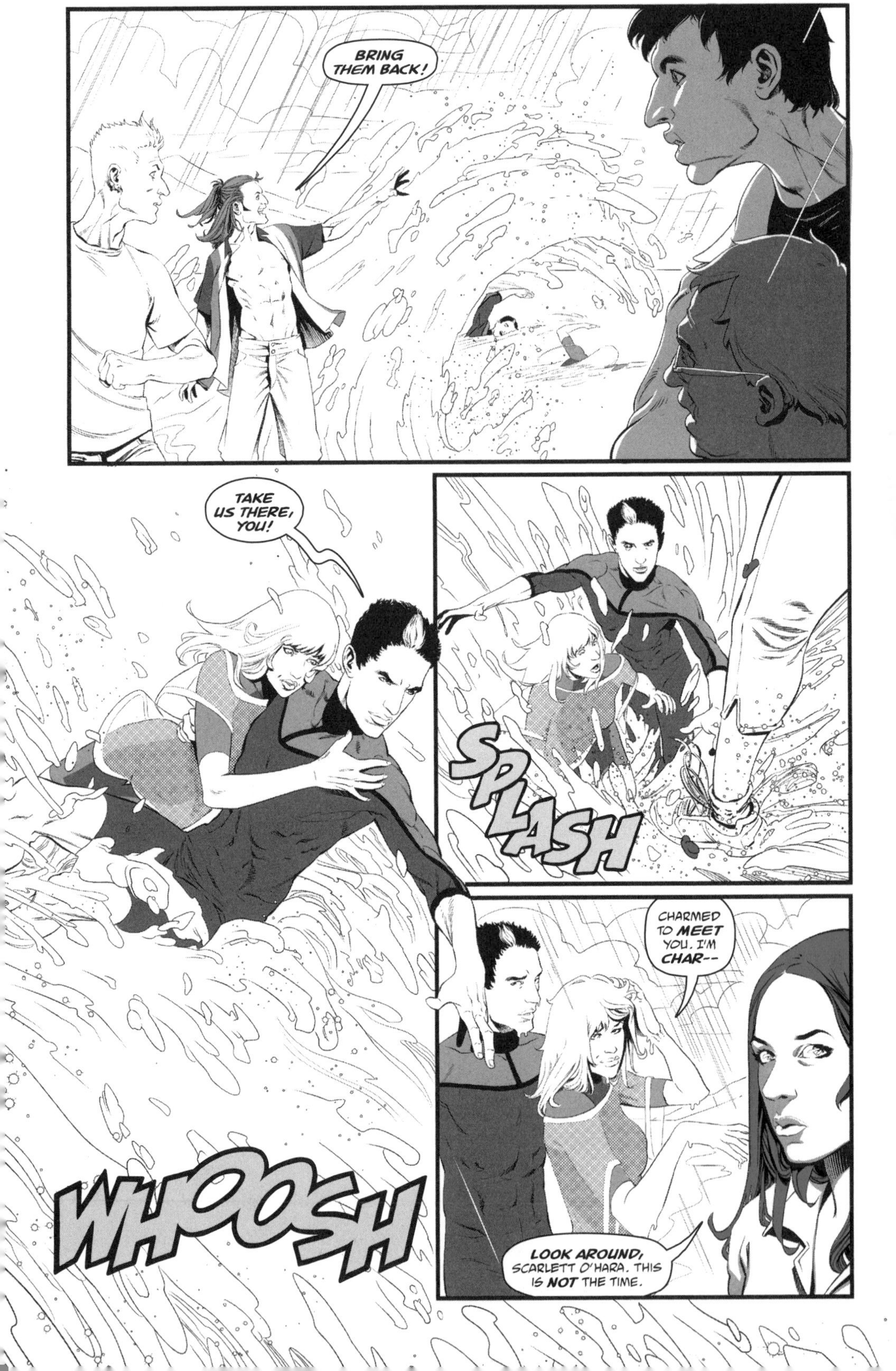
BRING THEM BACK!
TAKE US THERE, YOU!
WHOOSH
SPLASH
CHARMED TO MEET YOU. I'M CHAR--
LOOK AROUND, SCARLETT O'HARA. THIS IS NOT THE TIME.

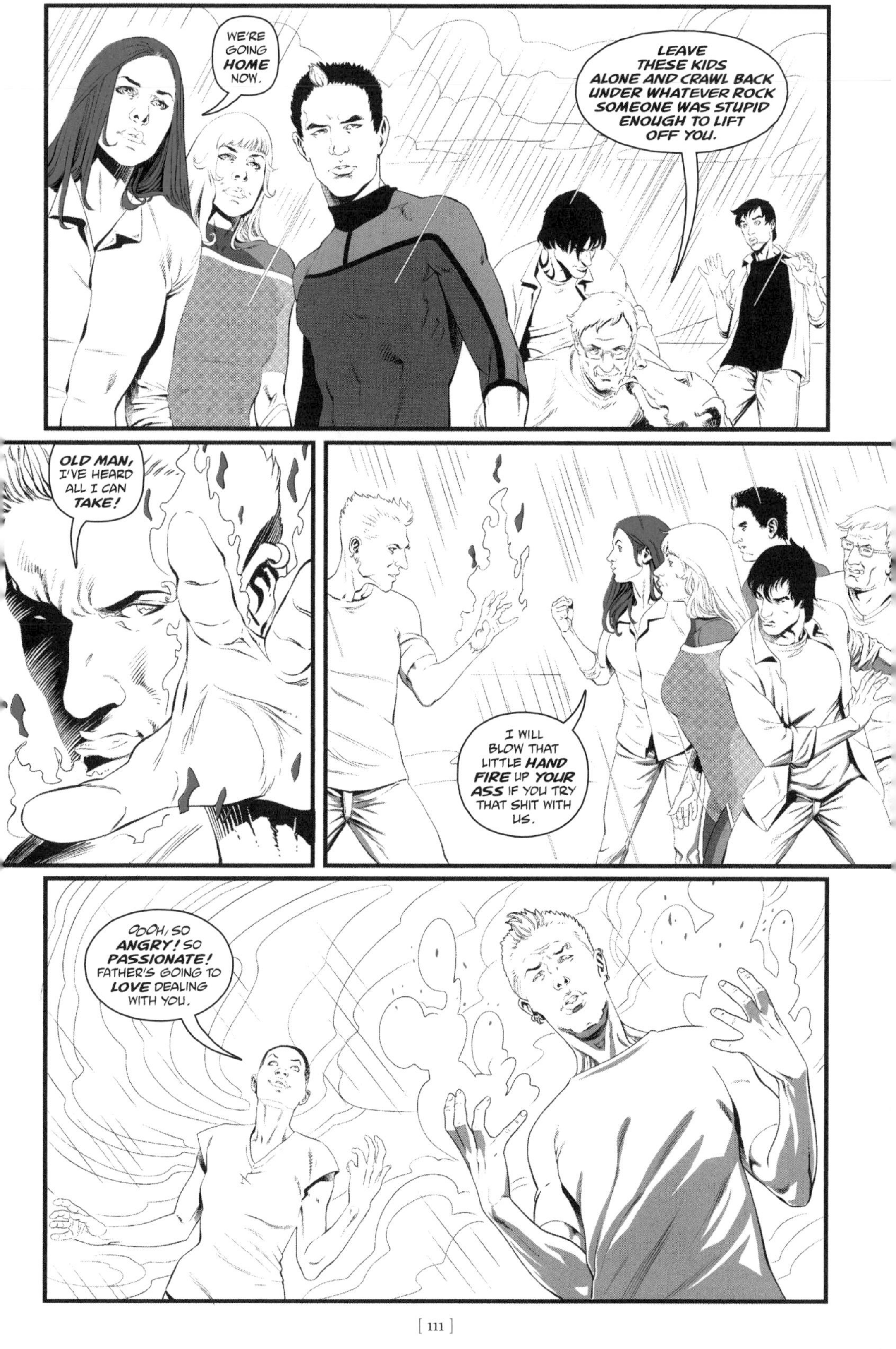
WE'RE GOING HOME NOW.
LEAVE THESE KIDS ALONE AND CRAWL BACK UNDER WHATEVER ROCK SOMEONE WAS STUPID ENOUGH TO LIFT OFF YOU.
OLD MAN, I'VE HEARD ALL I CAN TAKE!
I WILL BLOW THAT LITTLE HAND FIRE UP YOUR ASS IF YOU TRY THAT SHIT WITH US.
OOOH, SO ANGRY! SO PASSIONATE! FATHER'S GOING TO LOVE DEALING WITH YOU.

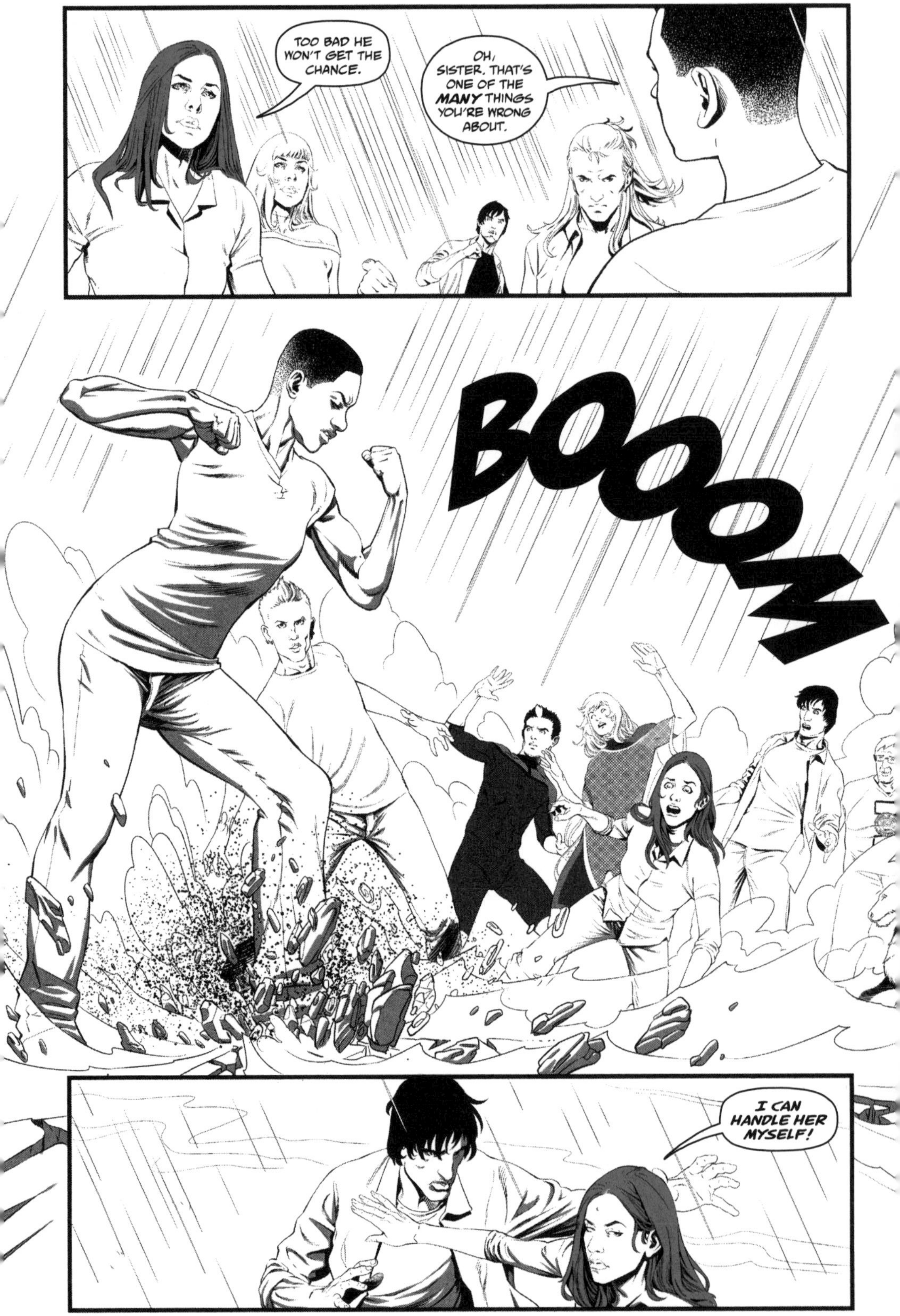
TOO BAD HE WON'T GET THE CHANCE.
OH, SISTER. THAT'S ONE OF THE MANY THINGS YOU'RE WRONG ABOUT.
BOOOOM
I CAN HANDLE HER MYSELF!

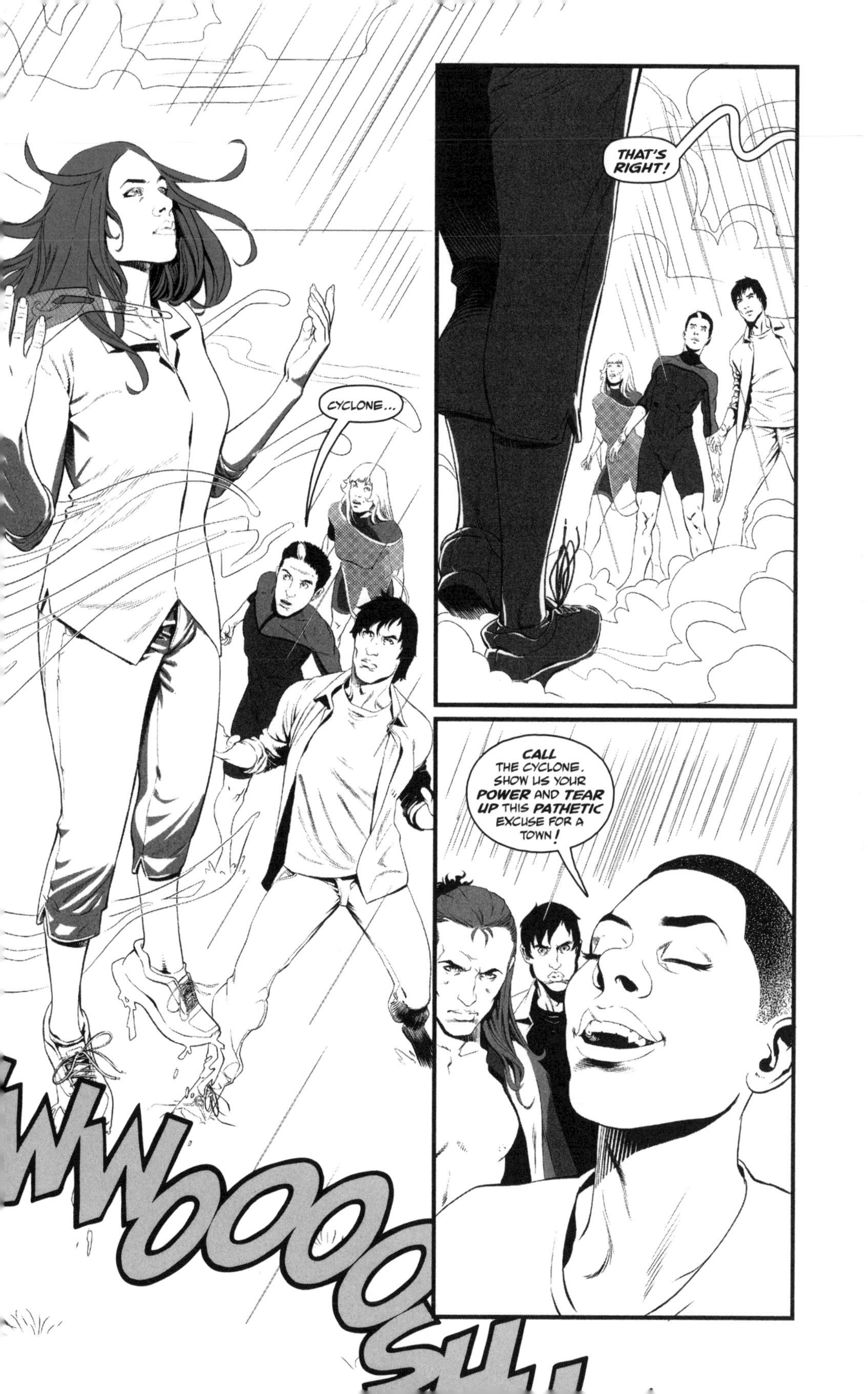
CYCLONE...
WWHOOOOSH!
THAT'S RIGHT!
CALL THE CYCLONE. SHOW US YOUR POWER AND TEAR UP THIS PATHETIC EXCUSE FOR A TOWN!

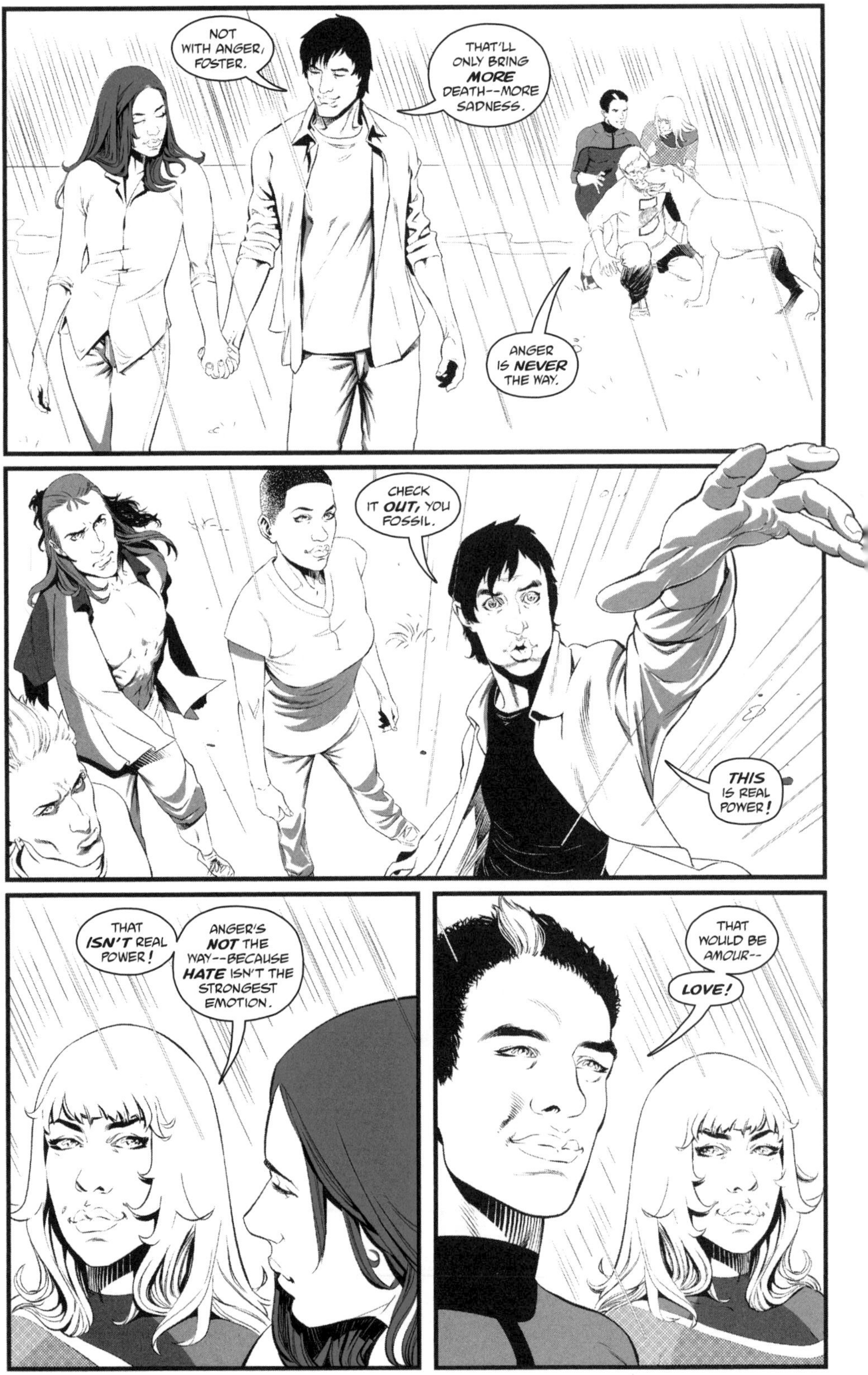
NOT WITH ANGER, FOSTER.
THAT'LL ONLY BRING MORE DEATH--MORE SADNESS.
ANGER IS NEVER THE WAY.
CHECK IT OUT, YOU FOSSIL.
THIS IS REAL POWER!
THAT ISN'T REAL POWER!
ANGER'S NOT THE WAY--BECAUSE HATE ISN'T THE STRONGEST EMOTION.
THAT WOULD BE AMOUR--
LOVE!

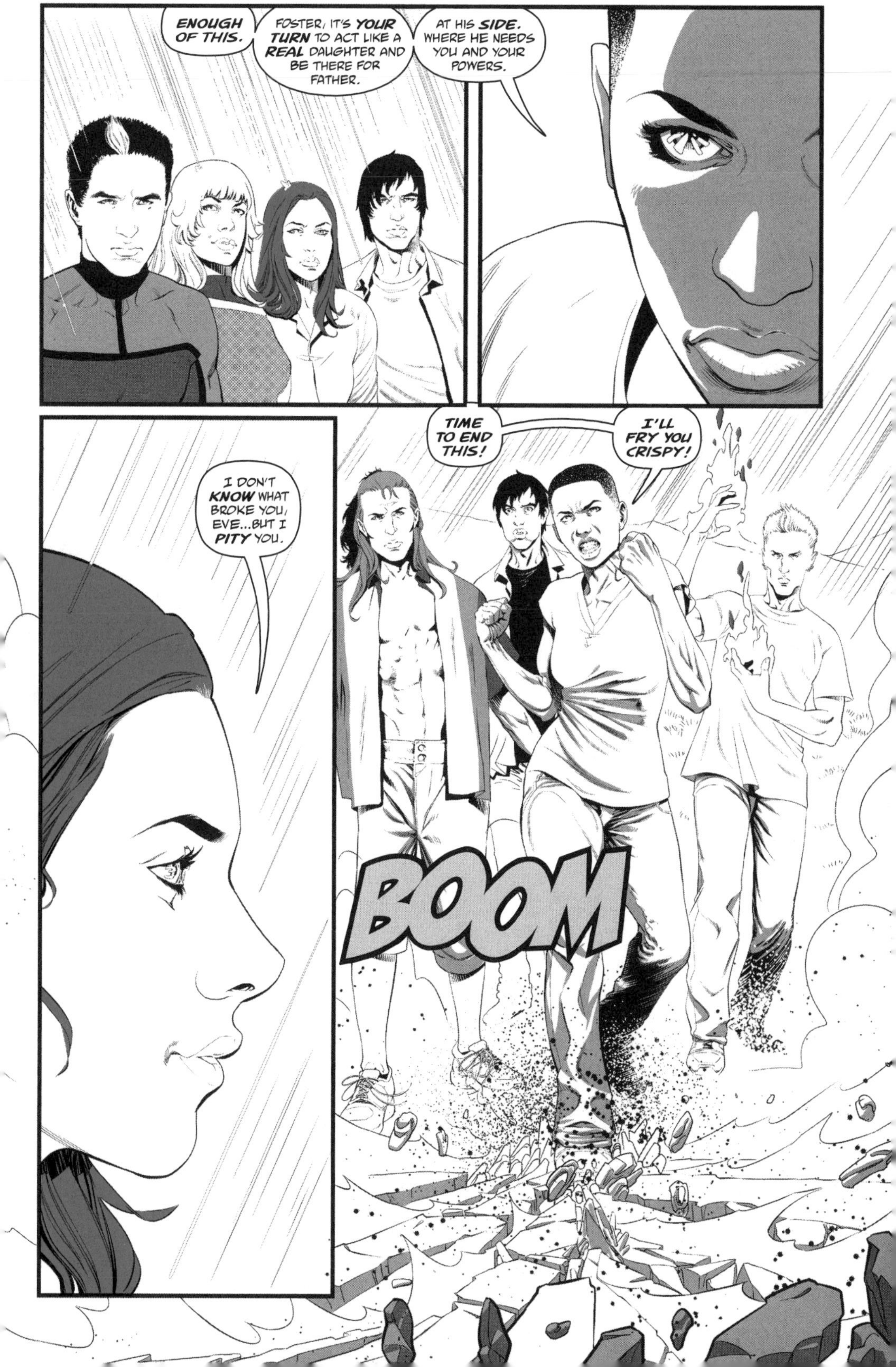
ENOUGH OF THIS.
FOSTER, IT'S YOUR TURN TO ACT LIKE A REAL DAUGHTER AND BE THERE FOR FATHER.
AT HIS SIDE. WHERE HE NEEDS YOU AND YOUR POWERS.
I DON'T KNOW WHAT BROKE YOU, EVE...BUT I PITY YOU.
TIME TO END THIS!
I'LL FRY YOU CRISPY!
BOOM

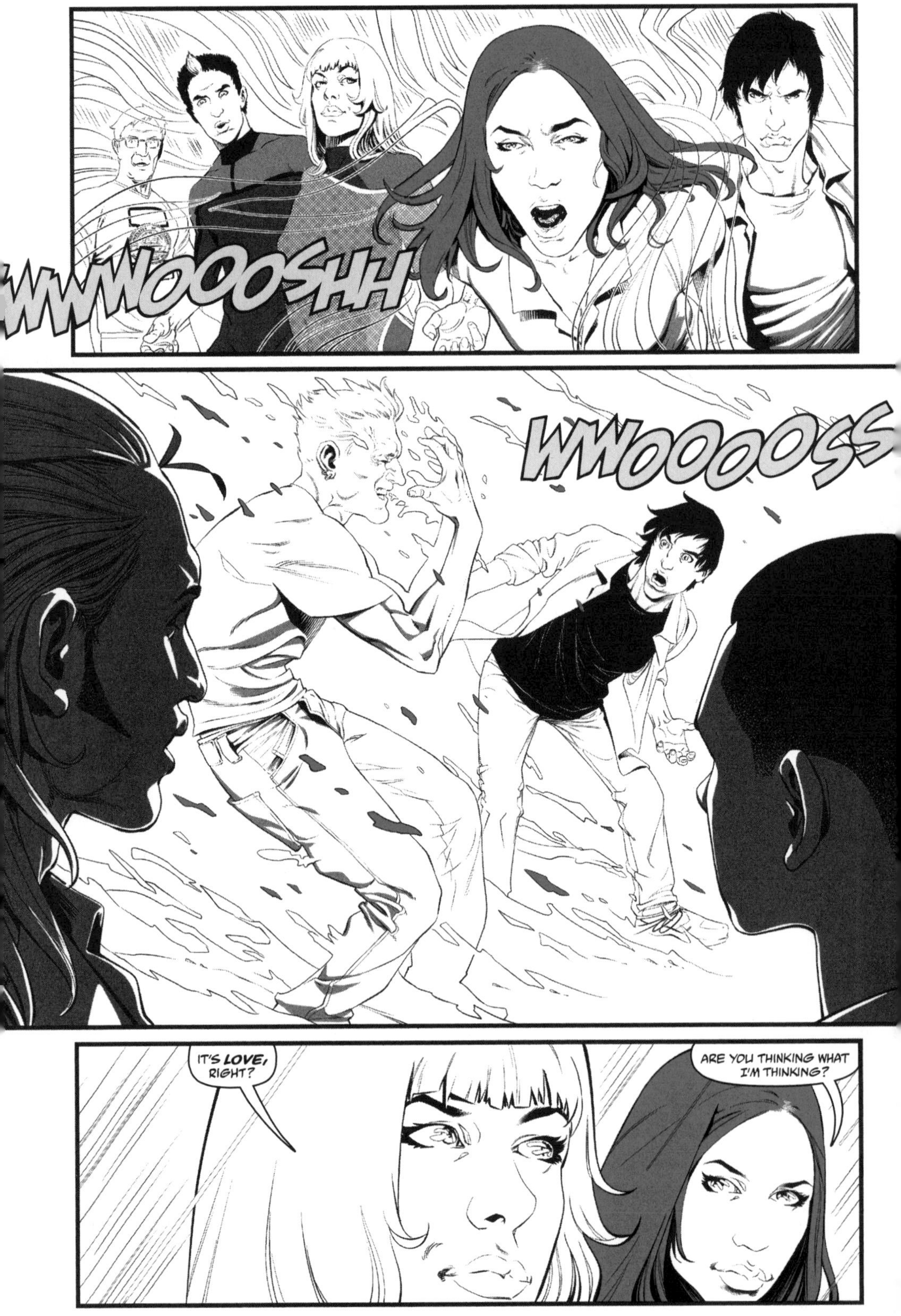
WWWOOOSHH
WWOOOOOSS
IT'S *LOVE*, RIGHT?
ARE YOU THINKING WHAT I'M THINKING?

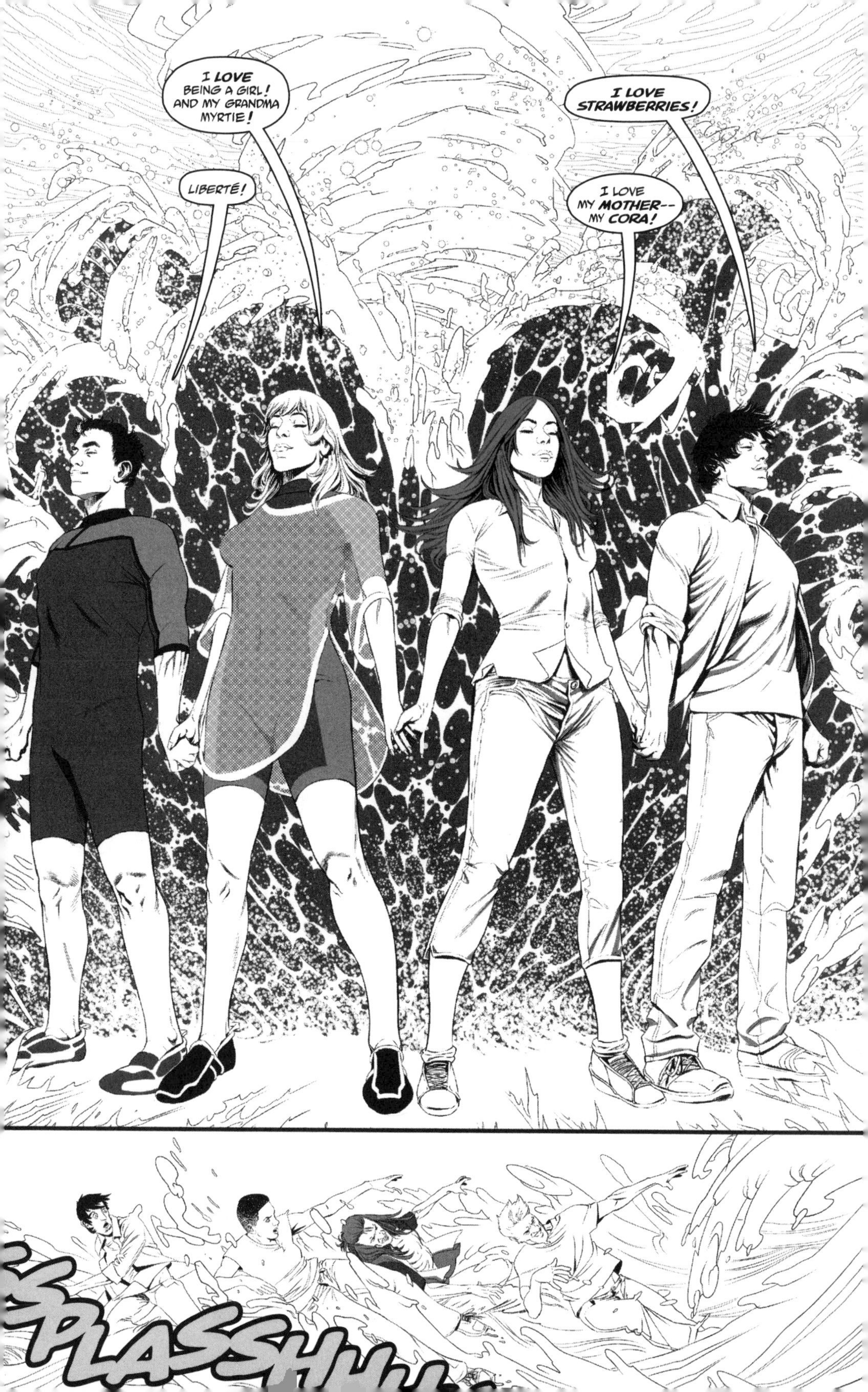
I LOVE BEING A GIRL! AND MY GRANDMA MYRTIE!
LIBERTÉ!
I LOVE STRAWBERRIES!
I LOVE MY MOTHER-- MY CORA!
PLASSH

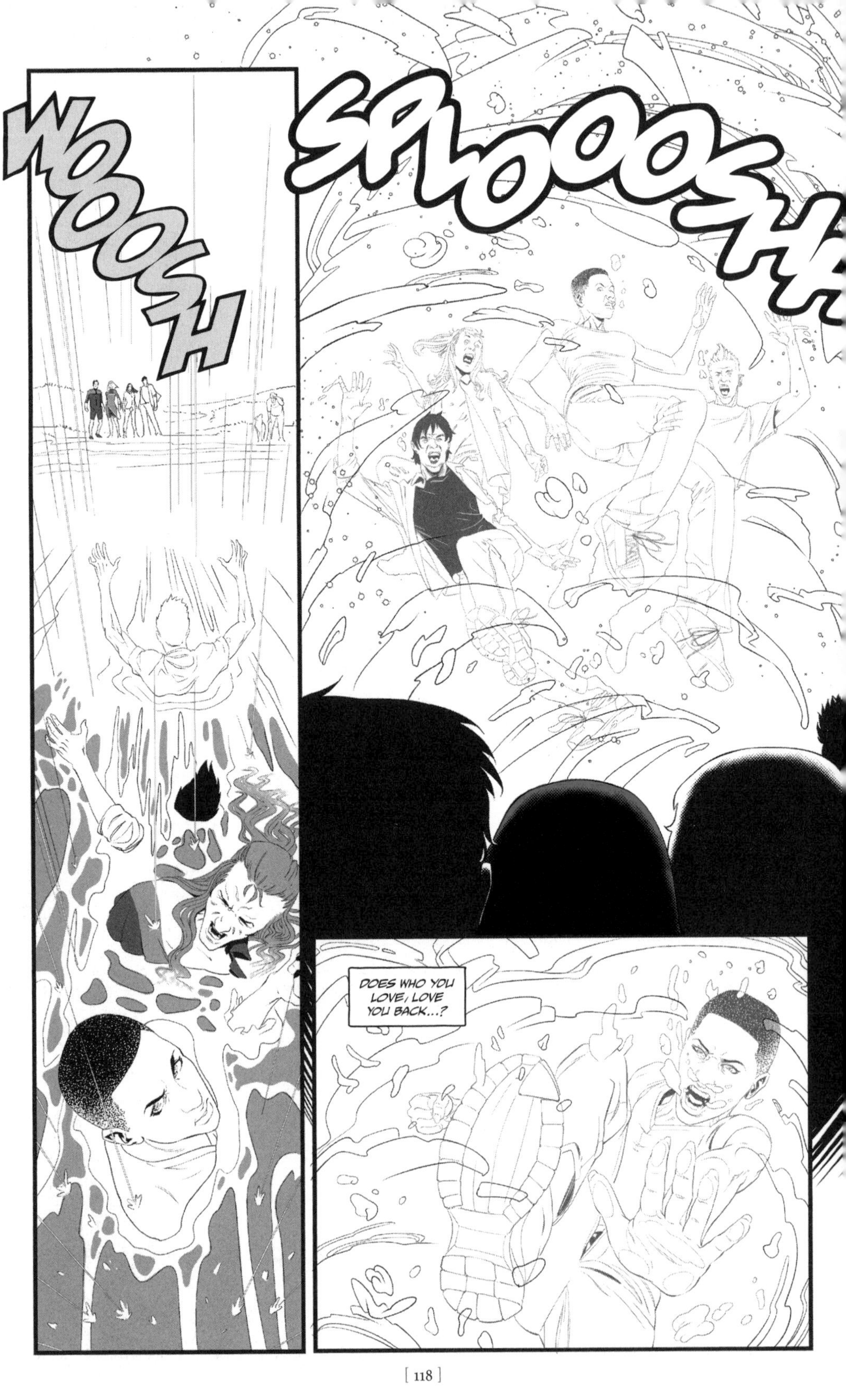
WOOOOSH
SPLOOOSHH
DOES WHO YOU LOVE, LOVE YOU BACK...?

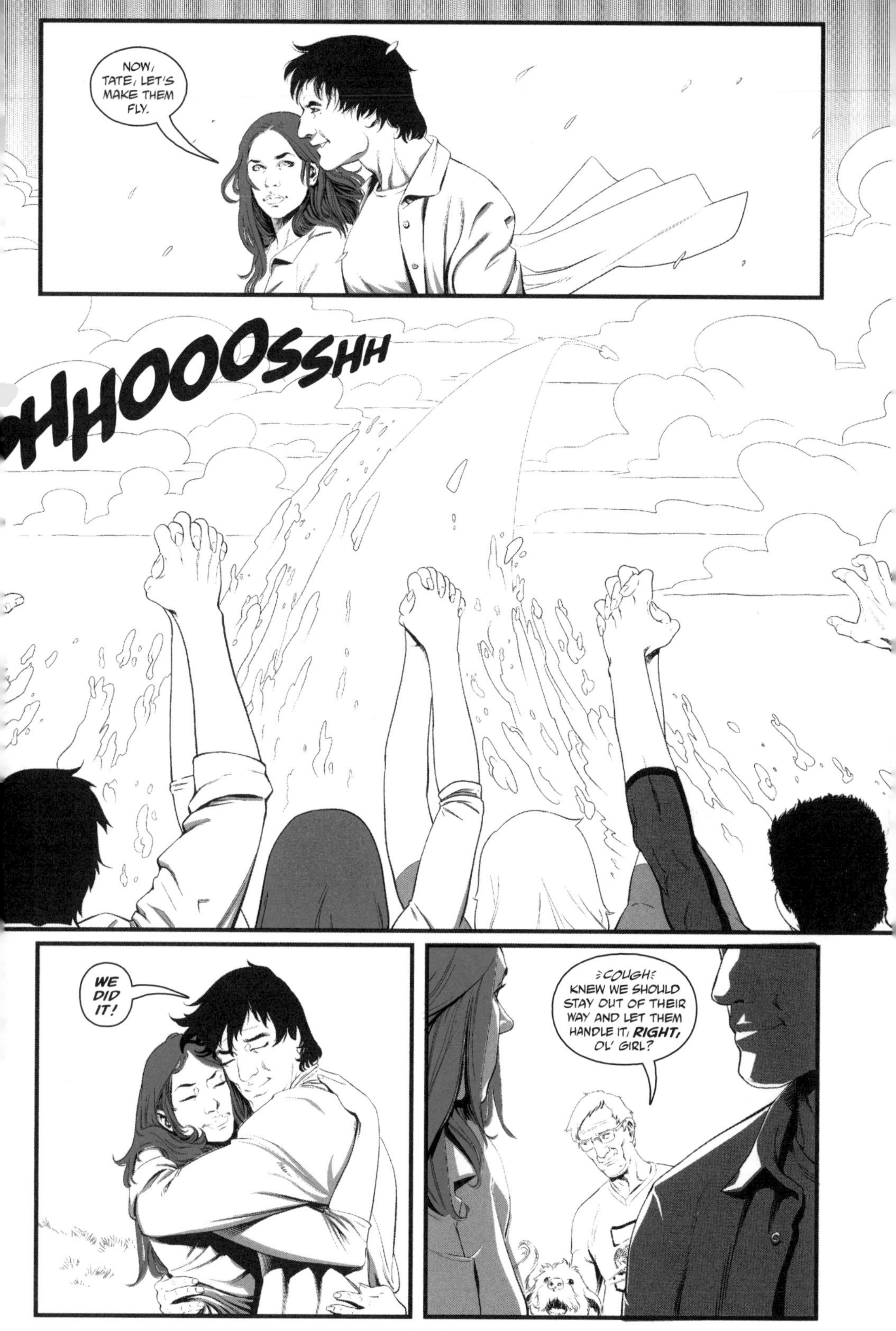
NOW, TATE, LET'S MAKE THEM FLY.
HHOOOSSHH
WE DID IT!
≈COUGH≈ KNEW WE SHOULD STAY OUT OF THEIR WAY AND LET THEM HANDLE IT, **RIGHT,** OL' GIRL?

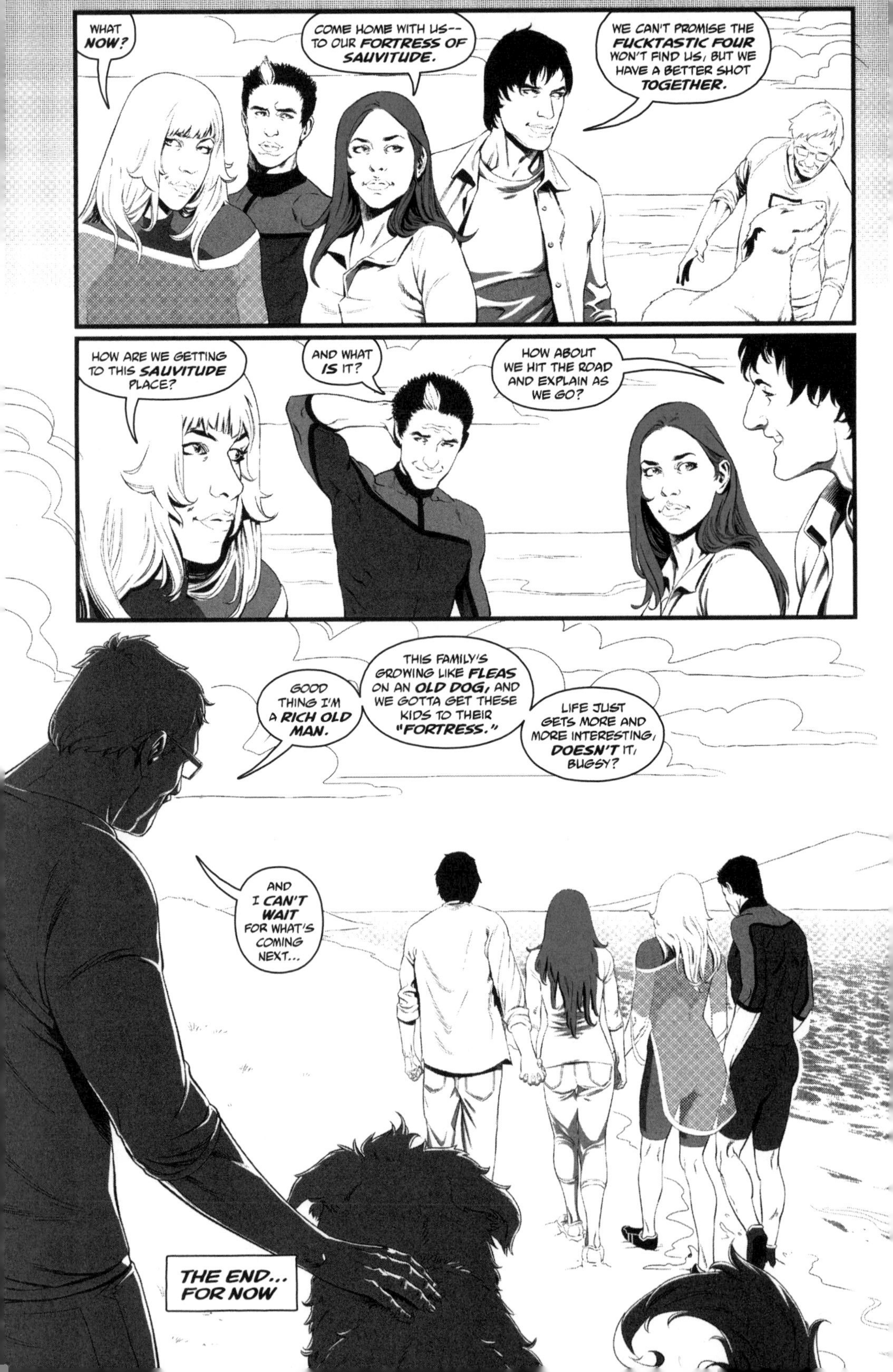
WHAT NOW?
COME HOME WITH US-- TO OUR FORTRESS OF SAUVITUDE.
WE CAN'T PROMISE THE FUCKTASTIC FOUR WON'T FIND US, BUT WE HAVE A BETTER SHOT TOGETHER.
HOW ARE WE GETTING TO THIS SAUVITUDE PLACE?
AND WHAT IS IT?
HOW ABOUT WE HIT THE ROAD AND EXPLAIN AS WE GO?
GOOD THING I'M A RICH OLD MAN.
THIS FAMILY'S GROWING LIKE FLEAS ON AN OLD DOG, AND WE GOTTA GET THESE KIDS TO THEIR "FORTRESS."
LIFE JUST GETS MORE AND MORE INTERESTING, DOESN'T IT, BUGSY?
AND I CAN'T WAIT FOR WHAT'S COMING NEXT...
THE END... FOR NOW